AWAKENING MACBETH

CARMEN AMATO

author of *The Hidden Light of Mexico City*

LAUREL & CROTON

CARMEN AMATO

Also by Carmen Amato

THE HIDDEN LIGHT OF MEXICO CITY

The Detective Emilia Cruz series
CLIFF DIVER: Detective Emilia Cruz Book 1
HAT DANCE: Detective Emilia Cruz Book 2
DIABLO NIGHTS: Detective Emilia Cruz Book 3
KING PESO: Detective Emilia Cruz Book 4
PACIFIC REAPER: Detective Emilia Cruz Book 5
43 MISSING: Detective Emilia Cruz Book 6
RUSSIAN MOJITO: Detective Emilia Cruz Book 7
NARCO NOIR: Detective Emilia Cruz Book 8
FELIZ NAVIDAD FROM ACAPULCO: A Detective Emilia Cruz Novella
THE LISTMAKER OF ACAPULCO: A Detective Emilia Cruz Novella
MADE IN ACAPULCO: 5 Emilia Cruz Stories

The Galliano Club series
ROAD TO THE GALLIANO CLUB
MURDER AT THE GALLIANO CLUB
BLACKMAIL AT THE GALLIANO CLUB
REVENGE AT THE GALLIANO CLUB

Praise for AWAKENING MACBETH

"The author expertly interweaves historical facts, drawn from the books Brodie is reading, into the character's bad dreams. Both Brodie and Joe are relatable characters; indeed, he's so perfectly flawed that many readers may fall in love with him, too . . . A suspenseful, paranormal romance." – *Kirkus Reviews*

"Manages to not be full of stereotypes. It was really an excellent read . . . I absolutely adored how smart [Brodie] was." – *Book Reviews Anonymous*

"An engrossing romance with a surprise paranormal twist . . . Carmen Amato has a real gift with the written word. Finding an author who can make you feel like you're in every room and situation that she talks about is golden." – *Stephanie Taylor, author of the Christmas Key series*

COPYRIGHT

AWAKENING MACBETH
Copyright © 2017, 2024 Carmen Amato. All rights reserved.

Published 2024 Laurel & Croton
Trade Paperback Edition

Identifiers
ISBN: 979-8-9891403-5-0 (print)
ISBN: 978-0-9853256-7-1 (ebook)

AUTHOR'S NOTE

My grandmother always said never wake a child abruptly.

"The soul wanders while we sleep," she cautioned us. "It needs time to come back."

For years I woke my children gently, even as I wondered why the soul would wander while we slept. What are souls looking for?

The question never left the back of my mind, until the day I finally realized the answer.

Love.

We're always searching for love.

But there's a dangerous side to love. Brokenhearted and grief-stricken souls wander in search of answers. That restlessness takes place in dreams where evil stalks in an unending quest for souls to steal, just like in that famous song about the devil going down to Georgia looking for souls to steal . . . in a bind because he was way behind.

As if stealing souls is a game.

If it is, are some souls worth more than others?

Keep reading if you want to know the answer.

In the meantime, wake those you love very gently. Who knows where they are wandering.

Carmen Amato
Wilson County, Tennessee
September 2024

CARMEN AMATO

PART 1

The bell invites me . . . for it is a knell
That summons thee to heaven or to hell.
(*Macbeth:* 2.1.63-5)

CHAPTER 1

"Right," Brodie Macbeth said out loud to her empty office, trying to ignore a tension headache.

She had to break up with Stanton tonight. He was on sabbatical from the university and leaving soon for California to film a documentary on presidential politics. If she didn't do it at dinner she'd have to wait weeks for another chance. Her students would break up with a text message but a tenured professor had to have higher standards.

Even if the tenured professor was about to be crushed by a lingering feeling of dead weight.

Brodie rubbed her forehead and stared at the cheatsheet she'd written for the occasion. Stanton was an intelligent, mature man. He'd appreciate her intelligent, mature approach:

Three years has been enough time to establish incompatibility.

It's time to take stock of our individual life goals.

This is an opportunity for our relationship to move to a more professional level.

"Dear Lord," Brodie murmured, her heart sinking into her toes. She had a doctorate in history and written a bestseller, yet she'd never read such drivel in all her life.

She moodily tapped the Johnny Cash bobble figure on her desk, making it nod jauntily at the framed photos lined up beside it.

Her dog Mouse in mid-Frisbee catch.

Brodie and her father when she'd graduated from the University of Virginia.

Brodie and her father when she'd received her PhD from Georgetown University.

Brodie and her best friend Diana Johnson 14 years ago on the night the two seniors led the University of Virginia women's basketball team to a wild screaming 82-80 victory over Duke for the southern division title.

The two women mugging for the camera were both athletic, but the resemblance ended there. Diana looked like an Egyptian princess with her slender build, dark skin, black eyes, and high cheekbones. In contrast, Brodie's muscular frame, pink and white complexion, dark blonde ponytail, and gray eyes pointed to ancestors who wore kilts and tossed cabers. The outdated basketball uniforms made both look taller than their respective 5'10" heights.

Johnny's head started running out of bob and she tapped it again.

The last photo was of Brodie and Stanton at the university provost's fund raiser last year. Stanton was ascetically slim and darkly Irish in an Armani tuxedo. With her long hair pulled into a severe bun, Brodie wore a black dress and flat shoes in an unsuccessful attempt to look narrower and shorter.

She and Stanton were standing side by side. But not touching.

Our whole stupid relationship in one photo. Brodie flipped the picture face down and threw herself back in her desk chair. Her head pounded.

The problem was that she knew just how the break-up would go. She'd begin with a carefully phrased opener. Stanton would pretend not to understand. Brodie would clarify that they really had no relationship besides being each other's trophy date for every university event. Stanton would bristle and get forceful, causing Brodie to freeze up, pull back, turn into a doormat-- anything to avoid an emotional confrontation. Stanton would spend the rest of the evening gassing on happily about how they were the power couple of the College of Arts and Sciences while Brodie made bread pills.

She picked a Lee Roy Parnell song from the music menu on her laptop, put her feet up on the desk, stared out the window, and mentally berated herself for being such a coward. It was late February, a few weeks into the spring semester, and the University of Virginia campus was glossed with a rare snowfall. Students used cafeteria trays to surf across The Lawn, the broad expanse of grass bordered by the Pavilions housing designed by Thomas Jefferson.

As Lee Roy started singing that he was country down to his soul, Brodie wished she was outside, too. In jeans and having fun. Instead she was in her stuffy office in Randall Hall wearing black pants and a beige twinset. And what could be more fun than trying to figure out how to extricate herself from a non-relationship?

The phone rang. "Dr. Macbeth," Brodie answered automatically, starting to doodle a chessboard on the cheatsheet.

"This is Sergeant Hank Falcone of the Boston Police Department," a deep voice said. "Is this Dr. Brodie Margaret Macbeth . . . uh . . . at the Corcoran Department of History at the University of Virginia?

"Yes." Brodie slowly lowered her feet to the floor. "Yes, it is."

"Dr. Macbeth, are you the author of *George and Martha*?" The voice on the other end sounded hesitant. "That new biography? We've all read it here at the precinct house."

"Yes," Brodie said. "That's me. How can I help you, Sergeant, uh, Falcone, did you say?"

"Yes, ma'am. I'm sorry to disturb you, ma'am, but I'm investigating a possible crime scene and your name has come up in connection with our investigation."

"You're calling from Boston?" Brodie verified. A bad feeling crept up her spine and made her forget the headache.

"Yes, ma'am," Sergeant Falcone said. "Are you acquainted with a Wallace Macbeth of 1296 Granite Castle Road, Charlottesville, Virginia?"

"Dr. Wallace Macbeth is my father," Brodie said, "And the head of the history department here."

"Dr. Macbeth, I regret to inform you that a man identified as Wallace Macbeth was pronounced deceased this morning at 10:40 am. He appears to have fallen out of a window of a downtown hotel."

"No," Brodie said, as the bad feeling turned into the sensation of dropping into a dark void. Without realizing what she was doing she stood up and bent over the desk as her stomach spasmed with tension. "Dad was at Harvard this morning. Giving a guest lecture. You can call their history department. I'm sure they'll tell you. He's very well known."

"The incident we're investigating concerns a white male, aged approximately 65. Six feet three inches tall, 190 pounds, with white hair and gray eyes. Wearing a blue wool sweater, plaid flannel shirt, and brown corduroy pants. Does that sound like a description of your father, ma'am?"

"Oh, God." Brodie's office shimmered around her, making the bookshelves and country music memorabilia hazy and indistinct.

"Dr. Macbeth," the police office said gently.

"How did you get my number?" Brodie asked, fighting for air against the vertigo. Suddenly Lee Roy's slide guitar was too much and she jabbed at the laptop to stop the music.

"There were three business cards in the deceased's wallet," Sergeant Falcone said. "Yours, that of a Dr. Stanton Sloane, also of the University of Virginia, and a Dr. Donald Pedder from Stanford University. We called you first. Do you know them?"

"Dr. Sloane," Brodie said. "He's a . . . a family friend."

"And Dr. Pedder?"

"I don't know."

"Dr. Macbeth, was your father married?"

"No," Brodie said, blinking with the change of subject. "My father's a widower."

"Would that make you next of kin?"

Brodie sat down in her chair before she passed out standing up. She gulped air and managed to say *yes*.

"As the next of kin to Wallace Macbeth," the police officer went on. "We'd like you to come to Boston and identify the body."

Again the room swam and Brodie breathed hard to prevent herself from passing out. "I can do that," she finally managed.

"Is there someone you can call to accompany you, ma'am?"

"Yes."

"Can you please me call as soon as you know your itinerary? We can have someone meet your flight." Sergeant Falcone gave her several numbers. Brodie's hand was shaking so badly that her handwriting was big and loopy as she copied them down.

This is all a mistake. Brodie broke the connection, found the information her father had given her before he'd left two days ago, and dialed his hotel. It was 4:00 pm; he would be back from giving his lecture at Harvard, and they'd have a good laugh.

The hotel operator put her on hold as soon as she asked for Dr. Wallace Macbeth's room. Light jazz played in her ear and then the hotel manager came on the line and regretted that he would have to refer her inquiry about this particular hotel guest to Boston Police Sergeant Hank Falcone.

The fight or flight instinct surged up and adrenaline pumped through Brodie's body. She disconnected and dialed an internal university number.

"Liz," she said as soon as the phone was answered. "This is Dr. Macbeth. Is Coach Johnson there?"

"She's in the gym," the Athletic Department secretary said. "Ooh, I'm glad you called. Do you remember Monica Corelli? She's the scout from Coach Johnson's old WNBA team. She was here Monday when you were practicing with us. She said she couldn't believe you never made it to the WNBA. You've still got it, Dr. Macbeth."

"Coach Johnson, Liz," Brodie said, trying to keep her voice from cracking. "It's urgent."

A recorded voice started talking about athletics at the University of Virginia. Brodie wound her long ponytail in her free hand, twisting it until her scalp stung enough to keep her from passing out or throwing up.

The recording was cut off by Diana's voice. "Brodie? What's up? Liz said it was urgent and that you sounded odd."

"I know this is bad timing," Brodie gulped. "Middle of the season and all. But can you go to Boston with me? Today?"

"Today?" Diana echoed in surprise.

"A police officer called from Boston." Brodie's chest tightened again and she had to stop talking. After a moment she went on, her eyes closed against the fear in her heart. "They said that Dad . . . or somebody . . . fell. There's a body. The person fell out of a hotel window. And the hotel said to call the police. I have to . . . go and identify it. The body. As soon as possible."

The sound of something heavy hitting the floor made Brodie start and look up. Sarah Gibbard, the history department's plump secretary, stood in Brodie's open office door, her face crumpling. There was an untidy pile of books by her feet.

"You're in your office, right?" Diana said in Brodie's ear. "I'll be over in five minutes."

Brodie put down the phone, swept around the desk, and hugged the secretary who was now weeping openly in the doorway. "Let's not buy trouble, Sarah," Brodie said. "Don't cry."

"Oh, no." Sarah sobbed into Brodie's shoulder.

"Maybe Dad got pickpocketed and somebody else had his wallet," Brodie babbled. "That person fell. That other person."

"But the police," Sarah said chokingly. "I heard what you said."

"It has to be a mistake," Brodie said and tightened her hold on Sarah. The woman had been Wallace Macbeth's secretary for nearly 20 years. "Please don't cry. It's a joke or something. Dad's fine. Really he is."

Sarah sobbed harder.

Brodie's teeth started to chatter from the adrenaline rush. Her mind jumped around crazily, desperate to find a different explanation.

Her father was aloof, eccentric, absentminded. He routinely

lost keys, wore clothes until they were threadbare, and was habitually late for their regular Wednesday night dinners. But he was also a brilliant historian, head of the Corcoran Department of History, and one of the University of Virginia's most respected and popular faculty members.

He was certainly smart enough not to fall out of a hotel window.

CHAPTER 2

"You're going to be a very wealthy woman, Dr. Macbeth," the attorney said.

His name was Smithfield.

Like the ham, Brodie thought ridiculously.

She looked around the modern glass box of a conference room as the two lawyers across the polished conference table spewed legal mumbo-jumbo at her and Diana: *estate tax* and *regrettable delay due to the investigation. Complications due to the decedent being born in Scotland* and *status as a naturalized U.S. citizen with continuing financial holdings in Edinburgh.*

The legalities of dealing with a suicide.

The last six weeks had been hideous. The awful trip to Boston, the police investigation and shocking verdict, the funeral, and a huge memorial service at the university. Brodie had drifted through all of it in a state of detached numbness, dry-eyed and dry-mouthed.

There'd been no energy left for breaking up with Stanton and so he'd been by her side during the funeral and memorial service, looking expensively mournful in a succession of dark Brooks Brothers suits. He was now in California filming his political documentary about something she didn't care about.

Ending things with him had become another entry on a continuing nightmarish to-do list that included today's final reading of her father's will.

"The advantage of having been an only child," Mr. Smithfield said ingratiatingly. He wore an expensive suit and too much hair gel. "I hope you consider our services as you enter the wealth management phase of your life."

Brodie stiffened; Diana squeezed her hand. Mr. Smithfield kept on talking.

The attorney, and his sidekick named Cooper, were part of a

slick and expensive practice in downtown Richmond, Virginia's state capital. Brodie had been surprised to learn that her father went to them to write his will and execute his estate. Wallace Macbeth had always used his old friend Judge Perkins in Charlottesville for his few legal transactions.

"Ah, yes," Mr. Cooper said with an awkward little cough. He was a big man with a shiny pink head. "What we mean to say is that you are essentially the sole heir. A relatively small but significant bequest goes to Dr. Katherine Macbeth of Edinburgh, Scotland. Your aunt, I believe?"

"My father's only sister," Brodie said.

"The will states that she is to inherit a landscape painting by Campbell Mackay that currently hangs in the living room of the house on Granite Castle Road in Charlottesville."

He looked at Brodie over the top of his half-moon reading glasses and she nodded.

"She will also receive Dr. Macbeth's share of the townhouse on Moray Place in Edinburgh, Scotland," the attorney said.

Brodie nodded again. Her aunt Kay had always lived in the stately townhouse in Edinburgh's New Town that had been left equally to her father and his sister by their parents. Brodie knew it well; growing up she'd spent every summer with Kay in Edinburgh while her father ranged all over the world looking for history and writing his books.

"Also, a minor bequest goes to the University of Virginia's library fund." Mr. Cooper looked up at Brodie. "The sum of twenty thousand dollars. But all of his books go to you."

"Okay," Brodie said distractedly, only because he seemed to expect her to say something. Twenty thousand hardly seemed like a minor amount of money.

Mr. Smithfield cleared his throat. "This leaves you to inherit the remainder of your father's estate. Namely the property on Granite Castle Road in Charlottesville, the contents of your father's office at the University of Virginia, his bank accounts in both the United States and Great Britain, and an investment portfolio managed by this firm. As you can see, this is quite a sizeable inheritance."

He passed a paper across the table to Brodie. She skimmed the paper, which listed Wallace Macbeth's total assets. Nearly $800,000 divided among several bank accounts in Charlottesville. Twice that amount in the Royal Bank of Scotland with another two million dollars invested in blue chip stocks. And the house was worth over a million dollars.

"Are you sure this is right?" Brodie felt dazed as she passed the paper to Diana. She'd had no idea her father had that kind of money. It was almost too much to take in. Her brain sought safe ground and fastened onto the house. "The house can't be worth that much," she protested. "It's in good shape, but it's just an old brick farmhouse with a rail fence and a gravel drive."

Diana passed the paper back to Brodie, her eyebrows raised in incredulity.

"Your father purchased the house over 30 years ago," Mr. Cooper said, as if Brodie hadn't grown up there. "It was assessed very fairly. Four bedrooms, three full bathrooms, large gathering areas. Not to mention four acres in that area. This is a very valuable property and would likely bring you a very fair price." He paused and the two lawyers exchanged glances. "I expect you'll be wanting to sell? Obviously, you can now afford to live anywhere. Our specialist in luxury properties has a few suggestions and would be willing to--."

"No," Brodie heard herself say. "I'll move in."

Diana shot her a look and Brodie felt at last there was something she could control. She'd never loved her townhouse off Rugby Road; it was close to the university but the yard wasn't really big enough for Mouse. The German Shepherd needed more room to run. And the Granite Castle Road house was *home*. It was the only house she'd lived in until she'd gone away to boarding school at the prestigious Madeira School outside Washington DC when she was 12. She always returned home at Christmas and Easter and for a week or two at the start of summer vacation before going to Edinburgh.

But even more than that, it was Dad's house. She couldn't just sell it to strangers.

"You wish to occupy the house?" Mr. Smithfield asked, his tone a mix of condescension and disappointment.

"Next week is spring break," Brodie said firmly. "I'll go to Edinburgh to give Kay the painting. When I come back, I'll move into the house."

Both lawyers shifted in their chairs. "There are two caveats," Mr. Cooper said slowly. His tie pinched his fleshy neck. "You must agree to read your father's collection of British histories. I believe the books are located in the Granite Castle Road house."

"Dad's books?" This was a legacy Brodie could understand. She nodded. "Yes, of course I'll read them."

Cooper nodded. "You must also agree to put the registration of your father's license plates in your name and use them on your own vehicle for as long as you reside in the state of Virginia. If you move from the state you cannot return the plates to the Department of Motor Vehicles but must keep them as personal property."

Brodie blinked. "I'm sorry?"

"Before you can claim any part of your inheritance, you must put his license plates in your own name and commit to lifelong ownership," Mr. Smithfield said. "Your father was very specific on this point. If you don't agree to these terms, all of Dr. Macbeth's assets revert to the state of Virginia."

"I don't inherit anything unless I use Dad's license plates?" Brodie asked in bewilderment, her control over events slipping away once more.

"That is correct," Mr. Smithfield said. He smoothed his red power tie.

"Is there something significant about the license plates?" Diana asked quietly, the first time she'd spoken since the introductions at the beginning of the meeting.

"Let's see." Mr. Smithfield found a piece of paper in the stack in front of him. "It's a Great Seal of Virginia plate. OFK 362. Your father was evidently very loyal to his adopted state, Dr. Macbeth."

"A Great Seal of Virginia plate," Brodie repeated. She couldn't recall her father ever discussing his license plates with the gold state seal in the middle. Or even the nondescript gray sedan that wore them. "Are you sure this is right? That my father's entire estate is pegged to his license plate?"

"It does seem rather unusual," Diana said.

"Yes, it does."

Mr. Smithfield peered at the date on the top of the long sheaf of papers that was Wallace Macbeth's will. "I remember distinctly when your father came in and made these arrangements. It was about six years ago and he was very specific."

"He planned all this six years ago?" Brodie asked.

"Yes," the lawyer said. "He was very emphatic. If you don't agree to the terms of the license plates, you inherit nothing."

"Do you know why he made out the will that way?" Diana asked.

"He said it was something you'd appreciate in time." The lawyer looked a little embarrassed and smoothed his tie again. "I certainly understand that this may all be rather upsetting. Given the nature of his death, you may be successful in arguing that your father was not of sound mind. If you wished to exercise your option to contest, that is."

Brodie felt her chest tighten. *Six years ago, Dad drew up a crazy will. Planned his suicide.* Over the years he'd revealed nothing. Wallace Macbeth had hardly been a demonstrative man but he'd been her father. She should have known why he'd do something like this.

The lawyer replaced the license information on the stack of papers in front of him. "Of course, we do have the change of registration form here. We can have our notary come in now if you'd like to sign."

In stunned silence, Brodie signed every piece of paper placed in front of her. In addition to the other half of the house in Moray Place, Kay got money to cover British taxes.

A law firm in Scotland would be notified that Brodie was coming to complete the paperwork next week.

Mr. Smithfield handed her a large legal file containing the deed to the Granite Castle Road house in Charlottesville, a copy of the notarized license plate registration, and other important papers. Suddenly Brodie was dizzy and suffocating in this glass prison. She scooped up her purse and coat and blundered her way out of the office suite, only dimly aware of Diana behind her.

The ladies room was just down the hall. Brodie dropped everything on the floor and fled into a cubicle. She didn't throw up, just stood hunched with her hands braced on the side partitions, trembling and gasping. It took a long time before the nausea and cold sweat passed and she felt steady enough to leave.

Diana was standing patiently against the restroom wall holding both their purses and the file. She'd hung their coats on hooks by the door. They were the only two people there. Brodie bent over a sink and splashed cold water on her face.

"You doing okay, sweetie?" Diana asked.

Brodie straightened up and looked at herself in the mirror above the sink. She'd barely eaten since the horrible trip to Boston and her severe navy suit and beige blouse hung on her like sheets on a clothesline. Her face was as white as the wall tiles. Her customary lack of makeup and jewelry didn't help.

"I look like an escapee from flight attendant school." Brodie peeled off her jacket and flung it to the floor. "How is it you always look so glamorous?"

Diana was wearing a black knit pant suit with a turquoise blouse and a multi-strand necklace of blue-green stones. Her hair was a spill of long thin dark braids that ended in tiny white beads. A two carat diamond engagement ring glittered above her wedding band. "Sweetie," she started.

"Do you know I've worn my hair like this my entire life?"

Brodie interrupted, an edge of hysteria in her voice. She started snatching bobby pins out of the thick braid she'd coiled into a bun that morning. They pinged faintly as they hit the tile floor. "Long and drab."

"You could cut it," Diana said, watching Brodie carefully. "Perk up the color."

"Cut it." Brodie gave a stretched-too-thin laugh as the braid snaked down her back. "Maybe even highlights. How about that? What a wild woman! *Highlights*!"

"I was wondering when you'd melt down," Diana sighed.

"I'm not melting down," Brodie insisted, wrestling with the stretchy band at the end of her braid. "I'm just sick of looking like a goddamned plain jane."

"You've held it together really well, sweetie," Diana said. She laid down the things she was holding and came to stand by Brodie so that they were side-by-side in the mirror. "Ray and I were talking. Maybe a little too well."

"*This was all a joke to him!*" Brodie shouted at Diana's unflinching reflection. "His license plates? His stupid license plates? What the hell is that all about?"

"I don't know," Diana shrugged.

"Why did he do this?" Brodie said furiously. "Why would Dad pitch himself off a Boston hotel balcony two hours before giving a guest lecture at Harvard?" She glared at their reflections. "His suit was laid out just like always before he took a shower. He was going to wear his St. Andrews tie. Why would a man lay out a glen plaid suit and his school tie and then jump out of a window?"

"I don't know what to tell you," Diana said sadly.

"The whole thing is like some sick joke." Brodie violently ripped out a handful of hair along with the stretchy band. "Except Dad didn't have a sense of humor."

Her stomach cramped, the nausea rose up, and she grabbed the sink to keep from falling over. Again she didn't throw up, just stood there until the feeling subsided, leaving her shivery and rubber-legged.

"You're going to get past it," Diana said and rubbed her back. "I'm here for you. Ray's here. The entire university is behind you."

Brodie splashed more water on her face.

Diana held out a paper towel. "You're doing great," she said. "But are you really sure you want to move?"

"Yes." Brodie mechanically put on her jacket and coat. Her father had been the only parent she'd ever known. He hadn't always been warm or demonstrative but he'd raised her, taught her to become a scholar and writer, been a valued professional colleague. He had a good life and a position he loved as much as a man like him could love anything. Nothing had gone wrong lately so *why had he done this*?

Diana smiled thinly; her dark eyes full of sympathy. "Don't you think you ought to talk to Stanton first? What's he going to say about it?"

"I don't care," Brodie said. She took the file folder and her purse and started toward the door. "We're over anyway."

"You're going to break up with Stanton?" Diana asked, not moving.

Brodie turned around, that dead weight pressing down on her again. "Don't tell me that doesn't make you feel like singing. He and I were never like you and Ray."

"That's an understatement." Diana leaned against a sink and took a deep breath. "If you're really going to break up with him, I can say this now. Stanton's never been nice to you and I wish you'd dumped that man's sorry ass years ago."

"Do you know the last time we did it?" Brodie asked abruptly. "October. *October*. He's so skinny I was afraid I'd snap him like a twig."

Diana made a choking sound.

"In three years I don't think we slept together more than a dozen times," Brodie heard herself blurt. "He wouldn't stay over at my place because he might encounter dog hair and die. His place is so full of priceless antiques you can't even sit down, much less have any fun."

"This would explain why you're in the best shape of your life," Diana said. "You work out with me twice a week and then there's the kickboxing classes, the five mile runs with Mouse, the marathon lap sessions in the pool. Not to mention why you're always free Saturday nights."

Brodie bit her lip. Stanton loved himself too much to love her and she'd always known it. Somehow her father's death made that thought even more bitter than it was.

She looked around at the white bathroom tiles and pushed herself away from the wall. "So here's the plan," she said, forcing her voice into the crisp but congenial tone she used with undergraduate students. "Edinburgh to get rid of the last legal details. When I get back I'll break up with Stanton, move into Dad's house, and start planning the department's annual symposium on music and politics. Everybody keeps asking if we're still having it this year."

Diana put her arm around Brodie. "That's a lot."

Brodie gave a forced bright smile. She needed to extinguish the emotions raging inside her, not let them out. "I'm good. Really."

Diana raised her eyebrows. "Really?"

Brodie propelled Diana through the door, unable to handle any more. "Let's go find a hair salon," she said, her voice sounding fake and sugary in her ears. "Someplace expensive. I'm rich, remember?"

CHAPTER 3

Brodie put her leather jacket and the expertly wrapped package containing the Campbell Mackay painting into the overhead bin of the flight to London. She settled into her aisle seat in the last row of the first class aircraft cabin without glancing at the occupant by the window.

Somehow today had even been worse than the day she'd stood in the morgue in Boston and said *yes, that broken body is Wallace Macbeth*. After dropping off Mouse at the kennel she'd gone to the house on Granite Castle Road to meet two of Cooper and Smithfield's legal minions and a notary. They'd witnessed the affixing of her father's license plates to her Volvo wagon and wrapped the Campbell Mackay painting, sealing it with a special label. Brodie signed affidavits that she was using the plates and transporting the painting to Edinburgh. Lawyers there would verify its delivery to Kay.

When everyone left Brodie walked through the house, the dusty rooms convincing her that her father was gone in a way that the funeral and memorial service had not.

It was real, it was true. He was never coming back and he was never going to tell her why he'd chosen to kill himself and make her use his license plates.

Throat and chest tight, she'd ended up in her father's den. It had been the room where Wallace Macbeth had really lived.

The room was dark and masculine with forest green walls. Like the rest of the house, the woodwork was oak. There was a big partner's desk and a walnut-colored leather sofa creased with the indentations of a thousand naps. A window at the far end of the room was covered in woolen draperies made from faded green, blue, and red Macbeth clan tartan. A butler's table sat in front of the window, supporting a silver tray laden with various bottles of Scotch, tiny dram glasses, and Waterford tumblers.

Her father's Napoleon versus Wellington chess set was on the coffee table in front of the sofa, each piece colorfully detailed and ready for the battle of Waterloo. Brodie and her father had played countless games of chess together; her father on the sofa, Brodie in the maple rocking chair with the University of Virginia seal.

Hundreds of books on British history marched across one wall, arranged in alphabetical order by author name. "Thanks for the books, Dad," Brodie had said out loud, her voice strained and thin in the silent room. She would read them all from A to Z. No cheating with her ereader, either.

The flight attendant came through with a choice of drinks. Brodie accepted a bottle of designer water and leaned back in her seat. Her hand reached up to adjust her braid, but of course it wasn't there. After the funeral, Diana had taken her to a fantastic salon. Her hair was now a chin-length bob with a platinum sheen and a feathery texture. The salon's makeup artist did Brodie's face, too, showing her how to play up the new hair color. She bought everything the woman recommended.

Brodie gave herself a mental shake and took the book from her carry-on bag. *Shakespeare* by British historian and novelist Peter Ackroyd would get her most of the way across the Atlantic.

She turned on the reading light over her seat.

"Say the bloody line, Burbage."

"Some time today."

The dream was real and vivid. Brodie was surrounded by men, all dressed as she was in the linen shirts, weskits, and hose of the Elizabethan middle class. Some, including Brodie, wore rough cloaks fastened around their throats with a crude metal clasp.

She was standing on the stage of the Globe Theater. The many-sided building was familiar; she'd gone to a play in the rebuilt Globe in London just last year with her aunt Kay. The wide stage was bigger than it had looked from the galleries where the audience sat. Grease lamps burned brightly on the edge. Two fancifully painted wooden pillars on either side held up a canopy decorated with stars and planets.

Dad is here. Brodie didn't know why she knew he was there, she just did. She was in the Globe to find him and make him answer all her questions. Tell her why he killed himself and left her such a puzzling legacy.

"Dad," she called, straining to see into the darkness beyond the guttering flames of the grease lamps.

"Burbage." A man stepped closer. "Are you daft? Say your line."

Brodie turned to look at the others on the stage. One man had a fabric horse head under his arm. No, not a horse head, a donkey head. "Is this *A Midsummer Night's Dream*?" she asked. "Are you rehearsing the play?"

"You'd be rehearsing it, too, if you weren't being so bloody daft," one of the men grumbled.

Brodie turned away impatiently. "Dad," she called again. "Dad!"

"Burbage, you daft bugger," a man complained.

"It's tha' doxy down ta Pig and Whistle in Hog Lane," another hooted. "She's fair addled his head."

"*Dad*," Brodie shouted.

One of the men grabbed her arm.

She swung her gaze to him in distracted irritation and recoiled in horror.

His eyes were white and diseased. The man wasn't blind, however; the cankered irises registered amusement and impatience at Brodie's reaction.

"Welcome to the game," he said.

"Shit," Brodie gasped, trying to pull back.

"Do you know who I am?" he asked, not letting go. He was in his mid-30's with flat brown hair and a trim beard. An unremarkable man except for the vile eyes and a grip like the bite of a horse.

"You're . . . you're Shakespeare," Brodie stammered.

He smiled icily. The effect made Brodie want to vomit. "Wouldn't it have been ironic if we'd been rehearsing *Macbeth*?" he asked.

"You know my name?" Brodie blurted.

"I know everything," the man said. The white eyes glinted in the yellow light of the grease lamps as he licked his lips. "Everything except what he told you."

"Let go of me," Brodie said and strained to pull away.

He hung on but his face tightened. The white eyes assessed her with a glazed, predatory quality. "You're staying in the game until I get my answer. You might get your answers, too, but I really don't care about that."

"The game?" Brodie looked around wildly for help but the actors on the stage ignored her.

"Let me put it simply," the man said, tightlipped against the effort of holding onto her. "Your father knew something about me and I'd like to know what it was. Because it helped him cheat the game. I had to take him out of the game because he cheated."

"Game?" Brodie asked in utter confusion."

"He made a sort of whistling sound as he fell." The man grinned, the white eyes full of evil humor. "Twenty stories, wasn't it?"

Brodie stopped pulling against his grip, too stunned to resist. "*What*?"

"Suicide?' The man licked his lips again. "Not murder at all."

"Are you saying my father was murdered?" Brodie rasped.

"*He cheated me*," the man shouted unexpectedly. "*For too long. And you know how.*"

"*Let go!*" Brodie shouted back.

She heaved away from him, finally breaking his hold. She spilled herself over the edge of the stage, and ran across the empty pit where people paid a penny to stand and watch the plays.

"You're going to tell me, bitch," the man screamed after her. *"Or I'll take you out, too."*

Brodie flew through the theater, the cloak streaming behind her as the men on the stage shouted for Burbage to return and finish the rehearsal. She found a door and shot out into a dank London evening.

The smell of London's Southwark district hit her hard, urine and manure and a too densely packed population. Brodie's heart pounded and her boots made a smucking sound as she headed for the river and the venerable section of Mayfair where she'd stayed a dozen times, the map of modern London in her head at variance with the scene in front of her. Shops and alehouses and stables and smithies and more shops lined the narrow streets. She was jostled by women in flounced dresses, apprentices in blue, children in rags, and men in doublet and hose or leather breeches.

The sound of the city was like the raucous hum of bees; the rattle of wagons, the clop of hooves, the squalls of street vendors, and the murmur of beggars. Brodie reeled from the sensory input.

Passersby frequently greeted her by tugging at their hairline and saying "Burbage." The men in the theater had called her that, too, and she realized people were taking her for Richard Burbage, Shakespeare's fellow actor and part owner of the Globe.

Evening lapsed into solid night. Brodie was scared and cold and lost in a city from the pages of history. The compunction that her father was near had gone. Over and over, Brodie tried to make herself wake up, but to no avail. She walked the filthy streets for what seemed like hours, trapped in this place mired in the past, her desperation growing.

She found herself on the banks of the Thames, under the trestle of a bridge. There were a few other people there, thieves and beggars and the destitute. They all stared at her sullenly. But Brodie was too exhausted to go on. She curled into a ball on the ground with the rough cloak around her legs. Several ragged people came toward her and she prayed they'd leave her alone. They passed, but then an old crone darted forward and grabbed Brodie's cloak.

Stunned, Brodie snatched at the woman's hand and suddenly they were rolling on the ground, locked together with the cloak twisting tighter and tighter around Brodie's neck. The woman's eyes were the same white as Shakespeare's.

Fear surged through Brodie's veins and she fought back with all the strength she could muster, even as her breath was choked off. Mud sucked at her and the river was too close.

The malevolence of the beggars and thieves watching the fight was like a tangible thing.

"Excuse me," the crone said in a gravelly baritone. "If I could just get by . . ."

Brodie struggled against a painful feeling of being turned inside out. The dream swirled and buffeted her. Rage thundered through her body, blotting out her thoughts and making her heart race. Blood pounded in her ears.

"Excuse me," the strange voice said again.

Disoriented and furious, Brodie forced her eyes open. A pair of enormous blue eyes stared into hers.

"*Who the hell are you?*" Brodie shouted.

Squint lines at the corners of the eyes crinkled in amusement. "The guy in the window seat who needs to go to the head."

A soft ripple of laughter circled around her. Brodie forced herself past the last vestiges of the nightmare and found herself back in her plush seat in the first class aircraft cabin. A tall man was standing beside her, stooping a little because of the curvature of the cabin ceiling. Brodie sucked in air as the anger receded, trying to reconcile the place she was in now with where she'd been just a second ago.

"Sorry to wake you," the man said. He had thick blonde hair and a trim country music goatee. Both were streaked with the brassiness associated with spending a lot of time in chlorinated water. "I had a big latte before getting on the plane. So if you wouldn't mind . . ."

Brodie blinked and her heart slowed. The man was obviously trying to move from the window seat on her right to the aisle on her left. She was blocking his way with legs, discarded shoes, rolling water bottle, and dropped book.

"Oh, God," Brodie said. Her fingers felt cold and clumsy as she gathered up the things on the floor then pulled in her feet. "I'm so sorry." she said as he eased past her to the aisle.

"No problem," he said and headed up the aisle, one hand on the ceiling to balance himself against the gentle motion of the aircraft.

Clutching her stuff, Brodie watched the man as he made his way toward the lavatories at the front of the first class cabin. He was wearing a long sleeved maroon shirt, faded jeans, and a woven leather belt. His shoulders were extremely wide and tapered to an excellent butt. He had the look of a professional football player; both lean and heavily muscled.

An elderly woman slid out of the first row of seats and slipped into the lavatory ahead of him.

The big blonde man stopped at the top of the aisle and turned around as if he'd known Brodie was watching. He looked straight at her, crossed his eyes, and grimaced at the lavatory door as if he was in dire straits.

Without thinking, Brodie leaned forward and mimed comic tears back at him.

He grinned and Brodie found herself grinning back. Their gaze held down the length of the cabin until the lavatory door opened and the elderly woman came out.

The man turned away from Brodie and she had another glimpse of his extremely excellent butt before he went into the lavatory. She sat back in the seat, still holding her book and shoes. One strange nightmare and she no longer had any dignity or self-discipline. She stowed her stuff in the seat pocket, even as the strange dream replayed itself in her thoughts. It made no sense but had certainly been the most frightening dream she'd ever had. She exhaled hard a couple of times and focused on staring out the window at the sight of clouds and sunset.

An expensive but worn leather knapsack was on the floor below the window. There was an oversized paperback book on the empty seat. The volume was a compendium by British humorist P.G. Wodehouse, one of a numbered series published in Great Britain. Surprised, Brodie turned the book to read the back cover. She loved Wodehouse and knew this particular edition had not been sold in the United States.

"Sorry, but I never lend out my Wodehouse."

Brodie looked up guiltily and her mouth went dry. If anything, the man was wider and taller and better looking than before. His shoulders were so vast he blocked her view of the seats on the other side of the aisle.

"I'm sorry," Brodie said and felt her cheeks flame.

He eased past her to his own seat, the excellent butt inches away from Brodie's nose.

"Are you a Wodehouse fan?" he asked as he fastened his safety belt.

"Yes," Brodie said, wondering if her face was red. "That's a wonderful edition. Where did you get it?"

"Great place in London called Hatchard's. On Piccadilly."

"I've been there," Brodie exclaimed. "It's one of my favorite bookstores anywhere."

"It's old," the man said, turning the book over. His hands were large and tanned and powerful with long, dexterous, big-knuckled fingers. No rings. "Probably bought the set about ten years ago."

"Are you planning to go back on this trip?" Brodie asked. Her mind raced, wondering who he was, what did he do, where he was from, why was he on this flight . . . was he married.

"Probably not. I'm just passing through Heathrow." He rifled a hand through his hair. His temples revealed a few gray hairs mixed with the blonde. There was a sapphire stud earring in his left ear with a tiny gold cross dangling below it. "Going to Edinburgh to play golf," he said.

"Oh," Brodie said. A pleasant tingle of excitement and attraction ran down her spine. "I'm heading to Edinburgh myself."

"For the golf?" He smiled and white teeth glinted inside the trim beard. The squint lines crinkled.

Kay had taken Brodie to Oslo one summer. The man's eyes were the same color as the sky over the fjord. It was like a deep, brilliant lacquer created from layers and layers of sea-swept Nordic light.

"No," Brodie said weakly. "Going to see my aunt. She lives in Edinburgh."

"Hmmm." The man pretended to think, showing the same easy humor as before. Brodie found herself torn between lust and laughter for no apparent reason. "I see a plump matron," he said. "She makes shortbread on Saturdays and calls you her 'wee bairn.'"

"Hardly." Brodie grinned. "She's an elegant orthopedic surgeon who teaches at the medical school. But I'm very impressed with your command of Scottish phraseology."

"Unfortunately you just got my entire repertoire."

The flight attendant came by to deliver menus and take before-dinner drink orders. Brodie ordered a Famous Grouse.

"Famous Grouse?" the man asked.

"It's a blended Scotch," Brodie said. "Very smooth."

"Do you mind if I follow your lead?" he asked. "I'm not usually a Scotch drinker but seeing as I'm going to Scotland it seems the thing to do."

"Absolutely," Brodie said. It was either say that or giggle like a nervous freshman who'd just met the captain of the football team.

The flight attendant flipped down their tray tables, covered them with white linen placemats, and went off to get their drinks.

Brodie opened *Shakespeare* again, hardly wanting to read but unsure if the conversation was over or not. She was conscious of the big blonde man shifting in his seat.

The attendant brought their drinks and small spinach quiche appetizers. Brodie saw the man raise his glass and inhale appreciatively. He turned to her and nodded. "I think you picked a winner," he said.

"*Slainte*," Brodie said and raised her glass. "To your success on the links."

"Is that the right thing to say? *Slainte*?" He touched her glass with his own and the crystal chimed. He sipped his Scotch. "Yes, that's very nice."

Brodie watched in a sort of stunned fascination as the man's muscular hand swirled the Scotch, making it coat the sides of the tumbler.

And then one of those hands was in the air in front of her. "I'm Joe."

"Brodie," she said faintly. His grip was firm and dry and swallowed her hand.

"That's an unusual name," he said. "Brodie."

"My mother's clan," Brodie said. "She was a Brodie from Forres."

"So I take it you've been to Scotland before," he said.

"Yes." Brodie caught herself staring at him and covered by taking another sip of Scotch. Those eyes were just *so blue*. "My family's originally from Edinburgh but my dad and I moved to the States when I was little."

"Where in the States?"

"Charlottesville. I still live there."

"I'm in Alexandria myself," he said, naming an historic Washington DC suburb.

The flight attendant came by to take their dinner orders. They both ordered the chicken.

Brodie fiddled again with the heavy book, not wanting to appear pushy or desperate. Women probably threw themselves at him in relays.

Joe cleared his throat. "We're probably on the same flight," he said. He reached into the storage pocket in front of him and pulled out an airline ticket. "Let's see. Are you on the ten o'clock connecting flight?"

"Yes," Brodie said.

"Well, how about that," he said.

Brodie took a big gulp of Scotch. "So you're going all the way to Edinburgh for golf," she said leadingly.

"With every expectation of disaster," Joe said. He smiled quickly, a wry sideways grin, and rumpled his hand through his hair again. The earring twinkled. "This is a reunion trip. There are four of us and every few years we get together and do something none of us is good at."

Brodie found herself smiling back. "College reunion?"

"No, I'm not a college man. These are my high school buddies."

"Really?" Brodie absorbed the fact that she was semi-flirting with a man who hadn't been to college. This was a first.

"Yeah," Joe said. "I went to high school in Athens. Greece is nuts about soccer and the four of us were the guys who didn't play. We were really tight and I guess we've stayed that way through the years."

Brodie cocked her head. "What were you doing in Greece?"

"My father was in the State Department and we moved all over. Ended up in Athens for high school. My buddies were diplomat kids, too."

"And they're in Edinburgh now?"

"No. Edinburgh just seemed about equal travel time for all of us. I'm the only American in the bunch and the only one in the States. Paulo is Italian and he's in business in Malta. Richard is Swedish. He lives in Stockholm now and works for a pharmaceutical company. Oscar followed his dad into Chile's diplomatic service. He's at their embassy in Paris."

"That's quite a story," Brodie marveled. "How long have you been doing this?"

He thought for a moment. "Every three or four years. We skipped a time there when I was in Iraq so I guess this is our eighth time in 20-odd years. Tells you how old I am."

"Iraq?" Brodie asked.

"Retired Marine Corps," Joe said.

Dinner was served on china with sterling silver flatware. A choice of wine was presented. Both Brodie and Joe accepted a glass of Cabernet. The lights dimmed in the first class cabin and there was the contented click of rich people eating.

Brodie and Joe chatted sporadically as they ate. Joe asked her about Edinburgh and Brodie talked about the castle, the Royal Mile shopping district, and the need to get away from the touristy areas and find a real pub. Joe was staying at the Dingerhoy golf resort outside Edinburgh. Brodie had never been there but knew it had two courses, a famous spa, and miles of nature trails. If Joe could afford a first class flight and the Dingerhoy, he was financially very well off.

The flight attendant cleared away dinner and brought coffee and cheesecake. The lights dimmed further and most people put on earphones.

"Movie time," Brodie said.

Joe punched the button for his overhead light, pulled out the entertainment magazine, and shared the list of movies. His shoulder briefly rubbed Brodie's before he pulled back. They decided to watch the same comedy film.

Joe turned out both overhead lights. Brodie slipped on her earphones, trying to ignore the fact that she was sitting in the dark with an incredibly attractive man.

The cabin was quiet as passengers either watched movies or slept. Brodie fidgeted; the movie was innocuous and not terribly funny.

Joe tapped Brodie on the arm. She lifted an earpad to hear him.

"Is it just me or is this movie pretty bad?" he whispered.

"It's pretty bad," Brodie whispered back. She felt like they were telling secrets in church.

"Do you play chess?" Joe asked, keeping his voice low.

"Yes, I do," Brodie said, unaccountably pleased.

"Excellent," he said and pulled out a small wooden travel chess set.

Wallace Macbeth had taught Brodie to be a good chess player; precise and methodical. But the man next to her was aggressive and gave no quarter. Brodie fought hard for every piece of his that she took off the board. They were each down to a handful before he was able to take her queen and surround her king.

"Checkmate," he said.

"Damn," Brodie muttered. She scanned the small board but there was no way out. She should have not played so defensively, but it was no use now.

"Best two out of three?" Joe asked, grinning.

"You're on," Brodie replied.

She won the next and lost the third just as the lights came up in the cabin and the attendant came to serve breakfast. The coffee was dark and rich and Brodie sipped it slowly, feeling the caffeine ripple through her bones.

The flight arrived in London right on time. When the plane had taxied to the gate and the seat belt light turned off, Brodie found her leather jacket and put it on. London and Edinburgh would be much cooler than Charlottesville.

Joe took a gray hooded sweatshirt and a tan suede barn jacket out of the overhead compartment and layered them on, flipping the hood over the collar of the jacket. He looked like a model in an outdoor outfitter's big and tall man's catalogue and Brodie had to hitch her jaw up before he saw her gaping at him. Even with her shoes back on he was at least five inches taller than she was. In the jacket his shoulders jutted like sandy cliffs.

They stayed together as the passengers filed out of the plane and into Heathrow, following the signs for connecting flights. Joe walked slowly, with a slightly rolling gait.

"Need to unkink." He flashed that rueful sideways grin as if he saw that she'd noticed the way he was walking. "Even first class isn't made for people my size."

They passed through passport control and were close to the security checkpoint for the flight to Edinburgh when Joe stopped and gestured toward a restroom sign. "I'll see you on the other side."

They were not seated near each other on the plane to Edinburgh. Brodie spent the short flight tapping one of her university business cards against her thumbnail, wondering if she should give it to him after the flight. She'd written Kay's telephone number on the back.

Maybe Joe was not interested in anything beyond a conversation and a chess game to ward off the boredom of a flight. Maybe he was just a friendly person. Maybe he was married and had six children. Maybe she'd be making a fool of herself.

Joe found her as Brodie waited at the baggage carousel.

"Need some help?" He had a golf bag over his shoulder and a large rolling suitcase with the handle extended as far as it would go.

"No, thanks. I just have this." Still holding the package containing the small landscape painting, Brodie snagged her suitcase off the conveyor and pulled up the telescoping handle. They started toward the exit.

"How are you getting to your aunt's?" Joe asked. "Do you need a ride?"

"No," Brodie said. "But thanks. My aunt is picking me up."

There was a small knot of drivers in the concourse looking for their clients. One was holding up a sign reading DINGERHOY.

"Well that seems to be for me." Joe introduced himself to the driver, then surrendered the rolling suitcase and golf bag. He turned back to Brodie. "It was nice meeting you, Brodie. Enjoy your vacation." He extended a small white card. "If you ever need your kitchen remodeled, here's my number."

Brodie produced her own card, hoping it wasn't limp with sweat. "If you ever get to Charlottesville, I'd be glad to show you around."

Joe took the card, shook her hand, then followed the Dingerhoy driver out of the concourse. Brodie watched him go through the big plate glass windows. He was still walking stiffly.

She glanced at the card Joe had given her.

BIRNAM WOOD
Bespoke Cabinetry
Joseph M. Birnam, Master Carpenter

PART 2

But this sore night
Hath trifled former knowings.
(*Macbeth*: 2.4.3-4)

CHAPTER 4

"We could go to the Balmoral for a late lunch," Kay said. She smoothed the front of her camel-colored Burberry trench coat and crossed her legs. Her shoes were camel suede loafers. The quilted Chanel bag on her lap matched the rest of her ensemble.

"Too fancy," Brodie said, as she set her shopping bags on the ground. "I'm just wearing jeans."

"I'm not having a plowman's lunch in a pub," Kay warned.

Brodie grinned and settled on the park bench. She and her aunt had spent the first half of the week in Edinburgh in law offices and banks, signing papers and transferring assets. Now it was Thursday and she and Kay were celebrating the end of legal hassles with an all-day shopping spree. Brodie tipped back her head and let the breezy sunshine play on her face.

Today was the first day she'd felt completely relaxed in a very long time.

They'd walked from the townhouse on Moray Place in Edinburgh's New Town to the shops on George Street and from there to the more popular Princes Street. The squash of tourists gawking at the dark spires of the High Kirk of St. Giles and the Scott Monument had chased them to the grassy slopes of the Princes Street Gardens.

From where they sat, they could see Edinburgh Castle looming over the Old Town, a magnificent pile of stone and history that dominated the Edinburgh skyline. As if to help their mood, Edinburgh's often overcast sky had given way to a rare, sparkling afternoon.

"How about tea at the Gunston House?" Brodie suggested.

"Let's talk for a few minutes before we decide," Kay said.

Something in her aunt's tone wasn't right. Brodie rolled her head to look at Kay. "Is everything all right with you and Keith?" she asked hesitantly. "He hasn't come by all week."

At 60, Dr. Katherine Macbeth was still a crisp, haughty beauty; tall and trim with the Macbeth family's gray eyes. She'd never married but for the past 20 years had maintained a relationship with a medical colleague, Dr. Keith McNeish.

"Keith's fine," Kay said. "I'd like to talk about how you're handling your father's death."

Brodie blinked. Kay was dangerously close to violating the Macbeth family's unspoken moratorium on discussing serious emotional issues.

"You really didn't say much when I came for the funeral," Kay went on. "I understand. Too many people were there. Now it's just us. So tell me. How are you?"

"I'm good," Brodie said brightly. "Just fine. Really."

Kay raised her eyebrows, prompting Brodie to go on. *And . . .*

Brodie gave an artificially cheerful *Yep, that's it* nod.

"Well," Kay said. "You've certainly never been a crybaby."

Brodie shrugged, still trying to look cheerful. There really wasn't anything to say. Her father had stepped off a balcony and turned himself into a crumpled dead shell. So she could have his Great Seal of Virginia license plates, a pile of books, and more money than she needed.

"Your father didn't leave a note, did he?" Kay asked.

"I would have told you at the funeral." Brodie bent down and fiddled with her shopping bags to signal that the topic was closed.

Diana would be proud of her. She'd bought a lot of new clothes, including a short cherry-red trench coat from the Karen Millen store to wear to some literary event she and Kay were attending tonight.

"Do you know why he did it?" Kay asked bluntly.

"Kay," Brodie said as she straightened up again. "There's no use in discussing it. What's done is done. Today was supposed to be our fun day. God knows we earned it."

"I need to talk about it," Kay said simply.

The Princes Street Gardens were like a long rectangular

bowl. The sides of the bowl were grassy slopes where couples went to find some rare Edinburgh sunshine, where kids played on the grass, where students sat on blankets and discussed literature and science. Kay wanted to talk but the beautiful Gardens wasn't a place for discussing her father's suicide. In fact, there was no good place for discussing suicide.

Kay looks old, Brodie thought suddenly. For years Kay had looked the same; elegant, statuesque, intellectual, ageless. But now her face was lined with sorrow and Brodie's father was to blame.

"Okay," Brodie said awkwardly. She slumped against the back of the bench and jammed her hands into the pockets of her leather jacket. "Why do you think he did it?"

"Your father was my big brother, not my best friend," Kay said, looking away. "He was absorbed in his own affairs. I saw him once a year. We talked less than once a month and generally the conversation was about you. Your grades when you were in school, things that you were writing, when he was putting you on a plane to Edinburgh. Never about himself."

"Dad talked about himself . . ." Brodie trailed off as she realized Kay was right, in a way. She recalled countless Wednesday night dinners. "He talked about his work, his students. All the time. But never what was going on inside his head. Is that what you mean?"

"Yes."

"Dad was always just about his research," Brodie said. "British history from Arthur to Churchill."

Kay shook her head. "No, Wallace was more than his work. He loved you very much. Too much, I sometimes thought. He wasn't demonstrative but he always wanted to protect you, shield you from too much real life."

"Not demonstrative. That's an understatement."

"He never got over your mother's death," Kay interrupted bluntly.

"That was 30 years ago," Brodie exclaimed.

"No one is strong forever." Kay turned to Brodie and her eyes were sad. "Do you understand what I'm trying to say?"

"Dad killed himself now because his wife died 30 years ago?" Brodie shook her head. "I don't see it. If Dad was that distraught he would have done it then."

"He had a toddler to take care of," Kay pointed out.

"So he waited 30 years?"

"He knew he could go," Kay said. "You were ready to handle life without him. You had money, a career, success."

"This is because of me?"

"And then you have Stanton," Kay continued approvingly. "He told me he knew you were safe with Stanton."

"Safe with Stanton?" Brodie echoed. It seemed an odd choice of words. *Established* maybe, or *professionally suited*. But *safe*?

"Your father was very pleased with your choice."

"About Stanton." Brodie stopped herself as Kay looked at her expectantly. "Well, um, we'll go into that later. What you're saying now is that Dad decided that I was set so he gave in to a 30 year bout of depression?"

"Yes." Kay twisted the chain handle of her Chanel bag into a knot, betraying how difficult the conversation was for her. "When your mother died Wallace lost a part of himself. He and Elizabeth had been having some trouble, I think. Then one day she's dead and they never got to fix whatever was wrong."

"They were having some sort of marital trouble?" Brodie had never heard that before.

Her father had always portrayed Elizabeth Macbeth as a saint. They'd met at the University of Edinburgh. He was a junior professor in the history department and she was studying economics.

"The real tragedy was how she died," Kay said, her gray eyes suspiciously watery. "A brain aneurysm at age 27. By the time Wallace woke up she'd been dead in the bed next to him for several hours. He was never the same. I think he wandered in the twilight until he knew that you were safe and then he walked over that balcony."

Brodie clamped her elbows to her sides, her hands curled into fists in her pockets. That wasn't the father she'd known; some tortured soul mooning over his wife's death until he finally killed himself over it.

She let the silence hang in the crisp air as Kay blew her nose and regained her composure, then turned to her aunt. "He never once said anything like that to me."

"Don't be naïve, Brodie." Kay straightened, her moment of weakness over. "You were his priceless treasure, the one thing he'd do anything to protect. Do you really think he'd tell you something like that?"

Brodie looked away, fighting unbearable sadness. There were a lot of students in the Gardens, young people in jeans and sweaters with backpacks full of books. On the flat, a couple was playing Frisbee. The girl couldn't catch the disc if her life depended on it but her boyfriend was laughing; she could do no wrong in his eyes.

Kay reached over and took Brodie's hand. "Have you seen a counselor?"

"You mean like a therapist?" Brodie asked. "A shrink?"

"A grief counselor."

"No." Brodie could not imagine sitting and pouring out her feelings to some stranger.

"You are experiencing grief," Kay said. "And that's something the Macbeths don't handle well. Are you having crying jags, bouts of indecision, sleepless nights?"

Brodie felt her face flush. "Nightmares," she admitted, feeling foolish.

She'd had another dream about Elizabethan England just last night. She'd been back at the Globe Theater searching for her father when Shakespeare had reappeared, an unremarkable man except for the hideous, corroded white eyes. They'd talked, more incomprehensible questions and mocking words that her father's death had been murder rather than suicide because Wallace had cheated and *what was his secret*, until Brodie ran away.

Like before, she couldn't wake up. She'd spent a terrifying night walking London's streets. The alarm clock had woken her, enraged and covered in cold sweat.

"About your father?"

"Sort of." Brodie gave an involuntary shiver. "I'm in London and I think I'll see Dad, so he can tell me why he . . . killed himself, but someone else talks to me about him."

"Go on," Kay said.

Brodie shook her head. "It's just that . . . they say that Dad was murdered."

"You know that's just denial," Kay said gently.

"Did Dad ever tell you some big secret?" Brodie blurted. "Something so fundamental and important it would change the way we live?"

"This is connected to a nightmare?"

"It just . . . I mean," Brodie faltered. "I wonder if there was something I should have known. I mean, more than him being depressed."

"You're having a normal reaction to intense and untreated grief," Kay said. She cleared her throat, the Macbeth mask of formality back in place. "It's not something you can resolve on your own. Tell me you'll see someone. I can make some calls for you, see if any of my colleagues here can recommend someone in the States."

Brodie shook her head. The last thing she wanted was everyone in Edinburgh thinking that Kay Macbeth's American niece was crazy. In some ways Edinburgh was as small as Charlottesville. An intimate city, as local writer Alexander McCall Smith once described it.

"I'm fine," Brodie said brightly. She stood up abruptly. "Let's find that tea."

☼

They ended up on the front terrace of a small restaurant behind the Saint Giles' cathedral. An awning protected them from the breeze but didn't block their view of the ornate church. The server brought finger sandwiches and a pot of loose-leaf Darjeeling.

"So, have I told you about this year's music and politics symposium?" Brodie asked as soon as the tea was poured. Kay looked vaguely startled at the choice of topic but didn't object, so for the next 30 minutes Brodie babbled furiously about the annual symposium and her students and the University of Virginia women's basketball team. Anything, really to keep Kay from talking about things that should just be left alone.

Nightmares about your father? This is just denial. Have you seen a counselor?

Kay was on her third cup of tea and her eyes were starting to glaze over when a group of dark-haired Gypsies started to wind their way around the tables on the restaurant terrace. Two women in layers of blouses and full skirts held out tarot cards while a man with a huge black moustache panhandled with an upside down tambourine. Several children of undetermined parentage, with runny noses and the furtive looks of pickpockets-in-training, trailed behind.

"Oh, for heaven's sake," Kay muttered, interrupting Brodie's spiel about Diana's coaching record. "Edinburgh is getting more beggars every day. They're all from Romania. Or Bulgaria. The European Union is getting entirely too lax."

"Fortune tellers," Brodie said. One of the women had stopped at a table to read tea leaves for a young couple. The Gypsy woman nodded vigorously and the couple laughed excitedly, clearly delighted with their fortunes. Brodie's chest tightened with jealousy.

"Now, Brodie." Kay pulled her chair closer to the table as the rattle of the tambourine neared. "It would really help if you saw someone."

"I told you," Brodie said, her eyes still on the happy couple exclaiming over a teacup. "I'm fine."

"So what would it hurt to get that validated?" Kay put her Chanel purse on the table, pulled out a smartphone and tapped on the screen.

"What?" Brodie saw the young man hand the Gypsy woman a British pound note. She tucked the bill into her voluminous skirts and said one last thing that made the couple laugh.

"Here he is." Kay put the open address book flat on the table and tapped a page. "Simon Proctor. Just the person. I'm sure he'll see you as a favor to me."

"Um." It had been a day of fun for that couple. Maybe they were tourists. *See the castle, have high tea, get your fortune told in an Edinburgh streetside café. Kiss in public. You don't care who sees because you're in love.*

"He's really excellent, Brodie. Consults in criminal cases all over the world. He specializes in serial killers."

"Serial killers?" Brodie echoed; her attention pulled back to her own table. "Kay, I'm not talking to some axe murderer expert."

"Really, Brodie," Kay said reprovingly. She indicated her phone. "I can make you an appointment right now."

"No, there are loads of other people I can talk to," Brodie insisted. The tambourine rattled loudly but she ignored it. "Diana. Even her husband Ray. Friends in the department--."

"Tell your fortune."

Brodie and Kay both looked up to see the dark-haired Gypsy woman standing by their table.

"Okay," Brodie said immediately, mentally thanking the woman for interrupting.

"Really, dear, these people are simply dreadful," Kay whispered, her hand protectively on her purse. "They smell."

"Don't be a snob, Kay," Brodie whispered back. She dug money out of her wallet and pointed it at Kay. "Five pounds for both. Her first."

The woman was older than she'd looked from a distance, with

wary dark eyes rimmed with thick black lashes. She was wearing a red print skirt, black boots, and a black sweater, with several shirts layered underneath. The skirt came to her ankles. "Yes, first," she said and deftly palmed Brodie's money.

"Good heavens," Kay said but she put away the smartphone. "You're wasting your money, Brodie."

The woman picked up Kay's empty tea cup and spat into it.

Kay flinched.

"You were done, weren't you?" Brodie murmured, suppressing a grin.

She got a frozen glare in return.

The woman swirled the saliva around the dregs of tea, then tipped the cup so that first Kay, then Brodie, could see inside. Bits of brown chard clung to the sides of the china in small meaningless clumps.

"Nice," the Gypsy said to Kay. "You have wealth. Order. Success."

"All true," Brodie said and gave Kay a significant look.

The Gypsy woman held the cup up to the light in an obvious bit of showmanship. "You look at a field of flowers. You look at it with someone special."

"Flowers," Kay said sarcastically. "How trenchant."

The Gypsy nodded. "Many many pale flowers. " She put the cup back on the saucer with a flourish, making her bracelets jangle.

"What else?" Brodie asked.

"Many many pale flowers," the woman repeated. "Beautiful flowers."

Brodie lifted her eyebrows in a question. That wasn't much of a fortune.

"Special," the woman said to Kay. "This is special thing for you."

Kay's lips compressed into a thin line of disapproval.

"You like flowers," Brodie said, trying not to laugh.

The Gypsy woman went through the spitting and swirling

routine with Brodie's cup, then stared into it with a sharp intake of breath. "You look for answers," she said softly.

"I guess," Brodie said. "I'm a history professor."

"You look for answers," the woman repeated and her dark eyes blinked rapidly. "You go to the dreams. I see it."

"I've had dreams," Brodie said slowly. Images from the Globe Theater flitted through her mind.

The Gypsy woman's eyes widened and she dropped the cup back onto the saucer. There was a sharp crack of china against china and the cup split in two, making both Brodie and Kay jump. Slimy dregs of tea oozed over the sharp edges of porcelain and onto the saucer.

The woman grabbed Brodie's left hand by the fingers and flexed her hand so that the palm was arched upwards. Brodie could feel her knuckles grinding together painfully and her wrist was strained but she didn't pull back.

"You have two," the Gypsy woman gasped. "Two lines of life."

"You're part cat," Kay said tartly.

But Brodie barely heard her aunt. The Gypsy woman had an iron grip on her fingers. A thumb pushed against the back of her hand so that the palm stayed taut. Brodie suddenly felt on the brink of discovering something important, something crucial to her very existence.

"Two lines," the Gypsy woman repeated. She stared into Brodie's face and Brodie stared back, unblinking, caught, poised on the cliff edge, waiting for the revelation. The woman's eyes were dark and unfathomable.

"Death walks here." The woman pushed a finger into Brodie's palm, imprisoning it between her own hands. "Death is very close to you."

"You're talking about my father," Brodie said.

"Death." The woman's voice dropped to a frantic whisper. "You talk to death. Someone you know is not what you think." She dropped Brodie's hand.

The tambourine rattled in Brodie's ear and then the woman was gone. The restaurant was suddenly silent.

"Charlatans," Kay sniffed. "You wasted your money."

Brodie sat back in her chair, massaging her hand. Her knuckles ached from being squeezed so hard. Her heart must have been pounding because she could feel the effect as it slowed. "Don't you think it was odd the way she asked me about dreams?" she said.

The waiter came and swiftly removed the broken cup.

"A fortune teller talking about dreams," Kay said wryly. "How original."

"Well." Brodie felt oddly disappointed. There was no revelation waiting for her. She'd merely had her fortune told about three months too late. "A little behind the time curve but still, to say that Dad--."

"One scary fortune, one happy fortune," Kay interrupted. "It's a formula. The woman is a charlatan."

"But your field of flowers." Brodie peered at the sludge in Kay's teacup. "Maybe she was talking about your vacation with Keith in June."

"We're going to Morocco," Kay said.

Betty, Kay's housekeeper, met them at the door as they walked in with their shopping bags. "There's a call for Miss Brodie," she said knowingly. "An American."

Stanton, Brodie thought and groaned inwardly.

Betty led her through the hall and into the living room, smirking the whole way. Short and stout and gray, Betty had been Kay's housekeeper for years, watching Brodie grow from tomboy to professor.

The receiver was lying on the desk. Brodie picked it up. Betty hovered, wiping her hands on her flowered apron, curiosity radiating out of her in waves.

"Thank you, Betty," Brodie said and looked at her significantly.

Betty winked and sidled out of the room, closing the door behind her.

Brodie squared her shoulders and put the phone to her ear. "Hello?"

"Brodie?" The voice was a gravelly baritone. "This is Joe Birnam."

"Joe." Brodie's knees got mushy. He had the sexiest phone voice in the world. She sank into Kay's leather desk chair. "Hello. How's the golf?"

"Pretty terrible." He laughed, a gruff chuckle. "All that yelling on the plane. I'm pretty sure that's why my game is so bad."

"This is what the professionals call deferred blame, you know." Brodie found herself grinning into the telephone. She leaned back in the chair and put her feet up on Kay's desk.

"Absolutely." Joe sounded the way a lion would if a lion talked; deep, masculine, dangerous. "I was hoping I could make you feel guilty enough to have dinner with me tonight."

He'd called for a date. Brodie swung her feet to the floor and jumped up in excitement, then froze. "Tonight? I'm so sorry. I'm going to a poetry reading with my aunt tonight at the Writer's Museum."

"Ah," Joe said slowly. "A poetry reading."

"One of my aunt's friends is the author," Brodie explained in a rush. "I'm sure it'll be terrible but I've promised her I'll go. Trying to fill those empty seats." But tomorrow Kay had her usual Friday night date with Keith. Brodie had been planning to spend the night with the BBC. She took a breath and crossed her fingers. "Would the invitation carry over to tomorrow night?"

"Most certainly," Joe said, then paused. "Maybe you'd like to come out here to the Dingerhoy?"

Joe's blue eyes, broad shoulders, and thick blonde hair rose up in her mind's eye. Brodie's imagination danced through the implications of an invitation to dinner at a resort . . . *hotel.* "Yes," she said, trying to keep her voice level. "I hear it's lovely."

"There's a very elegant restaurant in the main hotel," he said. "Or we could go casual in the clubhouse."

"Casual," Brodie said. "This is vacation time, after all."

"The clubhouse restaurant then," Joe said. "Good food, just a little more relaxed."

"That would be fine." Brodie sank into the desk chair again.

"There are some nice trails around here. Maybe a walk through the hills afterwards?"

"An evening ramble? Yes, I'd like that." Brodie clamped her free hand to her head to keep herself from flying apart. Every nerve she had was singing, just because some man she hardly knew had asked her to dinner.

"An evening ramble," Joe repeated. "Now why didn't I say that?"

"Stay in Scotland long enough and you'll pick up lots of quirky expressions."

"Just yesterday I aft gang agley," Joe said.

"Right on the golf course? You devil," Brodie flashed back and they both laughed. Joe had been imitating the Wodehouse character who often misquoted and mangled Scottish poet Robert Burns.

"Shall we say seven?" Joe asked. "Do you know how to get here?"

"I'll take a taxi."

"They pull up right at the main entrance. I'll meet you there."

"Tomorrow night, then."

"I'm looking forward to it," Joe said.

They said goodbye. Brodie replaced the receiver, jumped up, and did a crazy two-step around the room. Kay's theories and scary dreams and crazy fortune tellers were temporarily forgotten in a rush of girlish happiness.

The dance took her past the Campbell Mackay landscape painting her father had left to Kay. It was of a lavender field in

Provence. Kay had hung it over the loveseat.
The landscape was lush with many, many pale flowers.

CHAPTER 5

The taxi passed a small church off to the side. It was sheltered by a break in the soaring, leafy trees that lined the private road leading to the Dingerhoy.

I don't know how to do this, Brodie thought to herself in the back seat of the taxi and wiped sweaty palms on the knees of her pants. Her heart was thumping from a mixture of excitement and terror. It had been years since she'd had a real date and now she was going to a man's hotel. She and Stanton had just fallen into each other's company at university events and eventually had become a couple.

This was different.

The view widened and there was the Dingerhoy. The main hotel was a large Georgian house that had been tastefully expanded with additions that kept to the same architectural style. The front lawn was deep and sweeping and the sprawling golf clubhouse nestled behind a grove of trees.

Joe Birnam was right where he said he'd be. As the taxi crunched over the long, curving gravel drive to the Dingerhoy's ornate front entrance, Brodie saw him in the center of a small knot of men. He was the tallest, standing out in the tan suede barn coat and some baggy gray corduroy trousers, and again she thought that he looked like an advertisement for an outdoor clothing catalog.

The men were in some animated conversation, laughing and gesturing, but when Joe saw her in the back of the taxi he moved away from them. Their eyes met as the taxi slowed. Joe grinned broadly and Brodie couldn't help but grin back. The driver said something that she didn't hear.

Joe opened the door for her as soon as the vehicle came to a stop. Before Brodie could open her purse he'd paid the driver and asked the man to wait; his friends wanted to use the taxi to go into town.

He introduced her to them; Richard, a thin and serious bespectacled Swede; Paulo, the Italian who chided Joe for not sharing Brodie's company; and Oscar, the Brazilian who was a diplomat and who had come to Edinburgh from his country's embassy in Paris. They were intelligent, interesting men, joking about playing golf badly and attributing it to recent discoveries of various brands of Scotch. They were going to have dinner then go on a tour of haunted Edinburgh landmarks.

Brodie found herself smiling and laughing as they asked her for advice on restaurants along the Royal Mile. She told them about the streetside restaurant near St. Giles and laughingly warned them about Gypsies.

They finally shook hands all around. Richard, Paulo, and Oscar got into the taxi and it rumbled down the gravel drive. Brodie and Joe were left smiling at each other by the entrance door.

"Thank you for coming," he said, the blue eyes more unnerving than ever.

"Thank you for inviting me," Brodie said. There was a moment of mutual appraisal, and she knew they both liked what they saw.

"We decided on the clubhouse, did we not?" Joe asked.

"Casual, we said," Brodie reminded him.

"That's right," Joe said. "Although I must say you look much too nice for casual."

"Thank you," Brodie said. She had gone back to Karen Millen that morning and bought the entire window display; a cashmere cheetah print sweater, simple black pants, and teal leather loafers. She'd topped the outfit with the cherry pink trench coat and a purse just big enough for her wallet, a new toothbrush, and a clean pair of panties.

Joe put a hand on Brodie's arm to turn her towards the clubhouse on the other end of the resort and Brodie's heart thumped.

She felt like a freshman, out on a date with the captain of the football team.

☼

The clubhouse décor was devoted to golf, with antique clubs and old prints of golfers in plus fours adorning the wall. The lights were low but not dim; this was a setting for families and sportsmen. As the hostess led Brodie and Joe to a table, several heads turned. Brodie was conscious that she and Joe made a very striking couple.

The menu was a mix of French, Italian, and non-denominational modern fare.

"What do you recommend?" Brodie asked.

"Well, I can recommend the Shrimp alla Diavolo," Joe said. "Or the Chicken Saltimbocca. It's almost as good as mine."

"You cook?" Brodie asked, putting down her menu.

"It's a hobby," Joe said. "Now and then I run off to Italy. Hang out with Paulo and take a cooking class."

Brodie absorbed this fact. Joe Birnam was an intriguing man.

They ended up ordering the fried calamari appetizer to share and the two main courses he'd recommended. Joe selected a red wine and the waitress smiled and said she'd bring it right away.

"I owe you an apology," Joe said. "I sat next to you for eight hours on that damned plane and didn't recognize you as the author of *George and Martha*."

"That's quite all right," Brodie said. "Most people don't."

"I thought the book was terrific," Joe said. "I usually read military history, but my dad sent *George and Martha* for my birthday. I liked it so much I gave it to about six people for Christmas."

"So you were the spike in holiday sales," Brodie said laughingly.

The waitress returned with the wine, hors d'oeuvre plates, and a platter piled high with crisp circles of golden calamari framed by fat lemon quarters. Joe tasted the wine and pronounced it "just fine." The waitress beamed, poured them each a glass, and left.

"*Slainte*," Joe said holding up his glass and tipping it toward Brodie.

She touched her glass to his. "*Slainte*."

The blue eyes twinkled above the rim of his glass as Joe drank. The wine helped sooth Brodie's nerves but she was still tautly aware of everything about Joe Birnam and how attracted she was to him. In a starched white button-down shirt, Joe was a masculine, exciting presence. The big, dexterous hands made the flatware on the table look small. The sapphire-and-cross earring glinted in the low light.

"I'm going to tell everyone that I had dinner with the author in person," Joe said. He picked up a lemon wedge, deftly squeezed juice over the calamari, then heaped the small hors d'oeuvre plate in front of Brodie with the fried golden circles. "Although I have to say you look nothing like the picture on the back cover."

"It was old," Brodie said apologetically. The book carried an unsmiling black and white profile photo, hair in a severe bun.

"I remember thinking that the picture didn't fit with my image of the writer." Joe served himself some calamari.

Brodie put down her fork. "Why not?"

"You wrote history from the point of view of a relationship," Joe said. "It was real. They had problems. The people were vulnerable. You must be a very empathetic person to understand relationships that well."

"No." Brodie shook her head, trying to hide how surprised she was by his words. "I'm just a college teacher who tried to look at a historical figure in a way that I thought my students could relate to."

"And did they?"

"I have no idea." Brodie sighed and dipped a circle of calamari in cocktail sauce. "None of my books are required reading. The kids that read them are just gunning for extra credit."

Joe chuckled, then shook his head. The earring flashed. "I don't think you write for your students. I think you write because it's something you love to do."

"Guilty as charged," Brodie said, feeling as if her mind was open to him. It was an odd but not uncomfortable sensation. "I like finding odds and ends of history that don't mean anything by themselves. Like putting together a puzzle."

"Or a mystery," Joe said. He topped up her wineglass. "Always love a good mystery."

"Let me get this straight." Brodie realized she'd finished her calamari. "Wodehouse, military history, and mysteries. That's a pretty eclectic reading list."

"Yep." Joe picked up his wineglass. "My perfect book would be a P.G. Wodehouse murder mystery set in wartime."

"Already been done," Brodie observed. "Colonel Mustard in the drawing room with the knife."

Joe had been in the middle of drinking wine and he sputtered it back into the glass. They both started to laugh and the last bits of new relationship awkwardness melted away.

The main courses came and they ate and talked and talked and ate. Books segued into movies and movies segued into travel. Brodie considered herself well traveled but Joe had been just about everywhere.

His father's diplomatic career had started in Sweden where he'd met and married Joe's mother. The globe-trotting Birnam family had lived in Peru, India, and Spain where Joe had gone to elementary school with his older brother and younger sister. There were a few years in the United States, then when Joe was 11 the family moved to London and from there to Athens. He'd enlisted in the Marine Corps right after high school. Joe told her some funny stories about his early days as a Marine Security Guard at embassies in Mexico City, Cairo, and Tokyo but skimmed over wartime experiences in Kuwait and Iraq.

The candle in its little glass holder was burning low as the waitress took away their dinner plates and brought coffee and slices of a fruit tart. Brodie felt totally relaxed. She'd eaten her entire dinner without so much as one nervous stomach twinge. Joe Birnam was smart, funny, and easy to talk to.

"I'm really glad you gave me your card," Joe said, pouring cream into his coffee. "I'm glad we didn't have to wait until we were back in the States to do this."

Brodie felt herself blush a little. "Your card surprised me," she said.

"Why is that?" Joe asked.

"Two reasons really." Brodie ate a bite of fruit as she considered how to frame her thoughts. "First, your company name is Birnam Wood. That's quite a coincidence, don't you think?"

"I'm the Birnam," Joe said. "My cousin Marty is the Wood. Is there something unusual about that?"

"But my name is Macbeth and in Shakespeare's play the prophecy is that Macbeth is safe until Birnam Wood comes to his castle." Brodie put down her fork. "Macbeth is destroyed when the army comes disguised with the foliage of Birnam Wood. It's a real place, you know. Birnam's a village not too far from here."

"Damn." Joe leaned back in his chair. "That's not good. Do you think we're caught in some bizarre Shakespearean alternate universe?"

"I hope not." Brodie found herself smiling.

"Would it help if I told you the name is Dutch, not Scottish? As in van der Birnam."

"Your family is Dutch?"

"My dad's from this little town in upstate New York called Barneveld," Joe said. "Everybody up there is Dutch. Stuyvesant or de Groot or der Garry. My grandfather dropped the first part of the name during the Depression. Said a simpler name made it easier to find work. So I don't think the Shakespearean thing really applies."

"That's a relief," Brodie said and ate another bite.

"But you said my card surprised you for two reasons," Joe said. He laid his fork across his empty dessert plate. "What's the other?"

"Well, you do custom cabinetry and I think I might need to hire you." Brodie knew she was flirting outrageously and it felt *great*. "I'm moving into my dad's house and the kitchen is all original. Soapstone counters, about two feet of cupboard space, and a sink the size of Alaska."

"You live with your father?" Joe asked.

"He died in February. Suicide."

The words came out before Brodie knew it. She was suddenly appalled to find that she was shaking and blinking back tears. She dropped her fork and put her hands in her lap.

"I'm sorry to hear that," Joe said.

"No note, no nothing," Brodie said, unable to stop herself.

"It's all right to cry," Joe said quietly and reached across the table to touch her arm.

"Macbeths don't cry," Brodie said tightly. "We keep it all inside and then jump out of windows."

It was awful. Her throat was a solid leaden lump and her eyes burned and she was afraid to say another word lest she start sobbing like a little kid. As she fought for control Brodie kept her eyes across the room, on a family that had come into the restaurant a few minutes ago. The parents were probably in their mid-40's, with a boy and a girl who both looked to be 11 or 12. Every time one of them held up an index finger they all dissolved into laughter. It was a private family joke. Brodie wondered if the Birnam family had been like that. She and her father certainly never were.

She was dimly aware of Joe signing for the check. They sat in silence until Brodie felt strong enough to speak.

"I'm sorry for ruining your evening," she managed.

"It's not ruined at all," Joe said. His eyes were knowing and sympathetic. "How about that evening ramble now?"

"Thank you," Brodie said gratefully.

"No thanks needed." Joe stood up and helped Brodie on with her coat. By chance or design his thumb touched her cheek and brushed away a tear. She looked up and their eyes met.

It was the most intimate moment she'd ever shared with a man.

☼

It was nearly 10:00 pm when they walked out of the clubhouse. The sky was a clear gray twilight and the air was damp and cold. The hills beckoned in the distance, gray-green folds of land, lush and quiet.

"I keep forgetting how far north Edinburgh is," Joe remarked.

"It won't get totally dark until very late," Brodie said. "Not quite the land of the midnight sun, but close."

Joe pulled on his own coat. "Shall we work off our dinner? The trail starts over there and winds on for a couple of miles I hear."

"Sounds perfect."

He smiled and nodded at her, the blonde hair falling over his high forehead. By now his manner of rifling his hand through it was familiar.

They strolled down the clubhouse porch steps to the wide macadam path running in front of the Dingerhoy complex, heading for the fork in the path and the Nature Trail marker. Despite the cool night a large wedding reception was being held on the broad lawn in front of the main entrance. A bar was set up and the crowd milled around while a photographer took pictures of the bridal party.

The bride was wearing a simple but elegant white dress with a predominantly red tartan sash running from shoulder to waist, secured with a jeweled brooch. Female guests were in elegant dresses and hats while some of the male guests wore tuxedos. Most men were in full kilt regalia, including sporran, short jacket, and shoes that laced around the ankle.

"Men in kilts." Joe grinned. They stopped to watch for a moment. "Now I know I'm really in Scotland."

"My parent's wedding looked like that. I have a picture. My father in the Macbeth kilt, my mother wearing the Brodie sash."

"So all the different tartans represent different families?" Joe asked.

"Clans, actually," Brodie said. She discreetly indicated an older gentleman in a blue, green, and white open plaid kilt. "He's wearing the Forbes Dress tartan. And I think the bride's sash is the Grant tartan. Although it's a little bit like the Dalziel. Or the MacLintock."

"You know all the tartans?" Joe asked.

"I used to." Brodie nodded. "My aunt Kay made me memorize them years ago."

"I'm impressed," Joe said. Brodie wasn't sure if he was talking about her or the plaids.

On the outskirts of the wedding party an older gentleman in kilt and short jacket raised his glass to them. "Tha's a lovely lassie you've got there, laddie."

"I was just thinking the same thing," Joe called back.

Brodie felt the color rise in her cheeks.

"You're a Yank, eh?" The kilted wedding guest ambled toward them.

"Yes, sir."

"Come to steal our lassies, did ye?" The old gentleman was evidently in his cups. He beamed at Brodie. "She looks a sassy one."

"She is," Joe said conspiratorially.

"You'll have to watch yourself."

"I will," Joe promised.

"Good luck to ye, laddie," the old gentleman chortled.

Joe put his hand on Brodie's arm and they continued down the path away from the wedding.

"You're a lovely shade of pink, Sassy," Joe said.

"Oh dear," Brodie said. She touched her cheek; it was hot.

"I'm making it worse, aren't I?"

"Yes."

Joe laughed, the sound rippling into the open night sky. Brodie shook her head bashfully and stuck her hands in her pockets, her purse dangling around one wrist.

They walked in silence for a few minutes, skirting the golf courses, as the path unwound in front of them. The Dingerhoy wasn't exactly in a valley, but the rolling hills in the distance made it seem that way.

Brodie felt her equilibrium return as they walked. The hills were the sort peculiar to Scotland. They gave her the feeling of embracing enclosure and open freedom at the same time.

"A little better?" Joe asked.

"Yes."

"How's your mom handling it?"

"She died when I was little," Brodie said. "I'm a 33-year-old orphan. My aunt is the only family I have left."

"You and your dad must have been close."

"Yes. No. Sort of. He didn't get too close to other people. Mostly we were colleagues. He was my department head at the university."

They walked on. Here and there, Brodie saw sheep or horses grazing, and the coil of a stone wall.

"I know a little about loss," Joe said into the crisp night air. "Tell me if I'm right. First there's disbelief, then a sort of negotiation. You know, *I'll donate to charity and be a better person if you make this not be true, God.*"

"That's right," Brodie said quietly. "But it doesn't work."

"No, it doesn't." Joe's voice was quiet, too. "So then there's anger. The *why did you leave me* sort of anger. And only after the anger's done can there be grief. That's when the healing starts. Eventually there's acceptance."

"I can't get mad at Dad," Brodie said, surprising herself. "He had a goofy will, and I was mad at that, but to get mad at him . . ." She trailed off. The path rose gently and their pace slowed. There was no one else around.

"Ah," Joe said. "Maybe you're in the *how the hell am I going to cope with this* phase."

"You might have something there," Brodie said. Joe Birnam was opening a door she'd tried to keep closed but tonight she couldn't stop herself from walking through. "I just want it to go away so I don't have to cope with anything."

"Not wanting to but doing it anyway is the definition of courage," Joe said. His hands were in his pockets and he looked big and solid and reassuring in the suede barn coat.

"I don't have any more courage," Brodie said simply.

"Sure you do," he said.

"I lost a war I didn't even know I was fighting," Brodie heard herself say. "I should have known he was depressed. We worked together. Had dinner every week. I should have known him better."

"Maybe," Joe said. "But those guessing games never get you anywhere, believe me."

"I've got too many questions." Brodie didn't have the strength to pretend otherwise with this man the way she'd been able to with Diana and Kay and everyone else. For some reason she didn't understand, her defenses were gone tonight. She just wanted to put her face against Joe Birnam's chest and sob until she was exhausted and fell asleep.

"Hey." Joe stopped walking. "Let yourself grieve. You'll heal. You're pretty resilient."

"Resilient?" Brodie stopped walking, too. "How do you know? You've just met me."

Joe turned so they were facing each other. "There's steel in your eyes," he said.

Brodie looked down and shrugged. "So I have gray eyes."

"Listen to me." Joe reached out and tipped her chin up. His touch was very gentle. "This is an old Marine master sergeant talking. At times my life depended on knowing who could suck it up and keep going and who couldn't. When things get bad and there's fear in everybody's eyes, there's always a few who've got that something extra that says the fear isn't going to get them. You've got that look."

Brodie found herself caught by the force of his expression.

"You're serious," she murmured.

"Yes, I am," Joe said and dropped his hand. "I think you're made of some pretty stern stuff. But your father betrayed the trust between you. Maybe you need to let yourself get mad at him for that."

Brodie bit her lip. Joe was the first person to put it so succinctly and it pried open a floodgate of emotion. She found herself nearly overcome, barely able to nod. She started walking again.

"Something like this you have to take one day at a time," Joe said, keeping pace. "There'll be good days and bad days but after awhile you'll find that there are more good than bad. One day you'll wake up not expecting it to be a bad day. It's just another day. That's when you know you'll make it."

"I hope you're right," Brodie said shakily.

"Trust me," Joe said. "I am."

The hills rolled away from the path. The sun was a glorious ball of flame sinking below the rim of the hills. The Dingerhoy was far behind them now, the sounds of the wedding muted by the lush landscape.

Joe walked slowly, his hands by his sides. His gait was awkward as they started up another gentle incline.

"Still cramped from the flight?" Brodie asked.

"What?" He looked down at her.

"You seem to be limping," she said.

Joe halted. "I'm wearing a prosthetic."

Brodie stopped walking, too, not sure what he meant. "I'm sorry?"

"A prosthetic," Joe repeated. There was tension and unease in his eyes.

Brodie gave her head a tiny shake, still not getting it.

Joe reached down and raised his left pant leg high enough for Brodie to see that there was a slim metal pole instead of an ankle.

"Oh," Brodie said.

He let go of the corduroy and straightened up.

Brodie touched his arm. "Iraq?"

"Yes."

"When?" she asked softly.

"Five years, nine months, two weeks, and some odd days ago," Joe said. "Lost the leg above the knee."

"Will you tell me how it happened?"

He blinked, evidently surprised, then nodded and they started walking again, the air cool and damp around them. Joe tucked his hands in the pockets of the barn coat. The hills were closing in on them, throwing dark night shadows across the path. Brodie couldn't see his face.

"My second tour in Al Anbar," he said after awhile. "I took an IED. We were running a supply convoy to a fire base. I saw a dead animal in the road and swerved. It still detonated."

Brodie shivered.

"The Hummer flipped," Joe went on. "The guys got me out and the convoy formed up and had a nice little firefight. Luckily we had a Navy medic with our unit. Good friend of mine. Trey Morales. He got a tourniquet on what was left of my leg and kept me from bleeding out. Saved my life."

"You remember it?" Brodie asked.

"Yes. I never even lost consciousness." Joe was walking straight ahead, not looking at Brodie. "We'd been going through this crummy little village. Just a couple of cement hovels, really, and *blam*, the Hummer's crapping apart and on fire. Then I'm propped up against a wall and I know my leg is gone. I remember it seemed really important to tell Trey that I knew the leg was gone as if he wouldn't notice it otherwise. He's telling me, *I've got you, man, I've got you*. He's doing two things at once; getting a tourniquet on what's left of my leg and putting out the fire. I'm smoking. I mean I'm on fire. I remember seeing the smoke and being confused because it was as if I was a piece of meat on a barbecue spit."

Brodie focused on breathing. He was telling her this horrible story so simply, so plainly. There was no self-pity, no hopelessness, just the same wry humor that he'd shown before.

"It was because I was wearing synthetic compression shorts. After me they said nobody could wear them. Because when they catch on fire they melt your skin." He paused. They walked a little further. The twilight darkened around them before Joe spoke again.

"Trey manages to put out the fire but the next problem is that there's this old Iraqi guy running at us. Right through the middle of what had been the town square, I guess." Joe rumpled a big hand through his hair, making the cross below the sapphire dangle. "He's got the long robe on and a turban but he's got a rifle. He's running right at us, through the middle of the firefight. Crazy screaming *Yaw, Yaw*, at us and Carson, my corporal, shoots him. I'll never forget that moment. It's hot as hell, the Hummer's on fire. Trey is swearing under his breath, trying to get the tourniquet to tighten down on my thigh, I'm stinking like blood and charred meat, the noise of the firefight is deafening, and this guy is screaming *Yaw, Yaw* like a banshee. Then the chopper came and five minutes later I was at an aid station. I never saw Trey again. Never got to tell him thanks for saving my life."

"What happened to him?" Brodie asked, knowing the answer.

"He was killed by a sniper a week later," Joe said. He looked away from Brodie and she could see he had trouble talking about this part. "He's buried at Arlington."

"I'm sorry," Brodie said. "You two were close."

"You make friends differently in those circumstances," Joe said. "A wartime buddy knows you like no one else ever will. You can catch their eye in the middle of hell and you know what they're thinking and they know you. You keep each other strong."

"Did you negotiate?" Brodie asked. "Get mad before the grief?"

"I was willing to bargain my soul," Joe said. "I would have given anything to make the news of his death a mistake. And then I was mad as hell at him for leaving me just when I'd lost a leg and needed him. He'd saved my life and then disappeared. I was stuck alone with too many bad memories."

The path ended in a stone wall marking the boundary between the Dingerhoy and an adjoining farm. They both were surprised to find they'd been walking with Brodie's hand resting in the crook of Joe's elbow. They separated slowly and leaned against the wall.

"Do you have flashbacks?" Brodie asked.

"Nightmares once in awhile," Joe admitted, staring out at the hillside where some sheep were still grazing. It was truly dark now and their wool made white smudges on a dark background. "I'm back in that shitty little town and the old guy is running at us. Screaming words I don't understand. Other times I wake up totally surprised. *Hey, I'm missing a leg. What the hell?*"

Brodie gave a tiny shiver.

"I haven't talked this much about it in a long time," Joe said. "It actually feels kind of good."

"What's the hardest thing to deal with?" Brodie asked, feeling like he was inviting her into a place many did not go.

"Telling beautiful women," Joe said, with that now familiar wry grin and sidelong look.

Brodie flushed and shook her head.

"Okay," he said. "Not standing up in the shower."

"Seriously?"

"Yes," Joe said simply. "You have to accommodate the simplest things. But it's easier now. When I was in the hospital it took me awhile to realize what I was going to have to do, how I was going to have to live from now on. Damn, I was angry. I mean *really* angry. But one day I realized that no matter how I felt about it I was still going to be a one-legged man. I could be an angry and useless one-legged man, or I could be the best one-legged man there was."

"Not many people have the strength to think like that," Brodie said. Her own loss seemed puny compared to what Joe had been through.

"I'm not the only one," Joe said. "But I think I was luckier than most. No brain injury. The rehab center had a pool. I'd always been a good swimmer and as soon as I could stand the pain I was doing laps. It kept me in shape, got the swelling down. I still swim a couple times a week. Play water polo."

"So." Brodie looked at his profile; strong jaw, trim beard, high forehead. "Then you retired from the Marine Corps?"

"No." Joe bent and rested his elbows on the stone wall. He stared at the hills in the distance. "No, I went back to Iraq."

"You went back?" Brodie nearly fell over in shock. "What are you, made of iron?"

"Titanium, actually." Joe gave her another rueful smile and shrugged. "Maybe I needed to prove to myself that I was still the same as before but the point was that I was still a Marine. I'd passed all the tests; I could still do my job. And they needed unattached guys like me in Iraq." He paused. "I'm divorced. Brief marriage a long time ago. No kids. It was easier for somebody like me than for somebody worried about his family falling apart back home."

"So you went back to Iraq."

"Yes. Pulled a third hitch and saw enough dead bodies to last me a lifetime."

He stopped talking and they watched a shadowy figure on the hillside with the sheep. The fluffy smudges of white followed the figure toward the other side of the hill and disappeared over the crest.

"I think you are the bravest person I've ever met," Brodie said honestly.

Joe exhaled heavily. "I won the Silver Star my last tour in Iraq and the news people made a big deal out of it. You know, *one legged Marine able to leap tall buildings in a single bound.* Suddenly I was assigned some phony job at the Pentagon where they could show me off."

Brodie could imagine the public relations coup he represented; he'd pulled three combat hitches, won a major medal, lost a leg, and still looked like a recruiting poster. "That wasn't what you wanted, I take it."

"It gave me a good excuse for retiring," Joe said. "After 22 years it was time to do something else so now I'm a carpenter."

"I didn't know the Marine Corps taught people how to be carpenters," Brodie said, trying to coax out one of those sideways smiles.

Joe looked at her as if he knew what she was trying to do and a corner of his mouth lifted. "My parents bought this old house in Old Forge, New York when my older brother was born," he said. "We'd visit there every summer from wherever we were and Dad would add another room. When we kids got older, we helped. A real circus but we actually did pretty well out of it. I learned how to build things. My older brother Brian became an architect and my younger sister Rosemary is a nurse. You can guess why."

Brodie imagined the Birnam tribe; Mom and Dad showing their kids the world but bringing them home every summer to a place where they built something together. "It sounds wonderful."

"Surprisingly, the place is still standing. Mom and Dad retired there."

"But you didn't?"

"No," Joe said. He looked out toward the hills again. "I was a 40-year-old one-legged man who'd never lived by his own rules. I enlisted when I was eighteen and had either lived by my parents' rules or the Marine Corps' my entire life. I had to prove to myself I could live on my own terms." He turned to Brodie and leaned against the low stone wall. "I suppose that sounds pretty foolish, doesn't it?"

"No," Brodie said. She balled her fists on the top of the wall. "I know exactly what you mean. All my life it's been my father's rules or the University's rules. Sometimes living in Charlottesville is like living in a box."

"A box?"

"Don't get me wrong. Charlottesville was a wonderful place to grow up. There's mountains and the house . . . the university. It's meant a lot to me over the years to be part of it. But now . . . after . . ." Brodie started floundering and shook her head. "Since my father died . . . it's like the box is closing in."

"Maybe it's time to do something else."

"I have tenure," Brodie said helplessly. She rubbed a fist against the rough stone on the top of the wall. "Once upon a time it seemed that was all I'd ever want. "

They stood by the low wall for a long time, not speaking, the darkness deepening. Their shoulders touched and neither moved away.

"Tell me about resilience," Brodie finally said. "Say you weren't just humoring me back there."

"I told you," Joe said. "There's steel in your soul. I can see it in your eyes. You're going to face each day one at a time until there are more good ones than bad ones."

"Is that what you did?"

"Yes."

"Was today a good day?" Brodie asked softly.

"Yes," Joe said. "Today was a very good day."

They smiled at each other, very close together. Brodie's heart thumped and she willed him to come even closer, to put his arms around her and hold her hard against his chest.

"I think I mentioned I'm a bachelor," Joe said. He reached out and pulled up the collar of Brodie's trench coat, protecting her against the cool night air. "What about you? Is there anyone in your life right now?"

Brodie's thoughts slurred into slow motion as his eyes searched hers in the darkness. She and Stanton were over but there hadn't been any closure. It was a technicality but it was there and she knew she'd never be able to lie to Joe Birnam.

"Ah," Joe said into the silence.

"Another professor at the university," Brodie said unhappily.

"Been together a long time?"

"About three years," Brodie said. "But our relationship was . . . is . . . at a crossroads right now."

"Well," said Joe. "I hope it works out the way you want it to."

"Thank you," Brodie said, feeling wretched.

"Shall we walk back now?" Joe asked.

And just like that the evening was over.

Joe's limp was more pronounced as they headed down the path back to the Dingerhoy, as if he was tired and could no longer conceal it. Brodie shoved her hands into the pockets of the trench coat, silently furious with herself. She searched desperately for a way to explain what she'd meant by *crossroads*; words that would convince Joe that Stanton meant nothing to her any more. But all the explanations running through her head sounded crass and stupid and tacky, like excuses for why she wanted to cheat on her boyfriend.

The lights of the Dingerhoy made a glowing crescent against the night sky that grew larger as they approached. By the time they got to the hotel a fine mist had begun to fall and Brodie was shivering. Joe ushered her into the hotel and asked the concierge to call for a taxi. They were assured one would be there in ten minutes.

Joe asked if Brodie wanted to wait in the bar. Despite the cold and the rain she said, no, outside was fine. The bar was full of happy, noisy partygoers and the last drunken wedding guests.

They stood outside by the front entrance. There was only a

small overhang and they stood close so both could stay out of the rain. Brodie was very aware of Joe; the wide breadth of his shoulders, the faint scent of a spicy cologne, the rhythm of his breathing, the way he wasn't quite looking at her.

One of the wedding party in kilt and jacket dashed through the rain towards a car parked along the gravel drive. Amid laughter and singing, people in the car shouted for him to hurry.

"It's called *smirr*," Brodie said, wishing she had something better to offer.

"What?" Joe shifted to better protect Brodie against the rain, his back acting as a buffer against the weather.

"*Smirr*," Brodie said. "It's the word for this kind of rain in Scotland. You think it's just mist but you end up drenched."

"Ah," Joe said. He bent his head toward hers. "Look, Brodie. I hope your professor guy knows what a special woman you are. He ought to be fighting tooth and nail to keep you."

"It's not . . . like that," Brodie said. Joe was very near, one hand against the stone building. In the dark his eyes glittered like cobalt glass. "But thank you for saying so."

"Remember," Joe said. "One day at a time."

"All right," Brodie managed to say. If he came an inch closer they would be kissing. Her knees felt like jelly.

He reached out with his free hand and thumbed the line of her jaw, then touched her hair. "Your hair's like cornsilk," he murmured.

Brodie lifted her chin and held her breath.

"Taxi for Birnam!"

They both flinched at the loud voice. Joe pulled his hand and eyes away and Brodie leaned around him to see a big black taxi on the gravel drive, its headlights creating long cylinders of light through the dark rain.

"That's us," Joe called to the driver. The concierge popped out of the hotel entrance with a big umbrella and walked Brodie and Joe to the taxi. Joe opened the door.

Brodie got in and the taxi pulled away.

PART 3

Macbeth shall never vanquished be, until
Great Birnam wood to high Dunsinane hill
Shall come against him.
(*Macbeth:* 4.1. 92-94)

CHAPTER 6

"All right, then, here's the ten million dollar question," Diana said. She finished her last bicep curl and paused with the dumbbells in her hands.

"Go . . . on," Brodie panted. She bent her knees, moving into a deep squat as she held two 25-lb dumbbells.

"If he'd asked, would you have stayed?" Diana said.

"Yes," Brodie said, standing upright again. Her arms ached and her knees were wobbly as she replaced the dumbbells in their slot in the weight rack. She sucked in air, her heart rate staccato from the strenuous workout.

"It wouldn't have been, well, awkward?" Diana put her dumbbells in the rack, too. "He's only got one leg."

"No." Brodie collapsed onto the bench near the weight rack and found her sports bottle. She sloshed down some water with Joe in her mind's eye; the broad swimmer's physique, the big dexterous hands, the brilliant blue eyes. Whatever was missing or had been left badly scarred didn't matter. "No," she repeated, putting down the bottle. "He's in no way . . . diminished . . . as a man."

It was their usual Tuesday morning workout in the field house. Brodie was still fighting jetlag. She'd returned to Charlottesville late Sunday night and had been unable to sleep. Monday had dragged; she'd taught her undergraduate class, returned calls about the music symposium in May, and fetched Mouse from the kennel all while feeling like a zombie. Working out had to help.

"Fine," Diana said. "So let me see. The guy's a looker. Says the right things. He's clearly interested. Came right out and told you he's unattached."

"Divorced a long time ago," Brodie recalled. "He said it was a brief marriage. No kids."

"So why on earth did you say anything about Stanton?"

"Because not telling him would have been lying," Brodie said stubbornly. "We're still not officially broken up."

"You're kidding," Diana exclaimed. Two undergraduate girls milling by the Nautilus machines at the other end of the gym turned to look. Diana's glare sent them scurrying the other way. "You let *that* get in the way?"

Brodie sighed and busied herself with her gym bag, pulling out her boxing gloves. Far from the relaxing visit she'd envisioned, the trip to Edinburgh had left her with more questions about her father's death. The Shakespeare dreams haunted her and she was having a hard time finishing the Ackroyd book. The wrecked date with Joe Birnam was the icing on the cake.

Diana lowered herself onto the weight bench. "What's really going on here, sweetie?"

Brodie shifted to straddle the bench and face Diana. "Do you think I'm going crazy?"

"No," Diana said slowly. "Maybe you didn't want to sleep with Joe as much as you think you did."

Brodie shook her head. "This isn't about Joe." She looked around the gym. The two girls at the other end of the gym had been joined by two boys. A gym date. How cute.

She swung her eyes back to Diana who looked at her expectantly. Brodie took a breath and kept her voice low. "I've been having weird dreams," she said. "I've had a couple of really odd dreams where people talk to me about Dad. Kay thinks I'm obsessing about him the way he obsessed about my mother and she wants me to see a shrink."

"Let me guess," Diana said. "She believes his obsession is what caused him to kill himself after all those years."

"Yes," Brodie said.

Diana pointed at Brodie. "Always the same dream?"

Brodie shook her head. "I'm someplace thinking I'll find Dad, but then somebody with white eyes talks to me. Says all sorts of weird things."

"White eyes?" Diana frowned. "Is this person blind? An albino?"

"Neither." Brodie drank some more water, trying to sort out what she'd seen in those strange, too-vivid nightmares. "It's like . . . white rust. Corrosion of some kind."

"Sounds scary," Diana said.

"It is," Brodie said. "I know I'm asleep but I can't wake up and I'm sure I'm going to die. Worst nightmares I've ever had."

They sat silently on the weight bench while Diana thought. The two couples at the other end were giggling as the guys showed the girls how to work the Nautilus machines. The girls barely moved 20 pounds on the overhead press.

"Maybe the white eyes represent Stanton," Diana said finally. "Because you know if you stay with him it'll kill you."

"Well, if that's the case, here's the kicker," Brodie said. "Besides telling me I needed professional help, Kay said it was important to Dad that I was with Stanton."

"Kay said that?" Diana said in surprise.

Brodie nodded. "She thought Dad felt that he could . . .you know . . . go . . . because I was safe with Stanton. That's the word she used. Safe."

"Safe?" Diana echoed. She shook her head. Her braids were pulled back in a ponytail and the beaded ends clacked softly. "I don't buy it. If you two ever met a mugger Stanton would probably give him your purse, his wallet, and ask the guy if he wanted an autograph. Right after he peed his pants."

Brodie laughed in spite of herself.

"Kay is a nice person and I'm sure she means well, but there's a disconnect here," Diana said. She stood and stretched her back. "Maybe your dad told her he liked Stanton. Maybe he said *safe* meaning *financially secure*, something like that. After all Stanton's not exactly poor, is he?"

"That never occurred to me at all," Brodie said

thoughtfully. Diana's interpretation made sense. Although her father hadn't been overtly concerned with money while he was alive, his will had made it clear that amassing wealth had been important to him. No doubt he'd liked the combination of Stanton's family money, university salary, and sizeable television commentator income.

Diana shrugged. "Those nightmares are probably directly linked to Stanton. Any woman thinking she's got him around her neck for the rest of her life would have nightmares."

"So," Brodie said, feeling better. "I'm upset about Dad, upset about Stanton. Makes sense the two would get tangled in a nightmare."

"So what are you going to do?" Diana asked.

"Beat on the heavy bag for awhile," Brodie said. She hauled on the heavy boxing gloves and stood up. "Get rid of this jetlag. Clear my head."

"I mean about this Joe guy."

"Joe?" Brodie punched her gloved fists together and moved to the center of the gym where the 100-lb heavy bag dangled from a rafter. "Nothing. I blew it."

"So unblow it," Diana said. "Call Stanton, tell him it's over for good. Then call Joe. You said he gave you his business card."

"I'm not calling him." Brodie hefted a right hook into the bag. She felt the reverberation all the way up to her shoulder. "It would be too pathetic." She put a whine into her voice. "'I'm not a two-timer. Please date me.'"

"Coward."

"Yep." Brodie punched the bag again, putting her weight behind it.

Diana picked up her towel and water bottle. "So what's the moving schedule?"

"I'm meeting the interior designer at Dad's house tomorrow and we'll figure it out." Brodie jabbed at the bag again.

"Okay," Diana said. "Ray and I are just waiting for the word and we'll be there. See you later, sweetie." She disappeared into the locker room.

Right uppercut, left hook, right again, and then a jab hard enough to make the bag bounce. The chain suspending the bag from the steel rafter rattled.

Brodie beat the bag until her wrists were sore, her fingers were wrinkled inside the sweaty gloves, the jetlag had been pounded away, and it was time to be a talking head in front of 50 kids who were more interested in each other than in what she had to say.

But the workout hadn't really cleared her head. The same words had been running through it for days.

Your hair is like cornsilk.

CHAPTER 7

"I do not think that is a good plan," Stanton said. His voice in her cell phone was loud and testy all the way from Los Angeles. "The house is too far from The Lawn. And it's old. There's a lot to maintain. Is this some idea that your aunt put into your head when you were in Edinburgh?"

"Big dogs need a big yard," Brodie said, tucking the cell phone between her shoulder and ear as she tied the belt of the cherry red raincoat. "Mouse loves playing here."

"You can't make decisions based on that animal."

Brodie bit back a retort and sat down on a green wire settee. She was on the wide wooden porch of the Granite Castle Road farmhouse. The dogwood and crabapple trees would soon be covered in buds, softening the red brick exterior and green metal roof of the two storey house. Her brown Volvo wagon, sporting her father's OFK 362 plates, was parked at the top of the gravel drive that snaked through the opening in the split rail fence.

Mouse was sniffing ardently at something under a tree. The big German Shepherd had a creamy white belly and legs, and a black saddle. Brodie had dubbed the dog Mouse for her big, pink-lined ears.

"I'm not going to help you move," Stanton said stiffly.

"Okay," Brodie said, making a face he couldn't see. They both knew that Dr. Stanton Cabot Sloane II did not do manual labor. He was, after all, the Stafford Whitcomb Memorial Professor of American Foreign Policy, scion of the University of Virginia's Woodrow Wilson School of International Relations, and a noted political commentator.

"The house is too big for one person," Stanton persisted. "Too isolated."

"I grew up here, Stanton," Brodie said. "I can't sell the

house."

"I'm not saying you should sell it, Dr. Macbeth," Stanton said smoothly. He often used her professional title as a term of endearment and it never failed to irritate her. "You could make a bequest."

"What?" Brodie asked, glancing at her watch. It was almost ten o'clock. Mouse rolled joyously on the grass, paws bicycling the crisp morning air.

"A bequest to the university," Stanton said, sounding impatient.

"Dad left money to the library fund."

"You could donate the house," Stanton pressed.

"Donate the house?" Brodie echoed.

"Dean Slocum was telling me last semester that they're looking for a property to make into a writer's retreat. They want someplace a little out of the way and quiet. The farmhouse would be perfect." Stanton paused, as if trying to gauge Brodie's mood. "I'm sure he'd be sufficiently grateful."

Mouse got to her feet and trotted toward the house, fluffy tail waving. Cell phone still pressed to her ear, Brodie restlessly walked down the porch steps to meet the dog. "What do you mean, sufficiently grateful?"

"Well," Stanton said carefully. "I expect he'd want to do something in your father's honor in return. For the College of Arts and Sciences, I mean." He coughed discreetly. "Maybe a television studio. The Wallace Macbeth Memorial Studio."

"A television studio?" Brodie stopped walking and stood stock-still in the middle of the driveway. Mouse crunched over the gravel and pressed her head against Brodie's leg in a dog version of a hug.

"The International Relations and History Departments could share it. My department could train students to report on international events from the political perspective and your department's media studies program could use it to make historical documentaries."

"You're kidding, right?" The breeze played around the base of Brodie's neck. "You really think I'd trade Dad's house for a university television studio?"

"You need to think rationally about your decisions and not be so impulsive," Stanton said. "Making a bequest could have some very long term career implications for both of us."

For a moment Brodie considered breaking up with him right there and then, with the coward's cushion of long distance between them. But Stanton had been by her side at the funeral and had handled the press and planned the memorial service. As much as she wanted to, she couldn't dump him over the phone. "We need to talk," she countered. "About where we're going."

"I'll be back in Charlottesville in two weeks," Stanton said, not sounding surprised. "We're taping the segment on Clinton. I'll come for the weekend before I start doing the voiceovers. We'll talk."

"Okay," Brodie said and relaxed a little. The bad news might be that she had to wait another two weeks but the good news was that any emotional confrontation was safely put off for now. The breeze gusted and she put a hand to her head as her short hair rippled. "Uh, I forgot to tell you. I cut my hair."

"Cut your hair?" Stanton was clearly taken aback. "Am I going to like it?"

Brodie smiled grimly to herself. "No," she said. "It's pretty short."

"How short?" Stanton asked suspiciously.

"Very," Brodie said.

"I'm not happy," Stanton warned. "First the house, now this. What's happened to you?"

A blue van turned into the driveway, bouncing between the posts of the split rail fence. Mouse's ears pricked up like radar. "Stanton, I've got to go," Brodie said. "The interior designer is here."

"You hired a designer?" Stanton shrilled.

"Bye, Stanton," Brodie said. "See you in two weeks." She broke the connection and switched off the phone as a chic woman in black jeans and a mink jacket bustled out of the van. The woman had platinum bouffant hair, red lipstick, and a cardboard tray of takeout coffee.

Lydia Sue Crosby was one of the pillars of Charlottesville society. Her husband was on the university board. The Crosbys had attended both the funeral and memorial service for Wallace Macbeth.

"Brodie!" Lydia Sue gave her a double air kiss. "Your hair is fabulous! You should have been a model. And Mouse." She handed the coffee tray to Brodie and made cooing noises at Mouse who pressed close. Lydia Sue rubbed the dog's ears then hauled sample books and fabric swatches out of the rear of the van. "I've got loads of ideas. This house is fabulous! Let's start with the grand tour."

Brodie knew she'd done the right thing by calling Lydia Sue as soon as the double latte hit bottom. As the two women walked through the house, Lydia Sue kept everything on a very professional level, tactfully taking the emotional sting out of all the decisions Brodie had to make. The interior designer quizzed Brodie about how she would use each room, what furniture did she want to keep, and what did she want to bring over from the townhouse. When Brodie hesitated or floundered, Lydia Sue smoothly offered suggestions and solutions. Mouse followed them from room to room, the dog's nails clicking on the hardwood floors.

The living and dining rooms were relatively easy to deal with. Most of the living room furniture was old and unattractive and could be given to charity. The dining room set was dark and formal but it had come from the Macbeth family in Edinburgh so it would stay. Lydia Sue suggested a new chandelier and a new coat of paint. Brodie agreed as they passed through the swinging door to the kitchen.

"Well, well," Lydia Sue said, turning around slowly to take it all in. "Very vintage."

The kitchen still sported the glass-fronted white cabinets, stone countertops, and old oak furniture from Brodie's childhood. It had always been the domain of their housekeeper, Mrs. Weir, a battle axe from Inverness who'd moved to Charlottesville from Scotland with Wallace Macbeth and his toddler daughter. She'd retired to Scotland a few years ago but Brodie could still hear the woman's thick Scottish brogue snapping out instructions to finish oatmeal and do chores.

"I'm thinking bleached maple in here," Lydia Sue said. "Maybe a Shaker style--." She made a strangled sound. "Brodie! There's no dishwasher!"

I know a great contractor who could fix that. Brodie shrugged and pushed Joe Birnam out of her mind. "It doesn't really matter. I don't cook much."

Lydia Sue pointed to the refrigerator. "What's on the other side of that wall?"

"Dad used to have a housekeeper," Brodie said. They walked out of the kitchen and into a plain bedroom. "This was Mrs. Weir's room. The only bathroom downstairs is in here."

"If we redo the kitchen we can break through the wall and hook up a dishwasher." Lydia Sue looked around the bedroom then went to the window and parted the curtains. "Fabulous view of the dogwoods. This can be a very nice guest room. Maybe red toile?"

They went from Mrs. Weir's room into the den.

"This is the only furniture I want to keep," Brodie said softly.

Lydia Sue turned on the overhead light. The dark green walls glowed. Ancient leather book spines made for a muted and comforting collage.

"Dad always napped on this sofa," Brodie said. "First rule when I was little was never wake him up."

"Light sleeper?" Lydia Sue said, counting outlets.

"I guess." Brodie nodded. "He'd wake up really angry. He hardly ever got mad but waking him up made him furious." She pointed to the tartan-covered window. "He even nailed the curtains to the window frame so no light came through."

"Should we replace them?" Lydia Sue said, moving to the window. She slid a finger between the tautly nailed wool and the window frame. "Goodness, Brodie! These curtains haven't been cleaned in years. Moths have been feasting on them!"

"We can get them cleaned, can't we?" Brodie went over to Lydia Sue. The decorator eased nails out of the window frame. As more light came into the room Brodie saw how dirty and tattered the curtains were.

"I really want to keep them," she said. "It's the Macbeth clan tartan. Dad brought the fabric from Edinburgh."

"We'll find a fabric re-weaver." Lydia Sue stuck her pencil in her hair, grabbed her clipboard, and steered Brodie upstairs. They decided to enlarge Brodie's old bedroom and use the furniture from the townhouse along with a new upholstered rocking chair. The bathrooms would get a facelift.

They'd leave alone both Wallace's bedroom and another which contained all the papers and personal items that had come out of his office in Randall Hall.

With those decisions made they sat at the kitchen table to talk décor. Lydia Sue showed Brodie a soft sage velvet. "Maybe we can do a sofa in this for the living room and use your floral loveseats from the townhouse on either side. Form a U-shaped seating area around a larger coffee table. It would be fabulous."

Brodie fingered the velvet. "Can we do all this and get me moved in two weeks?"

Lydia Sue looked like she was going to have a stroke. "In *two weeks*?"

"Yes." Brodie nodded as Lydia Sue goggled at her. "Can you do it?"

"Omigod," Lydia Sue said. She took some short, jerky breaths and pulled out her cell phone. "We won't be able to do anything custom. Or the kitchen. Why two weeks?"

"It would just be good." Brodie flipped the pages of a sample book and studied a square of damask.

Lydia Sue stopped punching buttons and covered Brodie's hand with her own. "Are you sure you're all right? Do you want to talk about it?"

"No," Brodie said brightly. "I'm fine. Really."

Moving day was a carnival. Lydia Sue and her staff arrived just as the moving truck rumbled up to the farmhouse. Diana's husband Ray Hudson, who was the University of Virginia football team's defensive coach, brought a carload of football players to move furniture. Most of Diana's team came to help, too, and the move turned into an Athletic Department social event.

The flirting and jokes were loud, spilling from room to room, fortified by pizza and soda. Lydia Sue and her swarm of junior decorators seemed to be everywhere at once.

By six in the evening the house was decorated, polished, and organized down to the curtain pleats. Lydia Sue pronounced the house fabulous, hugged everybody, collected her people, and went home to soak her feet. The football and basketball players took off for a movie and more flirting.

Ray left to get Chinese food and to pick up dogs; Mouse had been with Puck, Diana and Ray's black Labrador Retriever all day. The two dogs were full of energy after being cooped up in Diana and Ray's townhouse and zoomed around the farmhouse in an orgy of investigation. Mayhem ensued around an empty pizza box in the kitchen before Ray broke it up.

Brodie, Diana, and Ray talked and ate their way through a pile of Chinese takeout. It was close to midnight when Brodie walked the couple to the front door. Puck resisted, unwilling to leave Mouse, and so Ray looped a hand around the dog's collar and encouraged him across the lawn to their SUV parked behind Brodie's Volvo wagon.

"My hero," Diana called from the porch as Puck flopped in all directions except forward, the dog's tail whipping the night air.

"You're going to go home and bang Ray like a drum, aren't you?" Brodie said mournfully, holding onto Mouse. Diana and Ray had a happy, enviable relationship. They seemed to fit together seamlessly.

"Pretty much." Diana smiled sadly, sensing Brodie's mood.

"Doesn't he have a brother?" Brodie sighed.

"Nope." Diana rubbed Mouse's ears. The two women grinned as Ray let loose with a string of epithets as he shoved Puck's rump into the back of the SUV.

"Do you want me to stay tonight with you, sweetie?" Diana asked. "This house has a lot of memories in it."

The hatch of the SUV clanged and Ray came back to the porch. He was big and solid, a muscular tank of a man in basketball shorts, Nike tee shirt, and cross trainers. His skin was dark and his shaved head gleamed. "That dog is dumb as wood," he said. "How many times has he gotten into that vehicle?"

"He's still learning," Diana said apologetically.

Ray looked from Diana to Brodie then stepped forward and put his hand under Brodie's chin. "Are you going to be all right here tonight?" he asked seriously. His big dark eyes searched hers.

"Yes." Brodie batted his hand away. Ray's eyes were like liquid chocolate, the kind to get lost in. Diana was so lucky.

"Don't you fib to me," Ray warned.

"I'm fine." Brodie rose up on her toes to kiss his cheek. "Diana just asked me the same thing. You guys worry too much about me."

Ray frowned. "Are you sure?"

"I'll be fine," Brodie insisted. "You go along home. Thanks for everything, both of you."

She waved as the SUV headed out, then locked the front door behind her. Without the crowd of people who'd been in the house all day, the place felt too big, too quiet.

Brodie drifted into the living room. It looked totally different than it had two weeks ago. Then it had been a shabby, cluttered space between the kitchen and the den. Now it was like a luxury hotel with cream walls, butterscotch linen draperies, dark wood entertainment center, her floral linen loveseats, a glass topped coffee table, and a mossy chenille sofa with linen toss pillows. Silver mercury glass lamps floated on mirrored end tables. A velvety rug with a faint vine design deadened Brodie's footsteps.

The dining room draperies were the same butterscotch linen and the walls were a faint smoke blue. The new chandelier was a riot of silver and crystal droplets.

It didn't feel like home at all any more. Suddenly Brodie was struggling with the questions she'd never be able to ask her father. *Why? Why did you do this? Why did you leave me with no word of explanation?*

Mouse pressed against her knee, as if sensing her pensive mood.

"We're going to be fine, sweet dog," Brodie said as she bent and stroked Mouse's head. "Yeah. We're unpacked, your bowls are in the kitchen, and you've got a big yard to play in. Much better than the townhouse. Let's go to bed."

She led Mouse into the kitchen and out the back door to do her business. When the big dog came back into the house Brodie started turning off the lights.

She lingered in the den. Lydia Sue's stylish hand had cleaned and tidied and added a rug but otherwise the room was still the same. Dark green walls, familiar leather sofa, mahogany desk, butler's table with a selection of Scotch bottles and Waterford tumblers.

The refurbished tartan curtains were open. The window reflected the night back at her.

Brodie drifted over to the bookshelves. She'd finally finished *Shakespeare.* The next book was *Endurance* by Caroline Alexander.

Mouse stretched out on the bedroom carpet as Brodie put on a big tee shirt, brushed her teeth, then curled into bed with the book. *Endurance* was the story of British explorer Ernest Shackleton's disastrous 1914-1916 attempt to cross Antarctica. His ship, the Endurance, had been caught in the pack ice below South America. After a harrowing year the ship was crushed by the ice. The marooned men survived on floes that moved north with the ocean currents, until the melting ice turned to slurry and they launched their three salvaged lifeboats. All reached uninhabited Elephant Island a week later. Knowing their plight to be desperate, Shackleton took a handful of men and sailed off in the largest lifeboat to find help.

Twenty-two men were left on Elephant Island with Shackleton's second-in-command Frank Wild. He kept them alive by creating a shelter from the two remaining lifeboats and killing penguins and seals for food. The hope that Shackleton and his crew would reach the whaling community on remote South Georgia Island was all they had.

Frank Hurley's original photographs were a riveting accompaniment to the harrowing story.

She was lying down, damp and agitated. Her feet felt as if they were burning, a rich hot pain that made her bite her lip to keep from crying out. Somehow, it seemed important not to reveal how she felt.

The place she was in was dark, with the sort of wet chill that weakens bones. The air reeked of a foulness Brodie couldn't identify; excrement, rotted fish, salt water, and something besides.

It was like the strange dreams she'd had before, vivid and substantial. And just like before, she knew she was there to find her father.

"Dad?" Brodie called out, trying to see through the

gloom. "*Dad.* I'm here."

"Yer da's in Wales, Perce," a man's voice replied. "Mick and Mack are going to take care of you just fine."

Brodie blinked and struggled to sit up, resting her weight on her elbows. The scene was the makeshift hut on Elephant Island that Shackleton's men had dubbed the "Snuggery." She squinted in the darkness, her senses almost overwhelmed by the smells as well as the sound of keening wind and pounding surf.

As her eyes adjusted to the lack of light she could see the low stone wall forming the base of the shelter. The roof was two arcs made of upside-down boats. She was in a sleeping bag under the largest arc. Nowhere was the roof high enough to stand upright. On a crate, an oil lamp guttered in the draft, giving off a stink like burning fish. The feeling that her father was there was strong and eerily familiar.

Several men squatted on their haunches around her in the odd shelter. Their clothes were dark and filthy from the long months of their ordeal. One man pulled off a blackened anorak to reveal a grimy undershirt and long, pale arms. He started taking surgical instruments out of a pan of water and laying them on a cloth smoothed over a crate. Brodie recognized him from the pictures in the Alexander book as Dr. J.A. McIlroy, often referred to as Mick.

She reached out and grabbed the front of his undershirt. "Do you know where my father is?"

McIlroy froze in surprise. Someone else detached Brodie's hand from his shirt.

"Perce, you've got nothing to worry about," a man's voice came from the dark beyond the oil lamp's flickering circle of light. "Mick and Mack are going to fix you up right."

Brodie squinted. The speaker was Frank Wild himself, a small imperturbable man with an unlit pipe clenched in his teeth.

"I'm here for my dad," Brodie said and tried to get out of the bag. The pain in her feet made her sink back with a small gasp.

"Easy, Perce, easy," Wild cautioned. "It'll be over soon."

"The chloroform won't bother you at all, Perce." A third man moved toward them. It was Alexander Macklin, the other surgeon on Shackleton's expedition.

Perce. They were calling her Perce. The whole strange dream came tumbling into focus. Just as in the Globe she'd been Richard Burbage, now she was being taken for Perce Blackborow, the youngest member of the Shackleton expedition. Originally a stowaway, Blackborow had become a real and well-liked member of the crew. His feet had been badly frostbitten during the open-boat journey to Elephant Island and the surgeons had amputated the toes of his left foot.

Macklin dropped onto his knees at Brodie's side so that she was flanked by him and Wild. "Tell me what he told you," he said and leaned into the light.

Terror rose in her throat. "*No,*" Brodie croaked.

Macklin's eyes were the same as Shakespeare's; a horrid corroded mess that radiated menace and made Brodie sweat.

"I knew you'd play again," Macklin said softly. "You're his daughter and you'd have the same questions he did. Why, why, why."

"What's wrong with your eyes?" Brodie heard herself ask hoarsely.

"You know, the game is quite exciting. Pieces on a constantly shifting board." Macklin mimed setting chess pieces on an imaginary board resting on Brodie's sleeping bag. "Your father was quite good. He really didn't need to cheat."

Brodie stared at him. There was nothing she could say that would make any sense.

"But he did, I know it." Macklin pretended to move the chess pieces, faking concentration over the board. The white eyes glittered and his tongue caressed his lips. "You just need to tell me how he did it. What was his secret?"

"Stop talking about my father," Brodie said, gasping as she tried to make herself wake up. She sucked in the oily, fishy air and tensed her body. *Wake up!*

Macklin showed her a small glass flask and a rag. "This is chloroform," he said, pouring fluid onto the cloth. "If you don't tell me how he cheated, your game will be over."

"What?"

"Tell me his secret."

"I don't know what you mean."

The cloth pressed over her face. Brodie gagged and struggled to push it away. Macklin shoved his other hand under her head, trapping it between his hands. Brodie flailed at his arms, holding her breath, sure that if she breathed in the fumes coming off the cloth she would die. She got hold of a corner of the cloth and Macklin pressed harder, crushing her head. He was killing her and Brodie's brain rang with the tolling bell of desperate survival.

She dug her nails into Macklin's hand. His grunt of pain was drowned out by a siren growing louder and louder as it came closer and closer.

Brodie struggled against a painful feeling of being turned inside out. The dream swirled and buffeted her. Rage thundered through her body, blotting out her thoughts and making her heart race. Blood pounded in her ears.

She woke with a small furious scream, tangled in the sheets and damp with sweat.

Reality as evidenced by pale mauve walls, her mahogany bedroom furniture, and the new upholstered rocking chair gradually replaced the vividness of the dream. She blinked at the clock as the last whiffs of oily, fishy salt air wafted away.

It was eight in the morning. She was alive.

The alarm clock sputtered into silence.

Brodie heard Mouse thump up the wide oak stairs and remembered that yesterday had been moving day. Which meant that today was Sunday, the day that she was having dinner with

Stanton.

"Damn," Brodie whispered.

CHAPTER 8

The Old Mill Room of the Boar's Head Inn was arguably the most elegant restaurant in Charlottesville. Soft music played, candlelight flickered, and contented diners murmured compliments to the chef for their 5-star meals. The tap of silver on fine china was hushed by the Olde Hunt décor.

"You went behind my back and I'm not happy," Stanton said. "It's not the best use of your father's property. But we can come back to that. You said you wanted to talk and I agree. We need to address some long term issues."

Brodie blinked at Stanton. It was too much to hope that he was going to break up with her but her heart gave a little flutter nonetheless. She sipped some wine and nodded at him to go on.

Stanton was as handsome as ever in a wasp-waisted European suit that emphasized his slender build and sharp features. They'd met at a university function just as *George and Martha* made the New York Times best seller list and Stanton started burnishing his academic credentials with guest appearances on a major news network. At first she'd been drawn by the combination of striking looks, professional success, and the self-assurance that came with his family's Houston oil money.

Now she just wanted him to understand that whatever it was they'd had, it was over.

"Your friendship with Coach Johnson." Stanton patted his lips with his cloth napkin and replaced it in his lap. "Is it really in your best interests?"

"You mean Diana?" Brodie was completely caught off guard.

"Hear me out," Stanton said. "You could take over as chair of the history department in a few years. The search committee will bring in an interim department head, everybody knows that. Then it'll be your turn. You're an alumni of the university. You're Director of Graduate Studies for your department. Your father was synonymous with the department. You'll have both name recognition and the sympathy vote."

Brodie put down her fork. "What does that have to do with Diana?"

"If you want to be head of your department," Stanton said carefully. "You have to cultivate the right people. Coach Johnson might not be the right people."

Brodie's mouth fell open.

"She's a coach, not a true faculty member," Stanton persisted. "She doesn't understand your situation. She's not the right influence. Look what she had you do to your hair. And that red dress. I can't believe you're wearing something that skimpy. You're a tenured professor at a prestigious university and she's got you looking like a harlot."

The waiter came by and asked if everything was all right with their dinner and Stanton said well, he was a little disappointed in the Cabernet used for the mushroom sauce but no, he didn't want a replacement, just coffee.

Brodie leaned forward as soon as the waiter had wilted away with their dishes. "Diana Johnson is my best friend," she said tightly. "You and I, on the other hand, are really just professional colleagues. Our relationship has run its course."

"What?" Stanton frowned.

"It's time to step back from the assertion that we are anything more than fellow academics," Brodie said, remembering the cheatsheet she'd made months ago.

Stanton rolled his eyes with impatience. "Is this because I can't make it to your symposium next month? I told you I was going to be very busy this entire semester."

"It's not about that, either."

"Then what are you talking about?" Stanton looked genuinely baffled. "After all, we're the power couple of the College of Arts and Sciences."

"God, Stanton," Brodie said in quiet exasperation. The difference between this meal and the dinner with Joe Birnam at the Dingerhoy was like night and day.

The waiter appeared and set down their coffee.

"Did you hear me?" Stanton said sulkily when the waiter left.

"Let's leave the university and my friends out of this," Brodie said.

"I don't see how we can," Stanton countered.

"Stanton, Brodie, so good to see you both."

Brodie jerked her head around to see Dr. Harry Casey, an adjunct professor from Stanton's department, with his tiny wife Lorna in tow.

"I said, Harry, that can't be Brodie, not with that hair," Lorna chirped. "But he said if it's Stanton it has to be Brodie and there you are. I hardly recognized you." She gestured at Brodie, taking in the red silk designer sheath dress, Hermes scarf, brown lizard slides, and cropped platinum hair. "So . . . *Mia Farrow*."

Stanton stood. He shook hands with Casey and gave Lorna a peck on the cheek. "Beautiful as ever, Mrs. Casey."

Harry Casey turned to Brodie. "We're so sorry again about your father." A shambling sandy-haired man, he touched her hand sympathetically, like a sad sheepdog.

"Thank you," said Brodie, and then Stanton went into his act, asking Casey if he had summer research plans, complimenting Lorna's nondescript hair, and downplaying his own latest appearance on network news talking about Congressional challenges to the power of the presidential veto.

"He was on when all the girls in bridge club were over," Lorna said ingratiatingly. "They all said he was so handsome but of course I told them he was taken."

"Why, Lorna," said Stanton. "I'm blushing."

"My, my," said Brodie. She didn't care for Lorna Casey. The woman was the mainstay of the Charlottesville gossip mill.

"Stanton's really getting the department some national attention," Casey said. "Dean Slocum's thinking about his television studio concept. I think it's brilliant."

"Umm," said Brodie as Stanton smoothed his Italian silk

paisley tie and tried to look modest. Harry Casey was so ready to hitch his wagon to Stanton's star it set her teeth on edge.

The Caseys eventually moved on to a table in the middle of the elegant dining room. Lorna waggled her fingers at Brodie before sitting down. Brodie curved her lips and waggled back.

"Well, I see a smile," Stanton said smugly. "Are you feeling better about things now?"

Brodie took a deep breath. The restaurant seemed smaller with the Caseys there. "We need to come to closure, Stanton," she said. "We really don't have a more significant relationship any more and it's time to acknowledge it. That's all I'm saying."

"Is this about sex again?" Stanton didn't look upset, just sure that he could talk her into a different point of view.

"It's an area of incompatibility," Brodie said carefully.

"I think your expectations are unrealistic." Stanton's voice was smoothly self-assured. "We're not teenagers. We're professionals who have put sex in its rightful place. You need to start acting your age and not be so . . . rabid."

"*Rabid*?" Brodie echoed in surprise.

The word came out a little too loud. Out of the corner of her eye Brodie saw a number of other diners stare at them, including Lorna Casey. Brodie's stomach cramped. By morning it would be all over the University that the power couple of the College of Arts and Sciences had been arguing at the Boar's Head Inn.

"You've been under a lot of stress and it's finally coming out tonight," Stanton said. He reached for Brodie's hand. "Once you get over Wallace's passing we'll get back to how things were."

"No," Brodie said. "This has nothing to do with Dad." His manicured hand was slimmer and more delicate than hers and she felt vaguely repulsed. No wonder she'd been having hideous dreams about him. Brodie pulled her fists into her lap as the restaurant's dark paneling and hunting print wallpaper closed in.

Lorna Casey swiveled her eyes at them and nudged her husband at the same time.

"You really need to think about what you're saying," Stanton said testily, obviously offended by Brodie's gesture. "We're good for each other's career."

The waiter brought the check in a discreet leather folder. Stanton handed the man his credit card and looked at Brodie, his mask of solicitude still in place.

"What's your summer schedule?" he asked.

Brodie knew Stanton was using the waiter's presence to distract her. "I'm teaching the graduate Survey of Historical Literature on Tuesdays and Thursdays," she said. "And having office hours for my dissertation students on Friday mornings."

The waiter left and Stanton pocketed his credit card. "A nice relaxing schedule," he said "The summer semester will help life get back to normal. You'll come over on Sunday and I'll make piña coladas, just like always."

"Stop it, Stanton." *Dad killed himself and I'll never understand why. Life will never be normal again. I hate piña coladas and I don't want you.* Brodie wanted to shout all that at him and more but didn't. She was an adult. A rich, accomplished adult. She could cut her hair and buy new clothes but some things would never change.

"I'm off tomorrow." Stanton had his smug look on, knowing he'd won a concession from her. "The voiceovers should take a week. We'll pick up the discussion then."

Madge Harper, head of the Alumni Affairs office, was at the Casey's table. All three eyed Brodie and Stanton. Lorna said something and Brodie saw Madge's face register surprise.

"We'll talk again when I get back," Stanton said, trying to get Brodie's attention. "Isn't that a good plan?"

Brodie watched Lorna and Madge gossip, swiveling their eyes at her then quickly looking away. She felt the dead weight settle on her shoulders again, heavier than ever. She wasn't going to make a scene in the middle of the Boar's Head Inn and Stanton knew it.

"I said, isn't that a good plan?" Stanton pressed.

"It's a ripping plan," Brodie said, defeated.

"I really wish you wouldn't use your father's British expressions," Stanton said reprovingly as he came around the side of the table to pull out her chair, keys to his Mercedes in hand. "I'm only saying that because I have your best interests at heart. It makes you sound pretentious, Dr. Macbeth."

CHAPTER 9

The alarm clock was clanging. Brodie struggled against a painful feeling of being turned inside out. The dream swirled and buffeted her. Rage thundered through her body, blotting out her thoughts and making her heart race.

She woke with a small furious scream, tangled in the sheets and damp with sweat.

Her heart was pounding so hard she thought she was having a heart attack. As she gulped air she tasted the tang of salty sea spray.

It had been Elephant Island again. She'd been outside this time, walking on the small spit of stony beach outside the hut made of overturned lifeboats. Shackleton himself was there and this time he had the corroded white eyes. Brodie had been faced with the choice of throwing herself into the heaving gray sea or having him shoot her with the long hunting rifle the explorer had managed to save from the wreck of the Endurance.

Or telling him Wallace Macbeth's secret.

It was hard to know which was worse; last night's dinner with Stanton or the nightmare?

Brodie turned off the alarm and sat up. Monday morning and there were things to do. Classes to teach and symposium plans to finalize.

"One day at a time," she said shakily as Mouse trotted into the bedroom.

On Thursday, Brodie worked out with Diana in the morning, then taught class. Afterwards, she grabbed a boxed salad to eat at her desk. As she walked to Randall Hall, the mid-April weather was mild and The Lawn was littered with students and Frisbees trying to pretend that spring break wasn't over. She could almost laugh at those foolish nightmares.

Of course, her father hadn't been murdered over some hidden secret. His suicide had been proven by the police investigation. Kay believed he'd done it. A gypsy had even confirmed it in a strange sort of way.

What she really needed was to be absolutely and finally rid of Stanton. It was too late for anything to happen with Joe Birnam, but being finally free of Stanton would end the dreams. She would write another cheat sheet for the next conversation with him. That way she wouldn't let him talk her into any more delaying action.

"Dean Slocum called," Sarah said as Brodie came up the stairs. The secretary's desk was positioned outside the bank of professors' offices. "He said I was to call as soon as you came in."

"Okay." Brodie propped her bookbag on Sarah's desk. "Did he say what he wanted?"

"No." Sarah looked at Brodie expectantly and Brodie shrugged in return.

Sarah dialed the dean's office and told whoever answered that Dr. Macbeth was in. As she listened to the response her eyebrows went up. Sarah disconnected and looked at Brodie. "The dean says he'll be here in 15 minutes."

The fact that the dean would come to Randall Hall rather than summoning Brodie to his office wasn't lost on either of them.

"Thanks, Sarah," Brodie said lightly.

She went into her office, turned on the lights, and dumped her bookbag on the desk.

"What the hell, Macbeth?"

Brodie whirled around to see Jackson Hull in her doorway. Hull was the driving force behind the department's interdisciplinary Media Studies program. He had longish gray hair, a red-veined nose, and horn-rimmed spectacles.

"Hello, Jack," Brodie said. She leaned against the edge of the desk and tried not to breathe in the cigarette fumes coming off his rumpled tweed jacket.

"Sloane tells me you're not pitching in with the television studio," Hull said.

"If you are asking if I'm donating my father's house to the university, the answer is no. I moved in. It's my house now."

Hull's face flushed with anger. "Sloane said you were on board. The house for the studio."

"He did, did he?" Brodie flushed with suppressed anger. Murdering Stanton would probably be better than sex. With him at least.

Hull pointed a tobacco-stained finger at her. "I liked your father, I really did. But he protected you, made you Director of Graduate Studies, kept your little music symposium limping along. I hope you know that's all over now. When I'm department head those perks are going to someone else and you're going to have to toe the line."

"Thanks for the heads-up, Jack," Brodie said evenly and nodded at her desk. "Now if you'll excuse me."

"You'd better let Sloane talk some sense into you, Macbeth," Hull snarled and walked out.

Brodie tossed the salad into the trash and sat down at her desk. Jack Hull was a jerk. Almost as big a jerk as Stanton. Who else had the famous Dr. Sloane told she was donating the house to the university? Was he still pushing the rumor, trying to build up enough pressure so that she'd do it even now? Now when he got back from California, in addition to convincing him they were truly broken up, she'd also have to make him understand she was keeping the house. It was going to be a dreadful conversation.

The comforting playlist of country music beckoned. She picked out Radney Foster's *Another Way to Go* and clicked the icon.

Howard Slocum, dean of the College of Arts and Sciences, walked into Brodie's office as Radney sang that he was tired of pretending, that there wasn't going to be a happy ending. Slocum was a big, rotund man with pronounced male pattern baldness and a steel trap mind. He and Wallace Macbeth had been friends and Brodie knew the dean was troubled by her father's suicide.

"I hear you moved into the big house," Dean Slocum said after giving Brodie a clumsy peck on the cheek. He sat in the upholstered chair next to the desk and Brodie settled uneasily into her desk chair.

"Yes," Brodie said. She turned off the music and waited for Slocum to ask about a possible bequest.

"That's great," Dean Slocum said distantly. He cleared his throat. "Brodie, I thought you should be the first to know that the search committee has selected a very distinguished academic to replace your father as head of the history department."

"Oh." She'd been so ready to hear Slocum say something about donating the house that it took a moment for the message to register.

"I wanted to tell you first." Dean Slocum glanced around the office, his eye resting on the framed Patsy Cline albums and the cardboard Grand Ole Opry model Diana and Ray had given Brodie for Christmas.

Brodie waited.

Slocum shifted in his chair. "The search committee has selected Dr. Donald Pedder. He's head of the history department at Stanford but he's originally from Virginia and wants to retire here. He's an Arthurian studies historian. Hasn't published too much lately but *The Round Table Bloodline* is a classic."

Brodie nodded. The Pedder name was familiar.

Dean Slocum ran his hand over the edge of Brodie's desk. "Dr. Pedder is not a young man and the consensus is that he'll be a caretaker for a few years." The college dean looked meaningfully at Brodie. "You would be his natural successor, especially if you maintain your publishing momentum. What's your next project?"

Brodie shook her head. The echo of Stanton's words made her uncomfortable. "I really haven't decided," she said. "This hasn't been a very creative time."

"I'm sure you'll be working on something terrific in no time soon," Dean Slocum blustered. "You've garnered a lot of the right kind of attention for the university. The sort a department head needs."

"You know Jack Hull thinks he's next in line." Brodie said.

"No," Dean Slocum said and made a dismissive gesture. "Jack's a good man, of course and his success is inarguable. The Media Studies curriculum is the best in the nation because of the way he's teamed with the international studies department and Stanton, of course." Slocum coughed discreetly in acknowledgment of Brodie's relationship with the revered Dr. Sloane.

"But Jack doesn't go down well with alumni," he continued. "You have the inside track as far as I'm concerned. You're a noted scholar on the Revolutionary War and a bestselling author. The music and politics symposium is very popular. Attendance and donations have gone up by ten percent every year you've chaired it. That makes you very appealing to our alumni base."

It was subtle but effective pressure: Brodie's publishing success led to alumni attention which in turn led to increased donations. Ditto the annual symposium. Her moneymaking abilities for the university were what mattered and she was better at it than Jack Hull. She was too young yet to get the department head slot, however, so Pedder would hold the job until Brodie had been around long enough. In the meantime, she was expected to keep writing because it made the university look good when a tenured professor published a bestseller.

It was the box she'd come to dread.

"Just a word of caution," Dean Slocum said. He stood up and Brodie did, too. "Pedder can be a little prickly. It's important for you to stay on his good side. He's very well respected and his recommendation will be pivotal when he's ready to retire."

"Good to know," Brodie said noncommittally.

"He'll be here in June," Dean Slocum said. "He wants to meet with everybody on Monday the tenth. It'll be a mandatory meeting. Before your colleagues scatter for the summer."

"Yes, of course," Brodie said.

"I know this has taken a terrible toll on you." Dean Slocum's face was full of sympathy. "You lost both a parent and a close colleague. Grace and I are here for you. Anytime you want to talk."

"I'm fine," Brodie said brightly. "Really."

CHAPTER 10

In front of the television with Mouse at her feet and a microwave dinner on her lap, Brodie called Stanton on the Saturday after his scheduled return.

He was supposed to have flown in the night before. She'd waited all day for him to call.

His voicemail clicked on.

This is Dr. Sloane. Obviously I'm unavailable. Leave a message.

Brodie held the phone to her ear and thought of all the things she could say.

Stanton, we're over.

Stanton, there's really nothing more to talk about.

Stanton, you're giving me nightmares.

Brodie said nothing. The voicemail timed out and she hung up the phone. "You can damn well call me," she said to the empty room.

Mouse made a grumpy noise and Brodie went into the kitchen to throw away the plastic entrée tray and let the dog out. It was a pretty night, with plenty of stars. The azaleas bordering the fence line were a riot of pink. The dogwood trees and daylilies would bloom in another week or two.

Mouse bounded up, tail wagging, the dog's eyes glowing like pinpoints of reflection. Her favorite plastic hedgehog was in her mouth. Brodie pretended to snatch the toy. Mouse leaped away before she could.

It was an old and often-played game. Brodie never got the toy. Mouse pranced around to show off the drooly piece of plastic.

At 11:00 pm, having finished *Endurance*, Brodie climbed into bed with *Fighter Boys* by Patrick Bishop from the shelves in the den.

The back cover described the book as "superb" and

"unputdownable."

Brodie was soon immersed in the air war over Britain in 1940. The young British pilots were scared and inexperienced. They fought and cried and were wounded and died until the Germans stopped coming out of the skies above the English countryside.

Stanton didn't call on Sunday, either.

Or Monday.

Or Tuesday.

On Wednesday, Brodie was in her office. She had a stack of papers to grade but she checked the university's instant messaging system instead and realized that Stanton was online. He was no doubt sitting in his office in Cabell Hall, not 200 yards away. He'd been the one who'd insisted they weren't over, that they'd talk. But apparently couldn't be bothered to call her.

There was a soft knock on her open door and Brodie jerked her head up from the screen.

Sarah Gibbard was in the doorway. "They took out the furniture in your father's office this morning," the secretary sniffed.

Brodie nodded, her anger with Stanton replaced by fresh pain over her father. *One day at a time,* she reminded herself. She forced a small smile. "The new chairman of the department gets new furniture, does he?"

"Yes," Sarah replied. She put a small yellow envelope, stenciled with a brown "M," on Brodie's desk. "I found this taped to the underside of a desk drawer," the secretary said.

Inside the envelope was an unremarkable key.

"Probably yet another emergency house key," Brodie sighed and stowed it in her purse. "Dad was always losing keys. There's a drawer full of them in the den."

Sarah left. Stanton was no longer logged into the university intranet. Brodie thought about calling his cell phone and graded papers instead.

At 5:00 pm she wandered out of her office to check her mail. The usual university notices were in her slot. Details about the upcoming graduation, a campus blood drive, and the university magazine with a feature article about an economics professor with the improbable name of Sabine Seagull. The woman had a mass of curly black hair and looked to be about 12 years old. She'd written a trendy book about the cost of identity theft entitled *How To Be You.*

Two envelopes stood out from the notices. Brodie turned them over as she went back into her office. The first envelope contained an invitation to accept a posthumous achievement award for Wallace Macbeth from the Royal Society in London. The award would be given during the Society's annual three day conference.

The Society hoped Brodie would say a few words about her father's legacy as a modern historian. She smiled wryly as she read the stiff, pompous note. It was just the sort of recognition her father would have been pleased to accept.

Brodie swiveled her chair to check the desk calendar. Graduation was in late May. The Royal Society event was in early June and the week before the history department's first meeting with Dr. Pedder. She could go to London, accept the award, see a play. Brodie grabbed a notecard and an overseas stamp and wrote out a brief acceptance.

The other envelope had a return address in California that she didn't recognize. She pulled out a piece of notepaper with the Stanford University crest at the top.

Dear Dr. Macbeth,
I write to you with mixed feelings; happiness that we shall meet at long last and sadness at the circumstances which will lead to it. Your father was a brilliant man and I feel I cannot

fill his shoes; nonetheless I look forward to being in Charlottesville this summer and assuming the post of chair of the history department.

Your father and I were friends, colleagues, and rivals(!) for many years. Last year we started a collaboration on the Arthurian myth in anticipation of a book to be published this fall. Your father was to send me his notes. Due to his untimely demise I must ask that you send me his material. It is of the utmost importance.

I look forward to receiving Wallace's research at your earliest convenience.

Sincerely,
Donald Pedder

Brodie read the note twice, the connection finally dawning. Pedder's business card had been in her father's wallet the day he died, obviously because of this joint project. But if her father had ever done research on King Arthur, Brodie had not found it. She got another notecard and wrote Pedder that she was sorry, but she was not aware of any research notes or materials pertaining to his request. But of course she was looking forward to meeting him in June.

"Knock, knock."

Brodie looked up to see Ellen Foster, an adjunct history professor, standing in the office doorway. "Hey, Ellen."

"What's keeping you so late?" Ellen asked. She was in her mid-60's, plump and grandmotherly in a white linen shirt and a pair of reading glasses on a beaded string around her neck. Her husband was a professor emeritus in the anthropology department; their children were grown and out of the house. "You and Jack Hull are the only two others in the building."

"I got a letter from Dr. Pedder," Brodie said.

"Really? Do you have his mandatory meeting on your calendar?"

Brodie grinned. "Is that a nice way of saying you think he's going to be a trifle difficult?"

"I never said anything of the sort." Ellen said virtuously.

"And I never would have inferred it." Brodie rolled her eyes. Ellen was a smart, friendly colleague with a good sense of humor.

"I was just going down to The Corner," Ellen said, referring to the short street which bordered the main campus. "Have you had dinner yet?"

"No, I haven't." Brodie put down her pen. "Are you single tonight?"

"Yes." Ellen pretended to take off her wedding ring and slip it into the pocket of her long khaki skirt. "Bob's at a conference and I hate cooking for one." She paused. "Are you waiting for Stanton?"

"No." Brodie smiled grimly.

"I thought maybe you were. You look nice."

"Thank you." Brodie was wearing the Karen Millen black pants and a gauzy white top. "But, no, I'm not waiting for anybody."

"I could use some company if you're free."

"That would be nice," Brodie said. "Thanks for asking." Ellen had just delivered her from another microwaved entrée or a salad from the grocery store. "Just let me log off."

"Okay," Ellen said. "How about I get my bag and meet you by the stairs in ten minutes?"

"Perfect," Brodie said and Ellen left.

Brodie finished her note to Dr. Pedder and found a stamp.

"So, I assume this Pedder is a buddy of yours," a male voice rasped.

Brodie looked up and her heart sank. Jack Hull was leaning against her doorjamb, an unlit cigarette in his mouth and a pile of papers under one arm. He was wearing a stained and rumpled blue hopsack suit that he'd probably bought in 1968.

"Hi, Jack," Brodie said.

"Slocum says Wallace and this Pedder were friends." The cigarette bobbed as Hull talked. "He coming here to do you a favor?"

"I wasn't on the search committee, remember?" Brodie shuffled some papers on her desk in an effort to look busy.

Hull snatched the cigarette out of his mouth and pointed it at Brodie. "You've got some deal worked out, don't you? Your dad's buddy comes to take care of the department then hands it over to you, is that the story?"

"There's no deal, Jack," Brodie said.

"First no bequest, now this." Hull narrowed his eyes. "Don't think this is over between us, Macbeth. I should have gotten the chair, everybody knows it. You're the one trying to keep me out of it and save it for yourself. Consider yourself warned."

"Don't be ridiculous, Jack," Brodie said but Hull was gone. She heard his footsteps scrape swiftly down the stairs. A thin odor of stale tobacco wafted in his wake.

Brodie mailed both notecards as she and Ellen Foster walked across the campus that Thomas Jefferson had built, shadows of the trees stretching across the stately colonial brick buildings. They ended up at The Varsity, a small diner sandwiched between a boutique bookstore and a store full of preppy clothing. They each had a beer with dinner, trashed Jack Hull, and speculated about Donald Pedder.

For a few easy, sociable hours Brodie was able to forget the dismantling of her father's office. And Stanton.

PART 4

Macbeth shall sleep no more!
(*Macbeth*: 2.2.40)

CHAPTER 11

Brodie had never dreamed music before.

The recording was crackly and took her a moment of hard listening before she recognized a radio with poor sound quality. She looked around, holding herself tightly, knowing that once again it was one of *those* dreams.

The sensations were familiar now; the strange vividness; the certainty that she was there to find her father; the connection to a setting of a book.

She was in a pub. It was dim and smoky and full of people chatting and drinking beer from dimpled glass pint mugs. The place had an old English feel to it, the sort of village pub that hadn't changed much in the past few hundred years. The walls were covered in peeling red damask wallpaper. The low ceiling was braced with dark wooden rafters. Heavy velvet curtains that had seen better days were pulled over the windows.

"Hoy, our Rose! Save a thirsty man, there's a good girl."

A group of men by the dartboard were gesturing at her. In contrast to their Fighter Command pilot uniforms, Brodie was wearing a printed cotton dress, a wool cardigan, and a barmaid's apron. There was a round metal tray in her hands. It was black and had a red lion painted on it with the words *Red Lion Basingstoke*.

The dream came into better focus around her, as Brodie made the connections. The Red Lion pub in Basingstoke had been a popular watering hole for British fighter pilots holding off the Germans in 1940. In *Fighter Boys*, Patrick Bishop had written that the British aircraft crews went out for evening fun in the pubs no matter how grim the day's aerial combat against German bombers and fighters.

Brodie took a deep breath of smoky air and staggered as a pub patron bumped into her. He mumbled an apology and helped her regain her balance. As before, the dream was too real, too vivid, too *awake*.

She slowly threaded her way to the waiting darts players, all of whom were in military uniforms. "Can I pull you some pints, boys?" she asked and collected six empty beer mugs.

"Refills all around, Rose."

She made her way through the press of customers to the scrubbed wooden bar. A stout, cheerful man of about 60 was behind the bar. His cheeks were flushed red with hard work and his eyes were a twinkling gray-blue. With his shirt sleeves rolled up above his elbows, meaty forearms flexed as he filled six clean mugs and set them on her tray.

"Fine crowd tonight, Rose." He jerked his head to indicate the sink behind the bar. "Mind I need some dishes washed."

"Bob, a swift half." A young man dressed in a Fighter Command uniform stepped up to the bar and tossed down some coins. A girl in a blue skirt and plaid jacket clung to his arm.

Balancing the tray, Brodie went back to the darts group and delivered the pints. As she made her way back through the crowd she scanned faces, looking for her father. The pub wasn't that big and after a few minutes she knew he wasn't among the patrons.

It was just like those other dreams; the initial certainty that he was there, the failure to find him, the utter frustration that her questions would not be answered tonight. Next she'd see someone with those strange white eyes.

Brodie felt wariness creep up her spine like cold fingers. She wove her way around the pub again, on the pretense of picking up dirty ashtrays. No one had the strange white eyes.

She was wiping up a spill on the bar when the door to the pub opened and three men in uniform walked in. One hobbled with the use of a cane. The other two were badly disfigured, their faces and necks shiny with raw scar tissue. All three had probably "walked out;" pilot slang for parachuting out of a burning aircraft. The worst had neither lips nor a proper jaw, the skin having melted away into the gumline. His hands were bandaged and Brodie wondered how he'd gotten into his uniform.

As they stood by the entrance, seemingly undecided if they should stay or not, the hubbub of the pub gave way to a disconcerted hush. The girl in the plaid jacket let out a little squeak of distress. Some of the older patrons looked shaken and uncomfortable, their eyes suddenly sweeping everywhere but at the sad knot of wounded men. One woman looked as if she might vomit. Only the boisterous darts group in the far corner seemed oblivious to the state of the newcomers.

Brodie swallowed her own shock at their horrific injuries and left her cloth on the bar. She went up to the pilot with the worst burns, looked straight at him, and smiled. "My darling," she said as warmly as she could. "How lovely to see you."

Brodie saw the gratitude in his eyes. There was a man inside the ghoulish face. Her heart twisted. Brodie put her hand on his lapel, leaned forward, and brushed what was left of his cheek with her lips.

"Evening, miss," he said, the word slurred by his facial injuries.

"Call me Rose." Brodie turned to the next wounded pilot. His face was a pulpy mass with a shocked expression due to the absence of eyelids and eyebrows. "And you. Welcome to the Red Lion. Lovely to see you." She kissed him, then the pilot with the cane. "Pints all around, boys?"

The three moved into the pub. For a moment the awkward hush seemed to blanket the pub, but then, as if everyone had taken their cue from Brodie, the conversations buzzed loudly again.

Brodie got three pints from Bob and delivered them to the table where the wounded pilots were sitting.

The dream went on for a long time. Like before, she couldn't wake up. Brodie filled beer glasses from the draft kegs, emptied ashtrays, mopped the bar, washed dishes in the sink behind the bar, set out snacks of cheese and crisps, and flirted with several pilots. She made sure the wounded men had full mugs.

At one point, talk in the bar stopped for a BBC news

broadcast. When it was over everyone applauded and then booed the Germans.

"'Ere, Rose," Bob said, tilting his head to indicate a bucket on the floor full of empty bottles. "Take the empties out to the bin before I break me neck."

Brodie picked up the heavy bucket, made her way past the bar to the small side door, and walked out into a cool, damp night. It was misty and overcast, too cloudy for aircraft to be aloft tonight.

There were a few cars parked in the alley outside the pub, the bulbous outlines of the 1930's vehicles creating voluminous shadows. No new cars in Britain; all manufacturing had been diverted to weapons of war.

The alley was paved with square stones, wet with a recent rain. The bottles went into crates stacked against the outside wall of the pub. Someone probably came through the alley and collected the crates every few days, Brodie mused as she stacked the bottles. They'd be reused. Nothing went to waste in wartime.

"Here we are again."

Brodie jerked her head around, brown ale bottle in hand.

It was a big man this time, leaning against an old Rover sedan, the bulky vehicle half hiding him. He was dressed in rough woolen pants and a patched coat. A tweed cap was pulled down over his forehead but not so low she couldn't see his white, corroded eyes.

"This is a stupid dream," Brodie said, her heart hammering. "I don't know who you're supposed to be but it's just stupid."

"You're tougher than I'd thought you'd be," he said in reply. "Given your two-faced mother and your cheating father."

"Shut up." This time Brodie would face down the white eyes, make the nightmare pop like a soap bubble.

"She's the one you really ought to know about." The man licked his lips. He had broad, blunt features and heavy eyebrows under the cloth cap. "I'll bet he never told you the truth."

"This dream is over," Brodie said firmly. "I don't love Stanton and I never will."

"Lizzie was fucking two men," the man sneered. "Married to Wallace but she didn't want to go to America with him. She wanted to stay in Edinburgh. With Ian. And she didn't know what to do. When her soul went looking for answers I took it with my bare hands."

"You're a liar," Brodie charged but Kay's words surfaced in her mind. *They were having some sort of marital trouble . . .*

"Dear sainted Elizabeth," the man snorted, his white eyes glinting. "Is that how he described her? He believed she was perfection when she was double crossing him with her panties on fire. She didn't make it through one night of the game. He never believed that I wrung her neck like a chicken's."

"My mother died of a brain aneurysm," Brodie exclaimed.

"But her soul got its neck wrung," he laughed.

"Are you saying you killed my mother?" Brodie's voice was shrill and her hand tightened on the glass bottle. "You killed my mother while she slept?"

"But back to him," the man said as if Brodie's question had never been asked. "He's dead and you know how he cheated the game. Tell me how."

"Did you kill my mother?"

The man moved away from the car, a knife in his hand, his frosted eyes unblinking and cruel as they cut through the darkness. "Tell me how your father cheated the game or I'll gut you like a fish."

Brodie threw the ale bottle at the man, catching him on the cheekbone. He made a guttural sound, spun backwards, and fell heavily. Brodie grabbed another bottle from the bucket but slipped on the wet stones as she threw and went down as well.

The second bottle missed the man and smashed loudly. Shards pinged off the cars. The man rolled across the stones and glass and grabbed Brodie's ankle. She screamed hoarsely as she groped for another bottle, for the bucket itself, for any weapon.

"Rose?" The side door opened, spilling out light and safety

and the hum of many people.

The man let go of Brodie, scrambled between the parked cars, and disappeared.

Bob's fat face frowned from the doorway. "You all right? Was somebody out there?"

"No, nobody," Brodie heard herself say. Her ankle throbbed and her throat was raw from the scream. "I slipped and broke a bottle. I'm sorry."

"Daft cow," Bob said kindly. "Must be tired. Long night. Take over the bar and I'll clean up the glass so no one pops a tire."

"Thanks, Bob. I am tired." Brodie picked up the empty bucket and stepped into the pub, not sure why she'd lied to Bob. She made a show of yawning, her heart still thudding in her ears.

☼

Brodie woke with the nightmare running through her head. It took several uneasy moments for the disorientation to pass and it didn't help that Mouse was standing by the side of the bed, panting in Brodie's face. Her bedroom was still dim. It wasn't quite light beyond the curtains.

After a few minutes Brodie put on shorts and a tee shirt, then headed downstairs.

While the coffee maker did its magic Brodie let the dog out into the back yard and watched the sun come up over the dogwood trees. She was going to take her cue from Stanton. He'd been back in Charlottesville long enough to call if he needed to talk any more about *them*. But he hadn't and she was going to take that as goodbye. She'd already said what she needed to say to him so as far as she was concerned, they were well and truly over.

Brodie took her coffee into the den. Her purse was there. Joe Birnam's business card was still in her wallet.

She sent him an e-mail thanking him for dinner at the

Dingerhoy. Told him she was taking his advice. One day at a time. Signed off with a simple *thanks again, Brodie.*

Then she fished out the little envelope with the "M" stenciled on it and dropped it into the drawer with the rest of the odd keys.

Brodie took Mouse for a run before heading to the university. There were a lot of little details to resolve for the music and politics symposium. If she kept busy she wouldn't think about her father or Stanton or Jack Hull or what it was going to be like to have this Dr. Pedder sitting in her father's office.

She wouldn't think about Joe Birnam, either.

CHAPTER 12

Brodie looked in panic at the clouds below the fuselage. The controls in front of her were totally alien, the yoke jerked in her gloved hands like a live thing, the roar and vibration of the engine thrummed against her heart, and the oxygen mask dug into her skin. She was going to crash this plane, this Spitfire, high over the English Channel.

Static filled her ears and a crackly voice said, "What was the secret?"

Another Spitfire was out there, its wing nearly touching the edge of hers. It was close, close enough for her to see that the pilot had corroded white eyes. Brodie couldn't breathe as panic bloomed into sheer terror.

Brodie gasped for air and then the Spitfire and the clouds turned inside out and rage blanketed the terror.

She forced open her eyes, knowing that she was finally awake, grateful and angry at the same time. The sheets twisted around her legs were soaked with sweat. The telephone on the bedside table rang again.

Brodie kicked away the sheet, sat up dizzily, and grabbed the phone. "Hello."

"This is Joe Birnam calling for Brodie Macbeth."

"Joe!" Brodie inhaled with a rush and looked at the clock. It was already 9:00 am.

"Did I wake you up?" Joe asked. "Do you sleep in on Saturday mornings?"

"No, not at all."

Joe Birnam laughed as if he knew she was kidding him and Brodie pressed her head to her knees. Even over the phone, Joe's deep gravelly voice made her weak.

"How are you?" she asked.

"Still recovering from vacation," he said. "I spent a week in

Paris with Oscar. He's living the good life over there."

"Paris," Brodie said. "How nice." She had a mental image of Joe Birnam in the City of Lights, the broad shoulders silhouetted against the Eiffel Tower.

"How about you?" Joe paused. "I got your email. Things working out back there in Charlottesville?"

"Yes," Brodie said. Her heart flopped like a fish out of water. "I'm . . . uh . . . past the . . . uh . . . crossroads. On my own. Taking it one day at a time."

"Is that what you wanted?" Joe asked carefully.

"Yes." *Absolutely.*

"That's great," Joe said. "Really great." He cleared his throat. "Well, I know it's short notice, but I'm having a house party next weekend. It's the Cherry Blossom Festival in DC and some friends are coming into town for it. Nothing big, just a picnic on the Mall. See the cherry trees. Hear some music. Pay our respects to the monuments."

"Sounds wonderful," Brodie said, sliding onto her pillows. They were clammy with sweat but it didn't matter.

"If you'd like to come, you could drive to my place Saturday morning," Joe went on. "We'll go into DC for the festival in the afternoon. Folks can head home after brunch on Sunday."

"Let me check my schedule," Brodie heard herself say.

He was inviting her to stay over Saturday night. She laid the phone on the bedside table, went to the bathroom and splashed some water on her face, then picked up the phone again. "Joe, that will work out fine."

"Super," Joe said.

They chatted for a few more minutes. Joe gave her directions to his apartment in Alexandria, the code to the parking garage, and instructions for parking in the right space. She should aim to be at his place around noon next Saturday.

When they hung up, Brodie dialed a number from memory.

"Wake up," Brodie nearly shouted after Diana mumbled hello. "We have to go shopping. I need some killer picnic clothes."

☼

The week flew by without another horrible dream. Saturday morning Brodie stashed her overnight case in the Volvo, dropped off Mouse at the kennel, and headed north on Route 28 with Brooks and Dunn's *Greatest Hits* filling the car. She drove north for three hours, passing through the small towns of central Virginia that were dotted with stately brick homes and anchored by the red Virginia clay. At Warrenton she left Route 28 and headed east on Interstate 66, the big six lane highway.

On the western fringe of the capital, following Joe's precise directions, she found the George Washington Memorial Parkway and followed the scenic road south to Alexandria, the DC suburb that still cherished its colonial roots.

She drove through the old town's historic streets to the newer outskirts. Joe's apartment building was part of a modern complex on the Potomac River. Brodie stopped at the entrance to the underground parking garage and punched in the code Joe had given her.

The gate barring the garage entrance swung open. Brodie hurriedly shoved her sunglasses up into her hair as she drove down the ramp into the dark garage. She parked in the number 21 spot, right next to a big white crew cab truck with BIRNAM WOOD BESPOKE CABINETRY lettered on the side.

The parking garage was at the basement level. There was an intercom buzzer by the door leading into the building. Brodie pushed the button marked BIRNAM.

"Hello." It was a woman's voice.

"This is Brodie Macbeth," Brodie said stiffly. "Here to see Joe Birnam."

"Oh, *Brodie*," the woman exclaimed as if they knew each other. "I'll buzz you in and tell Joe you're here. First floor. Apartment 1 D. D like Delta."

A buzzer sounded, releasing the locked door. Brodie picked up her overnight bag and walked into a well-appointed foyer. She took the elevator up one floor.

The door to Apartment 1 D was open. People were milling about. Sounds of clinking ice cubes, laughter, and country music filtered through.

Brodie shifted the overnight case to her other hand and slowly approached the apartment. The captain of the football team sure had a lot of friends.

Joe was suddenly in the doorway, filling it with wide shoulders and crinkly blue eyes. "Hi," he said warmly.

"Hi," Brodie replied and set down her bag. "Thanks for the great directions. I didn't have any problems."

Joe wore the cross and sapphire earring, jeans, and a gray USMC tee shirt. He looked good enough to eat.

"Thanks for coming. You look fantastic." He gently pulled Brodie's sunglasses out of her hair and held them out to her.

"Thank you," Brodie said, momentarily tongue-tied. She took the sunglasses. Her head was tingling where his hand had touched her.

"Pink is definitely your color," Joe said.

"It's what all the sassy girls are wearing this season," Brodie said, her tongue suddenly unraveling. She silently thanked Diana who'd helped select her pink linen top, matching pink espadrilles, and skinny denim crop pants.

"Those sassy girls," Joe said. "They really know how to make an appearance."

"We have certain standards to maintain," Brodie said.

He gave her his sideways grin, blue eyes crinkling in fun. Brodie grinned back and for a moment they just stood like that in the hallway, with party noises coming from the apartment behind him.

"Well, I guess I'd better introduce you to everyone," Joe said finally. He took her bag then turned so Brodie could go in the door ahead of him.

She felt his breath on her cheek as she went into the apartment.

There were only ten people there, not the crowd she'd first thought. Joe introduced her to Marty, his cousin and business partner, and Marty's wife Christine, who had answered the intercom. Next, she met Bill and Faith and Craig and Sue; Bill and Craig were both Marine sergeants stationed at Henderson Hall in nearby Arlington. Brad was also a Marine; he and his wife Gayle had driven up from Quantico and their suitcases were on the floor next to the sofa. The three active duty Marines were joking with Ken who was retired, like Joe. He and his wife Ellen had driven down from Pennsylvania.

"And now for the 25 cent tour," Joe said after the introductions had been made.

"You charged us 40 cents," Ken joked.

"You probably got to see the bathroom," Brodie offered.

"Yes," Christine said. "But it's another 10 cents if you want toilet paper."

"Could you lend me a dollar?" Brodie asked innocently and everybody laughed.

"Hey," Joe protested. "I invited Brodie here to be the straight man."

"Into each life, laddie," Brodie said with mock sympathy.

"Met your match, Joe," Christine said, laughing again.

The apartment was big. As Joe explained, he'd bought it years ago when he was stationed at Henderson Hall. He'd kept it as a rental property but renovated it when he'd moved to the area to work with Marty.

The living room was a wide open space with a high ceiling, clean white walls, built-in bookcases, and a classy, masculine feel. A deep brown leather sofa, two matching chairs, and a circular coffee table with a glass mosaic top were positioned in the middle, effectively separating the room into two. In the upper half, the seating arrangement faced a widescreen television flanked by twin French doors. One corner of that end of the room was set up as a gym, with a large multi-exercise weight machine angled toward the television.

Behind the sofa the rear half of the room was dominated by a long oak dining table. Brodie was no antiques expert but she recognized the craftsmanship and straight lines of Mission style and knew that the table was a very expensive piece.

Oak wood and masculine decor carried over to the kitchen, which was separated from the dining area by a long black granite counter. Next to the kitchen a short hallway lined with framed maps led to the master bedroom. Brodie had a glimpse of cream walls and a king-sized bed with a heavy square-spindled Mission headboard before Joe moved across the hall to an office with a modern metal desk and a rolling work table. There was a sofa with someone's luggage next to it.

"Joe does all the drafting work and blueprints. He's really talented," Christine said behind Brodie. She'd left the group in the living room to join Brodie and Joe in the hall. Marty's wife was a petite brunette in her late 40's. She obviously had a wicked sense of humor and Brodie liked her already.

"Brodie will be in the guest room," Joe said, throwing Christine a look Brodie couldn't fathom.

That room was on the other side of the living room. Joe set Brodie's bag on the floor next to a queen-sized bed covered by a striped comforter. There were more framed maps on the walls. He gestured at a door beyond the bed. "Bathroom's in there. Go ahead and freshen up. We'll leave in about 20 minutes. Two-car convoy."

"Twenty minutes," Brodie repeated. "Got it."

Joe turned to walk out of the room, then stopped. "I'm glad you could come."

"Thanks for asking," Brodie said, wanting to touch him. Just put her hand on his arm, let him know there could be more. A ripple of tension passed between them as if he'd read her mind and didn't know what to make of it.

"I'll just go get everything together," Joe said lightly. He walked out of the bedroom, his uneven gait barely noticeable.

☼

It had been a few years since Brodie had been in downtown Washington. There were more memorials on the Mall, that long stretch of green between the regal Lincoln Memorial and the distant Capital building, than when she'd been in high school. But the Washington Memorial was still the anchor, its spire still the tallest building in view.

The surrounding circle of flags fluttered in the spring breeze. The cherry trees were in full fluffy pink bloom and the area was crowded with tourists and festival-goers. Brodie adjusted her sunglasses as they walked across the grass, her brain replaying the moment Joe had eased them out of her hair.

They found the perfect gathering spot near the festival bandstand. Ken and Ellen volunteered to stay with the picnic supplies. The rest of the party fanned out to be tourists for an hour or so before the entertainment started and it was time to eat.

The group stayed together as they toured the big World War II memorial but by chance or intention Joe and Brodie were alone as they approached the Vietnam Memorial.

"This one always gets me," Joe said. He was wearing black Oakley wrap-around sunglasses. Brodie couldn't see his eyes.

"It was the perfect design," she said.

There were a lot of people milling about; parents with strollers trying to explain to their children what the dark stone wall symbolized, older people who ran their hands over the names etched into the granite, others who traced names onto paper or left small mementos.

Joe took a folded envelope out of his back pocket. Brodie watched as he awkwardly bent and placed it at the foot of the wall next to a small teddy bear and some flowers. "From Joe" was penned across the front.

"I leave something every once in awhile," Joe said to Brodie as they moved away to let others get a chance to look at the wall.

"You're keeping promises," Brodie said with a sudden certainty.

"That's right."

"To them or to yourself?" Brodie asked.

"Both, really," Joe said. "I guess I'm letting the ghosts know I'm doing what they couldn't. If I can keep it together . . . live a good life . . . then I've done what they never got a chance to do."

"It's a way of honoring them," Brodie said.

"Yes," Joe said softly. "I won't forget the ones who weren't as lucky as me."

Their arms touched and Brodie felt the pull toward him, stronger than ever. "We shouldn't," she said. "History has proven it time and again. When a society forgets its warriors, the society eventually decays."

They were away from the memorial now, walking across the grass in no particular direction.

"I like your perspective," Joe said.

Brodie wished she could see his eyes.

"I'm reading all my dad's books," she offered. "It's my way of honoring him."

It was a long minute before Joe replied. "Thank you," he said.

"For what?"

"I'm not sure," Joe said and the big shoulders shrugged. "For understanding, I guess. I'm just some old busted-up Marine but duty, honor, country . . . those things are still a big part of who I am. You seem to get that."

"Someday there'll be a memorial for your war, too," Brodie said. "People will see what your generation did and how you lived afterwards. Those promises will mean more than you know."

That now familiar ripple of tension passed between them again.

A veteran's group with a petition to improve health care and help homeless vets had set up a table. Joe and Brodie stopped and signed and Joe answered questions about his military service and where he'd seen action.

As they left, Joe took out a wad of bills. His hands were big and powerful as he dropped the money in the donations jar.

CHAPTER 13

Joe Birnam was an avid reader, a master carpenter, an interesting conversationalist, a well-traveled man, a Marine once and forever.

And a fantastic cook. His picnic food was fabulous. There were gourmet salads, roast pork sandwiches, some type of Asian chicken skewers, and Italian artichoke fritters.

The festival entertainment started with a famous comedian and ended with the National Symphony. Meanwhile, the conversation was lively. As in Edinburgh when she'd met his high school buddies, Brodie found that she liked Joe's friends very much and felt welcomed into their circle.

She caught Joe watching her from time to time and watched him, too, when she thought he wasn't looking. They were very *aware* of each other, Brodie thought.

It was after midnight before everyone got back to Joe's apartment and had coffee. Christine and Marty, and the two couples who lived in nearby Arlington went home, leaving Brodie, Joe, Ken, Ellen, Brad and Gayle in the apartment.

Brodie, Joe, and four chaperones.

The leather living room sofa opened into a bed for Ken and Ellen. Brad and Gayle were on the office sofabed.

To get to Joe's room from her own, Brodie would have to cross the living room past Ken and Ellen asleep on the sofabed. And if she knocked on Joe's door Brad and Gayle right across the hall were sure to hear.

He didn't knock on her door, either.

Brunch in the morning was as good as the previous day's picnic. Christine and Marty came back and once again Brodie found herself chatting and laughing with everyone. They picked apart the Sunday news shows and demolished Joe's eggs, sausage, waffles, and cantaloupe wedges. They argued politics.

Brodie especially liked Christine. As they talked she learned that Christine was a high school chemistry teacher. She and Marty had been married just over eight years; the second marriage for both of them. Children from first marriages were grown and gone.

At one o'clock, after helping clear away the brunch dishes, Brodie told Joe she had to be going. She needed to pick up Mouse before six when the kennel office closed.

"I'll walk you downstairs to your car," Joe said.

Brodie said her goodbyes and got a knowing wink from Christine. Joe picked up her overnight bag and they headed for the elevator.

"So I'm getting thrown over for a dog," Joe said teasingly as they descended to the basement floor of the apartment building.

"Mouse is super," Brodie said without thinking. "You'll have to meet her next time."

Joe blinked and Brodie felt an embarrassed flush creep into her cheeks. She was grateful when the elevator doors swooshed open. Joe unlocked the door to the parking garage and Brodie led the way to the Volvo parked alongside the big white truck. The parking garage was dim and quiet and cool. They were the only people there.

"Thanks for coming," Joe said.

"I had a nice time," Brodie said, suddenly worried that their farewell was going to be awkward.

She unlocked the Volvo, suddenly finding it hard to breathe. God, but he made her feel like a freshman.

"We never really had a chance to talk." Joe put her case in the back of the car then came around to Brodie. "About those crossroads."

"No, we didn't." Brodie's mind jumped around, trying to find a way to tell Joe that it was over with Stanton. She sagged against the side of the car. Everything sounded like she was asking Joe to be her rebound. *It's over with him. So now how about you, cowboy?*

"I guess it's none of my business," Joe said. He stuck his hands into the back pockets of his jeans.

"That relationship in Charlottesville is over," Brodie said. She looked down, fiddled with her keys, and pulled open the driver's door so that it was between her and Joe. "It was really over before I went to Edinburgh but we had plans to talk again. But that didn't work out."

"How are you feeling about that?"

Brodie looked over the rim of the car door window and caught the full force of Joe's eyes. They were vivid blue beacons cutting through the gray dimness of the parking garage. "Fine," she said firmly. "Stanton is a colleague, nothing more."

Joe frowned. "This Stanton wouldn't be Stanton Sloane, the professor guy on TV, would it?"

"The very same," Brodie said. She leaned into the car and tossed her purse onto the passenger seat. "He's a lot more shallow in real life."

Joe laughed and Brodie's stomach unclenched for a moment.

"So this changes things a little, doesn't it?" Joe asked.

"Between us, you mean?" Brodie replied cautiously.

"Yes," said Joe. He leaned against the fender of the car and crossed his arms. "Now that both of us are unattached, so to speak."

"Would you like to come to Charlottesville?" Brodie heard herself ask. "The first Saturday in May? My graduate seminar is doing a symposium on music and history."

"A university symposium on music and history," Joe said slowly as if he'd never heard of such a thing. "Are you speaking?"

"I'm the master of ceremonies," Brodie explained. "There are other presenters and a keynote speaker. All talking about music and how it has impacted history. Bob Marley in Jamaica. The music of the Civil War. Just the story of George M. Cohan and the music of World War I could be a whole symposium in and of itself." She was handling this badly, slipping into the comfort of professor mode.

Brodie gripped the rim of the car door window with both hands and plowed on. "It's an all-day event. The department does it every year and it's quite popular."

"I'd love to come," Joe said, his eyes still on hers. "If for no other reason than to see you in action."

"You might actually learn something," Brodie said, trying to sound like her knees weren't giving way.

The recurrent ripple of tension between them turned into a torrent.

"If I call, will you give me directions?" Joe asked.

"Yes, yes." Brodie felt herself blushing. "Call. Or I can send you an email with directions to the house."

"How about we do both?"

"That's good, too," Brodie said.

They grinned at each other over the car door, knowing that something was happening, letting the torrent pour over them.

"Go pick up your dog," Joe said. He leaned over the car door and kissed Brodie's cheek, his trim beard scratching softly against her skin. "See you in two weeks. Drive safe. Call me if you get into trouble on the road. Or if you don't."

CHAPTER 14

Joe called Tuesday night and they talked for an hour, Brodie curled up on the living room sofa with the phone pressed to her ear. He called again on Thursday. Both conversations were full of shared laughter and the anticipation of seeing each other again.

Brodie e-mailed him directions to the farmhouse on Friday, wishing the next week would flash by in an instant. She was sure that what hadn't happened in Edinburgh at the Dingerhoy would happen in Charlottesville in her bedroom. And she hadn't had a weird dream since the weekend he'd called to invite her to the festival.

Saturday afternoon she was cleaning up the den, replacing on the bookshelves the books she'd finished reading--Churchill's memoirs of World War II--when the phone rang.

Sassy, she expected to hear. *'Left onto my street at the oak tree?' Directions or a good country lyric?*

It wasn't Joe. It was a young woman with a down home Southern accent, asking if this was the Macbeth residence.

"This is Dr. Macbeth," Brodie replied, wondering if the caller was a student.

"This is Wanda from Munk's. Ya'll owe three months for ya'll's storage unit. Ya'll gonna pay that this week?"

"I beg your pardon?" Brodie asked in confusion.

"Ya'll gotta year contract and it's behind three months rent for ya'll's storage unit."

"I don't have a storage unit."

"Wally Macbeth?"

"I'm his daughter." Although to Brodie's knowledge no one had ever called her father "Wally."

"Well, if he don't pay, his stuff's gonna be con . . . con . . . confistaken."

"Confiscated," Brodie corrected automatically. She sat on the edge of the desk and pressed a hand to her forehead. "Are you sure you have the right person? Where did you get this number?"

"Wally Macbeth," the woman said stoutly. "His stuff's gonna get took."

"Okay, okay," Brodie said. She had no idea what her father would have placed in storage. "I'll come and pay. Where are you?"

"Munk's Storage on Chart Street," the woman said. "Ya'll gonna come before six? Office closes at six. Look for the big yellow sign with the brown M on it."

"Yellow sign with the brown M," Brodie repeated and hung up.

She opened the desk drawer full of loose keys and took out the envelope Sarah had given her. The yellow envelope was discolored where it had been taped to the underside of her father's office desk but the big brown M was clearly visible.

Brodie picked up Diana on her way to Chart Street.

"Moral support required," she said as Diana got into the Volvo. "Something doesn't feel right."

"For a storage unit?" Diana said skeptically. "It's probably full of old books."

Ten minutes later, as the Volvo juddered over railroad tracks and kept going through a run-down neighborhood in the southern part of the city, a worried look spread over Diana's face. "We might have to fight our way out of here," she said. "We should have brought Ray."

"And the dogs," Brodie said, hoping she wouldn't have to stop at any red lights.

Chart Street was a million miles away from the refined gentility of the university or the new commercialism of Charlottesville's rehabilitated downtown. They passed an asphalt factory; a shaky barn-like structure with railroad cars full of glinting black coal sitting idle behind it. Across the way, an adult bookstore's neon sign advertised XXX Hard Core.

A couple of women in tight shorts, tube tops, and stiletto heels lounged in front of the pawnshop next door, waiting for business and getting old before their time. The windows of both shops were covered by metal grilles.

A collection of beat-up trucks cluttered the parking lot of a no-name fast food place. A dumpster by the entrance overflowed with sandwich wrappers and paper cups, its sides covered in profane graffiti. A dozen teens with low-riding jeans and beer bottles slouched in front of the combination launderette and massage parlor and eyed the Volvo with malevolence.

The air smelled like sulfur.

"This is like a war zone," Brodie murmured.

"Why would your dad come down here?" Diana asked. "I mean, there are storage places in a lot nicer parts of town."

Munk's Storage was a series of low corrugated metal buildings fronted by rollup garage doors and surrounded by a rusted chain link fence. The entrance was a gravel drive rutted through to the dirt. Brodie drove through the opening in the fence, the Volvo bouncing hard in the ruts.

Gravel pinged against OFK 362 and the car's undercarriage before Brodie parked by a hand-painted sign reading "offise."

They didn't accept checks or credit cards. Brodie had to pay cash for three month's rent before being allowed through an inner fence blocking off the storage units. The two women walked past rows of garage doors before finding the right unit. The key from the envelope fit into the lock at the base of the door.

"Here goes," Brodie said. She wiped a sweaty hand on her jeans and hauled on the handle. The metal slats rolled up with a squealing protest of rust and heat.

Her father's storage unit was empty except for a battered cardboard file box pushed into a corner.

"That's it?" Diana said as they walked into the space.

Brodie found a light switch and a single bulb in the ceiling came to life. "Apparently."

She squatted down and opened the box. It was full of spiral-bound school notebooks. She picked up the one on top and rifled through the pages. They were all covered with her father's distinctive copperplate handwriting.

"Notes, I guess," Brodie said in bewilderment.

They escaped Chart Street, went back to Diana and Ray's place, and dumped the box of notebooks out onto the kitchen table. As Brodie and Diana began sorting through them, Ray handed around beers then went outside to grill burgers.

Most of the notebooks were yellow with age, the metal spirals bent. There were 20 in all, most containing two years' worth of brief diary entries. They started with the year the widower Wallace Macbeth had come to the United States with his daughter and ended about six months before he died.

Diana picked up a notebook at random. Brodie did the same. It was a European A4 size notebook with a stiff cover and thick spirals. She flipped through the pages, skimming her father's words. Wallace Macbeth had written of the move to Charlottesville, of the difficulty in getting Mrs. Weir to fly. Brodie was referred to several times as "the child."

Thank God the child looks like a Macbeth. If she was dark and small like the Brodies it would be too painful a reminder of what I have lost. She is a part of Elizabeth and for that I am grateful but she is a true Macbeth as well.

"Your mother was Elizabeth?" Diana asked.

"Yes."

"This is sort of mushy . . ."

Brodie looked over Diana's shoulder.

June 22: My thoughts constantly turn to Elizabeth. My life is hollow now, nothing fills my thoughts as she does and always will. Our life together was fate and fate has been ripped from me. I am deformed, voracious, restless.

In my dreams I long for her, to find answers, and then place my mouth on hers. I would close my eyes and breathe life back into her as she wrapped herself around me . . .

"Ohhhh-kay," Brodie said. "My dad's sex fantasies. Yuck."

She flipped through a third faded notebook, reading entries at random.

2 November: Once again I am filled with longing. This emptiness is a torment. The nights tease me and I don't understand what is happening.

30 November: I will not sleep again tonight. My dreams are too intense. Elizabeth was so close I could feel her presence. I long for her, to touch her, to pull her body against mine, to stroke her breast. She could answer my questions and then I would push deep inside her, rock both of us--.

"Eeeuu," Brodie said and closed her eyes.

"He actually used the word *loins* in this entry," Diana said faintly.

"Do you know what this means?" Brodie asked, shoving the notebook away in disgust.

"Your dad could have had a second career writing bodice-rippers," Diana said.

"No." Brodie drank some beer, realizing that her hand was shaking. "Kay was right. Dad was obsessed with my mother. It's like there was a side to him I didn't know at all."

Diana gathered up the notebooks, loaded them back in the box, and set the box near the front door. Brodie slumped in her chair at the kitchen table and picked at the label of her beer bottle.

"So your Aunt Kay was right," Diana said as she came back into the kitchen. She took plates and flatware out of a cabinet and brought them to the table. "Maybe not what you wanted to hear but you finally got some answers, right?"

"How could Dad have been this strange, obsessed man and I didn't know?" Brodie asked.

"He was very good at hiding his problems," Diana said. "Just look at where he kept his diary. In a storage unit in gangland." She drank some beer as she stood by the table. "And it kind of dovetails with the license plates, doesn't it, sweetie? Erratic behavior he kept well hidden."

"Remember what the lawyer said? Maybe Dad wasn't of sound mind." Brodie managed to shred a piece of damp label. "I wonder how hereditary insanity is."

"I know what you're thinking," Diana said. "When was the last time you had one of those Stanton dreams?"

"Awhile ago," Brodie said. "Before I went to Joe's."

"See?" Diana waved her finger at Brodie. "Your subconscious knows it's truly over with Stanton. You probably won't have any more."

"What were you all reading?" Ray asked as he came in the back door with a plate full of burgers. He was wearing an Atlanta Falcons apron and his shaved head gleamed from the heat of the grill. Puck was at his heels, looking hopefully at the plate.

Ray would like Joe, Brodie thought distractedly.

"Brodie's dad's diary," Diana said. She opened the refrigerator and got out cole slaw and potato salad.

Brodie pointed down the hall at the box. "Thirty-five years of sexual obsession."

"Whoa," said Ray, putting the plate of burgers on the table and sitting down. "Can I read it?"

"No," Diana said firmly. She kissed the top of Ray's head. "Don't joke. Brodie's really upset." She went to the sink, washed some lettuce, then brought a plate of it to the table.

"I guess that explains why he never remarried," she said to Brodie. "He was still in love with your mom."

Brodie tried to push her father's strange diaries out of her thoughts as they ate. Diana and Ray's kitchen was clean and inviting; sparkling white cabinets, granite countertops, dark blue walls, a splashy valance over the big bay window. The tablecloth was a coordinating stripe. All the rooms in the townhouse were decorated in bold color combinations. *A reflection of their personalities and relationship*, Brodie thought. *Vibrant, happy, complete.*

In comparison, she felt like a dour work-in-progress who'd had to hire a decorator. A work-in-progress with a thick streak of insanity in her family.

"So next weekend," Diana said leadingly.

"What?" Brodie pulled her thoughts back to the present.

"Joe's coming next weekend," Diana said. "Why don't you bring him over here for brunch on Sunday?"

"Yeah," Ray said. He slipped Puck a bite of burger. The dog swallowed it whole. "I ought to check him out for you."

"You don't have to check him out," Brodie protested.

"The guy picked you up on an airplane," Ray pointed out.

"In first class," Brodie riposted.

Ray threw up his hands in mock protest. "Just trying to do a friend a favor."

"Actually we thought we'd better feed him at least one meal while he's in town," Diana said. "Don't want the guy to starve."

"I can cook when I have to," Brodie said indignantly as both Diana and Ray hooted.

When she got home Brodie lugged the box of diaries upstairs and dumped it in the storeroom with the rest of her father's papers. She didn't know what she'd ever do with the notebooks. They were too personal and intimate to read but she couldn't just throw them away, either.

But at least she knew what had happened. Kay had been right. It was a strange, awkward closure but it would do.

One day at a time.

CHAPTER 15

Brodie was frightened, more frightened than she'd ever been in her life. The fear was like a greasy hand in her bowels.

"Tighten up that square, you lazy buggers! Monsewer's dainty horsemen are coming fer another kiss."

As the vivid dream took shape around her, Brodie realized she was in the heavy red and white wool uniform of a British redcoat. There was a clumsy musket in her hand and she was in a hollow square formation with hundreds of other soldiers. The square was four men deep and a hundred wide. She was toward the back but she could see over the shoulders of the soldiers in front of her. A muddy field stretched away from the military formation. In the center of the enormous hollow square officers rode nervous horses and bellowed orders, telling the men to look sharp, to stay close, to spit at the French.

Other British squares were staggered across a field like the red squares of a chessboard. Dead and wounded horses and soldiers littered the mud all around the British formations. There was a farm in the distance, built with the solid stone walls of rural Europe. The air was cloyingly dense with the acrid smell of gunsmoke and the sweet gumminess of spilled blood and sweaty bodies. Gunners in the far distance belched death from behind a smokescreen created by their cannons.

The smoke lifted in a slight breeze and Brodie suddenly realized where she was: Waterloo, 1815. Napoleon, Emperor of France, had been defeated in Russia and exiled to the tiny island of Elba, only to escape, regain his throne in Paris, rebuild his army, and convulse Europe in one, final cathartic battle.

Britain's Lord Wellington would defeat Napoleon at Waterloo, a tiny farm village in Belgium sited near a crossroads but would pay a terrible price to do so.

A cannon ball screamed out of the sky and savagely struck the opposite side of the square. Several men fell, creating a groaning, bloody hole that was instantly filled as the redcoats shuffled together again.

Brodie knew she was vulnerable in this dream in a way she'd never been before. Wellington's infantry had been torn to shreds by Napoleon's guns and cavalry at Waterloo; the British and their Prussian allies had very nearly lost the field. The square formation was Britain's answer to French cavalry but pitting infantrymen against horses was a horrific, bloody business. A wounded horse could slide into the side of a square and breach the line of soldiers, opening it to the slashing swords of the cavalry.

"Dad," Brodie shouted. She had to find her father and get both of them away from the battle. "Dad!"

"Shet yer gob!" the soldier next to her cried and jabbed his elbow hard into her ribs.

"Close up, close up," an officer in the hollow center bellowed.

Brodie looked around desperately, knowing she wasn't going to wake up. The wounded were dragged to the center. Their groans competed with the boom of the French guns.

"Here they come," someone yelled.

Brodie's heart stopped beating.

The French cavalry was a breathtaking sight. From far across the huge field the Cuirassiers in their heavy armor walked their huge horses forward. Behind them were the Red Lancers in bizarre square headgear and the Horse Grenadiers in tall black bearskin helmets. Brodie could see past them to the Carabiniers in white uniforms, Dragoons in green, and troops of Hussars with plumes in their hats. There were thousands of French soldiers, all coming to kill her and her father, too.

"Dad!" Brodie shouted, determined to find him before the assault. "*Dad*!"

"He'll be calling for his mam, next," someone jeered.

"Oh, this is good. Very good." A new voice came from behind the ranks of redcoats.

Brodie twisted around. A young officer on horseback loomed above the redcoats, the horse and his ornate uniform giving him power and stature. He reined in the animal, making the rearmost soldiers flinch as the nervous beast pawed the ground near them.

His eyes were white and corroded and totally familiar.

"Your choices of venue are always so extravagant," the officer said. His horse pranced nervously. "Quite exciting compared to your father. He was always so predictable. But it looks as if this time you've landed yourself in quite a mess. Tell me what you know and I'll help you get out of here."

"I don't know anything," Brodie said, her voice shaky with fear.

The rasp of metal on metal rang above the noise of the gathering battle as the officer drew his sword. He whipped it down, catching Brodie under the chin, forcing her head upwards. Brodie caught her breath in a ragged gulp as the redcoats on either side of her shrank back.

"Your father's not here," the officer said calmly. "He's left you holding the bag, so to speak. So you might as well tell me his secret. How he cheated the game."

"I don't know what you mean," Brodie said. The metal was cold on her skin and she was shaking so hard her teeth chattered.

"He told you something important," the officer said. "Stop trying to hide it. You can't possibly have succeeded this long unless he told you the secret. I'll get it out of you one way or the other."

"The toff's mad," a redcoat beside her murmured. "Tell him."

"Steady lads," another officer called from the safety of the hollow center of the square. "Wait for my word!"

A cannon boomed and the men in the square moved restlessly. The officer's horse neighed and skittered a step and the sword bounced against the underside of Brodie's chin. The ground vibrated, as if an earthquake rolled in waves deep inside the earth, and Brodie felt the upheaval deep in the muscles of her legs.

"In case you haven't noticed," the officer said, inching up the sword tip so that it pressed under Brodie's eye. His face was round and smooth but the eyes were old and diseased. "We haven't got all day."

The French cavalry had begun its charge in earnest. The ground shook beneath Brodie's feet, the sword point was too close, fear was grinding her stomach, and *she couldn't wake up*.

"Please," Brodie breathed. "I don't know what you're talking about."

A thousand hooves drummed along the ground and ten thousand men roared defiance and the sound of a sharp bark was like suction against Brodie's skin, pulling her away from the battlefield and the officer with the white eyes.

Dad! Help me! she wanted to scream.

The bark reverberated through the dream again.

Brodie woke up with a small scream, disoriented and enraged. It took her a long, excruciating moment to realize that sunshine was streaming in through the curtains and Mouse was barking in her face.

She sat up abruptly, her heart still hammering in her ears. For several long moments she fought for breath. The room wavered dizzily and she blinked hard to clear the battle of Waterloo from her vision.

"Dammit, Dad," she croaked. She found *Napoleon and the Hundred Days* by Stephen Coote on the floor by the bed and threw it across the room. "Why did you ever think I'd be safe with Stanton?"

PART 5

Stars, hide your fires! Let not light see my black and deep desires.
(*Macbeth*: 1.4.50-51)

CHAPTER 16

The week dragged but finally it was Friday night. Brodie glanced at her watch. It was still only 7:00 pm. Joe would be there in an hour. She gave herself a once-over in the hall mirror on her way to the kitchen. Subtle makeup. Skinny jeans, brown sandals, and a pale pink top. White lace underwear.

Playful and ready, Brodie decided and grinned shakily at her reflection. Joe would say something about the pink shirt. And hopefully take it off her later.

Mouse followed her into the kitchen, ears pricked up, the dog alert to Brodie's jittery mood. Brodie set the table with her nicest china and cloth napkins. Next, she opened the refrigerator and hauled out a disposable aluminum pan from DeLuca's Gourmet. It held two stuffed Cornish game hens, a wild rice pilaf, and maple glazed baby carrots, all artfully arranged on a potato gratin. All she had to do was heat the whole thing for a hour on low heat.

Dessert was strawberries and Cointreau liquor over orange sorbet in Mrs. Weir's cranberry glass bowls.

Brodie turned on the oven and slid in the pan. She poured herself a glass of mineral water and tried to think what else she should do. But the kitchen was sparkling, there was beer in the refrigerator and red wine on the counter, and the table looked lovely. The bathroom in Mrs. Weir's room off the kitchen was clean and she'd put out fresh towels.

"The other bathroom!" she exclaimed and ran upstairs. Mouse galloped up the stairs with her, nearly knocking Brodie off her feet as they went. Brodie put clean towels on the racks then gave her bedroom a final once over.

She stopped in front of the mirror over the dresser. "Maybe you're overdoing the sassy thing," Brodie said to her reflection. She traded the pink for a sleeveless black top. And found black slingbacks to replace the brown sandals.

The playful look was gone. This outfit said *you're in for a hot night, Joe Birnam.* Brodie put on some more mascara, fluttered her lashes at herself in the mirror and went back downstairs, her high heels making a sexy and confident *click* on the hardwood floors.

At 8:15 she was vibrating nervously between the front door and the kitchen, Mouse following at her side, when the phone rang.

"Brodie?"

"Joe?"

"Look, I'm going to be late. I'm still on Route 66."

"Oh."

"You might want to turn on the news," Joe said. He sounded tired and strained. There was a lot of noise in the background; sirens and people talking and someone crying. "There was a pretty big accident right in front of me and the whole road is blocked. Couple of people dead."

"Oh my God," Brodie breathed. She shot into the living room and found the television remote. "Are you all right?"

"I'm okay," Joe said. "They should have it cleared up pretty soon but I won't get to Charlottesville until pretty late."

"God, Joe," Brodie said. Scenes of wreckage filled the television screen, courtesy of a local news channel. "Do you still want to come?"

"I'll be there," Joe said. "Just keep the lights on."

"You be careful," Brodie said. "There's no need to rush. Dinner will keep."

"I'll call you again when I get out of this mess," Joe said.

Brodie sank onto the loveseat with the remote. The accident on Route 66 soon made the national news. A semi truck had fallen off an overpass and onto the westbound lanes of traffic, crushing cars and snarling traffic. At least four people were known to be dead, with a dozen injured. The road, full of travelers getting out of Washington for the weekend, was solid gridlock all the way back to the capital. Brodie thought she could see Joe's white truck as the television view panned over the accident scene from above, shot no doubt from a helicopter. The scene looked gruesome, a huge tangle of metal and tragedy.

An hour passed. Brodie paced between the front door and the television. The click of the high heels soon drove her nuts and she looked down at herself. "You look like a hooker," she said aloud and went upstairs.

A simple white blouse and flats said *no pressure, I'm ready whenever you are*. Brodie had just gone back into the living room when the phone rang.

"It looks like one lane is getting by," Joe said. The deep voice was even more tired. "With any luck I'll be out of this mess in a half hour. What are my chances of getting a beer when I get there?"

"Excellent," Brodie said.

After they hung up, she went into the kitchen. The food from the gourmet shop was starting to look a little dry. Brodie decided to baste the roasted hens in butter like the instructions said. It was an unfamiliar and complicated process to melt butter in the microwave and spoon it over the meat but she managed and slid the pan back into the oven.

She yawned but was determined not to fall asleep. The day had been a killer; there had been so many last minute details to attend to for the symposium; sound system checks, anxious graduate students to soothe, a mix-up in a speaker's hotel reservation, a dozen calls from the university catering service. She looked at her notes for the opening and closing remarks she had to make.

Her intro was simple; thank people for coming, tell them where the bathrooms and exits were, which rooms to go to for the small workshop sessions, what time lunch was served, and a few fun facts about the presentations they were going to hear. When it was over she had to do a quick recap, again say thanks for attending, and direct them to the dean's cocktail party. She made a few edits, then turned back to the television.

At 11:30 she basted the hens a second time, her movements clumsy with fatigue. She got melted butter on the white blouse; a greasy streak that didn't come off. "It was inevitable," Brodie said to Mouse as she plodded up the stairs. She changed into a comfortable university sweatshirt and sneakers.

She settled on the front porch at 12:30, phone in hand and Mouse at her feet, resisting the urge to gnaw her fingernails. It was a cool, starry night and she was glad for the sweatshirt. A fat crescent moon hovered above the trees.

Bright headlights swept into view and the big white truck turned into the driveway.

Mouse tensed. The German Shepherd's ears swiveled forward as the vehicle came to a halt.

Shaky with relief, Brodie started down the porch steps as the headlights switched off and the driver's door opened. Joe got out slowly, turning on the seat so that his right foot touched the ground first. Mouse gave a short, sharp bark.

"Hi," Brodie called and then Mouse charged Joe, 95 pounds of churning muscle and bared teeth, barking furiously.

"Mouse!" Brodie shouted, totally startled.

"Whoa," Joe said and braced himself against the side of the truck as Mouse reached him and reared up on hind legs, still barking madly. The dog's jaws were inches from his face.

As Brodie watched in astonishment, Joe caught Mouse's front paws. Man and dog stood together, looking like an incongruous dance team backed against the truck.

Mouse gave two more short, sharp barks, and then licked Joe's face with every evidence of great joy. The dog's fluffy tail wagged furiously.

"Hey, hey there." Joe turned his face away from Mouse's exuberant tongue and staggered a little, still supporting the dog's weight by her front paws.

Brodie reached them, got a hand under Mouse's collar, and dragged the dog down to all fours.

"I'm so sorry," Brodie said breathlessly. "It was just because it's dark and you're a stranger. I'm *so* sorry." Mouse squirmed and bucked, determined to get to Joe. Brodie had to let go of the dog's collar before her hand was shoved into Joe's crotch. Mouse pressed her nose into Joe's pants, drinking in his scent and keeping him pressed against the truck.

"This has to be Mouse," Joe said. He bent and ran his hands over the dog's head and back and Mouse quivered with pleasure, even as she sniffed his prosthetic leg. "She's gorgeous."

"Sit, Mouse," Brodie said sharply. Mouse lowered her hindquarters and gazed at Joe adoringly.

Joe straightened up and smiled tired at Brodie. The big shoulders slumped with fatigue and Brodie's heart gave a concerned lurch. "I'm just about beat," he said. "You're a sight for sore eyes."

For a moment Brodie thought he was going to hug her but he didn't.

"Come on inside," Brodie said hurriedly. "Dinner's in the oven."

Joe pulled a duffel suitcase and a bouquet of pink roses wrapped in florist paper out of the back seat of the truck. He handed her the bouquet. "I hope they're not dead."

"You really didn't have to bring me flowers," Brodie said, touched.

She led him across the dark yard and into the house, Mouse tight against Joe's side. His limp was very pronounced and Brodie wondered if he was in pain.

"Hungry?" Brodie asked.

"Starved," Joe said. "But there was talk of beer, I seem to recall. A hundred miles or so ago."

They went into the kitchen, Mouse following as if connected to Joe by an invisible string. Brodie opened two beers and handed one to Joe.

"Cheers," he said and lightly touched the neck of his bottle against hers before drinking.

Brodie sipped her beer, knowing that if she drank it too quickly she'd fall asleep in her dinner. Joe had no similar compunction, apparently, and drained his bottle in one long, exhausted swallow.

"Dinner's ready whenever you are," Brodie said.

"Let me wash up and change my shirt first," Joe said. He was wearing a white BIRNAM WOOD tee shirt and jeans. The tee shirt had flecks of what looked like rust stains across the front. "In fact, I think I'll just throw this shirt away. Do you have a trash bag?"

Brodie blinked, realizing what the stains were. "Of course," she said. She found a trash bag in the cupboard then opened the door to Mrs. Weir's room. It didn't seem like the right time to show Joe to her own bedroom. And he looked too tired for all those stairs. Not to mention anything else.

Joe disappeared into Mrs. Weir's room with his suitcase and there was the sound of running water. Brodie put the roses in a vase and checked on dinner.

After hours in the oven, the Cornish game hens looked like wire sculptures. The rice pilaf had acquired a hard crust and the glazed baby carrots had shriveled into short leather strips. Brodie lifted out the pan and plated the food, hoping it wouldn't taste as overdone as it looked.

A few minutes later Joe came out of the bedroom in clean jeans and a navy blue tee shirt, his damp hair curling over the neckline. Brodie handed him a fresh beer.

They ate quietly, Joe accepting a third beer halfway through. Mouse sat by Joe's chair, ears back and looking hopefully at his plate. But Joe was a thousand miles away. He complimented Brodie on the food and she wondered if he even knew what he was eating. The chicken tasted like wood, the rice was like eating nails, and the carrots were fibrous and chewy. Neither ate much and Brodie was relieved when she could replace the plates with the strawberries and sorbet.

Joe flinched when she set the dessert dish in front of him as if her motion had been too sudden.

Brodie slid into her chair, picked up her spoon, then set it down again. "Are you all right?" she asked.

"Yes, sure," Joe said.

Brodie reached out and touched Joe's left hand. It was resting on the table next to his dessert dish. And shaking.

"Shit," Joe said, his gaze following Brodie's touch. He shook his head. "I'm sorry."

"It's okay," Brodie said.

Joe's hand turned and closed around Brodie's. His grip was strong and warm despite the trembling. "It happened right in front of me," he said. "I was in the middle lane and watched that rig tumble right out of the sky. The semi fell on two cars and the rest slammed into each other. Somehow I got the truck onto the shoulder and started running toward the accident."

"Oh my God," Brodie murmured. She rubbed her thumb over his, feeling the shaking subside.

"I hadn't seen a dead body since Iraq," Joe said. His eyes were dark and troubled. "It brought back a lot of bad memories."

Brodie's swallowed hard. "How long until the police came?"

"There was actually one in traffic behind me. A county guy. We teamed up. Found two bodies and got a bunch of banged-up people out of cars and onto the grass by the shoulder." Joe blinked and rubbed his eyes with his free hand. "Look, Sassy, I'm not good company right now. I need some sleep. Can we start the weekend over tomorrow morning?"

"Of course," Brodie said.

"Thanks," Joe said. He made no move to let go of her hand.

"I have to be at the symposium no later than nine in the morning," Brodie said apologetically. "It means leaving here at eight forty-five. Do you want to come with me? If you want to sleep in, I can leave you directions."

"No," Joe said. "I'll come with you. I don't want to miss a minute of you doing your thing."

"You sure?"

"The weekend starts tomorrow morning," Joe said firmly.

"Tomorrow morning," Brodie echoed.

"I really appreciate this," Joe said. "You know how to give a man space."

"Take as much as you need," Brodie said.

"I like you, Sassy," Joe said. "Very much." He squeezed her hand and looked at her expectantly.

Emotions churned but no words came out.

Joe raised Brodie's hand to his lips, kissed her knuckles, then pressed her palm to his cheek.

Brodie closed her eyes and felt the air quiver around them.

Joe exhaled and gently let go of her hand. His chair scraped over the tile floor as he stood up and then the door to Mrs. Weir's room closed.

Brodie made herself clean up the kitchen, painfully conscious of Joe on the other side of the wall. When she passed the door to Mrs. Weir's room on her way upstairs she heard him snoring softly and wondered if he was dreaming.

CHAPTER 17

". . . Thank you all very much for making the university's tenth annual symposium on music and politics such an enjoyable and informative day," Brodie said into the microphone. "Please join us for the cocktail hour Dean Slocum is hosting in the garden. And on that note--pun intended--we are adjourned."

There was a ripple of laughter. From his seat in the audience, Joe winked at her. His blonde hair and starched white shirt stood out amid the sea of seersucker and khaki suits, the summer uniforms of the successful Southern academic.

They'd carried on a virtual conversation for most of the day, the communication flowing silently between Brodie on the stage and Joe in the audience. Unexpected humor at a speaker's witticism, appreciation for certain musical spots, support for Brodie's students, disdain for a particularly pompous academic--they'd shared it all.

Brodie smiled and raised her hand in a farewell gesture and stepped away from the podium. Applause swelled inside the auditorium.

As the audience trickled out, Brodie went backstage and hugged her waiting grad students. They'd all made well-received presentations. She picked up the purse she'd left in the backstage office, found the stage door to the main auditorium, and went up the aisle to the lobby.

Joe was waiting for her, tall and broad against the wall with a shaft of sunlight from the window playing across his body. Brodie's mouth went dry at the sight of him.

"You did very well, Sassy," he said and gave her that sideways smile.

"Thank you, sir." Brodie started to shrug out of her jacket and Joe's big hands were suddenly on her shoulders, helping ease it away. Their movements brought them close and Brodie couldn't help smiling back at him, loving the way the corners of the blue eyes crinkled and how his teeth shone white inside the trim beard. "But be honest," she said. "How bored were you?"

"Not at all," Joe said. "The opening and closing remarks were riveting."

"Of course." Brodie gave a laugh.

Joe flipped her jacket over his arm like a waiter with a towel. "The rest is a little blurry," he admitted. "Especially when that hefty lady was talking about Hitler and Wagner. But that was your fault."

"Me?" Brodie slipped the handle of her purse over her shoulder. "What did I do?"

"You had your legs crossed." Joe looked down at her in mock seriousness. "I got so distracted when you started bobbing your foot I never heard how the story ended."

"Glenn Miller joined up and we won," said Brodie.

She touched his arm and turned him toward the exit, sure that tonight would be the night she'd really get to know Joe Birnam. He'd obviously put last night behind him. "Can you stand a couple of minutes at the cocktail party?"

"Only if I get to take you out to dinner afterwards." Joe's fingers trailed down the inside of her wrist. "I think I'm looking at a woman who needs a drink, a solid meal, and the chance to put her feet up."

"That would be so great," Brodie said fervently as their fingers met. "How about a quiet place with fantastic steaks and a beer list as long as your arm?"

"I'd like that." Joe kept smiling and for a moment Brodie thought he was going to kiss her but then a noisy bunch of students came out of the auditorium and the moment slid away.

"Ten minutes, I promise," Brodie said softly.

They held hands as they crossed to the garden. A steel drum band was playing next to the skirted bar, giving the reception a Caribbean feel. Dean Slocum was with his wife just inside the gate.

"Brodie," he boomed as Brodie and Joe walked up. "A wonderful day."

"Thank-you, Dean," Brodie said. "Let me introduce Joe Birnam."

Slocum shook Joe's hand, introduced his wife Grace, then focused on Brodie again. "What a golden touch you have. Everything you do turns to success."

"What a kind thing to say, Dean," Brodie said. "But I have to say that it really was my students who--."

"*Darling!*"

Out of nowhere, Stanton swept down on them, resplendent in a pale blue seersucker suit, lemon yellow shirt, polka-dot bow tie, and white suede bucks.

Brodie froze in utter astonishment as Stanton ignored Joe, edged by Dean Slocum, and put his hand on the small of her back.

"Darling, the symposium was wonderful," he said effusively. "Dean, didn't you think the agenda this year was the best we've ever had?"

"Uh, Stanton," Brodie started but her brain was screaming *no, no, this can't be happening.*

"I'm so proud of you, darling." Stanton took his hand off Brodie's back in order to shake hands vigorously with Dean Slocum. "Howard, it was so good for you to host this little gathering."

"Yes, very kind for you to do this for the *department*." Jackson Hull followed in Stanton's wake like a tired tugboat keeping up with a racing yacht. He wore a rumpled khaki suit. The smell of old cigarettes hung in the air around him.

"My favorite event of the year," Dean Slocum enthused.

Joe's face had registered a brief twist of surprise when Stanton first appeared, but now the captain of the football team could have been a professional poker player. Brodie saw his expressionless face and her brain came to a grinding halt. She felt like an idiot, not knowing what to do, what to say, how to avoid a scene.

"Our Dr. Macbeth is really making a name for the university, isn't she?" Stanton cocked his head, radiating that insincere sincerity she knew so well. He turned his high beams onto Dean Slocum. "I wouldn't be surprised if the symposium resulted in some significant new alumni donations."

"Confidentially." Dean Slocum leaned forward conspiratorially. "That's already happened. Why do you think this is my favorite event of the year?"

Stanton and Hull laughed dutifully.

"Maybe this is a good time to reconsider my proposal for a journalism studio for the department," Stanton said.

Brodie felt the air rush out of her as she realized why Stanton had shown up. Why he was calling her *darling* in front of the dean.

"Inter-departmental activities are always popular with alumni," Hull pointed out, fumbling a cigarette package out of the pocket of his khaki suit. His eyes were small and brown behind the horn-rimmed glasses.

"How much do you think it would cost?" Dean Slocum asked.

Joe eased away from the group, his face still expressionless.

"Dean, we have to be going," Brodie said.

No one heard her.

Stanton had turned on his television commentator's voice and his audience was hooked. He started spewing figures to a rapt Dean Slocum.

"Where'd you get Paul Bunyan, Macbeth?" Hull asked, obviously amused at Brodie's discomfiture. His eyes darted between Brodie, Joe, and Stanton as he sucked on his cigarette.

"Dean, I have to go," Brodie tried again as Joe disappeared into the crowd.

"Darling, *mea culpa,*" Stanton said, with a sly grin that dared her to discredit him. "I won't be able to make dinner tonight. You go on without me. I have a million phone calls to make."

His audacity was unbelievable. Brodie's brain was inert with embarrassment. "Yes, well," she said lamely. "Good night."

She walked across the grass, her heels digging in at every step. Joe was at the bar but didn't have a drink in hand. "Ready to go?" he said.

They were quiet in the Volvo on the way to the Hardware Store, a downtown Charlottesville landmark. The two-story restaurant had once been a real hardware store. The antique tool bins and signs had survived a careful restoration and the reminiscent décor was part of the restaurant's considerable charm. Brodie and Joe were shown to a table on the mezzanine overlooking the first floor.

They ordered beer and steaks and made stilted small talk, mostly about what Joe had seen during a stroll around the campus during one of the breaks. Brodie didn't know she knew so much trivia about Jeffersonian architecture. She picked at her salad and ate a few mouthfuls of ribeye.

When they got back to the house they went into the kitchen and let Mouse in. The dog went straight to Joe and flopped on her back to have her stomach rubbed.

Joe bent awkwardly and stroked the dog's fur. "I think we need to talk, Brodie," he said.

"Yes, of course, yes," Brodie heard herself gabble. She needed some liquid courage. "Let's go in the den."

Mouse followed them to the other room.

Brodie flicked on the old overhead light. The dark green den walls glowed. She put on a Brad Paisley album, then poured them each a stiff Famous Grouse.

Joe sat on the sofa with his glass and looked at the ornate chess set on the coffee table. Brodie settled into the maple rocking chair and flicked on the desk lamp. It brightened the room considerably.

Mouse yawned and collapsed into a heap on the floor by Joe.

"Napoleon or Wellington?" Joe asked.

"Napoleon," Brodie said, trying to forget the awful dream in which she was a redcoat at the battle of Waterloo.

They played silently for a few minutes. Brodie tried to block out the tension in the room by focusing on Joe's strategy but she couldn't do it. Everything had gone horribly awry between them, thanks to Stanton, and she didn't know how to fix it.

Joe took one of her bishops and Brodie stared at the board. Joe could checkmate her in two moves. She moved her queen to defend the king, trying to set up a gambit. It wasn't much. Joe was a very good chess player and would figure it out.

But instead of taking his turn, Joe got up and turned off Brad in mid-guitar solo. He came back to the sofa and the old leather creaked under his weight. As he sat facing her, it was obvious that one knee was intact and that the other was a metal joint.

"Did I ever tell you about my marriage?" Joe asked.

"Not really," Brodie said, surprised at the subject.

Joe sipped some Scotch then studied the glass with its half inch of amber fluid. The heavy Waterford tumbler looked small in his hand. "I was stationed in San Diego," he said. "She was the hostess in a restaurant. We lasted all of a year. I shipped out to the Gulf and she ran off with another guy. I signed the divorce papers in Kuwait."

"I'm sorry," Brodie said. Somehow it felt like her fault.

"I won't ever be that other guy, Brodie," Joe said.

"What?" Brodie asked blankly. Then his meaning caught and she straightened up in the chair. "Is that what you think? That I'm still seeing Stanton?"

"Are you?"

"No."

"You sure about that?"

"Of course."

"Then why didn't he seem to know?" Joe moved a pawn.

"He only showed up to pitch his idea about some television studio he wants the university to build," Brodie said dismissively. She used her knight to jump the pawn in an attempt to threaten Joe's bishop. "He knew the dean was going to be there."

"You didn't answer my question." Joe took her knight with his rook.

"There's nothing to discuss." Brodie moved her last remaining bishop and made a show of studying the board.

"But if you say it's over, why didn't he know?" Joe asked, making a visible effort to keep his voice even. "And come to think of it, why didn't anybody else know, either?"

"Stanton and I are just professional colleagues at this point," Brodie insisted. She looked up from the chessboard. "We haven't talked since before I went to Edinburgh."

"You haven't spoken to him since you got back," Joe said.

"No," Brodie said. "Nothing. No contact." Surely that would show she wasn't a two-timer.

"Then how does he know you're not at that crossroads anymore?"

Brodie blinked, trapped by Joe's logic. God, she'd been an *idiot.* She should have called Stanton, made things final, not left herself so vulnerable.

"So tell me if I'm wrong here," Joe said. He leaned back. "I don't think you're lying to me but I do think that you avoided telling this jerk how you felt. Maybe you thought it would be messy. Didn't introduce me to him because it would have been embarrassing. Sat for an uncomfortable hour in that restaurant looking at your plate hoping I wouldn't bring it up and it would all go away."

He looked so smug Brodie wanted to throw the chessboard at him. Joe had seen right through her and the feeling was intensely uncomfortable. She shrugged and concentrated on the chess pieces.

Joe reached across the table and the tips of his fingers caught Brodie under the chin. "Fidelity and honesty are big issues for me," he said softly. "I won't be jerked around."

Mouse lifted her head and looked at them.

Brodie pulled back, torn between acute embarrassment and the thrill of Joe's touch. "What do you want me to say?" she huffed. "That I'm sorry I didn't introduce you? Well, I am. I'm sorry. And I'm sorry he was insufferably rude to you and I didn't say anything."

"Okay. Thank you." Joe nodded.

Mouse laid her chin on her front paws again and watched Joe. Brodie folded her arms. Out of the corner of her eye she saw him use his queen to take her bishop and put her king into check.

"Checkmate," Joe said.

"Fine," Brodie said.

Mouse made a grumpy sound and rolled onto her back. She wriggled against the carpet, leaving dog hair everywhere.

"You know," Joe said. "This isn't about whether or not you introduced me to your asshole ex-boyfriend. It's that if you live your life never telling people how you feel, how is anyone ever going to know where they stand with you?"

"Are you accusing me of being dishonest?" Brodie exclaimed.

"Do you think it's honest not to tell people how you feel?" Joe shot back.

"I was brought up to be discreet," Brodie countered.

"I noticed that last night," Joe said. "I told you how I felt and you were nicely discreet."

Brodie drank the last of her Famous Grouse and felt her nerves fray. The tension in the room swelled, magnified by the dark walls and heavy tartan draperies.

"Look, Sassy." Joe began lining up the chess pieces as if for a new game. "You've got a lot of stuff bottled up in there. Every time you clam up you add more until the bottle's got more than it can hold."

His eyes were intense and immediate. "Get in there, get it out. Get mad now and then. I know you're tough, but avoiding real life is eating you alive." He paused. "And isn't that what happened to your dad?"

Brodie slammed her empty glass on the table and clenched her fists. What right did Joe Birnam have to lecture her like this?

Joe got up to refill their glasses. His limp was very

pronounced as Mouse followed him to the table by the window and suddenly Brodie was 12 again and it was the worst day ever. Her father had come to pick her up at Kay's house in Edinburgh at the end of the summer and announced coldly that Brodie would not be going to middle school in Charlottesville with her friends but would instead be going to boarding school.

It had felt as if he was banishing her, cutting her out of his life. Brodie had protested tearfully and Kay had tried to ask why but it had been like talking to a wall. "Macbeths don't cry," Wallace Macbeth had said scornfully.

A week later Brodie had watched her father and Mrs. Weir drive away from the Madeira School. And didn't cry.

Joe put the refilled glass in front of her. "You need to learn how to speak from the heart, Sassy," he said as he settled once more onto the sofa with Mouse at his feet. "If you don't, you're going to miss out on a lot."

Brodie raised her glass to her lips and sipped, stung by the truth in what he was saying but also seething inside. *Who the hell did Joe Birnam think he was?*

"If I didn't care I wouldn't say anything," Joe said as if he'd read her mind. "Maybe everyone else in your life has let you get away with it. Maybe everything was all right until your dad died. But you're hurting now and I don't like watching you do this to yourself."

He put the last pawn in place on the board. The two miniature armies faced each other again, ready for battle.

Brodie kept her eyes on the glass in her hand. "Last night you said I gave you space," she said tightly. "Maybe you should learn to do the same thing."

The room got very quiet.

"Well." Joe tossed down some scotch. "So she can get mad."

Brodie reached out and turned off the desk lamp. The room shifted into gray night, spared total darkness by the dim overhead light.

Joe put his glass on the table and stood up. "As the song goes, the whiskey ain't working any more."

Brodie stared at nothing as he walked away.

Joe stopped in the doorway, his back to Brodie. "For the record," he said without turning around. "If I ever see that asshole again I'm going to pull his head off and beat the shit out of him with it. And if I make a scene, so much the better."

He left, Mouse at his heels.

When she heard the door to Mrs. Weir's room close Brodie swept her hand across the chessboard, furiously knocking the carefully placed pieces to the floor.

CHAPTER 18

Mouse barked again, a short, staccato *play with me* yip that came from outside the house. Brodie wound her way out of the tangled bed sheets and went to the open window.

Joe and the dog were in the back yard. They were playing fetch with the old plastic hedgehog, Joe lobbing it across the grass and Mouse racing madly after it. The dog brought it back to him each time, dropping it neatly at his feet and barking to remind him to throw it again.

"Traitor," Brodie murmured.

Joe's shoulders were so much wider than his waist that his tee shirt flapped loosely around his midsection like a flag at half mast. As he moved across the grass with the dog, the narrow shin pole of his prosthetic was evident through the thin nylon of his warmup pants . He had a bandana wrapped around his head to keep the hair out of his eyes and the sun caught the fine blonde hairs on his forearms. He looked big and powerful and fundamentally masculine and nothing like the other men who'd been in Brodie's life.

As she stared at him longingly, Brodie knew that she'd seriously messed things up last night.

She slumped into the upholstered rocking chair, hugged her knees, and confronted some ugly truths about herself. Maybe there was insanity in her family. Maybe she was a defective human being without the capacity to love. Maybe all she'd ever have in life would be books.

And hideous nightmares.

Brodie pressed the heels of her hands into her eyes. She hadn't been able to see what was upsetting her father, she hadn't had the courage to stand up to Stanton, and she'd let her chance with Joe go by.

It wasn't just Stanton causing these nightmares, it was

everything.

Her father had never shared a great secret. Strangers asking questions in her dreams about his secret represented her inherited inability to love and be loved.

Sniffling with sad self-awareness, Brodie went back to the window.

Down in the yard, Joe dropped to the ground and started doing push-ups, his artificial left foot hovering above the ground, his weight borne by his hands and right foot. Brodie counted 120 push-ups with the excellent butt going up and down like a machine before Mouse started licking his face and Joe collapsed in laughter.

When he started doing crunches on the grass Brodie put on yoga pants and a tee shirt and went downstairs. The roses Joe had brought were on the kitchen counter. They'd opened into a froth of pink petals and she inhaled their scent guiltily.

Joe had come to the weekend with the same expectations she'd had. Between one thing and another it had all turned into a mess.

The coffee was still hot. As Brodie poured herself a cup Joe came through the back door, tracked lovingly by Mouse.

"Hi," he said.

"Hi," Brodie replied, her knees suddenly wobbly. He smelled like grass and sunshine and testosterone. "Good workout?"

"We were just playing around." Joe topped up Mouse's water bowl then filled a glass for himself and drank it down.

"Great," Brodie said and buried her nose in her mug.

Joe turned on the faucet again and splashed water on his face. There was a sweat stain at the neck of his tee shirt but he wasn't even breathing hard.

He turned off the water, dried his face with a paper towel, and leaned against the counter. "So. How're you doing this morning?"

Brodie put down her mug and took a big breath. "I owe you an apology," she said. "I was rude and I'm sorry."

Joe pulled off the bandana and stuck it in his pocket but didn't speak.

That was as much as she could manage. Acutely aware of Joe's eyes on her, Brodie opened the refrigerator and hauled out a big box she'd gotten from DeLuca's Friday afternoon when she'd picked up dinner. *The Party's On Us* the box proclaimed. *Deluxe Fruit Fixings*.

"Brunch at eleven," Brodie said lightly.

She opened the box and stared at the contents in dismay. There was a pineapple, a container of strawberries, some kiwis, half a cantaloupe, a grapefruit, and a couple of apples and pears wrapped in tissue paper. *Damn.*

"What's the matter?" Joe asked.

"It was supposed to be cut up," Brodie said. "I told Diana I'd bring fruit salad and it was supposed to be already cut up. You know, in pieces. To eat."

It felt like the last straw. The weekend with Joe had been ruined, nothing had gone the way she'd hoped. He'd found out that she was some emotionally stunted wretch, they hadn't done anything more than hold hands, she'd had another hideous nightmare, and now she wasn't going to have any fruit salad for Diana and Ray's brunch. Brodie grabbed the pineapple, threw it back into the refrigerator, and found a big glass bowl.

"What was wrong with the pineapple?" Joe asked. He found a mug and poured himself some coffee.

"Everything else I can just bring over as is," Brodie grouched as she sorted fruit. "But what's Diana going to do with a pineapple?"

Joe put down his mug and opened the refrigerator door. "You promised fruit salad, right?" he asked, bending to look inside.

The butt was very, very excellent in those thin nylon pants.

"Yes," Brodie said faintly. *Life is so unfair.*

Joe came back to the counter holding the pineapple and a small watermelon Brodie had bought for the week ahead. "We keep promises," he said and the blue eyes went right through Brodie. "We say what we mean."

"I really don't cook," she said lamely.

"You don't cook fruit salad." Joe took the kiwi out of the glass bowl and lined up all the fruit on the counter. He found the ancient chopping board Mrs. Weir had used to knead bread and handed Brodie a clean dish towel and a sharp knife. "Hold the pineapple like this. Cut off the top and then slide the knife down the sides." He demonstrated slicing away the prickly skin, exposing the juicy yellow interior. "And then cut it into rings and then make the rings into rectangles."

"Rectangles," Brodie said doubtfully.

"You'll see."

He left the kitchen and came back a minute later with a pen. He traced a line on the outside of the watermelon, inserted a knife along the line and started cutting.

Brodie sawed at the pineapple and got the top off. She and Joe worked side by side for a few minutes, Brodie self-conscious and sticky-handed as she hacked at the pineapple until there was a tidy row of yellow rectangles on the chopping board.

Joe cut away a long section of watermelon rind, leaving a green tureen with the ends higher than the sides to reveal the juicy pink interior. He showed her a round tool, jammed it into the melon, made a twisting motion, and produced a perfect pink melon ball. Joe dropped it into the empty glass bowl and handed Brodie the tool. "Your turn," he said.

"Uh," said Brodie.

"What time is brunch?" Joe asked pointedly.

Jerk. Brodie took the tool and stuck it into the watermelon. It took her a couple of tries but she figured out the trick. When she was done and the glass bowl was full of melon balls she looked at Joe in triumph.

But Joe merely glanced at the bowl then handed her a grapefruit. "Small pieces," he said and gestured at the glass bowl. "No pits or skin. Same for the pears and apples. Then wash and halve the strawberries. Peel the kiwis and cut them up. Cantaloupe, too."

There was no way she was going to do any more chopping or cutting or melon ball making. "No," Brodie said. "That's it for me. I need to go get ready."

"You're not done here," Joe said shortly.

"You could help, you know," Brodie said, irritated. He was the one who was the great cook and he'd just stood there and watched her make melon balls.

"It was your promise," Joe said. He went and sat at the table with his coffee. Mouse put her chin on his right knee.

Jerk. I so don't want to sleep with you. Brodie bit her lip and jammed her thumb into the grapefruit skin.

When she was nearly done cubing the cantaloupe Joe got two carrots out of the refrigerator. He peeled and sliced them into thin reeds.

"Put some paper towels in the empty watermelon," Joe said. "You need to dry it out and then--."

"Put everything in," Brodie finished. "I'm not an idiot."

"Not the pineapple," Joe said.

He leaned against the counter, all muscle and blue eyes, and Brodie seesawed between lust and annoyance. A lecture last night, now telling her what to do in her own kitchen. She grabbed a paper towel.

But when everything was done the fruit mixture made a wonderfully delicious kaleidoscope of color in the watermelon tureen. Brodie couldn't help smiling in satisfaction. *I did that.*

Joe handed her a carrot straw and a rectangle of pineapple. "Here," he said and worked the pineapple onto the carrot. He stuck it in the middle of the cut fruit.

"It's a sail," Brodie exclaimed.

"Very good," Joe said. "You do the rest."

In a few minutes the watermelon was transformed into a Spanish galleon under full sail.

"Look at that," Brodie marveled.

"See," Joe said. "You got your hands dirty and you didn't like it. But you're tough. You did one thing at a time. You hung in there, figured it out, and made something pretty good."

Brodie went to the sink and washed her hands so he wouldn't see her face flush. "Is this some new-fangled fruit salad therapy?" she asked.

"Just using what was available," Joe said. "I'm a resourceful kind of guy."

Brodie dried her hands and turned around and their eyes met. "Thanks," she said.

"Hey," Joe said. He stepped toward her. "We're all learning. Taking it one day at a time."

For a moment Brodie thought he might put his arms around her and hold her tight and she desperately wanted to be that close to him. To hide inside his embrace, to be protected by his strength, to feel his heart beat against hers.

"Don't ever turn out a light on me again, Sassy," Joe said.

CHAPTER 19

Puck bayed in response to the doorbell.

Diana opened the door. She ran an eye over Brodie and Joe waiting on the doorstep.

"We're here," Brodie said unnecessarily.

"Ray," Diana called over her shoulder. "Come look at this. The Vikings have come to brunch."

Brodie glowered.

Joe laughed. "No raping and pillaging until after we eat," he said.

"Did Brodie cook breakfast?" Diana asked with mock sympathy. "I'll bet you're starved."

Joe grinned, shifted the watermelon ship to his left hand, and extended his right. "Hi. I'm Joe Birnam. We come bearing fruit salad."

"Diana Johnson. Really glad to meet you," Diana said. She shook his hand then relieved him of the watermelon ship and lifted her eyebrows in admiration. "This is too fabulous to eat. Are you some kind of food designer in your spare time?"

"Brodie made it," Joe said.

Diana's mouth dropped open. "Wow," she said. "This is a first." She gave Brodie an *is this for real?* look then flashed Joe a dazzling smile. "Come on in."

As they stepped over the threshold Ray appeared and Diana introduced him. "I hear you're a cook," Ray said to Joe. "Ready for some grilling? I've got some chicken going with my own special sauce."

"Molasses or brown sugar?" Joe asked.

"Both," Ray said. "And balsamic vinegar."

"Nice," Joe said admiringly, one master chef to another.

"Not too early for a beer for you?" Ray asked hopefully.

"It's five o'clock somewhere," Joe said.

"Right this way." Ray gestured for Joe to proceed him, then gave Brodie a thumbs-up before following Joe down the hall. Puck trotted after them.

"He's gorgeous," Diana whispered, watching the two men disappear into the kitchen. "You were right about that ass. Last night must have been fantastic. Did the earth move? Stars collide?"

"Yesterday was hideous," Brodie hissed. "Stanton showed up."

"At the house?" Diana asked, shocked.

The screen door rattled and they both automatically looked down the hallway. Puck had been left in the kitchen and was bumping the door with his nose and whining.

Brodie shook her head. "At the dean's cocktail party after the symposium. And acted like we were still together."

"Oh, no," Diana groaned.

The back door opened, Puck shot outside, and the door closed again. "Dogs love him," Brodie observed sourly. "Joe's a magnet for interesting people and dogs."

"So what happened?" Diana rested the watermelon boat on her hip.

"We left the cocktail party and then had this weird argument at home. He slept in Mrs. Weir's room." Brodie left her purse on the hall table and smoothed the front of her sleeveless black and white print dress.

"Did you make up?" Diana asked. "He seems to be in a good mood."

"Sort of."

"So now what?" Diana led the way into the kitchen, her silk top and Capri pants matching the decor.

"I have no idea," Brodie said morosely. She headed for the refrigerator. "What do you have to drink? Anything stronger than beer?"

To Brodie's surprise it ended up being a fun, relaxing afternoon. Joe and Ray talked animatedly, their conversation ranging from football to politics to entertainment to football. Brunch was served on the patio where they all talked and laughed and listened to jazz. They moved inside for coffee and the Sunday afternoon NASCAR race, Joe and Ray still arguing good-naturedly over football.

At four o'clock Joe said he had to be thinking about heading back to Alexandria. Back at the farmhouse he disappeared into Mrs. Weir's room to pack. Brodie changed into denim shorts and a plain white tee shirt.

She came downstairs in time to see Joe carry his suitcase outside, Mouse hovering close behind.

Brodie watched from the porch as he tossed the bag into the back seat of the truck. As Mouse inspected the truck, Joe turned around.

"I'm sorry this was such a weird weekend," Brodie said from the top step.

Joe walked towards her, moving over the gravel drive with only the slightest hint of a limp. By now Brodie knew that it was only evident when he was very tired or walking on an uneven surface. He stopped at the base of the porch, the same Oakley wraparound sunglasses he'd had at the Cherry Blossom Festival in his hand. Mouse pressed against his right leg. Crickets started an early concert.

"It was weird, wasn't it?" he said. His hair was pale gold in the late afternoon light. "But your friends were nice. Diana and Ray are good people."

"So what's next?" Brodie asked hesitantly, coming down another step.

Joe sighed and squinted toward the old dogwood trees. The crickets hushed their song. "Maybe old Stanton did us a favor, Sassy."

"How's that?" Brodie took another step down. Her face was level with Joe's.

Joe touched her cheek, surprising her. "Without Stanton showing up, we might have jumped into something we aren't ready for."

"Joe," Brodie said. She slid her hand over his. "How ready do we need to be?"

"I don't know, Sassy." Joe traced the line of her jaw, her hand riding on his. The big blue eyes were sad. "I only want you to be happy. Get past this thing with your dad. Be able to get the hell out of that box if that's what you want."

Brodie's heart twisted in her chest. That wasn't enough. She wanted to know if they'd ever really be together, skin-to-skin, the way she'd imagined. And he was so close, his hand gentle on her cheek. "Joe, please."

"If I kiss you right now, I might never stop," Joe said. His hand fell away.

"Would that be so bad?" Brodie asked, her voice a tight whisper.

Joe shook his head. "We've both got a lot of thinking to do."

He got into the truck. Brodie felt utterly miserable as it backed out of the driveway and turned down the road.

The crickets started up again, their chorus from the dogwood trees loud and insistent. Brodie stalked into the house and got her purse and car keys.

"Brodie," Stanton said uncertainly. "And the dog."

"Hi, Stanton," Brodie said. "Can we come in?"

"Well." Stanton glanced backwards at the ornate colonial interior of the house. He had on his usual Sunday afternoon outfit of khaki pants, apricot polo shirt, and paisley ascot. "This really isn't a very good time--."

"Do you have company?" Brodie interrupted, pushing past him. "Don't worry, this won't take long. Come on, Mouse."

The German Shepherd obediently followed Brodie into the house, nails clicking on the foyer's slate floor.

"Look, Brodie," Stanton said nervously. "I really have to ask you to leave. You can't bring that smelly animal in here."

"First things first." Brodie deliberately walked into the living room and watched Stanton blanch as Mouse trotted across the antique Persian rug to sniff a delicate Lladro figurine on a mahogany end table.

Stanton snatched up the porcelain sculpture. Mouse lost interest, stuck her nose into a Chinese cachepot holding a miniature orange tree, and sneezed potting soil over the carpet.

"I really must insist, Brodie," Stanton said. "We can talk some other time."

"But now's good for me," Brodie said brightly. "Just tell me what you thought you were doing by going to the dean's party and acting like we were still together. You were the one who wanted to talk again but you've been the invisible man. Yet suddenly you're calling me darling in front of the dean? You never called me darling. Ever."

Mouse rolled on the dirt with snuffling noises of joy.

"Dear God," Stanton murmured as Mouse got to her feet and shook herself, puffs of white fur flying off the dog and settling onto the rug like miniature clouds. He looked back at Brodie. "I was doing you a favor."

"Doing me a favor?" Brodie echoed incredulously. Mouse's tail sideswiped a delicate piecrust table, making it teeter, as the dog went to investigate the silk damask seat cushions of the Duncan Phyfe sofa.

"Shoo," Stanton said, stilling the table and rescuing a delicate bouquet of flowers in a silver cup. "Yes, I was doing you a favor. Showing my support. There are reputations to consider." He reached past Brodie to scoop up an elaborately embroidered toss pillow before Mouse could press her muzzle into it.

"You are so full of it, Stanton," Brodie said furiously as Mouse lolled on the rug again, leaving a coating of spiky hair in the nap. "You came to the party to strike while the iron was hot. The symposium is always Dean Slocum's big donor day and you knew he'd be feeling generous. It was a good time to hit him up for your stupid television studio so you can broadcast from campus and get more air time."

"That's a very unfair thing to say," Stanton said, kneeing aside a taffeta hassock that had come in contact with Mouse's tail.

"It's the truth, though, isn't it?" Brodie snapped. Mouse trotted into the dining room. Brodie followed. Stanton brought up the rear clutching pillows and bouquet.

"Well, just so it doesn't ever happen again," Brodie rattled on. "This is your official notice that we are over. So there's no confusion, here's why." She started counting off the reasons on her fingers. "I do not like you. I do not like your snooty family in Houston. We do not like the same music, movies, or television shows. We don't have the same sense of humor. You don't turn me on physically. Kissing you is like kissing a brother. Bland and a little weird."

Stanton's face reddened as Brodie went on. "So we are no longer dating and never will again. If anybody asks, we have broken up. The power couple is no more. I may take out an ad in --."

Movement on the other side of the sheers covering the dining room window caught Brodie's eye. She yanked the curtain aside. Out on the deck, a young dark-haired woman in a splashy Lily Pulitzer sundress was sitting at the umbrella table laden with a pitcher of piña coladas, two glasses, and a tray of hors d'oeuvres.

"Is that Sabine Seagull?" Brodie asked, staring at the scene. "From the Economics Department?"

"Um, yes," Stanton's voice betrayed his nervousness.

Brodie swung around to confront him. "You're on a date," she accused.

Stanton's angular face tensed.

"You're dating her," Brodie said in amazement. "How long has this been going on?"

"Her book is outselling yours," Stanton replied as if that

explained everything. He leaned on the dining table. "Really, Brodie, you've said what you came to--."

"*You came to the dean's party yesterday and wrecked my life,*" Brodie shouted. "*And all the time you've been dating someone else?*"

"Like you never used me," Stanton said nastily. "With your father gone, you'll be nothing on this campus without me towing you along. Now see if you get the project funding you want. Jack Hull's not going to help you. Someday he'll be head of the history department while you're still chumming with your illiterate coaching friends and listening to yodeling music."

Somewhere in the house a door opened and shut. Sabine Seagull came into the dining room. Up close she was a fatally attractive woman, with big green eyes, artfully tousled long dark hair, and luminescent skin.

"Are you coming back out, Stanton?" she asked, then blinked as she recognized Brodie and sensed the hostility in the room. "Dr. Macbeth. Hello."

"Dr. Macbeth was just leaving," Stanton spat.

"Are you sure you won't stay and have a piña colada with us?" Sabine asked. She had a soft, little-girl voice.

"Dear God," Stanton said, as Mouse curveted into the room, a tennis ball in her mouth.

"Is this your dog, Dr. Macbeth?" Sabine exclaimed. "How beautiful." She crouched down to pet Mouse, ignoring Stanton as he leaped to the buffet to get a napkin.

"Thank you," Brodie said. The situation was getting very surreal. "Her name is Mouse."

"Hello, Mouse," Sabine crooned, rubbing Mouse's ears and getting a damp tennis ball deposited in her lap in return.

"Don't touch that dog, Sabine," Stanton snapped. "You don't know where it's been."

Sabine looked up in surprise as Mouse backed away from her and pressed against Brodie's legs. "Stanton, you don't like dogs?"

"He doesn't like sex, either," Brodie said tartly.

Stanton's face turned vermillion.

Brodie clicked her tongue. "Let's go, Mouse."

The pie crust table fell over with a satisfying crash as they passed through the living room on the way to the front door.

PART 6

If it were done when 'tis done, then 'twere well it were done
quickly.
(*Macbeth:* 1.7.1-2)

CHAPTER 20

"Open it," Diana said.

Brodie fingered the padded mailing envelope with the BIRNAM WOOD return address. "It can wait until we've had dinner," she said.

"Huh," Diana said.

Brodie made a face, put the envelope on the kitchen counter, and opened the bag from the restaurant. Mouse settled down by the table as the tantalizing aroma of marinara sauce and chicken marsala wafted out. Ray was on a recruiting trip so the two women had ended their day by getting takeout and planning to watch a movie at the farmhouse. Brodie had found the big envelope wedged in the box when she stopped in the driveway to collect the mail.

Diana brought plates to the table and started serving out the chicken and linguine. "Would it kill you to open it now before I die of curiosity?"

"This food looks great," Brodie said. Mouse settled onto the floor next to her chair.

Diana rolled her eyes and sat down.

Brodie twirled her fork in the linguine. She and Joe hadn't spoken since the music symposium three weeks ago. But he'd been constantly on her mind as she'd read through the D-E section of her father's bookshelves, given final exams, posted grades, marched in the graduation ceremony, and hugged her seniors goodbye. And woken terrified in a cold sweat more than once after a hideous dream in which she was running desperately from white-eyed people ready to kill her for her father's secret.

Now she had to get ready for her trip to London and the history department's meeting with Dr. Donald Pedder, scheduled for the Monday after her return.

A blob of pasta hit her chin and fell into her lap.

"What the hell," Brodie exclaimed, and grabbed her napkin. She wiped her chin. "Did you just flick food at me?"

"Yes." Diana loaded her fork again and held it like a catapult. "Open that envelope and then call Joe Birnam. You have to talk to him before you go to London."

"Oh, yeah." Brodie scrubbed at the sauce stain on her new beige linen jeans. Mouse stood and sniffed her. "Advice from somebody who throws spaghetti. How old are you?"

"Old enough to know that men like Joe Birnam only come around once in a lifetime," Diana said. "What happened between you two, anyway? Start talking, sweetie."

"Nothing," Brodie said.

"It can't be Stanton," Diana said. "It's still all over campus that you broke up."

The university gossip mill had been relentless. Brodie gave up on the stain and doggedly cut into her chicken. "Never mind about Joe. I told you. We argued, we sort of made up. Bottom line is that we just didn't click."

"Liar," Diana said. She waved her fork menacingly.

"So what are you going to do, throw pasta at me like a 5-year-old?" Brodie demanded.

"I might, if you don't do something. You've been miserable."

"I'm not anything," Brodie growled and busied herself with the chicken again. Another blob of pasta hit her in the ear. She dropped her knife and fork in surprise and they clattered against the china plate. "Hey! Stop it!"

"Open that envelope," Diana said and flicked more pasta. This time it hit Brodie in the shoulder, the red marinara oozing over her pale green shirt like Christmas slime. Mouse started licking sauce off the floor.

"That's it," Brodie exclaimed. "This is war." She grabbed a fistful of linguine and hurled it across the table.

Diana averted her face just in time. The noodle grenade sprayed across the side of her head and down the front of her starched white University of Virginia polo shirt with Coaching

Staff written on it. Diana's mouth fell open in astonishment as marinara sauce dripped down her braids, then she snatched up a piece of chicken and shot it Frisbee-style.

"*No*," Brodie said, laughing and twisting aside at the same time. The cutlet sailed past her head and smacked onto the floor. Mouse galloped over and wolfed it down. Diana loaded her fork with more linguine.

Brodie held up her hands in mock surrender. "All right, I'll open it."

She scrubbed her hands with her napkin and opened the envelope. She pulled out a colorful book.

Fruit Garnishes Made Easy.

Brodie gave a short, incredulous laugh.

"A fruit book?" Diana said, picking strands of pasta off her shirt and dropping them on the floor for Mouse.

"It's sort of a joke," Brodie said, not sure if she wanted to laugh or cry. "You had to have been there."

She leafed slowly through the how-to book. *Fruit Garnishes Made Easy* gave instructions for making apple swans, orange peel umbrellas, and frozen grape pyramids, but there was nothing written in it from Joe. It didn't really matter; Brodie knew exactly what he was telling her.

"B-I-R-N-A-M."

Brodie jerked her head up to see Diana on the phone, calmly toweling her braids with her free hand. "Yes, that's it," Diana said. "Thank you." She pushed a button on the phone, then put it to her ear again.

"What are you doing?" Brodie squawked, knowing full well that Diana had just used directory assistance to call Joe. She lunged over the table. "Give me that phone."

Diana immediately surrendered it. "Here you go. It's ringing."

Brodie went to disconnect but froze when she heard a tinny "Hello?"

"Oh, God," she whispered. "He answered."

"Say something," Diana hissed.

Damn. Brodie put the phone to her ear. "Uh, hello."

"Sassy," Joe said, sounding surprised. "How are you doing?"

"Okay." Brodie closed her eyes. Joe's deep, gravelly voice made her want to put her head down and howl.

"That's good," Joe said.

Brodie couldn't think of anything else to say.

Diana held up *Fruit Garnishes Made Easy.*

"Thank you for the book," Brodie blurted. "It's a classic."

"I thought you'd like it," Joe said.

There was an awkward silence.

Diana flapped her hand in a *come on* gesture.

"I, uh," Brodie floundered. She could hear Joe breathing heavily on the other end and wondered what he'd been doing, what he was wearing, if anyone else was with him. Maybe he had a date over. He was breathless from kissing some woman. Kissing her instead of Brodie because there was no thinking involved. "Is this a good time?" she asked.

"Sure," Joe said. "Just working out. I can take a break." He paused. "You okay, Sassy?"

Brodie glanced around the kitchen, desperately seeking inspiration. It came in the form of the book she'd been reading over coffee that morning; *The Wives of Henry VIII* by Antonia Fraser.

"I'm going to London on Monday," she said. "I was wondering if there was anything you'd like me to pick up for you at Hatchard's."

"I'll have to think about that," Joe asked. "Why are you going to London?"

"I'm accepting a posthumous achievement award for my father from the Royal Society," Brodie said.

"Very impressive," Joe said.

"I've been doing that thinking we talked about." Brodie shut her eyes and screwed her courage to the sticking place. "Maybe if you've been thinking too, we could talk about it when I get back."

"Okay," Joe said slowly. "When are you traveling?"

She told him her flight arrangements. She would drive to Dulles Airport and leave her car in the long-term parking

"Why don't you leave your car in the garage here instead?" Joe asked. "Get a taxi to the airport. Then I'll pick you up on Saturday."

"At the airport?" Brodie said.

"Yes," Joe said. "Right at the place where people get off the plane and other people find them."

"All right." Brodie felt lightheaded.

"Do you remember how to get here and the garage code?"

They talked for a few more minutes as Diana stared. Brodie gave Joe her flight and hotel information and they agreed when the taxi should pick her up at his apartment building Monday afternoon for the flight to London. They said goodbye and Brodie broke the connection.

"Oh my God," Diana said. "I knew it!"

Brodie started to laugh. They were both covered in marinara sauce. Linguini was dripping off her blouse, Diana's braids were gummy, the floor was a mess, Mouse was burping garlic, and the remnants of dinner were ice cold. And it was all wonderful because she was going to see Joe Birnam again.

CHAPTER 21

She stayed at her favorite hotel on Half Moon Street, near Piccadilly. The Royal Society was predictably stuffy but the members touched her with kind and gentle words about her father. The medal was accompanied by two days' worth of speeches, a medal in a velvet-lined wooden box, and a testimony signed by all the members. Brodie gave a 30 minute talk on the role of the modern historian that was very well received.

The last evening she went to Hatchard's and bought Joe a set of Inspector Rebus mysteries by Edinburgh author Ian Rankin. Walking back to the hotel along the iron fence enclosing Green Park, Brodie's emotions ran the gamut from thrilled to terrified as she thought about Saturday.

Back in her room she put the glossy green bag with its old fashioned lettering into her suitcase. She stared at the floral wallpaper most of the night, trying to figure out what to say to Joe when she saw him on Saturday.

It was time to grow up but she wasn't sure she had the nerve.

Heathrow Airport was its usual organized chaos. Brodie got through security without mishap and found her gate. There was an hour before her flight.

She went into the restroom. When she came out of the cubicle, she washed her hands and dried them on the big roller towel. The towel machine was right next to a wall mounted vending machine. It sold perfume, tampons, tissue packets . . . and condoms.

One British pound each.

The thoughts that had been running round and round in Brodie's head fused into a solid tangle as she found some pound coins. The machine dispensed three small foil packets and she shoved them into the bottom of her purse. She walked out of the restroom with her face scarlet, not sure why she'd just done that.

The flight was both too long and too short. Brodie shifted restlessly in her seat for most of it, unable to sleep. She picked at the elegant first class meal, tried to watch a movie, and ignored the woman sitting next to her.

At Dulles Airport, Brodie got her passport stamped at Immigration and was the first passenger from her flight to pull her suitcase off the conveyor at Baggage Claim. Her stomach was tight as she passed through the Nothing To Declare doors.

The crowd waiting for disembarking passengers was relatively light. Her eyes immediately picked out Joe; taller and broader and more alive than anyone else. He was wearing jeans and a navy tee shirt, with his sunglasses tucked into the neckline. His arms were folded as he watched the doors, the muscles of his forearms veined and massive.

She gave a tiny wave and his face lit with a smile. Brodie crossed the concourse, pulling her wheeled suitcase behind her. As she approached, Joe held out his arms and suddenly she was pressed hard against him.

Brodie dropped the suitcase handle in confusion and Joe kissed her.

CHAPTER 22

It was a lover's kiss, deep and insistent.

Brodie closed her eyes and clutched at Joe's shirt. In response to her touch, Joe slid a hand to the back of Brodie's head, burying his fingers in her short, feathery hair.

His mouth tasted of cinnamon. His lips were soft even as the trim beard rubbed against her chin. His skin smelled tangy and clean and Brodie felt his heart beating against hers as if they were joined and sharing just one. The airport concourse faded into nothingness because in the entire world there was only her and Joe.

Then someone knocked into them. Joe staggered and broke the kiss. For a moment he held on to Brodie's upper arms to steady himself. Then let go as if he'd been burned.

Suddenly the kiss had never happened, except for the spicy taste in Brodie's mouth and the confusion and regret in Joe's eyes. The orderly chaos of the airport rushed to fill the space between them.

"Hi," Joe said briskly. He found the handle of her suitcase. "Is this all you have?"

"Yes," Brodie managed. "Just the one."

He led the way out of the airport to the big white truck in the parking lot. They hardly spoke as Joe drove, the truck cab full of careful tension.

When they got to his apartment he brought her suitcase into the guest room. Brodie followed with her purse.

"Are you hungry, thirsty, or tired?" Joe asked. He put the suitcase just inside the door, as if reluctant to walk further into the room.

"Yes," Brodie said. She moved past him to put her purse on the dresser. The three condoms inside made it feel like lead. "All of the above."

"Well, how about I open a bottle of wine and get some dinner started?" Joe asked. "You can lounge around for a while."

"Sounds good," Brodie said. "Give me a couple of minutes."

"Take your time," Joe said breezily and walked out.

Brodie stepped into the bathroom, splashed water on her face, then hung over the sink, remembering the kiss. It had been wonderful. Joe had kissed her like he meant it; seriously, intently, skillfully.

But now evidently wanted to forget it.

She took out the Hatchard's bag and went into the living room. The big screen television was on, the sound low, race cars whipping around a track.

Joe was in the kitchen, twisting a corkscrew into the neck of a bottle of red wine. He smiled tightly at her as he drew out the cork. The atmosphere in the apartment was like the uneasy calm before a storm.

To distract herself, Brodie drifted over to the bookcases. She hadn't really looked at his books when she'd been there for the Cherry Blossom Festival.

He had the full set of Sharpe novels by Bernard Cornwell, the Horatio Hornblower series by E.M. Forster, and about 30 books by P.G. Wodehouse. The rest of Joe's library was a tribute to detectives and testosterone with books by Tom Clancy, Dick Francis, W.E.B Griffin, Robert B. Parker, and Dale Brown. He had Craig Johnson's Longmire series and a bunch of Scandinavian mysteries as well. Ian Rankin would fit right in.

Several military histories that her father would have approved of made a nice counterpoint, however, including everything by Stephen Ambrose, a number of books by military historian John Keegan, and Liddell Hart's history of World War II. There were books, too, about the Marine Corps, woodworking, and the many places he'd lived. As well as *George and Martha*. Brodie ran her hand over the spines; most were well worn.

She felt a presence behind her and whirled around. Joe raised an eyebrow. "You look like you could use some of this," he said, handing her a glass of wine.

"Thank you." Brodie took the glass. She handed him the Hatchard's bag in exchange.

"Thanks," he said, evidently surprised. He took out the books. "*Fleshmarket Alley. The Naming of the Dead. Resurrection Men.* These look great. You really didn't have to get them."

"Ian Rankin's from Edinburgh," Brodie said. "Shows a different side of the city than you probably saw. His main character is this police inspector named John Rebus. Complicated plots. And you said you read a lot of mysteries . . ." Brodie felt herself trail off.

"I'm going to really enjoy these," Joe said. "Thank you." He put the books on the coffee table then stepped around her and opened the French doors leading to the patio. "Would you like to relax out here while I get dinner ready? I put out some chips and salsa for you."

"Thank you."

Unsaid words hung in the air like heavy humidity.

Brodie went outside.

The flagstone patio was brightened by glazed pots full of geraniums and ivy. Two chaise lounges with thick beige cushions flanked a square side table laden with snacks. Brodie eased herself onto one of the chaises and stretched, feeling her legs relax from the flight. She sipped her wine and munched chips and homemade salsa as she watched Joe through the French doors. He was moving around the small galley kitchen. Shadows from the television across the room played on the floor in front of the counter. Joe opened the refrigerator door and disappeared from sight for a moment, then came back into view holding a red pepper.

As he found a chopping board Brodie realized the kitchen was set up for the fewest number of steps. The thought made her sad.

☼

"You don't have a little neck," a male voice said. "But she did."

Brodie opened her eyes and knew it was another one of those dreams. She was in a dank place, with damp seeping down cool stone walls. It was a round room, and a gloomy one, with a single stained glass window set high above her head. She was kneeling at an altar. There was a plain white cloth on the altar and a large wooden cross on the wall. At either end of the altar the flames of tall candles on pewter plates sputtered feeble light.

Her dress was long, with a full velvet skirt. The waist was tight and it was hard to take a deep breath of the thick air.

She turned awkwardly on the kneeler, wrestling with the dress, knowing that her father wasn't there.

The speaker was Henry VIII, wearing an elaborately embroidered maroon doublet and cape. His flat velvet hat was endowed with a jaunty feather.

He was jowly and stout, with thick legs and heavy hands and diseased white eyes.

Brodie shrank back against the altar, as an all-too-familiar fear swept over her.

"You tell me what he told you," Henry said. He licked his lips as if looking at something good to eat. "And I'll make them stop."

"Stop the dreams?" Brodie asked as she looked around the room. He was standing in the only doorway.

"Stop your execution, Anne," Henry said.

It came together again, just like it always did when she dreamed like this. She was Anne Boleyn, Henry VIII's second wife who'd been beheaded. Brodie tried to push through, to will herself awake, to open her eyes and see a different place. But her eyes were already open and she didn't wake up and the fear was punishing.

"I'm not Anne," Brodie managed.

"Of course you're not. But you chose the place, not

me." Henry's white eyes glittered. "Come on. Tell me what your father knew. He told you how he cheated the game and I want to know how. It's a very simple request, don't you think? You've stalled very well so far. But tonight you have to choose. Either tell me your father's secret or have your game come to its inevitable end."

Long-forgotten words from a strange Gypsy woman came back in a rush. "Are you Death?" Brodie choked out.

Henry laughed. "You know who I am," he said. "He told you everything, didn't he?"

"I don't know what you're talking about." Brodie stood up, searching through the gloom for a weapon, anything that would let her get by him.

"Of course you do, you're not a stupid woman," Henry observed. "Your mother might have been a silly girl, but you're his daughter and you know what he did. You were the only one he cared enough about to tell." He folded his arms. "Wallace was a worthy competitor and it's too bad that I had to take him out of the game. But he cheated."

Brodie grabbed one of the candles and pointed the lit end at him. It was a thick beeswax stick as long as her forearm. The flame flared as the candle moved, throwing odd shadows across the stone walls. "Get away from the door," she said.

A slow, predatory smile spread over Henry's thick, moist lips. He moved aside to reveal two medieval executioners: big, muscular men in leather smocks and black cloth hoods. Two women wearing long period dresses sniffled in back of them.

One of the women carried a small fluffy dog. As Brodie watched in shock, remembering the story of how Anne Boleyn's dog had accompanied her to her execution, the dog wriggled out of the woman's arms.

One of the executioners grabbed the candle out of Brodie's hand. She tried to hang on but he wrenched it away and tossed the candle to the floor, cracking it into two pieces still joined by the wick buried inside the wax. The other executioner took

Brodie by the elbow and shoved her out of the room.

Henry stayed by her other side as they mounted a steep stone stairway. "Tell me what he told you," he said softly. "I'll make them stop. You'll keep your soul tonight."

"I don't know what you want." With every step, Brodie knew she was coming closer to her own death.

She couldn't wake up. She couldn't think of how to make this nightmare end.

She couldn't get away from the faceless, menacing executioner and his iron grip on her arm. He propelled her up the stairs, her skirts dragging, the small dog yipping at her feet, the ladies-in-waiting crying, the other executioner preventing her from turning around and running away. And when they got to the top they would kill her. She'd never wake up. The white eyes would glint in a victory she'd never understand.

Henry opened a door at the top of the stairway and emerged onto a parapet. It was twilight. Other people were already up there; a priest, gaudily dressed people of the royal court, a somberly dressed man with a sheaf of papers.

The executioner shoved Brodie toward a thick wooden block and forced her to her knees. One of the ladies-in-waiting unfastened the ruff around her neck. Brodie struggled to stand again and the two executioners joined forces to keep her kneeling and tie her hands behind her back. Brodie's heart beat so fast she was almost blind from the blood rush.

"Tell me," Henry whispered. "Save yourself. Tell me what your father knew."

One of the executioners hefted a long handled, two-headed axe. He flicked his thumb across the edge of the blade and nodded with satisfaction. The second executioner forced Brodie to bend until her head was on the block. He pulled her chin forward to expose her neck and Brodie gasped in pain and terror.

A basket was placed on the ground in front of the block to catch her head.

CHAPTER 23

"Hey there."

Something was touching her face. "*Get away from me!*" Brodie screamed.

"Hey," the faraway voice said again.

Brodie wrenched open her eyes, fury and fear rushing over her in equal waves. There was swirling darkness all around her and she didn't know where she was. "Goddammit," she gasped.

"Wake up, Brodie."

It was Joe, bending over the chaise lounge. Brodie focused first on his face and then beyond his shoulder. The sun was beginning to set, sending gray and pink lines across the horizon. Small solar lights around the perimeter of the patio glowed, illuminating the plants. On the other side of the French doors, Joe's apartment was brightly lit.

"Are you okay?" Joe asked. He looked concerned. "I came out to tell you that dinner was ready and you almost took my head off."

Brodie breathed hard against the effect of the nightmare. Even more than Joe's presence, the cool evening air reassured her that she was awake. "I'm sorry," she managed. "Must be jetlag."

"Are you hungry?" Joe extended a hand and helped Brodie stand up.

For a moment they were standing too close. Then Joe's face went blank and he took a step back.

"Dinner," Brodie said, not sure if she was going from one nightmare to another. "Perfect timing."

Joe picked up her empty glass and they went inside.

The dining table was set and the chandelier dimmed. Josh Turner sang from the stereo, the country singer's baritone like gravel on velvet.

Brodie sat down as Joe went into the kitchen. The oak table

gleamed with polish. Each place setting was an elegant composition of black linen place mat, cream linen napkin in a silver holder, heavy silver flatware, and recycled glass goblets. There was a matching water pitcher on a tray, along with salt and pepper shakers.

Reality. Brodie took a few deep breaths.

Joe set down plates laden with couscous, chicken, and peppers in a curry sauce. It smelled wonderful. He poured them both some wine. The light from the chandelier threw shadows across his cheekbones and made his hair glint as he put the bottle of wine on the tray and sat down.

"*Slainte*," Joe said and touched his glass to hers.

"*Slainte*," Brodie said and drank.

Joe dropped his napkin into his lap and started to eat with a sort of dogged determination, as if fortifying himself for an ordeal to come. But Brodie only managed a few bites in between sips of wine. Her nerves were still thrumming from the dream and the tension between her and Joe was the killing kind.

They hardly spoke. Josh Turner's music filled the void.

"This is great," Brodie said finally, pronging a morsel of chicken.

"Glad you like it," Joe said. "More wine?"

"Yes, thanks," Brodie said. He refilled her glass as she pushed the food around on her plate. If things with this man didn't get resolved soon she was going to turn into an anorexic alcoholic.

"So how was the weather in London?" Joe asked.

"Drizzly."

"Pretty typical for this time of year, I expect?"

"Yes." Brodie took a deep breath and thought about all the things that had kept her awake last night in London. She wasn't there to talk about the British climate or watch his self-imposed eating contest. "That was a nice kiss at the airport," she said.

Joe froze with his fork halfway to his mouth. He lowered the fork to the plate. "Ah," he said, avoiding Brodie's eye. "I stepped over the line with that. I'm sorry."

"Does there have to be a line?"

"I've been doing a lot of thinking," Joe said. "And yes, there does."

"Why is that?" Brodie asked carefully.

"There's a lot in the way, Brodie," Joe said. "Complications. We both come with more baggage than we should ask the other to cope with."

Brodie summoned all her courage. "It doesn't have to be that way."

Joe ate more chicken.

"Look, growing up, my dad didn't like to see emotion." She swallowed hard. "No crying, carrying on. No telling him . . . intimate things. I don't think I realized how much I'm like him . . . was like him . . . until he died. That night in Edinburgh talking to you was pretty much an exception. And so . . . Dad and I . . . well, there were things we didn't talk about and I never realized how depressed he was all those years. Maybe if he'd told me more of what was going on inside he'd still be around."

"Don't blame yourself," Joe said, his voice neutral. His plate was suddenly clean, the knife and fork laid neatly across it.

"No." Brodie shook her head. "What I mean is . . . I know I'm the same. You're the only person I've ever met who called me on it. I was mad. But you were right. I don't want to turn out like my father, keeping things inside until they kill me."

She paused. Joe's face was a mask.

"You told me I had to speak from the heart," Brodie said slowly. "Well, the heart says this relationship was never meant to be platonic."

Joe stared at the table.

Only Josh Turner broke the silence, singing about Loretta Lynn's Lincoln.

"You made me face up to the way I avoid things," Brodie ground on. Her palms were beginning to sweat and she wiped them on her napkin. "Like Stanton. After you left that weekend I went and told him how I felt, why it was over. The entire university knew that I told him goodbye and why. You can call Diana and ask. The gossip was incredible and I didn't care because all I could think of was that I'd hurt you."

Joe didn't move. Brodie felt herself winding down. She took another breath. "With us, there can be something really special. We both know it. Every time we've been together there's been that spark and . . . and it . . . it could be great."

It was the longest speech Brodie had ever made about her feelings. When she raised her wineglass to drink her hand shook so badly the wine slopped around the bowl.

"I'm glad to hear I've been a good influence," Joe said.

Brodie felt the floor slide away from her, just like it had done in the airport when he'd pretended he hadn't just given her the kiss of her life.

"I think you could be a lot more than that," she said.

Joe exhaled as if he'd been holding his breath. The gold and sapphire earring shone in the light from the chandelier.

Brodie twisted her napkin, wringing out enough courage for a last shot. "I said I'm sorry, Joe. It's hard to change but I'm willing to try. Isn't that why you sent me the book? To say that we should talk?"

Now Josh Turner was singing about turning down the lights, putting on some music that was soft and slow, waiting all day to be alone with her.

"I sent you the book because I wanted you to remember how strong you are," Joe said quietly.

"Okay," Brodie said, confused and starting to get a little angry. "Let's get back to the main point. I said I'm interested. That there's a spark between us that should be encouraged. What were you saying with that kiss?"

"Done with your food?" Joe suddenly stood up and gestured at her plate.

"Sure." Brodie watched in rigid shock as he picked up flatware and plates and went into the kitchen. She heard the rattle of dishes going into the sink. The coffee maker started gurgling.

Josh Turner kept singing, his deep baritone driving each song. He was singing with Joe's voice, Brodie thought distractedly, a husky voice that made women's knees go weak and their clothes fall off.

Joe came back to the table with dessert plates of cheesecake and sat down.

"I've been doing a lot of thinking, too," he said formally. "It's obvious that I don't fit in with your life and the university. Anything that would happen between us would not be good for your career."

Brodie's jaw dropped. He sounded so horribly like Stanton that she couldn't believe it.

Joe started eating his cheesecake. Again, his face betrayed nothing.

"So," Brodie said. "You think my career is more important than my feelings?"

"Let's be honest here," Joe said. His expression didn't change. "An academic career has certain . . . ah . . . requirements. And I don't own a blue and white striped suit."

"What does a seersucker suit have to do with anything?" Brodie asked incredulously. "I don't believe this conversation."

"You're an accomplished, professional woman," Joe said. The words came out mechanically, as if he'd rehearsed them. "A well known writer. Well respected in your field. You're comfortable in front of an audience full of other well respected professionals. I don't want you to get hurt by an inappropriate relationship."

"Joe," Brodie protested. "I don't understand why you would say such a thing. Like you think I belong in that box."

"I don't want you to get hurt," he repeated woodenly.

"So, so," Brodie sputtered, having trouble breathing. "You turn me upside down in Charlottesville, you kiss me like that in the airport, you get me to say things I've never said to anybody. And now you're telling me *never mind*?"

For a moment the blank mask lifted. Brodie was startled to see raw pain in Joe's eyes.

"Don't do this to me, Sassy," he said hoarsely and then the mask was back.

"I'm doing what you said I needed to do," Brodie said, but now she knew the conversation wasn't about her at all.

Joe shifted in his chair and stared down at his empty dessert plate. "I'm sorry," he said. "I hadn't planned on that kiss or you saying all this. For you to be ready and me not. I was just looking for this weekend to . . . you know . . . let us cut it off clean."

"What's really going on here, Joe?" Brodie asked.

"Shit," Joe said. He got up and went into the kitchen. China rattled. He came back and put two empty mugs on the table before slumping back into his chair.

Brodie waited.

"I started something with you I can't finish," Joe said. His eyes slid over her face and away. "I knew it would go this way the day I met you. But I just couldn't leave it alone. Believe me, I've tried."

"I don't understand," Brodie said.

"The truth is," Joe said slowly. "If I was able to give you a . . . a real relationship, I would." He toyed with the mugs. "I'd give it all I have for as long as you'd let me."

"Joe--," Brodie started.

"But I can't," he interrupted flatly. "I can't go down that road with you. I thought I could but I can't. Don't ask me to."

"Oh, God," Brodie breathed. "Your injuries. From Iraq. Is that what this is all about? Because you can't . . .?"

"No." Joe looked startled at her implication. "Things work. But the neighborhood's bad."

"So?"

"Women don't spend a lot of time in that sort of neighborhood."

"I don't care."

"Your last boyfriend probably had a manicured dick," Joe said roughly. "And I've been *on fire*."

"Is that what this is about? You think that matters to me?" Of course he did. She was the woman who went through life avoiding difficult things and keeping others at arm's length. The woman whose last relationship had been all about show.

"I spent more time in the burn ward than I did in rehab," Joe said. "Think about it. The wrapping might be nice but what's underneath is going to scare you away."

Brodie shook her head.

"I have better luck with nurses or women who are in the military." His voice was flat. "They've seen it all before. But even they don't stay long."

"You're not being fair," Brodie protested.

"It might not feel that way to you now, but it will in time."

"You're assigning a reaction to me." Brodie felt anger bubble up again.

"It's tempting to change my expectations," Joe acknowledged and rearranged the mugs some more. "But I've already let myself get too involved when I should know better. Some one night rodeo with you won't be enough. I want all or nothing."

"And you've decided on nothing."

"Better me than you. And better now than later."

Brodie's anger erupted into a froth. "You said we could talk but all you're doing is shutting me out."

"It's better for you this way," Joe said. "Let's talk about something else."

"You told me not to avoid real life, but isn't that what you're doing?" Brodie demanded.

"This is real life," Joe said with finality.

The last song ended and the apartment filled with silence. Joe's face was inscrutable. Brodie put a bite of cheesecake into her mouth. The crust was thick and crumbly and the filling was rich and creamy. She had difficulty swallowing.

The Josh Turner album began the first song again. The rolling banjo and mandolin introduction of "Would You Go With Me" pulsed through the emotionally charged air and then Josh started singing.

Would you go with me/If we rolled down streets of fire

Brodie stood up, shoving back her chair with a squeal of wood on wood. She ran into the guest room, scrabbled through her purse for the condoms, came back to the dining room, and slapped them down in front of Joe.

"The offer's on the table," she said. "I'm going to take a shower. I'll be out in 30 minutes. You can give me your final decision then."

Joe sat like a statue, his unblinking gaze on the small foil packets.

I gotta know/Would you go with me?

CHAPTER 24

Brodie stood in the shower and let the hot water drum against her skin. The one time she had the guts to say how she felt to a man and everything had backfired.

The thought of walking into the living room and having him say *thanks, but I told you no* was almost more than she could bear. She should just get dressed and leave. Her car was in the apartment building's garage. Home in four hours, free of Joe Birnam forever.

But if she left, she'd always wonder. And there were too many unanswered questions in her life already.

Brodie stepped out of the shower, toweled her hair dry, and slipped into the pale blue silk kimono robe she used for traveling. Her hands shook as she tied the belt.

She opened the guest room door and walked cautiously into the living room. The room was dim; lit only by the kitchen light. The stereo was off and the air was empty and silent. The dining table was clear. The condoms were gone.

Brodie padded barefoot across the living room to the kitchen. The dinner dishes were stacked neatly in the sink. The coffee maker was off.

The apartment appeared empty. It didn't seem like a thing he would do but maybe Joe had run away. Brodie's stomach cramped. She was never saying anything remotely important to a man again.

"Hello?" she called, her voice thin and nervous in her ears.

"Brodie?" Joe's voice filtered through from the hallway. "In here."

She followed the sound of his voice to the master bedroom. The door was slightly ajar. She pushed it open.

Joe was sitting on the end of the bed. He was wearing a dark green terry robe that was long and hooded, like a boxer's. His earring twinkled in the light of the bedside table lamp and his hair was damp. There was a condom packet next to him.

Brodie blinked. It was like looking at an optical illusion. As Joe sat on the bed, the hem of the robe fell to his knees. Below it there should have been two bare legs, each with a bulging runner's calf, a bony ankle, and a high arched foot. But there was just one.

The air prickled for a tension-filled moment as Joe stared at Brodie staring at him.

And then Brodie hurled herself across the room into Joe's arms and he crushed her against him. His heart was beating savagely and his arms were a refuge and Brodie found herself balanced on his right thigh. She wrapped her arms around his neck and buried her face in his shoulder.

"I'm sorry, Sassy," Joe said against her hair. His voice cracked. "You really put yourself out there and I was a jerk."

"Yes, you were," Brodie said, her voice muffled by his robe and the lump in her throat.

"All I could think of was how torn up I was going to be if you couldn't handle it," Joe went on.

"So you tried to push me away?"

"It was better than saying I was scared shitless." Joe kissed her hair. "But it doesn't matter. One night with you is worth anything that happens."

"Don't you dare make me cry," Brodie sniffed into the terrycloth, her arms still locked around his neck.

"Hey." Joe jostled her a little. "We're going to have some awesome, sweaty, athletic sex here."

"I know."

"Everything's going to be all right."

Brodie loosened her hold and leaned back to see his face. "I should be saying that to you," she said.

Joe stood her up so she was facing him. "You say anything you like," he replied.

Brodie saw the permission in his eyes. She bent and unknotted the tie of his robe, willing herself not to react, no matter what was underneath. This was Joe. They were together. Finally.

She eased the cloth over his shoulders and let the robe fall onto the bed behind him.

Joe had the powerfully defined body of a man who had done hard physical work for many years. His chest was deep, with the distinctive slope of the competitive swimmer. The shoulders were dense and heavily muscled. The well-developed laterals of his back were a thick flare that pulled the skin taut against his ribs. His body hair was blonde.

There was a red and gold Marine Corps tattoo on his left bicep. It was close to his shoulder, with *Semper Fidelis* written in script underneath. The tattoo was the size of Brodie's palm. His upper arm was so wide that it would have taken four tattoos to span its width.

Brodie brushed her hand across his chest and Joe shuddered slightly. She slowly dropped to her knees in front of him and let her hand travel down his torso.

Instead of a navel, a corrugated belt of reddened flesh ran across his waist. Below it his abdomen was a patchwork of shiny discolored burns, grafted skin, and uneven scarring. His right hip and leg had escaped war unscathed, the ropy muscles and fine blonde hair a glaring contrast to the other side of his body.

The scarred left leg ended just above where his knee would have been, the bottom of the stump a smooth curve of skin. Brodie could see where part of the outer thigh muscle had been sliced away, leaving a narrow faded red divot. The left thigh was only slightly thinner than the right, however, and Brodie marveled at how much work Joe had done to rehabilitate that side of his body after such a horrific injury.

Gruesome scarring continued around the inside of the left thigh. The hair at Joe's groin had been mostly singed off and the damage was extensive. As Brodie's fingertips continued south, however, his body's response assured her that everything was in working order.

She spent a long time looking at and touching his scars and the coarse grafted skin. The startled flush of adrenaline that had coursed through her body at first glance gradually abated.

Brodie lifted her chin and defiantly met Joe's eyes. "Let me get this straight," she said. "An earring *and* a tattoo?"

A slow smile spread across his face. "I'm going to get you out of that box if it kills me," Joe said.

"It just might," Brodie replied and let Joe pull her down beside him on the bed.

CHAPTER 25

"Sweet Jesus," Joe murmured into Brodie's bare shoulder.

She helped him stay balanced as he eased out of her. He rolled onto his back for a long moment, breathing heavily, then continued a quarter turn away from her. Brodie heard him grunt softly and knew he was getting rid of the condom.

The blankets were on the floor. The sheets were a rumpled knot. The room was dark except for the small light on the bedside table.

Brodie cautiously stretched out her legs, feeling as if she'd run ten miles. They'd come together like two storms colliding; intense, titanic, muscular and full of movement. Brodie had never made love like that before, talking and laughing and shifting positions and abandoning every inhibition she'd ever had.

She'd climaxed long and hard as Joe's hands and mouth evoked wave upon wave of blinding sensation. He'd slid into her as the spasms abated, heating her like a furnace. Running her hands greedily over his shoulders and arms and sides, she'd compensated for his imbalance and their rhythm had a wild, rocking motion. It seemed to go on forever and then Joe wrapped his arms around her shoulders, bringing their heads together. Brodie had buried her hands in his hair and locked her heels behind his back. His climax had exploded inside their embrace and they rode it together; a rapturous secret sheltered by their bodies.

Joe flopped onto his back again and Brodie turned on her side to face him.

"Hey," he said, his chest still heaving as he lay splayed out next to her. His shoulders took up more than half the width of the king-sized bed.

"Hey," Brodie replied.

"Not too shabby." Joe grinned and drew in another lungful of air. "For a first time."

"Not shabby at all," Brodie said, figuring that was the understatement of the year. She reached out and pushed damp hair off his forehead. His face and chest were misted with sweat.

Joe exhaled contentedly.

Brodie sat up. "Don't go away," she said. She slipped on the blue silk kimono and went into the kitchen. She found a big mixing bowl, brought it back into the bedroom, filled it with warm water from the bathroom sink, picked up a clean washcloth and towel, and brought everything to the bedside table.

Joe's eyes followed her as she sat on the side of the bed and dampened the washcloth. He closed them as she gently wiped his face. She dried him with the towel and kissed him on the mouth.

She worked her way down his body in sections, bathing away sweat with the washcloth, then toweling him dry. Each section ended with a kiss. A kiss on each palm and arms were done. A kiss in the hollow of his neck.

He *was* a Viking, Brodie thought as she soothed the washcloth over his chest. Her own Norse warrior whose body bore testament to the battles he'd fought and to the narrowness of his escape from death. There was dignity in the way Joe carried his scars. He was maimed, marked, powerful, beautiful. She pressed her lips into the shallow depression between his pectoral muscles.

Brodie took her time, turning a simple sponge bath into a ceremony celebrating her new-found familiarity with Joe's body. She wanted to know everything about him. How the muscles of his shoulders rippled like liquid, where the hair was blonde and where it had been scorched away, how the grafted skin of his left thigh felt both slick and grainy, how very long his right leg was.

She'd just finished his abdomen and gently kissed the strip of corrugated skin when she realized he was shaking.

"Are you cold?" she asked, looking up.

Joe lay with his forearms crossed over his face, hiding it. "No," he replied, his voice muffled.

Brodie continued, washing his left hip and moving down the short thigh. She kissed the base of it and inside the scarred muscle, then turned her attention to his right side. She ended with a kiss on the top of his foot.

"There. All done."

Joe didn't say anything or move. His arms still hid his face.

Brodie brought the bowl and towels into the bathroom and returned to sit again on the side of the bed. Joe reached for her then and Brodie was stunned to see the salt tracks of tears.

"Sassy, I never expected--," he started, his voice thick.

"Let's not talk right now," Brodie whispered as she slid down onto the bed beside him. She pressed against Joe so that they were lying spoon-fashion, her hips curled into the curve of his body and her back pressed into his chest.

He draped his arm across Brodie's waist and she held his hand very tightly. If they spoke now she'd start blubbering that he was the best sex she ever had, that she never wanted to leave him, that she loved him.

Brodie closed her eyes and felt Joe's breath against her neck. She hadn't been ready for his emotions to be so close to the surface. And even less ready for her own.

They stayed unmoving for a long time. After awhile their breathing synchronized.

Brodie felt Joe's hand move. In the semi-darkness she watched long strong fingers untie her robe and ease it away. "You're very beautiful, Brodie Margaret," he said, his voice rich and low in her ear. "In every way."

She watched his hand caress her, playing with her breasts so that she couldn't help arching against him. Her breathing was like little gasps when the big hand slid between her thighs. Joe stroked her, finding just the right spot, and the muscles in her hips and legs tightened involuntarily. Brodie was still staring at his hand, fascinated by the play of veins in his forearm and the deliberate strumming of his fingers, when the tension and the tightness broke and she cried out and bucked against him again and again.

When the spasms subsided Joe picked her up to straddle him. He found another condom and they made love silently, the room quiet except for the ticking of a clock and their labored breathing. Brodie pulsed against Joe, leaning forward with her hands on his shoulders, her breasts swinging above him. Joe kept his hands on her waist, lifting her, making her ride him, his biceps swelling hugely with each upward thrust.

Their eyes were transfixed on each other as they rocked. Brodie was mesmerized by Joe, by the way his chest flexed as he moved her up and down, by the heat inside her, by the way his eyes shone like a lake at night. They were glittering blue water in the half-light, clean and pure and deep, beckoning her to dive in. She felt an inexorable pull, an insistence to abandon herself and follow his soul wherever it led.

Brodie gasped as she felt him thicken inside her. His eyes opened wider and she couldn't hold out any more and he thrust his hips upwards and choked out *"Brodie."* Then Joe came hard, his body jerking, and Brodie surrendered and fell into the blue, blue depths.

CHAPTER 26

"Tired?" Joe asked.

"A little," Brodie said. She gave up trying to hide her yawn behind a slice of bruschetta piled high with chopped tomato, eggplant, and olives.

"Want to do it all over again next weekend?" Joe asked. He ate a stuffed mushroom.

"Yes," Brodie said simply. They'd known all day that this was just the beginning but somehow it was nice to say the next step out loud.

"Good," Joe replied and they smiled at each other.

Brodie had thought to leave Sunday morning to pick up Mouse at the kennel before it closed, then get her notes organized for the mandatory departmental meeting the next day with Dr. Pedder, the new chair of the history department. But the kennel assured her Mouse was fine and could stay another day. And she didn't need to prepare anything for Dr. Pedder; if he wanted to know about her role as the department's graduate student adviser, he'd ask.

The change in plans meant that she and Joe stayed in bed most of Sunday. They talked for hours, read the newspaper, and made love. Brodie felt completely at ease with Joe, unselfconsciously and surprisingly content and relaxed.

She saw him in the bright light of a summer day, naked and exposed and on crutches. She watched him put on one of his five different prosthetic legs. She realized he liked to lie on his right side, could fall asleep almost on demand, and woke fully alert. She found out that he was tidy and organized, faithful to the habits of his long military career.

They left the apartment late in the day to find some dinner.

Joe's favorite restaurant was a small old-fashioned Italian place with vinyl checked tablecloths, sepia photos of Italian immigrants, and a beat-up mahogany bar that ran the length of the room. Several people had said hello as they'd walked in and Joe introduced her to Viola, the ample hostess, and her son Tony who seemed to be the only waiter for all ten tables. Older patrons at the bar waved as if Joe was a popular political candidate and gave Brodie openly appraising looks. Without being asked, Tony stocked them with a carafe of red wine and a big plate of bruschetta and stuffed mushrooms.

Brodie bit into a slice of crisp bread topped with tomatoes and peppers. She had on jeans, clogs, and his tee shirt. Joe wore baggy cargo pants, a striped cotton shirt, and the slack expression of a man who was totally and happily sated. His jaw line bristled with a golden five o'clock shadow. Brodie knew he didn't have on underwear.

"Do you want to come to Charlottesville?" she asked.

"Is this an invitation?" Joe licked his fingers and Brodie enjoyed a couple of heartbeats of pure lust.

"Yes," she said. "I promise it won't be weird."

"Then I accept," Joe said. He reached for a second slice of bruschetta and frowned. "But I can't come until Saturday. I've got a water polo match Friday night. Last match of the season. I can't miss it."

"Oh," Brodie said, disappointed. She considered. "Summer schedule starts this week. I'm done at noon on Friday. I could be here by four."

"If you came here we'd have Friday night together," Joe said. "But that's a lot of driving in one week for you."

"I don't mind driving," Brodie offered. "Then I could come to your match."

"You sure you want to? Our club isn't the Olympics."

"Can I ask a favor, though?" Brodie took another bite of bruschetta.

"Sure."

"Could I bring Mouse? I hate to put her back in the kennel so soon."

"Of course you can bring Mouse." Joe put a mushroom on her plate. "I'll give you the spare key to the apartment so you can let yourself in if you get there before I'm home from work."

"Okay," Brodie said, a little stunned by how offhandedly Joe had said that. Having a key was a huge step. In three years she'd never had a key to Stanton's house and he'd never had a key to hers.

"So I guess we're past platonic," Joe said.

"Platonic?" Brodie savored the mushroom stuffed with sausage, breadcrumbs, and garlic.

"That's what you said last night," Joe said. "That this relationship wasn't supposed to be platonic."

"Was I right?" The second bite of mushroom was even better than the first.

"Yes, but I have this rule. You know. We talked about it in Charlottesville." Joe studied the appetizer on his own plate, obviously trying to decide how to phrase what he wanted to say. He finally looked up. "If we're together, we're together for as long as it lasts. There's no room for anyone else at the same time. For either of us. It's just you and me and wherever this thing takes us."

"Exclusive," Brodie said. *A key and commitment.*

"*Semper Fidelis*," Joe said softly, his eyes searching hers.

"Okay. Good rule. Excellent rule." The unexpected intensity of the moment was almost more than Brodie could stand. She ate the rest of her mushroom and attempted to lighten the mood with some weak humor. "So what's past platonic? Are we going steady? Are you my boyfriend?"

"No." Joe reached out and wiped a crumb from the corner of her mouth. He licked it off his finger. "I'm not your boyfriend, Sassy. I'm your lover."

"Okay," Brodie said weakly. *He was her lover.* Lovers got keys and commitment.

"Thanks for not letting me fuck this up," Joe said. "I'm still wondering why you didn't just punch me in the head and walk out last night."

"I thought about it," Brodie admitted. "Not punching you. Walking out, I mean."

"I hope you're glad you didn't." Joe reached across the table and laced his fingers with hers.

Brodie gave her head a tiny nod. "It seems like a long time ago, doesn't it? Instead of just yesterday."

"Here we go," said Tony. They both looked up as he slung down huge plates of lasagna, a boatload of meatballs, and a basket of garlic bread. A shaker of parmesan cheese came out of his apron pocket. "You two need something else?"

"Thanks, Tony," Joe said. "You thought of everything."

Tony went to another table and Brodie busied herself with her lasagna, a little overwhelmed by the interrupted conversation. The layered pasta was piping hot and loaded with creamy ricotta cheese and a subtly spicy sauce.

Joe took a slice of garlic bread then slid the basket across the table to Brodie. "You're some piece of work, Sassy," he said.

Brodie glanced up from her plate. "How's that?"

"Even after all you've given me this weekend," Joe said, cutting into a meatball with the edge of his fork. "You still can't say 'I like you, Joe.'"

"A couple of condoms sure made a big impression," Brodie said, suddenly engrossed in selecting the perfect slice of garlic bread.

"That's not what I'm talking about and you know it," Joe said seriously. "What you gave me was unconditional acceptance. That's a lot more than this old crapped-out Marine ever expected." He ate half a meatball.

"Stop it," Brodie scolded, surprising herself.

Joe nearly choked. "What?"

"This poor old Joe act," Brodie said, feeling a hot prick of annoyance. She wasn't going to have anyone talk about Joe that way, least of all himself. "You went to war and lost a leg and a best friend. It was a terrible, traumatic thing to happen. But you also changed history and the effect is going to be felt for generations to come. Don't cheapen that."

"Uh," Joe said, taken aback by her vehemence.

"The pity party is officially over because there's no way I'm ever going to believe it," Brodie continued, pointing at him with her garlic bread. "You're in incredible shape. You play *water polo*. You've got the stamina of a man half your age and the experience to know what to do with it." She had the good grace to blush but kept going. "You're a true craftsman with a successful business. Unless you're living on credit, which I highly doubt, you're hardly poor. You have a nice home and everywhere you go you seem to have wonderful friends who think the world of you. Not to mention that my dog adores you. So knock it off."

Joe put down his fork. "Thanks for the advice."

"The problem seems to be that you've got this photograph in your head," Brodie heard herself roll on. "How you looked six, eight, ten years ago. You keep comparing yourself to it and you expect that I'm doing the same thing. But this is my frame of reference." She made a sweeping motion to indicate all of him, crumbs flying from the garlic bread still in her hand. "A man who's got some history etched on him. Who's got the courage to live by his values. You. Right *now*."

They stared at each other for a couple of heartbeats then Joe wiped his lips with his napkin. "Okay," he said. "Point taken."

Brodie cut into her lasagna and felt her blood pressure return to normal.

"Funny how this turned out to be a conversation about me," Joe remarked a few minutes later.

"It needed to be said." Brodie focused on her food, wondering if she'd gone too far.

Joe reached across the table and pronged a meatball off her plate. "I've opened a Pandora's box, haven't I?" he asked. "Right on my own head."

Brodie looked up to see that he was grinning that sideways

grin that made her knees go weak. "Eat your dinner," she admonished happily.

His phone rang just as they came back to the apartment. Joe tossed his keys on the dining table and answered in the kitchen. Brodie drifted over to the sofa, not wanting to eavesdrop.

"It's my mother," Joe called and beckoned to her. He tucked the phone between shoulder and ear and got out glasses and a bottle of brandy as he listened to the person on the other end. Brodie climbed on a barstool as he asked about his father's bad back and discussed something cryptic about his brother Brian, the eldest Birnam sibling.

"Mom, I know we talked about me coming up for the Fourth," he said as he poured Brodie a tot of brandy. "But Brodie and I have decided our relationship is no longer platonic and I'm hoping that means my weekends are booked for the foreseeable future."

They grinned at each other as he listened to the response. "That's right," he said. "She's here now. We just got back from a late dinner."

Brodie sipped her brandy. It was obvious that he'd talked about her to his family and the thought was somehow both thrilling and unnerving.

Joe leaned his elbows on the counter and winked at Brodie as he listened. "Okay," he said into the phone. "So the perfect spot is going to get snatched up by mafia people from Jersey. I can't help that." He listened some more and sighed. "Mom, everybody is always there. Rosemary and Evan live five minutes from you. Brian and Jenna are just down the road. Every family event is a circus. That's hardly a compelling argument." He sipped his brandy and rolled his eyes as he listened again. "Okay, stand by," he said.

Joe pressed the phone to his shirt to muffle sound, leaned across the counter, and kissed Brodie. "Would like to come to New York with me for the Fourth of July weekend? Canoe on the lake, eat my mother's potato salad, watch my dad murder steaks on the grill? My brother wants me to look at some investment property. I've been putting him off for about as long as I can."

"Are you sure you want me to come?"

"Yes," Joe said. "I'd like that."

"Okay then," Brodie said. It was amazing how fast things with him had moved. A key, commitment, meeting his family. And somehow it all felt right in a way that wouldn't have been possible with anyone else.

Joe put the phone to his ear again. "Okay, we'll come. Tell Dad we're bringing Brodie's dog, too. Big German Shepherd named Mouse."

Brodie tugged at his shirt, appalled. "I can't bring Mouse to your parents' house," she whispered. "She sheds like mad in the summer."

"It's okay," Joe mouthed to her. He promised his mother he'd call later in the week, broke the connection, and grinned at Brodie's discomfiture. "They love dogs. Dad's going to go nuts over Mouse. And you. Everyone is."

Much later, Joe turned out the bedside table light and they spooned together with Brodie's back against Joe's chest. She tucked his left thigh tight behind her own and Joe draped his arm over her shoulders. They pulled up the blanket and were happily and comfortably exhausted.

The air conditioner hummed. There was the faint sound of distant city traffic but the apartment had been a quiet lovers' oasis all day. The atmosphere still lingered, intimate and embracing.

"I like you, Joe," Brodie said into the darkness.

"I know, honey," Joe said and kissed the back of her neck. His arm tightened around her. "I like you, too."

Brodie slept without dreaming.

PART 7

Not in the legions
Of horrid hell can come a devil more damned . . .
(*Macbeth:* 4.3.55-56)

CHAPTER 27

Brodie pushed open the door of the conference room. She was carrying a BIRNAM WOOD stainless steel travel mug, the key to Joe's apartment was in her purse, and she was wearing the good suit she'd worn to the Royal Society because at five o'clock that morning it had seemed a better choice than jeans and a tee shirt. She'd just driven four hours on three hours of sleep, her muscles felt like a train wreck, and her mood could only be described as euphoric.

Her body had come for Dr. Pedder's meeting but her thoughts were back in Alexandria, back in bed that morning when Joe had opened his eyes and said, "This is like Christmas."

The room was nearly full. Ellen Foster waved at her from the far side of the table. Brodie sat down next to her.

"Don't you look nice," Ellen said admiringly. "Trying to win brownie points?"

"No." Brodie drank some coffee. "It's all I had. I got back from London on Saturday but stayed at Joe's. He lives just outside Washington."

"He's the big blonde guy who came to the symposium?" Ellen asked. "You have good taste."

"Thank you." Brodie smiled, secretly longing to gossip like a teenager. *He's my lover. He's wonderful. I have the key to his apartment right here.*

Ellen leaned toward Brodie. "He made Stanton look like a stick of beef jerky," she murmured.

By the time Brodie could speak again Ellen was engaged in conversation with the person on her other side. Ted Merkel was also a tenured professor and the department's Director of Undergraduate Studies. Brodie drank some more coffee and looked around the room. The entire department hadn't been together since the memorial service for her father. But everyone had obviously taken Dean Slocum at his word that the meeting with Dr. Pedder was to be mandatory. There was a full house of 25 people.

At the other end of the table, Jack Hull slouched behind a copy of *Chronicles of Higher Education*. Jane Goldstein, who taught Ancient Greek history, was next to him. Sixty years ago Jane had been a Rhodes Scholar and Brodie wondered if the woman was ever going to retire.

Alongside Jane, Keith Bixtree sat like a statue. Keith was the mainstay of the modern European History discipline and had the personality of a sequoia tree. On his other side, Linda Colms and Aaron Fox, the two professors who ran the African Studies program were talking animatedly. Rumor had it they were dating again.

The four Asian Studies professors were grouped together, a small sub-department of their own. Brodie was friendly with Linda Zhao, who was a long-distance runner as well as a fellow Georgetown University graduate school alumni, but only knew the other three professors socially.

Across the table, Damien Mendoza looked away from Brodie when she nodded at him; he was the senior professor teaching Latin American history and had accused Wallace Macbeth of nepotism when Brodie was named the department's Director of Graduate Studies. But her appointment had been made by the tenure committee. Everyone knew Mendoza didn't get the role because he hadn't published anything in ten years.

The rest of the chairs were occupied by associate professors, adjunct professors, and instructors who taught a wide range of history courses from Medieval Italy to the U.S. Civil Rights Movement. Several of the younger teachers looked nervous to meet the new department chair who would decide if they were retained to teach another semester, were given more important courses to teach, or eventually recommended for tenure.

Ellen looked meaningfully at Brodie's watch. "Think he's changed his mind?"

It was 15 minutes past the hour.

"I would," Brodie said.

And meant it. At that moment, Brodie knew for certain that she never wanted to be chair of the History Department. She didn't know how her father had done it all those years; dealing with Jack Hull's tobacco-edged ego, Jane Goldstein's shrillness, Keith Bixtree's wooden expression, Damien Mendoza's political machinations, and everything else that went into leading a department full of academic prima donnas.

The conference room door crashed open, everyone started in their seats, and a stocky man with a bald head and aviator glasses bounded into the room. "All here?" he asked exuberantly.

He moved swiftly to the speaker's podium at the head of the table, put a leather portfolio on it, and beamed at one and all. "So great to see you. I'm Donald Pedder. Call me Don."

"Dude," Ellen said under her breath and Brodie tried not to laugh.

Donald Pedder looked like an aging surfer who'd taken a wrong turn and ended up in Charlottesville by mistake. In contrast to the sea of khaki pants and polo shirts around the table, he was wearing a loud blue Hawaiian print shirt, long white board shorts, and red sports sandals. Even his bald head was deeply tanned and he was obviously in very good shape. Brodie put his age at a fit 65.

"I can't tell you how much it means to me that you are all here," Pedder said. His voice was strong, evidently accustomed to rising above the crash of waves. "Before we get down to business, I'd like to extend my condolences to all of you for the loss of your colleague and my friend Wallace Macbeth. Wallace was a uniquely gifted historian. While I can never fill his shoes, I hope to help guide our department to some significant achievements over the next few years." He smiled and nodded and Brodie watched as a few nodded back.

"So." Pedder rubbed his hands together briskly. "Let's go around the room and have some introductions."

One by one, as he walked around the table and shook hands, the various professors introduced themselves and answered a few questions from Pedder as to their background, recent publications and research, what courses they'd taught the past year, and which they would teach in September. Everyone watched the little interview show as it circled the table, the more junior teachers looking distinctly nervous as Pedder came around.

Jack Hull glowered as it was became clear that Pedder was both pleasant and personable and had taken the trouble to become well informed about his new teaching staff.

"And our very own Dr. Macbeth the Younger," Pedder exclaimed as he shook hands with Brodie. His grip was tight, as if he was testing her strength. Brodie squeezed back hard. He smiled and dropped her hand as if satisfied, then turned back toward the rest of the people in the conference room. "Let me all say this now, before I forget, *George and Martha* officially sold its millionth copy last week."

There was a smattering of applause and Brodie smiled her acknowledgment and thanks.

"This fair damsel's publisher," Pedder continued energetically. "Has agreed to celebrate these million copies with a reception right here at the university in August at the end of the summer session. What makes this even more special is that the publisher has promised to donate five dollars from every book sold between now and then to a suicide prevention charity. The university will match the contribution."

Before Brodie could say anything, Pedder moved to Ellen and shook her hand, the tinted lenses of his glasses glinting in the fluorescent lighting.

When he was done with the introductions, Pedder moved back to the speaker's podium and talked about the university's budget, the department's budget, the number of freshmen they could expect to see in the fall, his philosophy of teaching, and the college professor's moral duty to shape young minds. Then he went on to say that he'd be moving into his new house over the next few days and into his office the following week. His office hours would start the week after.

Pedder opened the floor to questions. Most were predictable; Damien Mendoza asked about reallocation of responsibilities among the teaching staff, a younger professor asked about tenure voting practices and was Pedder going to change them, another younger member of the group asked whether Pedder was available to act as a peer reviewer for staff members who were writing for academic publications.

Jack Hull continued his silent glower.

It was nearly one o'clock when there were no more questions and Pedder closed his portfolio and said he wouldn't keep them any longer. He wished them well with summer plans and would see them all at the reception for *George and Martha* in August.

"Don't wait for me," Brodie said out of the corner of her mouth to Ellen as people started getting up and collecting their things. Ellen nodded knowingly and went ahead.

Brodie edged out of the line moving past Dr. Pedder as he stood by the conference room door.

"Dr. Pedder," she said. "Can I have a word?"

Jack Hull grunted something unintelligible as he walked past Pedder. He was the last one out of the room except for Brodie. The smell of cigarettes lingered in his wake.

Dr. Pedder gave a slight cough and then his mouth twitched. "He teaches the History of Suavity, I suppose."

Brodie tried to suppress a laugh and failed. "Jack Hull expected to get the chairmanship."

"I heard something like that." Pedder smiled. He had a wide, Slavic face with tight skin and prominent cheekbones.

"Dr. Pedder," Brodie began.

"Don," He corrected her.

"Don." Brodie smiled awkwardly. "I . . . uh . . . appreciate the initiative in contacting my publisher and arranging this charity drive and reception, but I really wished you'd asked me first. I'm not comfortable with these arrangements."

"Oh dear." Pedder looked genuinely distressed. "Are you saying you didn't know?"

"No."

"Howard told me he'd consulted you," Pedder said. "Obviously there's been a miscommunication."

"Dean Slocum set this up?" Brodie asked.

"Why, yes." Pedder nodded. A tuft of wiry grey hair showed at the neckline of his shirt, curling between the flamingos and palm trees of the patterned fabric.

Brodie sighed. Dean Slocum, always on the lookout for ways to showcase the university.

"Feeling a little sandbagged?" Pedder asked.

"Yes," Brodie admitted. "I'd prefer not to have my father's passing be used as an attention-getting device for the university."

Pedder raised a hand. "Now, now, let's not be too hard on Dean Slocum. This whole thing benefits a wonderful charity. And your publisher was quite sure that it would raise a significant amount of money." He paused. "If you could see your way to going through with it, this money would help a lot of people."

This is a kind-hearted man who walked into a problem not of his own making on his first day. "I'll think about it," she said.

"If I could bother you on another topic, Dr. Macbeth," Pedder said. He gathered up his papers and leather portfolio from the podium. "You very promptly responded to my note asking about your father's research and I appreciate that. But I have to wonder if there wasn't something you overlooked."

Brodie shook her head. "No, I'm very sorry. My father kept very neat research records both at home and here at the university. He had nothing on King Arthur, I'm sure."

"Would you take it amiss if I went through his office?"

"It's yours now," Brodie said. "It was cleaned out months ago. They even put in new furniture for you."

Pedder seemed to blanch under his tan. "His notes were thrown away?"

"No, I kept most of his notes," Brodie said. "I have his material at home."

"Have you read everything?" Pedder pressed. "Was there anything unusual?"

"No." Brodie considered. "Most of what I have are early drafts of his books, copies of articles he used as references, and typed notes he dictated to his secretary. His focus was British history, of course, but mostly nineteenth to early twentieth century."

"I hate to seem persistent," Pedder said. "But may I impose to the extent of looking through that material? Your father had said he'd come across some truly new revelations and I was so counting on his contribution. The publisher is breathing down my neck. I feel I really won't have anything of value until I get your father's research."

"I don't think you are going to find what you're looking for but you're welcome to look."

"When would be a good time?" Pedder said anxiously.

Brodie tried not to yawn. "Maybe Wednesday afternoon?"

"Excellent," Pedder beamed. He opened his portfolio and copied down Brodie's address and telephone number. "You are kindness itself, Dr. Macbeth."

Brodie walked out of the building and into a wall of Virginia summer heat. Her reprieve from the box had been all too brief. But at least she was seeing Joe on Friday. She grinned in spite of herself as she walked to her car. Four days away.

So if Pedder wanted to read a bunch of old notes about the decline of Pax Britannica, he was welcome to do so.

And one more university cocktail party wasn't going to kill anybody.

CHAPTER 28

Dr. Pedder rang Brodie's doorbell promptly at two o'clock, just as she'd finished lugging all of the boxes containing her father's academic notes to the living room. Mouse skittered ahead of Brodie to the front door.

"It's not Puck," Brodie said with a grin.

She opened the door and blinked at the sudden technicolor of Pedder's outfit. He was wearing striped board shorts, an ikat print camp shirt, hiking sandals, and a straw Panama hat. An enormous red SUV sat in the gravel drive behind her Volvo.

Pedder beamed genially at her, the wide face under the hat brim even more tanned than it had been two days ago. Without the tinted glasses he had worn at their initial meeting his eyes were a dark, nearly pupil-less brown, accentuating his Slavic looks. *Yul Brynner goes Hawaiian,* Brodie thought and suppressed a giggle.

Pedder held out a box. "You're a coffee drinker, I take it?"

It was a gift pack of designer coffees. "You really didn't have to do this, Dr. Pedder," Brodie said.

"Call me Don."

"Of course. Come in," Brodie said. She stepped back to let Pedder pass into the house.

"I'm not really a dog person," Pedder said hesitantly, holding his leather portfolio in front of his chest as if for protection.

Brodie looked down and realized that Mouse was standing sideways in front of her, effectively blocking Pedder from entering the house.

"Come on, Mouse," Brodie said. She clicked her tongue and hauled at Mouse's collar. Pedder gingerly edged past the dog.

"We'll go in the living room," Brodie said and led the way. Mouse trotted behind her. Pedder walked slowly, looking all around him, as if the farmhouse was a museum.

"I heard this used to be your father's house," he said. "It's very elegant. Not quite what I expected."

"Thank you," Brodie said. "It's all thanks to the decorator I hired when I moved in a few months ago. If you need help settling in your new house I'd be glad to give you her name."

"I'd like that," Pedder said and then stopped short as he saw the pile of boxes on the living room floor.

"It's everything." Brodie gestured at the boxes. Mouse sat on her foot. "Everything is in a separate archive box by subject or by article. There are about 60 of them. Dad was very organized."

"Is this everything? You're quite sure?"

"Yes," Brodie said. She'd brought down every scrap of paper except the box of old diaries. "Would you like some coffee? Might make the job go a little easier."

"If it isn't too much work," Pedder said. He eyed Mouse. The dog stared at him, ears pricked up and panting a little. "And the dog?"

"I'll keep her out of your way."

"I can't thank you enough for letting me look," Pedder said as he took off his hat and sat down on the sofa. He took a pair of reading glasses from his shirt pocket. "It really is key that I find your father's research."

Brodie called to Mouse as Pedder opened the first box. The dog followed her into the kitchen. As the coffee machine did magic Brodie opened the back door for Mouse. "Here. Go outside. He's probably going to spread papers all over the place. If I let you stay inside you'll walk all over everything."

Mouse stood in the doorway and stared at the grass, then looked up at Brodie as if to say *I've never seen this place before in my life.*

"Go do your business," Brodie said. "You haven't been out since this morning. You're going to blow up."

Mouse backed away from the doorway and sat down.

"Go. Outside." Brodie made a *let's go* motion.

Mouse gazed over her shoulder to the doorway to the living

room, her pink tongue showing a little.

"Oh, for goodness sakes," Brodie said. She closed the door and glared at the silent dog. "Just don't bother our guest. He's going to be annoyed as it is when he doesn't find anything. He doesn't need you shedding all over him, too."

She poured Pedder a mug of coffee, put it on a tray, and added Mrs. Weir's green transferware sugar bowl and creamer.

Pedder was frowning over a sheaf of old mimeographed papers when she brought the tray into the living room. "Remember when copies were purple?" he asked. "Of course not. You're too young for that sort of thing."

Just as Brodie bent down to place the tray on the coffee table, Mouse stepped in front of her. For an awful moment Brodie thought she was going to pitch everything into Pedder's lap and then she found her footing and got the tray down safely on the table, although she had to reach over Mouse to do so.

"Mouse," Brodie snapped as Pedder instinctively recoiled. She grabbed Mouse's collar and made the dog sit next to her as she dropped onto one of the floral loveseats.

"Does your dog ever bark?" Pedder asked as he picked up the mug of coffee.

"Only when we play fetch," Brodie said. "Otherwise she's pretty silent. But she gets her point across. Today she's annoyed because I haven't paid her enough attention. We didn't go for our run this morning."

"Oh, dear. Have I messed your schedule?"

"Not at all. It's too hot to run."

Pedder sipped coffee and opened another archive box.

"I'll just be in the den if you need anything." Brodie said and indicated the doorway.

He looked up and smiled. "Thank you."

Brodie went back into the kitchen, a hand under Mouse's collar. "Outside time," she said forcefully and opened the back door.

Mouse backed away from the door and stood there panting.

Brodie pointed outside. Mouse didn't move. Brodie flapped her hand at the dogwood trees. Mouse didn't move. Brodie shoved on the dog's hindquarters. It was like pushing a cement mixer.

"Oh, never mind," Brodie said in exasperation. She took Mouse into the den with her. The dog settled sideways across the doorway like a furry speedbump as Brodie turned on the laptop.

There was an email from Joe in Brodie's inbox. They'd talked on the phone most of the previous night. She'd never, ever, had such a free-wheeling, suggestive conversation and his email made reference both to it and to the coming Friday night. Reading the email gave Brodie a happy thrill. Her lover was waiting for her, thinking about her.

There was an email from Kay, too, and some spam to delete. Brodie did a little online surfing, trying to get ideas for a hostess gift to bring to Joe's parents. Maybe a lifetime supply of lint rollers for all the dog hair Mouse was going to donate to their upholstery.

Brodie logged off, then leaned back in her chair and found her place in the latest book from the den shelves. *A History of the English People* by Paul Johnson. She read a chapter before her mind wandered to Joe.

Joe in bed, Joe scrambling eggs, Joe nonchalantly handing her his key. *Semper Fidelis.*

"Hello?" It was Pedder. He was in the hallway.

Mouse was still blocking the doorway. The dog's velvety muzzle rested on her front paws. One eyebrow flicked up as Brodie looked past her to Pedder, then Mouse rose into a taut crouch, her body poised for trouble.

"Mouse," Brodie snapped. She rolled the desk chair to the doorway and tugged on the dog's collar. "Sorry," she said to Pedder. "You must have surprised her awake."

"I needed a break." Pedder moved into the room, careful not to step too close to Mouse. He took off his reading glasses and looked at them, then shook his head and gave a rueful chuckle. "The eyes give out first, you know. If I wear my glasses I can drive but not read. If I wear my contacts I can drive, but I need reading glasses. And when my eyes get tired I have to go home and take off the contacts and find the glasses that are just for watching television."

Brodie smiled in sympathy. "Any luck with Dad's notes?"

Pedder shook his head. "Not yet, but I still have boxes to look through." He looked around the den. "This room is more of what I pictured Wallace Macbeth's house looking like."

"This was Dad's study," Brodie said. She gave another tug on Mouse's collar and the dog slowly sat down.

Pedder walked over to the window and fingered the cleaned and repaired tartan, then held up the various bottles of Scotch. "Your father's favorite was Balvenie single malt, wasn't it?" he asked.

"Yes. The 12-year-old sherry cask," Brodie said. She stood up and signaled to Mouse to stay. "How did you and my father meet, Dr. Pedder? He never mentioned you to me but I know he knew you because your card was in his wallet when he . . . uh . . . died."

"Was it?" Pedder seemed sad. He went over to the bookcases and studied the titles. "I miss him a great deal. He was a marvelous man. Brilliant."

"How long did you know him?" Mouse came and sat on Brodie's feet, the dog's ears pricked up.

"Oh, ages." Pedder continued to browse the books, tipping them to get a half look at the cover, then aligning the spines. "Would your father have left any notes in this room?"

"The decorator cleaned it out," Brodie said. "Anything of value was put in the archive boxes."

"And your father never mentioned his research on Arthur?" Pedder neatly aligned all the books whose authors' last names started with R-T.

Brodie shook her head. "I'm sorry. Not a word. I have to admit I don't think he ever really did the research."

"He did." Pedder turned around. "We talked about it every

time we met."

"Which would have been . . ." Brodie let her words trail off.

"Oh, every conference, every guest lecture, you know," Pedder said vaguely.

"Even if you never find anything at least you can tell your editor that you tried," Brodie pointed out. "Who is it, by the way?"

Pedder was studying the books and it was a moment or two before he replied. "Raymond Kensington. From Endicott Scholastic."

"I've heard of him. Ellen Foster in the department has a contract with them for her book on Civil War uniforms."

"What about your father's computer?" Pedder asked abruptly.

"You mean did Dad have a computer with notes on it?" Brodie thought for a moment. "I think they took it out of his office when they took out the old furniture. Sarah Gibbard, the department secretary, would know what happened to it. And she probably has some files, too. She used to type a lot of things for Dad."

"Didn't he have a home computer, too?"

"No."

"Oh." Disappointment tightened Pedder's lips.

"Your best bet is to talk to Sarah," Brodie said.

Pedder put his reading glasses back on. "Well, I'll be getting back to work."

Brodie looked at her watch. It was nearly eight o'clock. "I didn't realize it was so late," she said. "Would you like a sandwich or something?"

"Oh, I've imposed enough," Pedder said. "You don't have to cook, too."

"Sandwiches aren't cooking," Brodie said.

She made big sub sandwiches and a pitcher of iced tea while Pedder looked through more boxes. He was a pleasant and entertaining dinner companion, telling her about his photography hobby and making her laugh with his opinions of the differences between the California and Virginia lifestyles.

He left at 10:00 pm. Mouse followed him out onto the porch. A squirrel ran across the top rail of the fence and the dog dropped into attack position; ears back, haunches and front paws bent in a low slink.

Pedder got into the flashy SUV and backed out of the driveway. When the vehicle was out of sight Mouse trotted to the nearest tree and peed for what seemed to be an eternity.

CHAPTER 29

Brodie knew that Joe was a smart, aggressive chess player. But Friday evening she realized just how fierce a competitor he was.

The water polo match at Joe's sports club was a no-holds-barred event. Joined by Marty and Christine, Brodie sat in the bleachers alongside the Olympic-sized pool and watched Joe lead his team to a hard-fought 2-1 victory. He swam in long wetsuit shorts and left crutches by the pool's edge, but in the water his handicap was nonexistent. Joe scored both of his team's goals, his long reach making him a formidable player. Despite the silly caps that made all the swimmers look alike as the water churned around them, Brodie easily identified Joe by the trim goatee and colorful tattoo. She cheered herself hoarse.

They had dinner with Marty and Christine after the match, getting home long after midnight. Mouse had made herself at home while they were gone, and they found the dog asleep on the guest room bed.

Sunday passed in a happy blur. Joe headed off to work at seven o'clock Monday morning. Brodie walked Mouse around the Alexandria waterfront before driving home in the afternoon.

Joe came to Charlottesville the following Friday. They stayed in bed late Saturday morning. The afternoon was hot and sticky but they threw on shorts and Brodie directed Joe downtown. She felt like a tourist as they cruised the specialty shops and bought things she never did; garlic olives, ciabatta bread, artichoke hearts, and a type of steak that necessitated a serious discussion with the butcher in DeLuca's Gourmet.

Brodie wasn't sure how it happened, but the steak purchase led to a long kiss in the wine section. As she and Joe pulled apart Brodie realized they had an audience. Lorna and Harry Casey were staring open-mouthed at them from the gourmet cheese cooler.

"Village idiots?" Joe murmured.

"Yes."

"Do we care?" Joe asked.

"No," Brodie said.

Diana and Ray came over for dinner. Joe complained good-naturedly about Mrs. Weir's ancient cookware but made three different appetizers, spinach-stuffed flank steak, baked potatoes, and grilled vegetables. The evening was perfect, all of them talking and laughing, the dining room finally losing its formal gloom. They moved to the front porch as the night air cooled. In the moonlight they pointed out constellations to each other and watched Puck and Mouse chase squirrels.

Joe left early Monday morning and Brodie would have been heartbroken if it wasn't for the fact that she'd see him on Friday for the start of the Fourth of July weekend.

CHAPTER 30

"I thought you said this was a quiet little town," Brodie said.

"Tourists," Joe explained. "People come up here for the lakes and the mountains. In the summer they outnumber the locals ten to one. A lot of them like it enough to buy property. They stay a couple of weeks every summer and rent out the place the rest of the time."

The big white truck had left the interstate in Syracuse, with Joe's map of upstate New York open on Brodie's lap. Mouse had been a model back seat passenger. She obeyed all Joe's commands to sit, stay, lie down, and stop licking the driver's ear as they travelled north on small, two-lane state roads, aiming for the village of Old Forge where Joe's parents lived on the shore of First Lake. The dense forests, winding roads, and sparkling, unspoiled lakes of the Adirondack Mountains region were enchanting. Joe told her the area was commonly called the North Country.

They reached Old Forge's main street about nine o'clock, just as darkness fell and the air cooled to sweater temperature. It was a busy place, with people thronging the sidewalks in front of stores and restaurants.

"My brother Brian wants to build a small condo complex about 30 miles further north," Joe went on. "In Blue Mountain Lake. There aren't too many roads that come into the Adirondacks and it's at the intersection of two of them. In 20 years it'll be the new Old Forge."

A mile past the downtown area he swung the truck off the state road and onto a narrower paved one. Through the trees Brodie saw houses and beyond them, the seductive sight of moonlight glimmering on water. The truck turned down a gravel lane marked with a sign reading *Camp Hazy Harbor* and stopped by a sprawling cedar shingle house lit by several outdoor lights.

"Hazy Harbor?" Brodie asked.

"In the morning you see the mist over the lake," he said. "It's great to take a cup of coffee out to the dock and just sit."

"Sounds nice," Brodie said.

Joe leaned over the kissed her. "Nervous?"

"A little."

He grinned and stroked her cheek and Brodie kissed him back. They broke apart and got out of the truck. Brodie opened the rear door on her side to let Mouse jump down while Joe got the suitcases out of the truck bed.

A door banged, there was a shriek of delight, and Joe's mother flew out of the house, followed closely by his father. Brodie found herself hugged like a long-lost friend and hustled inside. A fuss was made over the Monticello estate wine she'd brought as they sat down for a late night supper of chili and cornbread in a modern but homey kitchen with scrubbed pine cupboards and a table as big as Texas. Mouse found a bowl of water on the floor near the back door and lapped at it.

"What else does Mouse need?" Inger Birnam was almost as tall as Brodie, with close cropped sandy-gray hair, a still-trim figure, and Joe's startling blue eyes. A slight accent betrayed her Swedish origins. Inger was in her early 70's, Brodie knew, yet her attitude and movements were of a much younger woman. She wore jeans, a red corduroy shirt, and the same style of clogs Brodie had.

"She ate when we stopped around six o'clock," Brodie said. "I brought her food and bowls. She should be fine."

"We have some leftover steak," Joe's father said. He angled out of his chair and went to the refrigerator.

Joe might have gotten his eyes from his mother, but he'd inherited size from his father. Peter Birnam sagged a bit at the hinges now, but he still had a strong jaw, wide shoulders, and Joe's deft, big-knuckled hands. His eyes were dark blue above wire framed reading glasses. He was bald on top and the white fringe left below was cropped short enough to show the skull.

"I think she's going to get spoiled here," Brodie said.

"Everyone does," Inger said. "That's the fun part of being a grandparent." She passed Brodie the basket of cornbread as Peter put a plate of chopped steak on the floor. Mouse skittered over the linoleum to him.

Brodie found herself surprisingly at ease. The comfortable atmosphere stemmed from Inger and Peter's relationship, she decided as she spooned up the last of the excellent chili in her bowl. They were totally in tune and happy with each other, even after fifty years of marriage and the stress of diplomatic life. Inger and Peter often touched each other; quick little pats of affection that spilled over to Brodie or Joe.

"So what are the weekend plans?" Joe asked as he carried empty bowls to the sink. He was tired and his limp was evident. "Do I get some time to show Brodie around before the hordes descend?"

"You're going to give Brodie the wrong idea," Inger said reprovingly. She brought a chocolate cake and a tub of gourmet ice cream to the table. "Don't listen to him. Brian and Jenna have four nice healthy boys. They're just like Brian and Joe when they were young."

"Loud," said Peter. "But they're balanced by Rosemary and Evan's girl."

"Caitlin is ten and she's an angel," Inger said and passed Brodie a huge wedge of cake topped with a scoop of ice cream the size of a bowling ball.

"Nothing like her mother at that age," Joe said. He accepted his own mammoth dessert. "Rosemary was rotten. She'd do things and then somehow work it out so that Brian and I got blamed when all along *we* were the angels."

Peter sputtered, Inger rolled her eyes, and Brodie laughed.

The rest of the family was scheduled to come over on Saturday afternoon. Sunday would be recovery day. On Monday Brian would take them to Blue Mountain Lake to see the land and meet the realtor. Rosemary and her husband Evan Cunningham, Old

Forge's doctor, would host a Fourth of July picnic on Tuesday. Afterwards, everyone would watch the village's Fourth of July fireworks.

It was after eleven when Brodie and Joe said good night and walked down the hall. He opened a door to a big bedroom with pine paneling and a colorful patchwork quilt on the bed. Brodie saw her suitcase.

"I'm beat," Joe said. "I always forget what a long drive it is."

"Sleep tight," Brodie said. She went up on her tiptoes to kiss him good night.

"You, too." Joe gave her a long, sexy, sleepy kiss, then sat on the bench at the end of the bed and pulled off his shirt.

"What are you doing?" Brodie asked.

Joe unbuckled his belt and yawned. "I take off my clothes before I go to sleep. It's sort of a routine."

Brodie gave him a look. "Shouldn't you do that in your room?"

"This is my room." Joe waved his hand at a doorway across from the bed. "I always stay in the room with the bathroom."

She realized his suitcase was in the far corner. "Then where am I sleeping?"

"Where you always sleep. With me."

"We can't sleep together in the same room," Brodie said uneasily. "Not in your parents' house."

"Let me guess." Joe let out a laugh and pulled her down onto the bench beside him. "The dour Scots. Your dad would never have approved."

"Never." Mrs. Weir's sharp tongue came to mind. *Miss Brodie, just what do you think you're doing?*

"Sassy, you kill me," Joe said. "In case you haven't noticed, we're not a couple of teenagers. And my parents know it."

They were spooned together with the lights out when Brodie caught her breath. "I didn't let Mouse out to do her business," she said.

"Dad will do it," Joe mumbled.

"What kind of guest dumps her dog on the host?"

"The asleep kind."

Brodie wriggled out from under his arm, pulled her silk kimono over her nightshirt, and padded into the hallway. Lights were on in the living room. It was a comfortable room, with an enormous Oriental rug, two brown velvet sofas, a giant scrubbed pine coffee table, a game table surrounded by upholstered chairs, and bookshelves full of *objets* picked up from around the world. One wall was taken up by a fieldstone fireplace, another was decorated with a sheet-sized tapestry, and a wide screen television dominated a third. Off to one side, angled to face the television, Peter Birnam reclined in a big leather chair. Mouse was stretched out on top of him and he was rubbing her creamy belly.

"Oh, my," Brodie said in surprise.

"Still up?" Peter had to cock his head above Mouse's to see Brodie.

"She shouldn't be bothering you like that," Brodie said. "She's not allowed on the furniture."

"No wonder I had to cajole her," Peter said.

Mouse tipped an ear at Brodie but didn't move. Brodie couldn't suppress a grin and Peter grinned back.

"She's being very good," he said.

"You're spoiling her and she's only been here a few hours."

"We spoil everybody."

"At least I should take her outside to do her business," Brodie said.

"We'll do it together." Peter put down the recliner's footrest and Mouse scrambled off his lap.

As they turned to walk out of the room Brodie realized the back wall was covered in photographs. Many were old photos of the Birnam family; Inger and Peter and their three tow-headed children in various cities around the world. Joe was easy to pick out in all the photos. His eyes were lighter than those of either Brian or Rosemary, as was his hair, and he always looked directly into the camera.

The family photos gave way to individual high school graduation pictures of all three Birnam children. Then there were college graduation pictures of Brian and Rosemary. Further down there were several pictures of Joe in uniform. One showed a very young Joe in dress uniform posing by a flag. He was the epitome of the Marine Corps; big, strong, tight-jawed. "He could have been a recruiting poster," Brodie murmured.

"He was a hell of a Marine," Peter observed. "Scared his mother to pieces every time he went away to war but he always said it was what he knew how to do and he could do it better than most."

"I believe it," Brodie said.

Several other photographs captured Joe in military gear in the desert. Some had a jumbled cement background that Brodie assumed was a building in Iraq. In all of them Joe was clean-shaven and even more heavily muscled than he was now.

Brodie touched one picture frame. In the photo Joe was wearing full desert camo gear, complete with body armor, assault rifle and a sidearm weapon in a holster on his right thigh. He was holding his helmet, revealing barely a quarter of an inch of sunbleached hair above a deeply tanned face and dark sunglasses. A red bandana was tied around his neck. A very handsome Latino man stood next to him, also in body armor and holding a helmet. His had the Navy medic insignia on it. They were both smiling at a line of dun-colored camels.

"Was that his friend Trey?" Brodie asked.

"Yes," Peter replied. "They were as close as brothers. What a loss when he was killed."

"Joe told me that Trey saved his life."

Peter nodded. "He left everything to Joe, too. Trey didn't have much of a family and Joe got his military insurance and everything. You know Joe's earring?"

Brodie turned to look at Peter. "Yes."

"That was the stone in Trey's high school graduation ring."

Trey Morales was shorter and leaner than Joe. His black crew cut was Marine Corps high and tight. He had a wide, dazzling smile and deep, dark, smoky eyes. He looked as if he'd be fun in bed and got a lot of chances to prove it.

Brodie and Peter let Mouse run around the trees for a few minutes. Joe was sleeping soundly when Brodie crawled back into the bed. She snuggled against him, inhaled the crisp air from the open window, and fell asleep as if drugged.

CHAPTER 31

Brodie and Joe drank their morning coffee on the boat dock and watched the morning sun burn the haze off the water. First Lake was small enough so that they could see across to the opposite shoreline. The whole area was thickly wooded but here and there houses and boat docks interrupted the line between trees and water.

The Birnam's house was set back from the water by about 200 yards. The land sloped down to the water and a winding path led from the back deck to the dock. Several canoes lay in a row under the shelter of a small boathouse near the dock.

Mouse's nails clicked as she paced from one side of the wooden dock to the other, her attention riveted on the water below. The lake was clear and only about four feet deep at the dock. Small fish occasionally darted by, swimming close to the surface above the rocky lakebed. The dog didn't bark when she saw the fish, but occasionally put out an agitated paw as if to swipe at them.

Brodie could see Inger at the kitchen window. They waved at each other and five minutes later Joe and Brodie watched his mother come down the path with a plate of coffee cake.

"Let me guess," Brodie said. "Hazy Harbor is not the place to be on a diet."

"You got it," Joe said.

The coffee cake was excellent. Brodie watched the houses along the lake come to life. It wouldn't be warm enough to swim until the afternoon, but people were out on their docks, reading the newspaper, checking their boats, soaking up the lake lifestyle.

The mellow mood lasted until noon when the hordes descended. Most of the mayhem was caused by Brian and Jenna's boys. They were all big blonde athletic kids who didn't have a shyness problem. In contrast, Rosemary and Peter's daughter Caitlin was small and quiet, staying close to her mother. Her father was on duty at the clinic and would come later.

"Okay," Peter shouted after about an hour. "I'm taking out the canoes. Who's coming with me?"

"Granddad! Me!"

The boys cannoned out the kitchen door. Joe looked at Brodie and she gave him a *go ahead, I'm fine* nod.

Joe grinned. "I'd better go lend some adult supervision." He pointed to his brother. Brian was shorter and softer than Joe. Both he and his wife Jenna had cheerful, relaxed personalities. "You there. Somebody's got to keep the kids in line."

"What about Dad?" Brian protested.

"I'm talking about Dad," Joe said. "Let's go."

"Finally, some girl time," Rosemary said when the men and boys had left the house. Trim like her mother, with shoulder length honey-colored hair pulled into a ponytail, she had a friendly, wide-open personality that was impossible not to like. "Anyone for a cup of tea?"

"Me," Jenna said.

"A tea party?" Caitlin asked hopefully. The little girl had elected to stay in the house rather than jump in a canoe with her cousins.

"Exactly," Inger said. "Brodie?"

"Sounds great," Brodie said.

As Caitlin clambered up on a chair, Rosemary filled the teakettle, Jenna found the tea bags, and Inger stacked mugs on a tray. As she brought it to the table the china clinked as if her hands were shaking.

"All right, Mom?" Rosemary asked.

"Of course," Inger said brightly.

Brodie helped set out the mugs and spoons, uncomfortably attuned to the atmosphere. Something had unsettled Inger. Rosemary and Jenna felt it, too, Brodie was sure.

The only one immune was Caitlin. She propped a large doll

on the table for Brodie's inspection. The doll was wearing a colonial-era blue taffeta dress.

"She's beautiful," Brodie said to the little girl. "What's her name?"

"Felicity," Caitlin said. "She's from colonial Williamsburg. Do you know anything about colonial times?"

"A little," Brodie said, conscious of Inger watching her.

"Uh huh." Caitlin had cornflower blue eyes and a blonde cloud of curly hair. "Well, Felicity lives in colonial Williamsburg and she loves horses and she gets to ride a foal named Patriot. And go to the governor's ball. Do you want to see her other clothes?"

"Sure."

"Thanks," Rosemary murmured as Caitlin ran off to find her doll clothes. She poured tea into mugs. "All these boys. She feels like there's no one to play with."

"I tried," Jenna said. She had short dark hair and the artistic hands of her architectural profession. "Four times."

The back door opened and Joe came into the kitchen. "Hey, honey," he said to Brodie. "Can we take Mouse?"

"In a canoe?" Brodie asked. She went to the big kitchen window over the sink. Mouse was trotting agitatedly from one canoe to the other as they bobbed in the water alongside the dock. "You've got to be kidding."

"She'll come in the big canoe with me and Todd and Jim," Joe said referring to Jenna and Brian's two oldest boys.

"She's not going to sit still in a canoe," Brodie said, turning to Joe.

"I'll just tell her to stay," Joe said. "She's very good for me."

"I know," Brodie admitted. "But there's no way she's going to behave in a canoe."

"She'll be fine, honey." Joe folded his arms and looked down at her as if he knew best.

"Okay, Ahab." Brodie waggled a finger at him. "Go ahead and take her. But if Moby Dick upsets your boat and you fall in and get rusty, don't come crying to me."

Joe kissed her, bending her backwards over the counter, then let go so fast Brodie had to grab the rim of the sink because her knees had done that damn rubbery thing again, right in front of his mother and everybody. The back door banged.

At the table, Rosemary poured more tea. Jenna sipped hers. Inger sat very still.

"Why is Uncle Joe's leg blue?" Caitlin asked into the silence.

"He likes that one best for sports," Brodie said. Joe had been wearing cargo shorts, a sleeveless tee shirt, and his blue titanium prosthetic. She went back to the table, hoping her face wasn't pink with lust.

"He got his real leg lost in the war," the little girl said as if giving Brodie important news. "In Iraq. Mom told me."

"Caitlin," Rosemary said.

"I know," Brodie replied to the little girl. "But he can do pretty much anything he wants with his new legs. Did you know he has five?"

"He does?" Caitlin's eyes opened wide.

Brodie nodded and stirred sugar into her tea. "Maybe he'll wear the black one tomorrow. It's very cool. Makes him look like RoboCop. Ask him to show you how the knee joint can flip up like this." She flapped her hand upwards. "And he's got some funky collapsible aluminum crutches for first thing in the morning when he doesn't have his leg on yet."

"Cool," Caitlin breathed.

Brodie picked up her mug and realized that Inger, Jenna, and Rosemary were staring at her openmouthed.

"Well," Brodie said uneasily, putting down the tea untasted. Maybe she had said too much about how she had seen Joe *first thing in the morning* to a child. She knew they shouldn't be sleeping in the same room in his parents' house. "I should go outside and see how Mouse is getting along."

"Good idea," Rosemary said thickly. She cleared her throat. "I'm pretty sure we don't want to miss this. Come on,

Mom."

Three canoes were heading slowly for the opposite side of the lake. Shouts and laughter filtered back to Hazy Harbor. It was clear Mouse wasn't being as good as Joe had promised.

The dog stood up in the boat then settled back into a sitting position. The canoe turned. Brodie saw Mouse stand again and stretch her snout toward Joe. Joe pointed and said something indistinct, then Mouse clambered over one of the boys toward him, making the narrow canoe rock crazily. Inger gasped, Rosemary snorted, and Mouse leaped toward Joe.

The canoe wobbled, then flipped. Mouse, Joe, and the two boys shot out of the craft as if from a slingshot, hitting the water with the sound of a spouting geyser that carried all the way to the dock.

They bobbed to the surface, laughing and spitting, then struck out for shore. Joe swam on his back at first, making sure that the boys were all right but they were smaller versions of him and wearing life vests. Mouse paddled next to Joe, riding low in the water like a giant wet rat. Brian and Peter turned their canoes around, secured the overturned one and the paddles, and started making for the dock as well.

Inger had beach towels at the ready. She handed one to Brodie as Joe and the boys hoisted themselves onto the deck. Joe sat on the edge and wiped his face with a corner of the towel as Brodie squatted next to him.

"You got to help me up," he whispered.

"Oh, God," Brodie whispered back, helping him out of the bulky life vest. "I knew something like this would happen."

"Just help me." Joe leaned heavily on her as he slowly got his right foot under him. He stood up, not using the prosthetic but letting Brodie take most of his weight. Rivulets of water ran off him. "I don't want to worry Mom, but I'm really messed up."

"Oh, God," Brodie said again, trying not to stagger. Draped over her like this, Joe weighed a sodden ton. Her tee shirt and shorts soaked up cold lake water.

"Really messed up," Joe murmured, as if he was in pain. "Honey, you were right."

Brodie wasn't sure how much longer she could keep him upright, much less get him up the stone steps to the house. "Can you walk at all?"

"I don't know," Joe said. "I'm too busy crying." He hugged her closer, totally drenching her, and raised his voice. "I mean *crying*."

"Crying?" Brodie echoed. Then she heard Rosemary and Jenna burst into laughter and realized that she'd been well and truly had.

"Get off me," she said to Joe but it was hard to sound indignant when she was laughing so hard. Joe stood up straight, shaking with hilarity, and then Mouse shook herself, spraying cold water over everybody.

The laughter spread, the adults wiping at tears and the kids doubled over with hysterics without really knowing what was so funny. Mouse shook herself again then rubbed wet fur against everybody in a friendly way just in case anyone had some leftover steak handy.

Wearing dry clothes, the intrepid boaters went out again. Still damp, Mouse stayed in the house with Caitlin as the little girl watched cartoons in the living room. Brodie walked into the kitchen in clean shorts and shirt, planning to offer to vacuum up the dog hair on the carpet, only to see Inger crying silently at the table while Jenna and Rosemary sipped tea and patted her arm.

"I'm sorry," Brodie said, backpedaling. "I just thought I'd--."

"I just made a fresh pot of tea." Rosemary pulled Brodie to the table and made her sit.

Inger attempted a watery smile and blew her nose. "Don't mind the old lady."

"Is everything all right?" Brodie asked uncomfortably.

"Couldn't be better," Inger said. "We were just discussing the menu for tonight."

The three women started talking about salad options to go with roast chicken. Brodie added sugar and stirred her tea, quite sure that Inger had not been crying about what food to serve her family.

"Ambrosia salad," Jenna suggested.

"That's an idea. We haven't done that in awhile." Rosemary hopped up and opened her mother's refrigerator. "You've got a lot of the right stuff. Whipped topping."

"Nuts?" Jenna asked a little too gaily.

Brodie stared into her cup and desperately tried to think of an excuse that would get her out of the room.

Rosemary rifled through a cupboard. "Walnuts. And a can of pineapple."

Inger dabbed at her eyes with a tissue. "Can't do ambrosia with canned pineapple. Only fresh."

"Just drain it really well," Rosemary said, putting the can of pineapple on the table.

"It'll be soupy," Inger said, starting to tear up again. "Your father hates soupy salad."

"Mom," Rosemary said gently. "It's okay." She kissed her mother's cheek and crossed to the sink to refill the teakettle as Jenna put her arm around Inger's trembling shoulders.

Jenna looked at Brodie, evidently bent on distracting her from Inger's tears. "What do you think? Can we do ambrosia with canned pineapple?"

"I'm really sorry," Brodie said. She eased her chair away from the table. "I don't cook."

"You don't cook?" Rosemary asked, clanging down the teakettle. "At all?"

Inger lowered her tissue in surprise. Jenna blinked and her mouth formed a tiny O.

"Uh, not really. Just sandwiches. Hardboiled eggs. Joe showed me how to do a fancy fruit salad once but generally it's better if I just watch." Brodie slid to the edge of her chair. "I should check to see if Mouse caught a cold--."

Jenna snorted and Inger made a noise, halfway between a laugh and a sob.

"Lord," Rosemary exclaimed. "Could you *be* any more perfect for him?"

"What?" Brodie felt herself blush.

"I mean, just *look* at the two of you," Rosemary said. "You and Joe look like a magazine ad for happy beautiful people. Joe hasn't been this comfortable with anyone in *forever*. I mean, he's so totally relaxed that he's himself again. He's even wearing shorts and let me tell you, we all nearly died of shock at that." She flapped a hand in Brodie's general direction. "You're athletic. You can take a joke. You're smart but not snotty. *And* you don't cook. I mean it's *perfect.*"

"Joe hates other people cooking when he is," Jenna chimed in. "He has to be in control of the kitchen. Of course he's a great cook, so I'm not complaining. He can make dinner at our house any day."

"I'm with you about the cooking thing," Brodie said, looking from Rosemary to Jenna. "But go back to the shorts. What are you talking about?"

"Joe never wears shorts when he comes home," Rosemary explained. "Not since he lost his leg."

Jenna nodded. "This is the first time we've seen his prosthetic."

"But Joe swims . . . he always wears shorts . . ." Brodie trailed off.

"Not here," Rosemary said. "And he doesn't talk about . . . you know . . . when it happened. But there you were, talking about artificial leg colors like it was no big deal. And that could only be because that's the way he talks about it with you."

"Joe lost more than his leg." Inger blew her nose. "Sometimes I've thought that he lost the leg and we lost him. But now . . . he's . . ."

"Oh." Brodie looked around the table, the situation becoming clear. Joe's family loved him unreservedly but she knew why he'd kept them at arm's length better than they did. "You know," she said awkwardly. "Maybe he's had a harder time coping than he lets on."

"But he should be able to talk to his own mother," Inger said. "To let it all out."

"Inger, you're the last person he can show how he feels," Brodie said, struggling to find the right words. "He comes across as this tough guy but Joe's been . . . afraid."

"He's been to war." Inger nodded. "That's natural."

"No." Brodie shook her head, still groping for how to express what she knew to be true. "Joe's not afraid of fighting or war or anything like that. Probably not even of dying. The one thing that can really hurt him is . . . is what the people he cares about think. Nobody else matters, just the people who are important to him. He's carried around this fear of rejection that probably none of us can really understand."

"Rejection from his own family?" Inger's voice was sad.

"That's who can hurt him," Brodie said softly, meeting Inger's eyes. "And he's been really afraid of that kind of pain."

"But maybe he's over it?" Rosemary asked. "He finally trusts us? I mean, if he's wearing shorts now."

"I think Joe's going to be fine," Brodie said. She raised her cup to her lips, knowing her face was pink, surprised at how much she'd said. But she knew what was in Joe's heart and she knew Inger needed to hear that her son wasn't lost at all. "You're all so important to him. I know he's had a hard time talking but it doesn't mean he doesn't care."

"He's talked to you," Rosemary said.

"Yes," Brodie said. "We've talked and . . . um . . . I guess a lot of things have come out. But please don't tell him I told you."

"Your secret's safe with us, Ishmael," Rosemary said.

Brodie and Inger both laughed, spilling their tea, and the tension was broken.

"Who's Ishmael?" Jenna asked.

As Rosemary explained about the narrator of *Moby Dick*, Brodie and Inger wiped up the spills. And somehow, between the table and the sink, Inger hugged Brodie tight and whispered, "Thank you."

CHAPTER 32

The land that Brian Birnam had his eye on was five acres of forest bordering the northeastern edge of Blue Mountain Lake. They hiked from the dirt road to the water's edge along a rough path through the towering pine trees. It was several degrees cooler in Blue Mountain Lake than in Old Forge, and a world away from Virginia's heat and humidity.

On the craggy shoreline, standing on a flat rock with Joe's arm around her waist, Brodie felt like a pioneer. The lake was surrounded by low mountains that undulated in muted shades of gray, blue, and green, making for a dazzling view. The sun reflected off the surface of the water so that the air seemed to glitter and the breathtaking view stretched to the horizon. It was serene and unspoiled.

A sanctuary.

"It's gorgeous," Brodie breathed.

"Amazing," Joe agreed.

"You look like you belong here." Brodie craned her neck to look up at him. "

Joe gave her the sideways grin. "Well, thank you, ma'am. I'll take that as a compliment."

"You should build right here. The view is fantastic."

"But remember, it gets about 20 feet of snow in the winter."

"It would be like a winter paradise." Brodie could imagine the landscape coated with snow, lush and white and frosty.

She sat on the rock with her arms around her knees as Joe and Brian discussed wells and septic system capacity. Her eyes were drawn to the water. This was the blue depths she'd seen in Joe's eyes and she couldn't help but feel a strong, elemental pull.

After half an hour they got back in the truck and drove back to the village. Blue Mountain Lake was comprised of a public boat dock, a tiny beach, a post office, a scattering of houses, and a secluded shoreline motel with an upscale-looking sign. And the museum.

It had been a revelation to turn the corner at the intersection of the two narrow state roads and see the huge Museum of the Adirondacks. It was a complex of modern and vintage log structures spread over several acres of land, complete with a restaurant, parking garage, and a miniature lake. The entrance building was impressive, taking up the equivalent of two city blocks.

The realtor met them at the museum restaurant. Brodie listened to the three men talk about septic surveys for a few minutes then whispered to Joe that she'd look around the museum for awhile. He nodded knowingly and gave her a wink.

Brodie walked slowly through each of the museum's several buildings, impressed at the quality of the displays. Everything was both well researched and attractively laid out; the history of the logging industry, the luxury hotels of the 1920's, the wildlife, the opulent stagecoaches and trains that once upon a time ran through the wooded mountains.

The large gift shop had an enormous display of both fiction and nonfiction books about the local area. Brodie put a copy of Walter Edmonds' classic *Drums Along the Mohawk* in her basket, then added several books by local authors dealing with the Revolutionary War in upstate New York. Just the places described in the back cover blurbs made her sense of history come alive: Oriskany, Saratoga, Fort Ticonderoga.

By the time Brodie reached the cashier her basket was full of books, birch-wrapped candles, a country plaid apron for Joe, and a mauve Pendleton wool throw for her bedroom. She paid and hauled her shopping bags outside.

The museum buildings were arranged so as to create a large, loose courtyard surrounding the miniature lake. People strolled through the courtyard on their way to the theater or the cabins displaying antique willow furniture. Brodie settled onto a bench and looked around. The waters of Blue Mountain Lake twinkled between the folds of the foothills and the mountain sat majestically in the distance. Bird calls carried on the crisp air.

The tranquility of the place rippled through her bones and Brodie closed her eyes. There were no boxes in this remote, unspoiled place. No Dean Slocums, no Jack Hulls trying to use her or trip her up. Just a warm, kindhearted family that had welcomed her with open arms. And lakes with the soothing lap of water against the shore. There were soaring trees, too, so tall that they made tunnels to drive through, with a strip of blue sky unwinding above.

But mostly, there was peace.

That had to be why she was sleeping so well. As the sun played on her face, Brodie realized she hadn't had one of those strange, white-eyed dreams since the weekend she'd come back from London. Joe had apparently blotted out every subliminal thought about Stanton. Brodie thought of Ellen Foster's comment. *He made Stanton look like beef jerky.*

The bench creaked as someone sat down next to her. "Come here often?" Joe's voice asked.

"Only when I'm trying to pick up lumberjacks," Brodie said without opening her eyes.

"Then today's your lucky day," Joe said. She felt the back of the bench bow as he leaned against it. "I'm wearing a plaid shirt."

Brodie looked at him from under her lashes and her heart flopped in her chest. Sometimes all he had to do was smile and Brodie would be reminded all over again that he was her lover, the only thing that truly mattered a damn, the one thing she'd give her life to save.

"Are all these bags yours?" he asked, sliding his arm around her shoulders.

"Yes," Brodie admitted, leaning against him. "How'd things go with the realtor? Are you going to buy the land?"

"I don't know," Joe said. "Brian's right, it's a prime location and it would be a great investment. But the septic study isn't done and until we know how many units we could build we're not going to make an offer. Maybe we'll wait to buy until this winter. Prices always come down then."

"When everything's buried under 20 feet of snow."

"Exactly."

As they drove back to Hazy Harbor, everyone in the car was quiet.

CHAPTER 33

"Jesus Christ! Jesus fucking Christ!"

Brodie jolted awake, blood pounding in her ears.

"Trey! Trey!"

She flicked on the bedside table light and tried to get her bearings.

"Jesus fucking Christ!" Joe shouted again. He was sitting upright, his eyes glassy and his chest heaving as if he'd just run a marathon. He churned on the bed, reaching for a leg that wasn't there. *"Christ, Trey!"*

"Joe, wake up." Brodie scrambled over the patchwork quilt, pushed aside his flailing hands, and grabbed his shoulders. "You're all right," she said urgently. "Look at me."

"Trey!"

"Joe, look at me."

Joe yawned abruptly with a harsh gasp and coughed and blinked. Brodie watched as awareness replaced the glassy stare. His body calmed as he hauled in more air and coughed again.

Brodie settled back on her heels and felt her heart rate slow. "You awake?"

"Yeah." Joe passed a trembly hand over his face. "I was yelling, wasn't I?"

"You're okay."

"Christ." Joe coughed again and shivered. "I could see that old guy coming at us, screaming. I swear I could even smell the fire."

Brodie shivered, too, and ran her hands up his arms as if to warm him.

"It was the fireworks," Joe said. "Sounded like Fallujah."

"Mouse thought so, too," Brodie said, trying to bring him back to her. They'd had a lot of fun at Rosemary and Evan's Fourth of

July picnic earlier that night. The Cunningham's house was on the opposite side of First Lake from Hazy Harbor and had afforded a perfect view of the fireworks going off from the town barge anchored in the middle of the lake. But the loud bangs had spooked Mouse. While everyone else had oohed and aahed over the spectacular display, Joe had sat on the living room floor with 95 pounds of nervous dog in his lap.

"Sorry to be so much trouble," Joe said. "What time is it?"

"Five o'clock," Brodie said, squinting at the clock. She got him a glass of water from the bathroom and climbed back on the bed. "We were going to get up early anyway. We've got a ten hour drive ahead of us."

"Did I scare you?" Joe asked. He drank down the water.

"You startled me," Brodie said carefully.

Joe put the empty glass on the bedside table. "There's a difference?"

"It was just a nightmare, Joe," Brodie said. "I've certainly had plenty of those."

Joe pulled Brodie against his chest and drew a big, shaky breath. "God, you're fearless."

There was a rustle in the hallway outside the door, then a discreet tap. "Joe, Brodie?" Peter Birnam's voice filtered in. "Everything all right?"

"We're okay, Dad," Joe called. "Nightmare. It's over."

"Okay," Peter said uncertainly. "Your mother and I are going to make some tea."

"Thanks, Dad." Joe gave a quiet laugh. "Give us a couple of minutes."

"Take your time."

"Let me guess," Brodie said as Peter's footsteps died away. "Tea is your family's comfort food."

They sat in the kitchen in robes and drank tea and had breakfast with Peter and Inger. By seven o'clock Joe and Brodie had the truck packed and Mouse loaded into the back seat.

"You're like a ray of sunshine," Inger Birnam said as she

hugged Brodie. "Come anytime."

"You don't need to bring this big galoot, either," Peter Birnam said, hugging Brodie next.

"I had a wonderful time," Brodie said truthfully. "Thank you so much."

"You take care of this young lady, you hear me?" Peter hugged his son.

"As much as she'll let me," Joe said and kissed his mother.

They headed south in the big white truck as Mouse flopped around restlessly on the back seat. A light rain pattered the windshield as Joe whistled with the radio and Brodie yawned next to him.

"Did you really have a good time?" Joe asked, taking the exit onto the main highway near Syracuse. "You kept getting sucked into the kitchen for girl talk and the whole domestic thing."

"No, it was nice," Brodie said. "Rosemary and Jenna are great. It was like being in *Little Women*. You know, Marmee and a house full of girls. I always wanted sisters."

"You did?"

"And a mom," Brodie sighed. "The whole thing with tea and circling the wagons round when somebody needs support, and well, just being there for each other. Your mother is great."

"It must have been tough to grow up without a mother, honey," Joe said. "But your dad was there, right?"

"When I was little." Brodie curled up her legs on the truck seat and leaned her head back. She smiled as her memory reached back to girlhood. "I remember being really little, maybe four or five, wearing a fancy dress and walking through campus holding his hand, feeling so grown up. It was always such an occasion to go to his office or look at the books in the library. Sometimes we ate in the cafeteria and the food always seemed so exotic compared to what Mrs. Weir made."

Joe chuckled. "I'll bet you were a very cute kid."

"I had long blonde braids and was always too tall," Brodie grimaced. "But Dad made me feel really special. He called me his Scottish rose and let me stay up when he had students and professors over. Mrs. Weir thought he was too indulgent because I'd always fall asleep and he'd carry me upstairs to bed." Brodie paused, her memories turning sad. "Then I got sent away to boarding school."

"You never told me that." Joe sounded surprised. He turned off the radio.

"Summer after sixth grade." Brodie swallowed hard. "I'd spent the summer in Edinburgh with Kay, the same as always. Dad had gone to Germany, I think, for some research in a library there. When he got back, he announced I'd be going away to boarding school. Whoosh, a week later he and Mrs. Weir dumped me at the Madeira School."

"You hadn't known?"

Brodie shook her head. "It was a total surprise. I thought I was going to seventh grade with all my friends."

"Christ," Joe said.

"I came home at Christmas and everything had changed. Dad and I were suddenly two adults who had a professional relationship."

"Christ," Joe said again.

"And that's the way we stayed." Brodie closed her eyes and listened to the rain and the hypnotic sweep of the windshield wipers. "He was remote and polite. I tried to get back what to we had before in the only way I knew how."

"Success as a history professor, too."

"He couldn't ignore that," Brodie said. "He was proud of me. We had dinner together once a week. But talk was always about work."

"Maybe your dad had a hard time coping with his little girl growing up."

"I wasn't ever his Scottish rose again," Brodie said tightly. "And then he died."

"I'm sorry, honey." Joe's hand found hers.

Brodie clutched his fingers and swallowed hard again. "I've

never told anyone about how I ended up at boarding school. How bad it hurt. Not even Diana."

"I'm your lover, honey," Joe said seriously. "You're supposed to tell me stuff."

His certainty helped her sadness dissipate. "You get that from your family," Brodie said. "You all grew up telling each other everything. Your parents taught you how. I think they're wonderful."

"You know," Joe said. "If you want my family, you've got to take me, too."

"Well." Brodie pretended to think. "If I have to."

"You know," Joe said into the rearview mirror to Mouse. "She tries to hide it but I think she likes me. In broad daylight and everything."

"Shut up," Brodie murmured.

Joe laughed. They held hands all the way to the Pennsylvania border when Mouse decided it would be nice to ride in the front seat, too, and it took a certain amount of shoving to convince her otherwise.

PART 8

Come, love and health to all.
(*Macbeth*: 3.4.87)

CHAPTER 34

Summer was BIRNAM WOOD's busiest time of year and it was difficult for Joe to take time off so Brodie went to Alexandria every weekend.

It was just easier. Her schedule was much more flexible. And his apartment was so inviting, with its openness and large-scale furniture. Plus it had the amenities in the bathroom and kitchen that made life easier for Joe. But mostly the apartment in Alexandria just somehow felt more *right*, as if the old farmhouse in Charlottesville wasn't ready for so much happiness.

Brodie loaded Mouse into the car Friday after her office hours, and arrived before Joe got home from work. There was always a note and something unexpected on the dining room table. Joe's surprises were intended to make Brodie feel at home; a new toothbrush, a pink chenille bathrobe, bowls for Mouse, a 20 pound bag of dog food.

When Joe came home in the evening, the precious hours started to fly by, full of walks along the waterfront, talking and sightseeing, occasional nights out with Marty and Christine. He took her over to the big warehouse where BIRNAM WOOD was located. The place was as well organized as Joe's apartment, with a neatly appointed conference room and office area set apart from the busy shop floor.

They swam at his sports club several times, challenging each other to laps then playing around in the deep end like a couple of teenagers. Brodie ignored the questioning glances in the locker room from women who'd seen her in the water with a one-legged man.

There were moments of perfect peace, too, when Brodie just lay in Joe's arms on the sofa reading or watching a movie, or in bed hearing nothing but the sound of his heartbeat and the ticking of the clock. And there were moments when she realized anew the sort of man she was with, when he showed her the numerous medals, qualifications, and citations from a highly decorated military career.

One Sunday afternoon he let her read the Silver Star citation. They sat on his bed with an open box of military memorabilia between them. Brodie's eyes blurred as she read *conspicuous gallantry* and *repeated rescues under fire* and *disregard for his own life.*

"A night attack. The medic was killed immediately," Joe said. "I grabbed his bag. For about the longest six hours of my life I got all the wounded to a safe zone and did triage. Kept praying I wouldn't get hit in the prosthetic. If I got hit anywhere else I figured I could keep going but if the leg broke I wouldn't be able to move fast enough to do anybody any good."

He fingered the ribbon on the medal. "I swear Trey was with me that night. It was as if he was whispering in my ear, telling me what to do. That's why not one of those guys died."

His eyes were bright. Brodie put down the citation and held him close and let him know that she understood.

Brodie took to spending Mondays at the Library of Congress. The books she'd picked up in Blue Mountain Lake spurred research on the mostly forgotten revolutionary battles in upstate New York and before long she felt the first hints of excitement that meant a new project was coming together.

The new book would be bigger than anything else she'd done; it would be a biography of the land and the people who'd fought to make it theirs. Many of the key players in New York's revolutionary history were Dutch emigrants and Brodie scribbled notes about Peter Gansevoort and the siege of Fort Stanwix and General Nicholas Herkimer who'd lost a leg like Joe at the battle of Oriskany. As the life drained out of him, Herkimer had sat under a tree and directed his colonial troops to victory over the

British.

One afternoon she found a reference to a Lieutenant Johannes van der Birnam. At Joe's urging, she called Inger and Peter that night and shared her find. They were as excited as she was and Inger promised to scour the local library.

The next Friday night Inger called with the news she'd found an old genealogical survey and Brodie talked to her for an hour, both thrilled with the discovery. Joe weighed in with military tactics and they pored over maps spread over the oak table and tried to reconstruct obscure military engagements. Her publisher sent her a contract for the new book sight unseen.

But as the hot summer days raced by, and Brodie started in on her father's books by authors whose names started with "P," she began to dread the start of the fall semester. It would mean less time with Joe.

While she would teach only one graduate class, Brodie knew that university responsibilities would take up much of her time. After all, she was the department's graduate studies advisor and would again organize the annual music and politics symposium. Then there was the endless round of fundraisers, departmental meetings, and faculty cocktail parties.

At least Dr. Pedder had gotten himself organized in Randall Hall fairly quickly, with office hours on Tuesday afternoons. Brodie often ran into him. He'd decorated his office with some excellent photographs of sunsets over water that he had taken himself and seemed unaccountably pleased when Brodie complimented him on them.

The issue of her father's research on King Arthur came up now and again, Pedder ever hopeful that she would find an overlooked box of research material. Brodie heard from Sarah that he'd tracked down her father's ancient computer and made the university support staff print out everything on the hard drive, all to no avail.

The *George and Martha* reception was scheduled for the last Friday of the summer session. The day before Brodie worked out with Diana, taught her final summer session class, and then holed up in her office to grade papers and look at the files on two applicants for an Asian Studies position vacated by a junior professor who'd unexpectedly left to do relief work in Tibet. Brodie had promised Linda Zhao that she would serve on the interview panel.

"Knock, knock."

Brodie looked up from the papers on her desk to see Ellen Foster standing in her office doorway. "Hey, Ellen," she said. "Come on in. When did you get back from Richmond?"

"Yesterday." Ellen dropped into the upholstered chair and adjusted her striped cotton shirtdress. "Had to be here in time for your reception tomorrow."

"Thanks, I really appreciate it."

"How many people?"

"About two hundred at last count." Brodie grinned at Ellen's surprise. "Sarah asked me who besides the department I wanted to invite. I gave her a handful of names and figured it would be the usual wine and cheese thing. Dean Slocum had a different plan."

"A big deal, huh?"

"I think so," Brodie said ruefully. She leaned back in her chair. Last summer she would have been wearing a navy polo shirt and a khaki skirt. Now she was wearing a lime green sundress. "But it's for a good cause."

"So who did you invite?" Ellen asked.

"Diana Johnson and her husband. The Crosbys. Joe."

"Joe." Ellen's eyebrows wiggled. "Things going well?"

"They are," Brodie said, unable to suppress a grin. "He's coming late because tomorrow's Friday and he has to work but he'll meet me there."

Ellen opened her purse and extracted a folded letter-sized piece of white paper that she handed to Brodie. "I need a favor. Tell me what you think."

Brodie unfolded the paper. It was a letter from Endicott

Scholastic Publishers saying that due to the untimely death of editor Raymond Kensington, all titles currently in development were frozen. Endicott Scholastic would be contacting all authors at a later date to determine the disposition of their work. In the meantime, authors were requested not to contact the company but to allow the Endicott Scholastic corporate family to deal with the passing of their esteemed colleague.

"Oh, dear," Brodie murmured. She peered at Ellen over the top of the letter. "They're not saying if they're still going to publish or not."

"That's my point." Ellen looked distressed. "I'm sorry he passed away but the letter leaves me hanging. I have a contract with them but haven't delivered the manuscript yet. Does the letter mean that I'm free to get a new contract with somebody else? If not, how long until they assign a new editor? A year? A week?"

"Did you check their website?"

"I haven't had a chance."

Brodie quickly found the Endicott Scholastic corporate website. "They've got an In Memoriam column," she said, scanning the homepage. "Raymond Kensington shepherded more than two hundred books through the publishing process for them. Then it just says what your letter says."

"Great." Ellen sighed and put the letter back in her purse.

Brodie leaned forward, elbows on the desk. "Ellen, maybe you should call a lawyer."

"I probably should."

"You know," Brodie said. "Talk to Dr. Pedder first. Raymond Kensington was his editor, too."

"For that book on King Arthur he was writing with your father?" Ellen asked.

"Yes, although I doubt Dad ever got around to doing his part of it," Brodie said. "Dr. Pedder's never found anything Dad did."

Ellen stood up. "Well, maybe I'll go see surfer dude and see if he knows anything."

"He's a good guy," Brodie said. "If he knows anything he'll help."

Ellen headed for the doorway. "So tomorrow night in the dean's garden."

"Seven o'clock," Brodie confirmed.

Ellen stepped back toward Brodie's desk. "You know, Dean Slocum might have turned it into a media circus but that doesn't undermine your achievement," she said. "*George and Martha* is a great book. A lot more people understand the roots of this country because of it."

"You still have to come tomorrow, Ellen."

"Damn." Ellen winked at Brodie and left.

Brodie turned back to the computer screen. On a whim, she did a quick search for the late editor and clicked on a news report from the *Cincinnati Herald.*

Raymond Kensington had died of a brain aneurism.

CHAPTER 35

Brodie had been to plenty of university receptions in this very garden, enclosed by Jefferson's famous serpentine brick walls, but nothing as elegant as the *George and Martha* charity event that night. There was a string quartet playing, white linen-swathed buffet tables featured an ice sculpture of a dove while smaller skirted circular tables were set out for those who wished to sit. A big cardboard check covered by a cloth waited for the momentous unveiling.

Two hundred well-dressed people were chatting, sipping champagne, and eating crab puffs and bacon-wrapped oysters. Waiters in tuxedos and white gloves circulated with more hors d'oeuvres and trays of champagne flutes.

"I thought you said this was going to be a tacky disaster?" Diana asked, strikingly elegant in a white slubbed silk cocktail dress.

"I know," Brodie said wonderingly. She was wearing an outrageously expensive pale gray silk dress Diana had talked her into buying. The layers of sheer fabric clung to her body like a sin and highlighted her pale hair. "Sarah kept saying the Dr. Pedder was making most of the arrangements and that it was going to be the best party the university had ever seen. But I didn't really believe her."

"Is that him?" Diana asked and made a discreet motion.

Dr. Pedder was across the garden talking to a short, frail-looking man in a dark suit. The professor was wearing a pale peach linen suit and white suede Gucci loafers. His bald head gleamed as if he'd polished it.

"That's him," Brodie said, trying not to laugh.

"He looks like a Eurotrash hairdresser," Diana said.

"He's sort of a character," Brodie said. "But I think he's just what the department needed. Somebody to shake things up. And he sees right thorough Jack Hull so I really like him."

Ray walked up to the two women and held out champagne flutes. "Here's to the two best looking women here," he said.

"You clean up pretty good," Brodie said as she took one of the flutes. Ray was wearing a classic charcoal gray suit, a white shirt, and a red foulard tie.

"You're not too bad yourself." Ray touched his glass to hers and Diana's in a toast. "So where's Joe?"

"He should be here any time," Brodie said. "I hope he didn't run into bad traffic." *Or decide not to come because the last university reception he attended was a total disaster*. She drank her champagne.

"A little nervous, are we?" Diana said, eyeing Brodie's empty glass.

"No," Brodie said stoutly. A waiter came by and she exchanged her empty flute for a full one. Diana raised her brows triumphantly and Brodie pretended not to notice.

"You two want some shrimp?" Ray asked.

"Flag down the waiter with the little rumaki things," Diana suggested.

Brodie sipped her champagne and looked around. Dean Slocum was chatting with Pedder, obviously entranced with the man's ability to focus attention on the university. Her eyes wandered to the garden gate but Joe still wasn't there. She checked her cell phone. He hadn't called or left a message.

Dr. Pedder bounced over. Brodie hastily put her cell phone back in her tiny shoulder bag and introduced him to Ray and Diana. He seemed delighted to meet them and spoke knowledgably about the university's sports record. Pedder's dark brown eyes sparkled with delight when Ray offered to give him a tour of the football facilities and introduce him to the head coach. Ellen and Bob Foster joined them. Pedder was like a magnanimous host, remembering names and personal details.

Brodie looked around the garden again and there was Joe, framed in the gate.

He had on a long black western frock coat, a white band-collar shirt, and jeans with a subtle black design on the outer seam. As he scanned the crowd, he rumpled his hair away from his forehead and Brodie caught the blue flash of his earring. His other hand held a pink corsage in a clear box.

"It's finally happened," Brodie murmured.

"What?" Diana looked at her.

"I'm going to the prom with the captain of the football team." Brodie handed Diana her glass and floated across the garden to Joe.

"Hi," she said. "Come here often?"

"Hi," Joe said, his eyes crinkling at the corners in the way that Brodie loved. "God, Sassy, you look incredible."

"Thank you." Brodie kissed his cheek then rubbed off a faint lipstick smudge. "You look very handsome."

"Thank you, ma'am," Joe said. "You said wear a jacket."

"I know." Brodie stepped back to look at him again and smoothed the frock coat's lapel. The fabric was a fine thin wool. "This is gorgeous."

"You're the gorgeous thing here." Joe ran a finger across her exposed collarbones. "Can we go home now? This dress is giving me ideas."

"That's why I got it," Brodie said. "But we have speeches and music first."

"I know," Joe said and handed her the corsage box. "This is for you."

"Thank you." Brodie took out a wrist corsage and slipped her hand through the bracelet.

As twilight settled on the garden, the mini lights wrapped around the trees came on, giving the reception a soft fairytale feel. Dean Slocum made opening remarks, then Dr. Pedder mounted the podium. He peppered his short talk with both humor and candor, managing to both congratulate Brodie and express condolence for the loss of Wallace Macbeth.

Joe and Brodie stood together, his arm around her

waist. Pedder wrapped up his remarks and turned the podium over to Lance Avery, head of the company that had published *George and Martha*. Avery gave the book's publishing statistics: a second printing ordered after only six weeks of sales, nearly 2,300,000 books sold in less than a year, the first non-fiction book published by his company to be translated into fifteen languages in the first year of publication.

Avery said a few more words about how Brodie was the easiest author his company had ever dealt with, his enthusiasm over her new project about New York, and how glad he was to make this contribution to a charity that was so close to her heart. He then invited Brodie to the podium with him and she stepped up for a short speech thanking Avery for his support and Dean Slocum and Dr. Pedder for organizing the reception. When her formal remarks were over, she and Avery moved to the little curtain hiding the enormous cardboard check that would go to Vale of Hope.

Brodie pulled the string, the fabric slid away, and everyone started applauding. Brodie stepped back to look at the amount. The check was for $475,000.

Arnold Petrillo from Boston's Vale of Hope charity stepped to the podium and said some effusive words of thanks, nearly choking with emotion at the amount. When he stepped away from the podium he hugged everyone, including Brodie. She said the wrap-up bit, thanking everyone for their support, welcoming Dr. Pedder to his new post, and wishing Petrillo luck in carrying out his important mission in Boston. When the speeches were over Brodie walked back to Joe.

But the focus was still on her and the reception got lively. Brodie found herself talking to a reporter from a major news magazine, executives from the publishing house, city functionaries from Boston, the mayor of Charlottesville, and other academics. Joe started talking to Ray at some point and was introduced to other members of the athletic staff.

After an hour of being the center of attention, Brodie found herself trapped in a corner talking to three professional charity fundraisers. Joe was across the garden. A sea of people surged between them as the chatter of well fed guests competed with the string quartet. She could see the back of Joe's head because of his height but she couldn't tell if he was alone or talking to someone.

"Excuse me," Diana said, edging into the group of people with Brodie. "Can I borrow our guest of honor for a moment?"

Brodie made her excuses to the charity consultants and let Diana lead her to the bar. "Thank you," she said under her breath.

"You looked like you needed rescuing," Diana said. She ordered them both tonic water with lemon.

"I did," Brodie admitted. "They were from some Boston group that helps subsidize Vale of Hope. Nice, but I think I'm running out of things to say to people who are in a fundamentally depressing field."

"I hear you," Diana said and handed Brodie a glass. They moved away from the bar and watched the crowd.

"This was so much nicer than I'd thought it would be," Brodie said. She was actually enjoying herself, despite the crush of people. "But I've lost Joe. I hope he's not counting the minutes until he can get out of here."

"Don't worry," Diana said. "He's with Ray. And Dr. Pedder. Over there."

Brodie took a step to the right. Through a break in the crowd she could see Joe and Ray talking with Dr. Pedder and two other men she didn't recognize. All were holding beers and laughing and gesturing, their expressions backlit by the fairy lights in the trees. "Wonder what they're talking about," she said.

"They look pretty chummy, don't they?" Diana asked, craning her neck to see over the crowd. She turned back to Brodie. "You do realize that every woman here tonight wants to sleep with Joe, don't you? And every man wants to be him. Maybe not Ray. But the rest of the suits."

"True." Brodie watched Joe with the fierce pride of

ownership.

"It's the cool jacket."

"And the earring," Brodie reminded her.

"All thanks to me and my linguine." Diana grinned and held out her glass. "To you. Health, wealth, and happiness."

"Thanks." Brodie touched her glass to Diana's, drank, then traced a circle on her palm with the damp base of the glass. "I have all three, don't I? Especially the last. I'm so happy I feel guilty."

"Guilty?" Diana asked. "Why on earth should you feel guilty?"

Brodie refocused on Joe. She was glad he was having a good time because he'd taught her so much. Like how to speak from the heart. She took a breath. "I'm the happiest I've ever been. I've got money and a good job. A great new research project. And Joe."

"So where's the guilt coming from, sweetie?"

"All this happiness less than a year since Dad died doesn't seem right." Brodie toyed with her swizzle stick. "Joe said it would be like this, that one day I'd wake up and my first thought wouldn't be that Dad was dead and how was I going to survive."

"So you feel guilty because you're moving on and not mourning for your father any more?"

"Something like that." Brodie shrugged. "It's not this visceral pain any more. It's almost like I'm supposed to be thinking about him more than I do."

"You'll always love him," Diana said gently. "But you've moved on. Circle of life and all."

"I know." Lance Avery caught Brodie's eye and waved. Brodie raised her hand in acknowledgement. Avery started toward her but got waylaid by Ellen Foster. "But then there's guilt on a whole other level, too."

"You're confusing me, sweetie." Diana said, frowning.

"Dad . . .well." Brodie looked at Diana. "Dad would not have liked Joe."

"You don't know that," Diana exclaimed.

"Think about it," Brodie gulped, wanting Diana to say she was wrong but knowing she was right. "I know Dad liked Stanton. His degrees. His television career. His family money. Kay said so. But I dumped him and fell for a blue collar guy whose family comes from the middle of New York nowhere. Money-wise Joe's extremely comfortable but Dad wouldn't see it that way."

One of the executives from Avery's company looked to be walking toward them. Diana stepped in front of Brodie, blocking his view, and the man veered away.

"You can't go around living your life as if your dad was here telling you what to do," Diana insisted. "Trying to do that gave you those horrible Stanton nightmares."

"I know, I know." Brodie jabbed the swizzle stick into an ice cube, breaking the point. "But I can't help feeling hugely guilty because it's a relief that Dad's not here to tell me he disapproves of Joe. What kind of daughter thinks that?"

"You were a good daughter and you know it," Diana reproved her.

"He wanted that license plate to make me think of him every single day but I don't anymore."

"What's the plate number?" Diana asked.

"OFK 362," Brodie said immediately.

Diana handed their empty glasses to a roving waiter and shook her head at the offer of a glass of champagne. The waiter moved out of earshot.

"So the thing he wanted you to remember is still there," Diana said and tapped Brodie lightly on the side of the head. "It hasn't gone away just because you're living your life. You deserve to be happy."

Brodie took a deep breath. "I do, don't I?"

"Just look at yourself, sweetie," Diana exclaimed. "Six months ago we would never have had this conversation. And you'd never have worn something as fab as this dress."

Brodie felt a blush creep up her cheeks. "I've changed a lot, have I?"

"In a way, I think your dad knew he could go because it was time to let you live your own life," Diana said. "That's just what you've done. By living the life you were meant to live, you're remembering your dad every day in probably the way he really wanted you to."

"Oh," Brodie said, suddenly grappling with a rush of emotion.

"I think it has a lot to do with Joe," Diana went on. "I've never seen you let yourself be so happy. You *glow* when you're with him. So don't beat yourself up playing the 'what if' game. You don't know what your dad would have said about Joe. Just be happy and leave it at that."

Brodie swallowed hard. "Okay."

"Take my advice or I'll throw linguine at you," Diana warned.

Brodie laughed and hugged Diana, knowing that her friend was right. There was nothing to be gained by asking more questions that would never be answered.

They broke apart and watched the knot of men across the garden. Pedder was obviously telling a fishing story. He mimed casting a rod then fighting a fish at the other end of the line. Joe and Ray and the other men were all laughing. "It's like watching a beer commercial," Diana said.

"Nobody in a beer commercial would wear a peach suit," Brodie observed.

"True."

Pedder mimed winning the tussle and finally reeling in the fish. There was some group discussion then Joe handed Ray his beer and mimed taking the hook out and throwing the fish back in. Brodie and Diana heard Pedder's laughter all the way across the lawn.

"This is going a lot better than the last university reception Joe attended," Brodie said.

CHAPTER 36

Brodie and Joe were lazy on Saturday but summoned enough energy on Sunday to take the tour at the White Lion winery near Monticello. The tour was relaxed and friendly as they strolled with the guide through the rows of vines stretched across the foothills of central Virginia. They saw the copper vats ready for the grape harvest, the bottling machine, the corking machine, and the bins of stamped corks waiting to be pressed into bottles. They finally ended up in the cool vaulted tasting room. They sampled several varietals, swishing and spitting and eating cheese between samples to cleanse the palate.

Joe was very knowledgeable and made Brodie laugh with descriptions of wine he didn't like. *Pine sap, possibly, with a hint of dung beetle.*

They had a late lunch on the restaurant terrace overlooking the vines. The hills fell away below them, the land rippling into higher, blue-gray undulations in the distance.

"I have to leave really early tomorrow morning, Sassy," Joe said as he finished his steak sandwich. "You wouldn't believe this house we're going to be working on. The kitchen alone is going to be as big as my entire apartment. We've got the first meeting with the client at ten o'clock."

"God," Brodie sighed. "I'm beginning to hate Mondays."

"Me, too." Joe leaned back in his chair. "You still coming on Friday?"

"Yes," Brodie said. "I'm on the interview panel to replace Dr. Hong and we're interviewing on Wednesday and Thursday. Mouse and I will be at your place on Friday." She picked a nut out of her pecan chicken salad and ate it. "Are you sure you can stand us for a whole two weeks?"

"You bet," Joe said and gave her that sideways grin. "I'll expect supper on the table at six, my slippers and pipe by my chair, and Mouse sitting quietly with the newspaper in her mouth when I get home every night."

"How about if I meet you at the door in just an apron while Mouse digs up the plants on your patio?"

"Even better."

Brodie grinned and crunched a forkful of salad. She would stay at Joe's until the beginning of the fall semester. She'd work on her research while Joe was at work and when he came home they'd just relax. The thought of so many days together was like a forbidden luxury.

The waitress took away their plates, swept crumbs off the long white linen tablecloth, and went to get dessert and coffee. They angled their chairs away from the table so they could take in the magnificent view of vines and rolling hills. There were only a few people on the terrace; other couples who had come for a late romantic lunch at the elegantly skirted round tables and were taking their time over dessert and the spectacular vista.

"This is lovely," Brodie said. She tugged down the hem of her red skirt and put her sandaled feet up on the low stone balustrade that edged the terrace. Her toes were red, too, and her white linen blouse had a bow at the waist and Joe was with her and the world loved lovers. The green vines of the winery stretched away from the restaurant in rows that undulated over the hills and blurred in the distance. The peaceful landscape gave her a feeling of freedom, of space, of never being hemmed in.

"You get the feeling that the vines just stretch on into heaven," Joe said, echoing her thoughts. He eased out his right leg and put his foot up on the balustrade next to hers. The breeze rippled the stone-colored cotton of his pant leg and the tiny gold cross below the sapphire earring twinkled in the shaded sunlight. He was wearing a black polo shirt. The banded sleeves hugged his biceps and Brodie's heart gave a lurch just looking at him.

The waiter brought coffee and apple pie and tiny glasses of the winery's signature dessert wine.

"Almost as nice as Blue Mountain Lake," Brodie said, stirring her coffee. "That place was so incredibly peaceful."

"You think Blue Mountain Lake is nicer than this?"

"Absolutely," Brodie said. She cut into her pie. "Speaking of, any news on the land?"

"Well, yeah," Joe said. "I haven't told Brian yet, but the deal's off."

"Why? What happened?" Brodie asked, oddly disappointed. She took a sip of coffee with her eyebrows raised.

"New York," Joe said. He fiddled with his spoon. "I won't be that far away from you for that long."

Brodie put down her coffee cup. "I'm not going anywhere. I'll wait."

"But I won't." Joe pushed aside his untasted coffee, then stretched his arm across the table. "Hold my hand, honey."

Brodie slid her hand into his. Joe's grip was warm and strong.

"Being with you," he said. "The way we are. It's more than I ever thought I'd have."

"Me, too," Brodie said softly.

"After Iraq," Joe went on. "I kept reminding myself that I was one of the lucky ones. I'd survived and could pay tribute to those who hadn't. I had a family who cared. I had friends so there was always something to do. You know, background chatter to keep myself from thinking too much." He rubbed his thumb over hers. "But I always knew a big part of me would be dead."

Brodie knew he needed to say these things. Over the summer, since the night she'd chastised him in the Italian restaurant, he'd occasionally made a remark as if a weight had rolled off his shoulders.

"And then I met you and we stood outside in the rain at the Dingerhoy and something changed," Joe said. "You had that silky hair and that body and so much to say and no way to get it out. I knew I should walk away, that you had the power to hurt me like no one else on earth. But I couldn't stop thinking about you. I wanted to be the one who found out everything about you."

"That's just what you did." Brodie squeezed his fingers.

"You made me see that there was someone out there who could accept me for who I am now. That healed me. I'll always love you for that. And for about a million other things, too."

Brodie felt her throat tighten. The vines shimmered in the distance.

"So I guess you know where I'm going with this," Joe said. "I'm not getting down on one knee and I don't have a ring in my pocket but I'm offering you everything I've got. My heart, my soul."

"Are you proposing?" Brodie quavered, her heart suddenly banging in her chest.

"Yes, I'm proposing." Joe drew her hand across the table and kissed her palm. "I love you, Sassy. I want to marry you. We'll have a good life together, I promise."

Brodie's mouth dropped open.

"But if that's too much too soon we could just live together," Joe said, evidently amused at her reaction. "Hell, I'll even settle for being next door neighbors who sleep together every night if you need your independence."

Brodie hitched up her jaw with difficulty.

"I've been thinking we could find a house that's somewhere in the middle of the commute for both of us," Joe continued. "Maybe Warrenton. With a big yard for Mouse."

Brodie pulled her hand out of his and stood up. The fine china and silver flatware blurred against the white linen tablecloth. Her body felt alive with sensation but she couldn't breathe. She gripped the edge of the table to steady herself because she was shaking as if she was caught in a storm.

Joe stood up, too. "Where are you going, honey?"

"I don't know," Brodie said blankly and then she moved around the side of the table, unwittingly dragging the tablecloth with her. As the plates and coffee cups and tiny glasses and silver spoons and forks clattered together and spilled onto the terrace floor, she walked into Joe's arms and kissed him with all the meaning she could put into it.

"Is this a yes?" Joe asked when they finally broke the kiss.

"Yes," Brodie whispered. "*Yes*. I love you."

"Damn," Joe said wonderingly. "I never thought I'd hear you say that."

"I know," Brodie said around the lump in her throat. "But I love you. So much." She sucked in air. "In broad daylight and everything."

Joe laughed then, and Brodie laughed too, feeling lightheaded and giddy and incredibly happy.

Behind her the waiter coughed discreetly. "Is everything all right, sir?"

"We'll take a bottle of your finest champagne," Joe said, still holding Brodie close. "To go."

"Yes, sir!"

The other diners on the terrace started to applaud and say congratulations and Brodie felt her face get pink and Joe laughed again and it was the sound of freedom.

"I can't wait any longer," Brodie said.

They'd left a trail of clothes from the front door. By the time they'd reached her bedroom they were both naked and breathing hard.

Joe sat down in the upholstered rocking chair and Brodie straddled him so that her legs dangled over the curving fabric arms. The wrapping securing his prosthetic to his left thigh was under her hip; there'd been no time to take it off. Joe found a condom and pulsed into her. Brodie's eyes opened wide and her thighs tensed around his ribs.

Joe started to rock the chair.

By the tenth rock, they were both trembling.

By the fifteenth they were glistening with sweat and staring at each other wild-eyed.

Brodie was wound so tight her body was vibrating like a steel guitar string. She was soaring but tethered. Spiraling out of control but still safe in Joe's arms.

They both climaxed on the next rock and Brodie collapsed against Joe's chest.

"Hey," Joe said after awhile.

"Hey," Brodie said, her mouth against his shoulder.

"Remind me to get this chair bronzed."

"Okay."

Brodie looked up. The big blue eyes crinkled tiredly. The torrent hit her broadside; excitement, risk, bliss, joy, and Brodie started to cry.

She cried hard, helpless with emotion, crying for all the things she had now and never had before. She cried, overwhelmed by the fulfillment she'd thought was for other people, a happiness she'd only ever dreamed about with a man who'd given her strength and hope and the courage to be who she wanted to be. She cried because she was angry at her father, because she missed him, because she hadn't cried at the funeral, because she felt guilty for not knowing him well enough, because he hadn't been the kind of parent that Inger and Peter Birnam were, because she could finally grieve for him.

And because her father would never see her have the love he'd once known with his wife but had been unable to share with his daughter. Brodie cried even as Joe got rid of the condom, turned her so that she was sitting sideways on his lap, and covered her with the Pendleton throw from the basket on the floor.

He rocked the chair and rubbed her back as she sobbed. The tears were cathartic, releasing years of pent-up feelings. They washed away reserve and bitterness and a loneliness Brodie hadn't even known was hiding deep inside.

She cried herself dry, until there was nothing left except a few hiccups and a feeling of exhausted peace. Brodie wiped her wet face with her hand. "I'm sorry," she sniffed.

"Nothing to be sorry about," Joe replied.

"It wasn't because of you," Brodie said.

"I know." Joe smiled. "You needed it. A lot of bad stuff came out."

"You can read my mind sometimes." Brodie nestled back into the warmth of his body.

"I try." Joe kissed her forehead. "Feel better?"

"Yes."

They rocked quietly for a long time until Joe's stomach growled and they realized it was past eight o'clock.

"How about I cook us something to go with that champagne?" Joe asked.

"Sounds wonderful." Brodie eased off his lap. "And poor Mouse is still outside."

Joe readjusted his prosthetic and they both pulled on shorts and tees. He yawned sheepishly as he opened the bedroom door and gestured for Brodie to go ahead of him.

"Wait a minute," Brodie said. "I need to tell you something."

Joe leaned against the wall and raised his eyebrows questioningly.

"You know," Brodie said awkwardly. "Since we met I haven't been with or cared for any other man."

"That's okay, hon--," Joe started.

"No, it's not," Brodie interrupted. "I *hate* that you ever doubted me, even for a minute. There hasn't been anyone but you and there never will be anyone in my life except you. You need to know that. And when I say *know*, I mean you should know it here--" she touched his forehead "--but mostly I want you to know it here." She rested her hand on his chest and Joe pulled her close.

"I do know," he said, his voice thick with emotion. "You didn't have to tell me. But it means the world to me that you did."

"*Semper fidelis*," Brodie said softly. "I will only ever love you."

"I will always honor you as my lover and my wife," Joe said, as if he was taking an oath. "I love you and I will never be unfaithful to you."

Brodie cried again, but this time it was from sheer happiness. Joe wiped her cheeks and kissed her. Mouse circled from one to the other the entire evening, sensing the excitement between them.

CHAPTER 37

"We went out to White Lion on Sunday," Brodie said, keeping her voice casual. She dumped her sports bag on the floor next to the bench. She and Diana were alone in the field house locker room. "The restaurant is really nice."

"Oh yeah?" Diana asked. She started working her locker combination. "What did you have?"

"Chicken salad with pecans," Brodie said airily. "Joe had the steak sandwich. We had apple pie for dessert and that's when he asked me to marry him."

Diana jerked around, the beaded ends of her braids clacking. "What?"

Brodie shrugged, trying to be nonchalant when everything inside her was screaming and dancing. "He asked me to marry him. You know, proposed."

"*Proposed*!" Diana shrieked. "What did you say!?"

"What do you think I said?" Brodie felt her face wreath into a huge smile. "I said *yes*."

Diana grabbed her by the shoulders. "You said yes on Sunday! And you're just telling me now?"

"I was going to call," Brodie confessed. She'd spent Monday morning giggling to herself and then had fallen asleep on the sofa. Joe had called in the evening and they'd talked for two hours. "But I think I was in a daze yesterday."

Diana tossed back her head, let out a scream of delight, and Brodie found herself yelling back in utter joy. They did a crazy jig around the empty locker room until they were both breathless.

"So when?" Diana asked. "When are you going to get married?"

"We were thinking of a fall wedding," Brodie said. "So, um. Soon."

"Where? In the university chapel?"

"No," Brodie said. She plopped down on the bench in front of the lockers. "I want to get married at Hazy Harbor."

"Where?"

"Joe's parents' house," Brodie explained. "A fall wedding on the dock, with the leaves turning colors. The lake behind us. God, it would be beautiful."

"It sounds gorgeous," Diana said, sitting down, too.

"But the bad news is, I'm probably going to be moving to Warrenton," Brodie said. "We want to find a house that's halfway for both of us."

"We'll still hang out." Diana hugged her again. "I'm so happy for you I can't even say how much."

"Be my maid of honor?"

"I'd love to."

"You're going to have to help me plan everything."

"You know what?" Diana asked. "Let's bag this workout and go downtown instead. Buy bride's magazines and check out that new stationery store. I hear they do fabulous invitations. You've got a lot to do if you're going to get married in a couple of months. Damn, I planned my wedding for a year."

Brodie stood up. "I feel drunk."

The euphoria lasted all day. Brodie and Diana cruised through nearly every store in Charlottesville to get wedding ideas. Late in the day Diana dropped off Brodie at Randall Hall laden with her sportsbag, a book on ultimate receptions, three bridal magazines, and a collection of catalogues and pamphlets from floral shops. The old building wasn't air conditioned and as Brodie hauled her stash up the stairs the load got heavier in direct proportion to the increasing warmth of the upper floors.

"Hello, Dr. Macbeth." Sarah Gibbard held out a sheaf of telephone message forms.

"Hi, Sarah." Brodie juggled her load to take the message slips. "Place feels kind of quiet."

"Not too many people here," Sarah said. "Almost everyone is gone until the start of the fall semester."

"Are you recovered from the reception?" Brodie asked. Sarah had helped Dr. Pedder put it together and had enjoyed herself thoroughly at it. Brodie made a mental note to send Sarah flowers or something as a thank-you.

"Your boyfriend's really handsome," Sarah said, coming around the side of her desk. "Somebody said he's a country music star."

"He's not but I'll tell him you said that." Brodie grinned. She'd introduced Sarah to Joe shortly after the check unveiling and the secretary had actually gaped at him. No doubt the campus gossip mill was grinding merrily, comparing Joe to Stanton.

"Can I talk to you privately, Dr. Macbeth?" Sarah asked.

"Sure."

Sarah gestured for Brodie to go into her own office. The secretary shut the door behind them.

Mildly curious, Brodie put her sportsbag on the floor and the shopping bag full of books and magazines on the desk. "What's up, Sarah?"

"It's Dr. Hull," Sarah said. "He made me type up a letter of complaint to the Ethics Committee. He says Dr. Pedder was behaving in an inappropriate manner at the Mousetrap on Sunday night."

"Dr. Pedder was at the Mousetrap?" The popular local nightclub was generally regarded as a graduate student hangout during the school year. Younger faculty kept it alive during the summer when there were few students in town.

"With Dr. Seagull from the Economics Department," Sarah said.

"Okay." Brodie swallowed laughter. The randy old coot. Sabine Seagull had to be thirty years younger than he was.

"Dr. Seagull gets around, doesn't she?" Sarah looked at Brodie expectantly, obviously hoping for something juicy and repeatable about Stanton.

"Sarah, let's not gossip," Brodie said. "Dr. Seagull and Dr. Pedder are none of our business."

"Dr. Hull is concerned that he's not setting the right example," Sarah sniffed. "California morals, he called it."

Brodie shrugged, the effort not to laugh nearly killing her.

"Well." Sarah smoothed the collar of her blouse, obviously disappointed in Brodie's lack of strong reaction. She opened Brodie's office door. "I was just about to leave for the day. Do you need anything?"

"No, not a thing," Brodie said, moving around the side of the desk. "You have a good evening, Sarah."

"Good night, Dr. Macbeth."

Brodie sat at the desk, finally letting herself chuckle as Sarah's footsteps clicked down the stairs. It was going to be fun to watch from the sidelines as Pedder and Hull battled over the coming year. But if she had to choose sides, her money was on surfer dude.

There wasn't much in the way of email. Linda Zhao had sent a note giving the place and time of the first Asian Studies interview. Tomorrow, at eleven. Brodie called Linda to confirm, then read through the applicant's file. He was impressive on paper, Brodie wondered if he'd be the same in person.

She left the office at seven o'clock. The hallway was dark and stuffy. The early evening had done little to cool the sticky Virginia heat. All the doors to faculty offices were closed and the building felt empty and somber. But Brodie was glad to see a thin rime of light showing around Pedder's not-quite-closed door. She needed to say thanks. Not only had Pedder thrown a very elegant reception but he'd worked hard to make Joe feel welcome.

Brodie juggled her load to tap on the partially open door. "Don?"

The door swung inward and Brodie put her head around the opening. Pedder's desk was in the middle of the long narrow room. He was leaning back in his chair with his sandaled feet up on the desktop. His brown-tinted glasses were pushed up on his forehead and he was asleep, his mouth open a little and his hands folded comfortably on his stomach. The window shades were down and the desk light was on, illuminating his clothing and throwing shadows across the large framed photographs on the walls. Pedder was wearing another wild combination of printed board shorts and striped shirt.

Brodie grinned and started to back out of the office, easing the door shut as she went.

The hinges squeaked.

Pedder's eyes flew open and he sat up.

Brodie gasped and dropped the shopping bag. The book and magazines spilled out onto the floor.

Pedder vaulted the desk, yanked Brodie into the office, slammed the door shut, and turned to confront her.

His eyes were white and diseased. They were the same eyes Brodie had seen so many times in her dreams. Corroded with white scales but not blind. But this was not a dream. It was *real*. The air went out of her lungs, the world spun, and Brodie gaped at him uncomprehendingly.

"Well, well." Pedder pulled the tinted glasses off his forehead and tossed them across the room to the desk. The white eyes stayed locked on Brodie.

She opened her mouth but fear and confusion blocked words or action. He had *the exact same eyes* as all the people in her strange dreams.

They'd all had *his eyes*, she realized, her thoughts tumbling wildly. As if his eyes and his consciousness had inhabited each different person in each different dream.

"I was waiting for you," Pedder said, blocking the door. "It was time to take those annoying contacts out. Show you what you're up against."

Brodie managed to find her voice. "Who are you?"

"It's time to tell me what your father knew, Brodie," Pedder said.

Despite the pounding fear and uncertainty, Brodie wasn't surprised by his words. But she didn't understand.

Pedder licked his lips, a slow languorous taste with his tongue. "He called the game a quest, you know. A quest to find out why his precious Elizabeth had died. I told him, but he kept pretending he didn't believe me. We played for more than 30 years."

"In every dream I had," Brodie breathed. "It was you, wasn't it? Being who you needed to be to fit into each dream."

Pedder's broad face twisted with impatience and he suddenly slammed his hand against the heavy wooden door. The sound was the like the crack of a whip. "*Tell me what you know*," he shouted.

"Oh, God." Terrifying and unreal connections came together in Brodie's head. "My father had dreams, too. That's what you mean by playing the game. He played a game with you in his dreams."

"Hide and seek," Pedder snickered. "Cat and mouse."

"The dreams are the game." Brodie started to shake and broke into a sweat as she realized where the connections were leading. "Get killed in the dream and you're dead in real life. Because your soul's been stolen."

"How clever." Pedder's voice was laced with sarcasm. "As if you didn't know."

"That's what happened to my mother. You said so." Brodie involuntarily crossed her arms as if to protect herself. This idea, this concept, this crossover between dream and reality was too ludicrous to believe. But she did. "You killed her in a dream. You took her soul and she died. She died in her sleep."

"And then Wallace had questions and he played the game and he *cheated*."

"You killed him in Boston, didn't you?" Brodie's voice rose

uncontrollably. "Just like you said in the dream. You threw him out of a window."

Pedder laughed. "Donald Pedder was distraught to hear that his dear friend and colleague Wallace Macbeth had jumped to his death in Boston."

"Why?" Brodie's entire body was telling her to get out, to get away but Pedder was in the way and her legs weren't working. "Why didn't you just take him . . . in his dreams . . . the game . . . like you took my mother?"

Pedder's face twisted in fury and Brodie had a flash of insight, a historian's sudden understanding of a pattern of behavior that was more than what it appeared to be on the surface.

"In all those years," she gasped. "You couldn't. Dad was too good, too smart. He was too good *at your own game.*"

"*Shut up,*" Pedder screeched.

"He was better than you," Brodie said, sure of what she was saying. "That's really what you want to know. That's the secret you need to find out. *Why was Dad better than you at your own game?*"

"*He thought he was Arthur and Lancelot and Galahad, all rolled into one,*" Pedder roared, his face suddenly beet red. Brodie shrank back as spittle flew from his lips. "*But he was Pellinore. Pellinore and the damned Questing Beast.*"

"*He was a good man,*" Brodie shouted back as anger surged ahead of fear and confusion. "And you killed him because you couldn't steal his soul."

"*I didn't want it!*" Pedder's voice was full of fury. His eyes were like white hot coals in a circle of blood. "*I had your mother's.*"

"And Raymond Kensington, Ellen's editor." Brodie's mind spun like a water wheel, terror sloshing off and getting scooped up again by the next revolution. "You killed Raymond Kensington because you knew Ellen would find out that you weren't writing a book about King Arthur. That nonsense was just an excuse to go through my father's research notes. But you didn't find what you were looking for and that man died for nothing."

"Collateral damage," Pedder said, suddenly flippant.

"I'll have you arrested," Brodie said shakily. "Charged with murder."

"On what evidence? That you had nightmares?" Pedder folded his arms, now eerily calm. "Certainly not in your father's case. The Boston police found no evidence of foul play. A cut and dried case of suicide."

"Are you really Donald Pedder?" Brodie realized her teeth were chattering.

"Still so slow to catch on." Pedder looked at his hands as if they were new. "Donald Pedder. I forget what his quest was but I took his body, too. The one before was getting old. It's tricky to go from one to another and only the strongest bodies work, you know. The weak ones just fall apart and there you are, with a mess. Of course it's funny but not if it happens to you."

"You're evil," Brodie breathed around the terror in her heart. "You're Satan."

To her surprise Pedder laughed gaily. "What a wonderful coping device the word *Satan* is. It lets simple souls believe there's only one bogeyman out there."

He licked his lips at her and Brodie was reminded of an animal stalking its prey. He was toying with her, breaking her, making her soft enough to swallow in one bite.

"You came here to find out what my father knew," she parried weakly. "But there isn't anything to find out. If he knew how to cheat at your game he didn't tell me. So you can go back to hell or wherever you came from."

Pedder casually walked to his desk chair and sat down, pulled an antistatic cloth out of a drawer, and made a show of polishing his glasses with it. "We have a deal to discuss," he announced. "You tell me how your father cheated the game and Joe Birnam can keep his soul."

Horror washed over Brodie in a cold wave.

"It's quite a fair trade," Pedder said. His eyes glittered speculatively. "After all, the soul of a warrior is the biggest prize in the game. Warriors' souls get insulated by pride and patriotism and discipline. Dedication to duty. They're hard to come by."

"He didn't tell me," Brodie cried. "I can't trade Joe for *something I don't know.*"

Pedder shrugged indifferently. "Then the Marine's soul is mine. Maybe you'll get to watch."

"I'll kill you before I let you touch him." Brodie lunged for the desk, grabbed Pedder by the shirt front, and hauled him forward, her own screams resonating in her ears. He dropped his glasses and grabbed her wrists. They grappled awkwardly, the desk between them, and Brodie realized he was more than strong enough to have pitched her father out of that Boston window.

"Excellent," Pedder hissed, the white eyes victorious. "You'll be in jail for killing Donald Pedder and every night in your dreams you'll see me toy with Joe Birnam's soul. I'll drag it out, take him bit by bit until he's a shambling fool who can't even remember his own name."

"*No!*" Brodie tore herself away, forcing Pedder to let go or be dragged over the desk. "*You leave us alone.*"

"You should have more respect for who I am," Pedder spat. "I pull on the threads of weakness that run through families. Generations upon generations. I pull the string and uncover madness and infidelity and unrequited love and heartbreak and all the things that make souls try to find answers to questions they never should have asked in the first place."

"I don't care," Brodie breathed. "Leave Joe alone."

Pedder pointed at her. "Your thread started unraveling a long time ago when Macbeth killed Duncan to become king of Scotland. That's when the Macbeths had guts. Now they just read and imagine themselves to be knights and kings."

Brodie fumbled blindly for the doorknob, adrenaline surging through her body like an overdose of heroin.

"You think about my offer," Pedder snarled. "I'll be in touch."

"Take mine instead," Brodie heard herself say. She leaned her forehead against the door, frightened and desperate. "Leave Joe alone. You can have my soul instead."

"That's not the way the game works." Pedder sounded like he was talking to a 2-year-old. "Your soul is worth nothing compared to his."

Brodie turned around to face Pedder again. "Touch him and I'll kill you. I don't know how, but I will."

"My, my." Pedder laughed and licked his lips, the predatory look oddly at variance with his surfer clothes. "Saber-rattling from a woman without a sword."

Brodie wrenched open the door and stumbled out of the office, her legs numb with panic. The air was sharper and colder in the hall. She took the stairs two at a time, hugging the banister to keep from falling.

"You forgot your *bridal* magazines, Dr. Macbeth." Pedder's laughter followed her all the way down.

CHAPTER 38

Brodie vomited into the toilet bowl until there was nothing left to bring up. The bathroom spun and Pedder's laughter echoed in her ears. She clung to the cool porcelain and tried to breathe past the dizziness and nausea. Slowly, slowly, the bathroom stopped spinning.

She let go of the toilet seat and slumped against the wall, the tile floor cold against her bare legs. Every light in the house seemed to be on. Across the hall, her skirt, top, and sandals were in a heap on her bedroom floor. Her purse and car keys were there, too. Mouse stood uncertainly in the doorway to the bathroom.

Brodie had no memory of driving home, letting in the dog, or taking off her clothes.

Mouse walked cautiously into the bathroom, her nails clicking, and nuzzled Brodie's shoulder. Brodie put her arms around the dog and buried her face in the thick, comforting fur.

"I'm scared, sweet dog," she whispered. She felt utterly defenseless in the face of a thing that was too big, too evil to truly comprehend.

Mouse suffered the hug for a few minutes then pulled away. Brodie blinked hard and forced herself to stand up, using the wall for support. When she felt strong enough, she climbed into the shower and let the hot water pelt her. Joe had left some shower gel on the tub rim and Brodie lathered herself thoroughly with it, as if his spicy scent could somehow wash away the stain of the horrible conversation with Pedder.

As she stepped out of the shower and wrapped a towel around herself, Brodie realized two things.

First, the situation was no product of an overactive imagination or indigestion or distress over Stanton. It was real and horrifying and true.

Second, she knew she couldn't risk sleeping again until she'd found out what her father knew.

Wallace Macbeth wouldn't have gone without leaving something that would let her save Joe.

☼

June 28: I was so close to Elizabeth I swear I could smell her perfume. We were in a large chamber decorated with hanging tapestries. He told me she would come, but she did not appear.

September 3: Elizabeth had always loved Malory. Such a diversion from economics. This time I waited for her in a meadow. There was a jousting target and bales of hay. The sun was warm on my back and made me yearn for her all the more. He was on a horse but did not approach. He stayed at a distance and we stared at each other . . . Sometimes I think he is the Keeper of these vivid dreams. Like a custodian.

January 9: I'm beginning to realize that if he is there, no matter in which guise he appears to me, then Elizabeth will not come into the quest. His presence prevents her from coming to me but I do not understand why.

January 29: The child is brilliant. I combed her hair last night as she read to me. Johnny Tremain. *She says it is her favorite book. We talked about the Revolution, hopefully I did not bore her with the British point of view. Fourth grade is passing quickly.*

February 2: Mrs. Weir insisted on cleaning the tartan today and I had to refuse. She burned dinner in retaliation but the curtains are not to be taken down. I need the darkness.

Brodie put down the notebook and drank more tepid coffee. It was nearly dawn on Wednesday and she'd read through the first ten years or so of her father's notebooks. They'd confirmed what Pedder had said.

Wallace Macbeth's obsession with his dead wife had led him into dreams he called a quest. Just like Brodie's dreams in which she was sure she'd find her father, Wallace believed he would see Elizabeth but never did.

Instead, Wallace became fascinated by his interaction with the inhabitant of his dreams he called "the Keeper." Wallace and the white-eyed Keeper discussed philosophy, right and wrong and love and hate. There was none of the deadly intent and urgency of Brodie's dreams. If Wallace knew he was talking to pure evil he did not acknowledge it.

"How could you have done this, Dad," Brodie said out loud to the den. Mouse, lying in front of the sofa, pricked up her ears and looked questioningly at Brodie.

The rest of the notebooks beckoned but Brodie felt lightheaded from too much caffeine and not enough food. She took her empty cup into the kitchen and let Mouse out to do her business. The backyard was green and inviting, the sun was rising, and it was hard to believe that the whole grisly nightmare of Pedder and stolen souls and murdered parents was true.

But it was and she couldn't stay awake forever. Brodie shouted for Mouse to hurry up and finish. The dog bounded across the grass to her, ears up in alarm, and Brodie locked the back door behind them.

She dumped dry food into Mouse's bowl and made herself a sloppy ham sandwich, her movements jerky with stress and fatigue. Her stomach was tight but Brodie managed to down a few mouthfuls.

March 1: I pushed my way in again. There were tapestries on the wall. The floor was stone. Through an archway I could see rolling hills and I wondered to whom they belonged. Elizabeth was close but of course I did not see her.

March 21: The walls were adorned with crossed swords, most so heavy I could not even hope to lift them. Armor was on mannequins. The leather of the armor's inner pieces was soft and well-used.

April 8: The dreams are too vivid sometimes. I woke shouting this morning when the alarm went off. The child came to my room, her eyes huge with concern. I explained I'd had a nightmare and she went to make the morning coffee. It is hard to believe she is so grown up. Sixth grade. Middle school and teenage boys loom ahead.

May 16: The child won the essay prize for the best historical discourse on colonial Virginia. The prize is $200 and she is elated. We bought a new dress for the award ceremony. She wanted to wear stockings but Mrs. Weir has said stockings are inappropriate for age 12.

"Old bitch," Brodie said out loud. "No wonder I was such a fashion disaster." She dug her fingers into her eyes, took several deep breaths, and kept on reading.

July 8: My love for Elizabeth is unabated. I love her as much now as I did the day we married. I must consciously put thoughts of her aside, like today as the child and I head for Edinburgh. She will stay while I research the archives in Berlin.

July 20: The archives are immense. My research is at once both monotonous and enthralling. I pore over microfiche every day. I shall not write much, my eyes are tired at the end of the day.

August 9: I'm tired of Berlin, tired of this country's reluctance to admit the past and its obsession with cleanliness, as if that could cleanse the country's soul. And I am tired of being alone with stacks of books. I dreamed last night of the place where I go to see Elizabeth. The Keeper was there and we talked of the Holocaust. He played devil's advocate again. Why do I force myself to dream such things?

August 20: It is nice to be back in the UK, although London is still too big and noisy for my taste. I called Edinburgh and the child seemed happy.

August 22: I hardly know what to write. My breathing is still erratic. I fear stroke.

I ran into Ian Fergusson by accident in the museum's reading room. I had not seen him since Elizabeth's funeral. He is unchanged, still a fine looking man. We exchanged greetings and then he begged my forgiveness for his relationship with Elizabeth the year she died. I was speechless as he talked on and on, seemingly unaware that I had not known of their affair. As he talked I realized that the Keeper was right--Elizabeth had planed to leave me for Ian, that she had not wanted to come to America with me and the child. Ian talked on, a man who'd been holding too much inside for too long. I left stumbling with shock, without bestowing the forgiveness he craved.

I can think of nothing now but that the Keeper's words were true. Elizabeth was unfaithful to me and went looking for answers and he murdered her soul with his bare hands as she dreamed in her sleep lying next to me. I went looking for answers when she died and have ended up in the dreams as well. The Keeper could haven taken me, too, but all these years I have unknowingly distracted evil from its pursuits with dialogue.

It sickens me but I am intrigued. I have been in the presence of another dimension of the psyche. I have transcended my own mortality for 11 years. I have seen a dark soul incarnate.

August 23: I wandered the streets of the city last night, afraid to sleep, having revelations that at once frighten and calm me. I have realized that the only way to protect my daughter, to keep her out of the dreams, is to never have her love deeply. After all, love is what drove both Elizabeth and myself to seek answers. Elizabeth loved another and I loved her. Both loved too deeply.

The only solution is to teach the child not to love in this way. She must be brought up to live safely without the sort of passion, that if thwarted, leads to a quest for answers.

"Oh, God," Brodie murmured. She sat back in the desk chair as tears rolled down her face. The memory of that terrible day in Kay's living room rushed back, the images fast-forwarding in a blur of caffeine and despair.

Wallace had come back to Edinburgh from London determined to create a new daughter who could live without love. Boarding school was just the first step in his campaign to keep her safe.

No wonder her father had liked Stanton; he'd known the relationship was passionless.

Safe with Stanton.

Her phone rang. Brodie started so hard she nearly bit her tongue. She stayed on the sofa, panicked that it was Pedder.

A minute later she checked her voicemail messages.

"Brodie? This is Linda Zhou. The interview started half an hour ago. I hope you'll be joining us soon."

"Oh," Brodie said dully and looked at her watch. "Sorry, Linda."

She deleted the message, dried her cheeks with the back of her hand, and kept reading in search of the clue that would save Joe's life.

Brodie finished the last notebook shortly after seven in the evening. She closed the cover and put all the notebooks back into their box with mixed feelings of grief and incredulity.

Despite what her father had learned the summer that she was 12, he hadn't ended the game with Pedder. Six months after packing Brodie off to boarding school he'd written of sending himself back into the quest and facing down the Keeper as if they were two boxers in a ring. He'd done it again and again.

Over the years the dreams became more menacing and violent. Six years ago he'd met Pedder at an academic conference and realized the professor from Stanford was the Keeper. The knowledge prompted him to make out a new will and store his diaries at Munk's but he hadn't stopped pushing his way into the increasingly dangerous dreams.

Instead, Wallace Macbeth had relished these death-defying conflicts as welcome diversions from the slow pace and snarky politics of academia. He'd lived a second secret life, full of risk and drama, carried out in countless naps on the den sofa or at night in his bedroom.

Brodie looked around the den. The house felt tainted, dirty.

She stumbled into the kitchen. She'd gone more than 36 hours without sleep. Fatigue was gaining on her fear, making her numb with apprehension.

"How did you survive so many dreams, Dad?" she muttered as she opened a can of soup and dumped it into a pan. "Of course you figured out how to cheat. Or you would have died in your sleep, too."

Her brain felt wrapped in cotton wool, but something resonated through the fluff. *I pushed my way in again.*

"You got in, Dad," Brodie thought out loud.

Mouse clicked across the floor and sat down on Brodie's foot. Brodie absently leaned against the dog as she swirled the chicken and noodles around with a teaspoon. "He went in by choice," she said to Mouse. "So it stands to reason he figured a way out."

The thought was staggering and she dropped the spoon into the soup.

"That's it, Mouse!" She swept down and hugged the dog. "That was the cheat. Dad figured out how to wake up. He could come and go and somehow Pedder never knew he was doing it on purpose."

The phone rang. She let it go to voicemail again.

Joe's deep voice made her pulse rate go up. *"Hey, Sassy, it's me. Just checking to see how the interview went this morning. Call me when you get home. I love you."*

Brodie slowly stood up. She might know what her father had done but until she found out how he'd done it, the knowledge was useless. Hours of exhaustion and she still had no weapon with which to defeat Pedder and keep Joe safe. The thought made her nearly hyperventilate as the soup boiled up and spilled over the pan.

Brodie managed to turn off the heat and shove the pan off the stove. It overturned onto the counter. Boiling liquid splashed her hand and the spoon clattered to the floor.

Cold water against the burn helped her stay in control. As she stood by the sink with her hand under the faucet, Brodie realized that her father had given her a weapon, after all.

It was the same one he'd used to keep her safe for a very long time. Maybe it would keep Joe safe, too.

She threw some paper towels onto the spill and put a bag of frozen corn on her burned hand. Then she sat at the table, took a deep breath, and autodialed Joe's number.

"Hello," Joe answered on the second ring.

"Hi."

"Hey, honey. How was the interview?"

"Interview?" Brodie had a hard time talking around the lump in her throat.

"Weren't you interviewing for the Asian Studies opening today?" Joe asked. "You said today and tomorrow."

"I didn't go."

"What's the matter?" Joe asked, his voice suddenly full of concern.

"I can't come on Friday," Brodie said. Her chest clenched and she wondered if she was going to have a heart attack before she did what she had to do.

"The interview time get switched? Damn. Well, come on Saturday."

"I can't come at all," Brodie ground out.

"What? What's going on?"

"I don't think we should see each other any more." Someone else had to be saying these words. Brodie felt disembodied, as if she was watching herself destroy something priceless.

There was a long silence on the other end of the phone. Brodie closed her eyes and felt the tears seep out.

"I don't understand." Joe said finally.

"We can't see each other any more," Brodie said.

"What's going on, honey?"

"Don't call me again," Brodie whispered and hung up.

He called a minute later, the phone trilling facedown on the kitchen table.

Two minutes later, the phone rang again. Then a third time.

The sun dipped and darkness lengthened across the yard.

Brodie sat at the kitchen table and sobbed. Mouse sat and watched her.

Brodie woke with a start. She'd slept for two hours without dreaming. It was pitch black outside. Her face was seamed from the napkin and spoon she'd put on the kitchen table when she'd heated the soup. The frozen vegetables used to treat her burn had thawed.

Mouse whined and scratched at the back door. Brodie let the dog outside for a few minutes, then dragged herself upstairs.

She turned off her cell phone and left it on her dresser, then pushed open the door to her father's bedroom. The room was just as Wallace Macbeth had left it before going to Boston all those months ago: tarnished brass bed, worn ivory chenille coverlet, old ornate Victorian dresser and nightstand, antique oriental carpet. The windows were covered by both slatted wooden blinds and dark blue draperies. The air felt heavy and dank.

Brodie snapped on the lights and got to work. She spent all Wednesday night methodically rifling through everything in her father's bedroom. She slit open the linings of his suit coats, emptied every drawer, ran her hand inside every shoe.

At dawn she staggered out of the room empty-handed, leaving clothing heaped on the floor and the mattress slashed. The burn on her hand was red and angry and hurt like hell.

☼

"Hey, sweetie. I'm at the gym. Where are you? Call me on, okay?"

In the kitchen, huddled over yet another pot of coffee, Brodie listened to Diana's voicemail and endured a wave of hopelessness. It was noon on Thursday and she'd been awake nearly 50 hours. A cold shower and clean shorts and tee shirt had helped but she was at the end of her tether.

Joe had left four messages, each one progressively more angry. Linda Zhou and Sarah Gibbard had left messages as well.

"Uh, sweetie," Diana's voice went on. "Look, I ran into Linda Zhou in the locker room. She said you didn't make it to your interview yesterday and you never called her. You're interviewing somebody else this afternoon and she's wondering if you're going to be there. Can you call her?" There was a pause. "Okay, well, talk to you later."

Mouse pushed her nose into Brodie's lap and shoved agitatedly. When Brodie absently patted the dog's head, Mouse stropped her forepaws on the kitchen floor and jumped around.

"Okay," Brodie said tiredly. "I know. You need a change of scenery. Me, too." She walked through the living room and unlocked the front door. Mouse charged out.

Brodie slumped onto the green wire settee on the porch and watched Mouse run around like a lunatic, sniffing all the familiar places the dog hadn't investigated in days; a particular upright of the split rail fence, the chipmunk hole under a magnolia tree, the flower pot full of impatiens wilting waterless in the southern noon heat.

The Volvo was parked on the gravel drive. OFK 362 mocked her.

Brodie's thoughts barged around aimlessly, a cacophony of exhaustion. What had the lawyer said? *I remember distinctly when your father came in and made these arrangements . . . He said it was something you'd appreciate in time . . . Given the nature of his death, you may be successful in arguing that your father was not of sound mind.*

Brodie stretched out her legs and let her head tip forward to stretch her neck. Her whole body was sore and aching. Despite everything she'd been through and learned, she didn't believe her father had been driven insane by either his obsession with his late wife or by his games with Pedder.

Her head came up slowly. Pedder hadn't thought her father was warped. He'd been afraid of Wallace Macbeth and the knowledge Wallace had possessed, knowledge that Brodie didn't share.

On the other hand, Pedder had ridiculed her father.

He thought he was Arthur and Lancelot and Galahad, all rolled into one . . . But he was Pellinore. Pellinore and the damned Questing Beast . . .

Brodie sat bolt upright. Her father had been able to send himself into a quest dream and it was always to a place with stone walls and tapestries.

"Camelot," she choked out. No wonder Pedder was determined to find her father's research about King Arthur. Mouse stopped sniffing and stood alert, ears and tail pricked up high.

Your thread started unraveling a long time ago when Macbeth killed Duncan to become king of Scotland. That's when the Macbeths had guts. Now they just read and imagine themselves to be knights and kings.

"Mouse," Brodie screamed, rocketing off the settee. The dog bounded up the porch steps. Brodie wrenched open the door and nearly tripped over the dog in her haste to get inside.

She tore through the house to the den, fatigue forgotten, and breathlessly searched the bookcases for books about King Arthur. There had to be something in the second half of the alphabet--she'd already read through the authors with names starting with P and there'd been nothing about Arthur so far.

At the bottom of the last bookcase she found a dog-eared

edition of *The Once and Future King* by T. H. White.

It was the only work of fiction on the shelves.

Once and Future King.

O. . . F . . . K . . .

OFK 362.

"Oh, God," Brodie rasped. She found herself gulping for air as she dropped onto the sofa with the thick book. It only took her a few moments to find page 362.

PART 9

The night is long that never finds the day.
(*Macbeth:* 4.3.239)

CHAPTER 39

. . . He unharnessed the horse and spancelled him. Then he took off his own armour and hung it neatly on a nearby tree with the shield on top. After this he ate some bread which the girl had given him, drinking water from a stream which ran beside the pavilion, stretched his arms out until the elbows went click, yawned, hit his teeth with his fist three times, and went to bed. The bed was a sumptuous one with a coverlet of red sandal, to match the tent. Lancelot rolled himself in it, pressed his nose into the silk pillow, kissed it for Guenever, and was fast asleep.

There was a faint pencil mark on the side of the page but the passage had no relevance and Brodie kept on reading. A man woke Lancelot who grabbed his sword and confronted the intruder.

"Now," cried the man, and he aimed a furious swipe at Lancelot's legs. The next minute he had dropped his sword and was holding his stomach with both hands, doubled up and whistling. The cut which Lancelot had given welled over with blood which looked black in the moonlight, and you could see some of the insides of the stomach with their secret life laid open.

Brodie continued reading to the end of the scene on the next page, then put down the book and blinked hard. The page was a clue, she was convinced of it. The pencil mark confirmed it. But there was no discernable connection to dreams or Pedder or her father or anything else.

Lancelot had gotten lost and taken refuge in the sumptuous pavilion. He'd taken care of his horse, ate, yawned, and went to sleep. The man who'd come upon him owned the pavilion and had mistaken Lancelot for a common thief.

The altercation ended amicably, with no real damage done despite the ominous description of the man's cut. The man who had surprised Lancelot was named Belleus and became one of

Arthur's knights of the Round Table.

Brodie shook the book violently. Nothing fell out. "Dammit, Dad."

She re-read the passage again and again, trying to make some connection between page 362 and her father's diaries. She went through the notebooks again, comparing them to the book, trying to match words and phrases or find some code. The afternoon passed without a clue.

Brodie threw the useless book onto the coffee table, agitated beyond endurance, and poured herself a double Famous Grouse from the bottle on the butler's table. She'd been so sure that *The Once and Future King* would tell her how her father had cheated the game with Pedder. How he'd moved in and out of the quest dreams.

Now she was adrift, worse off than before. Some of the Scotch slopped on her chin as she slammed it down.

The alcohol burned her throat and exploded like a bomb in her empty stomach. Brodie clanged her glass on the silver tray, making the bottles and glasses jump.

"*Dad!*" Brodie shouted. "*Why didn't you just tell me?*"

Anger and exhaustion coursed through her and she lurched to the bookshelves and began flinging her father's books off the shelves. They hit the floor with sharp thuds. First the B's, *Fighter Boys* and its neighbors, then on to the C's.

Churchill's smug *I-won-the-war* tomes splattered off the shelf and her phone rang.

"*I will kill you,*" Brodie screamed, sure it was Pedder.

"Brodie?" Joe said at the other end of the connection.

Brodie froze with the phone in her hand. "Joe," she said.

"We need to talk."

"No."

"What the hell is going on, Sassy?" Joe demanded. "We're talking marriage one day and the next you say we're over? I don't think so."

Brodie found herself back at the butler's table. She took a swig of Famous Grouse directly from the bottle.

"I told you not to call me anymore," she said into the phone and broke the connection.

The phone rang two minutes later. Brodie stood in front of the window. It had gotten dark and she hadn't noticed. She took another gulp of Famous Grouse as the phone rang again.

The fifth time he called Brodie answered. "Stop it, Joe," she said.

"You owe me an explanation," Joe said. "Let's hear it."

"Where are you?" Brodie asked, worried that he was talking and driving at the same time, on his way toward Charlottesville. Toward Pedder.

"I'm on the waterfront," Joe said. "Watching the boats. I'm coming to Charlottesville tomorrow. For some answers."

"You can't come here," Brodie nearly shouted. "*No.*"

"What's going on? You can't just drop this bombshell and expect I won't have questions. Talk to me, honey."

"I'm sorry." Brodie closed her eyes, tipped up the bottle of Famous Grouse, and drank. "We're just over, okay?"

"Are you drunk?" Joe asked.

"Not yet," Brodie said grimly and belted down another one.

"Just what the fuck is going on, Brodie," Joe snapped.

The Scotch was starting to insulate her and suddenly Brodie knew how to keep Joe safe.

"Okay," she said thickly. "Here's the scoop. I've been seeing Stanton all this time. We never really broke up. Me and Stanton. Sorry."

"You're lying," Joe exploded.

Brodie stared at the reflection of a liar in the window and drank some more Scotch. "Nope."

"I don't believe you."

Brodie swayed and watched herself. She was nicely framed in Macbeth clan tartan. A design from the days when the Macbeths had guts. "You have to."

"*You have to?*" Joe echoed incredulously. "*What kind of shit is this?"*

"*Shit, nothing,*" Brodie shouted. "I told you not to call and you didn't listen."

There was a long silence. Brodie imagined Joe rumpling his hair, the blue eyes cold with anger.

"All right, let's just calm down here," he said. His tone had gone from furious to controlled. "Something's very wrong. You're scared. What's the matter? Are you having second thoughts about getting married?"

"I told you. I've been seeing Stanton all this time."

"You really think I'm going to believe this garbage?" Joe asked. "That our whole relationship was a fake?"

Brodie didn't reply.

"Did you fake last weekend?" Joe pressed.

No. I love you. I have to protect you. "We never had anything," Brodie mumbled. She pressed the cool glass bottle of Scotch against her forehead. "You . . . you were just some fun."

"I don't believe you."

"Too bad."

"*Too bad?*"

"Yeah. Stay away from me, cowboy."

"*Fuck this,*" Joe roared.

There was a whistling sound in Brodie's ear, then a splash and a gurgle. The connection buzzed nosily and then went dead.

"*Goddammit,*" Brodie shouted. She turned awkwardly, unstable with hard liquor and bottomless despair, and threw both phone and Famous Grouse across the room. The phone cracked into the doorframe but the bottle banged into the bookcase nearest the door, bounced off a leather-bound spine and dropped to the floor. Amber fluid gurgled out and the room filled with a sharp, yeasty scent. Mouse appeared in the doorway, nose twitching as she sniffed the puddle of Scotch.

"Get away from that," Brodie shrieked and staggered towards the startled dog.

She tripped drunkenly on the crazy patchwork of books strewn across the floor, overbalanced, and went down hard. Her head smacked into the corner of the coffee table. Pain dazzled her eyes for a moment and churned through her brain.

Blackness closed in.

CHAPTER 40

The smell was cloying and earthy and it took Brodie a moment before she recognized it as mold.

It was a dream, and she knew she would not be able to wake up. Nor would she find her father.

Brodie blinked hard and a dim room came into focus. It was a spacious chamber with stone walls and a high ceiling. There were several smoke-darkened tapestries on the walls. One small window was fitted with closed wooden shutters.

The furnishings were sparse for such a large chamber. A bed shrouded by blue and gold woven curtains dominated, with a bearskin blanket, a round oak table flanked by two leather covered chairs, and several wooden trunks inlaid with a gold royal crest. A metal plate and goblet stood on the table; the slices of cheese and mutton on the plate looked moist and fresh.

Several thick candles illuminated the room. Crossed swords hung from crude iron fixtures above an open hearth. There was a crackling fire but it did little to chase away the chilly dampness that rose up from the floor.

Brodie walked to the window and opened the shutters. There was no glass behind them, just a deep opening that revealed a drizzly twilight. She was high above a wide emerald meadow that undulated away from stone walls. There was a lush forest beyond. The land was damp with rain and seemed fresh and new.

"Camelot," Brodie whispered to herself.

Her father's dream had become her own.

Opening the window didn't dispel the moldy smell and Brodie realized it was coming from herself. She was wearing a maroon velvet gown that puddled on the floor. The bodice was stiff with embroidery and the sleeves trailed well beyond her fingertips. The skirt hung heavily around her waist, making her hips ache from the weight. She pulled up the velvet hem to discover two layers of armor-like linen underneath. The bottoms of both layers were slimy with mold. She was wearing short leather boots and could feel the damp floors through the thin soles.

Brodie dropped the skirt with a grimace of disgust and looked around the room once more. Maybe going to his dream was what her father had intended for her to do. Maybe his secret could only be revealed to her in Camelot.

But whatever happened, she needed to be ready. She hauled a chair across the floor to the fireplace. Standing on the springy leather, she wrestled one of the heavy swords out of its holder. It was too heavy to handle easily from her awkward position and slid out of her grasp. The sword clattered to the floor as Brodie splayed herself against the chimney to avoid being sliced apart.

"My lady?"

A young woman in a simple linen dress came into the room from a curtained doorway and looked shocked at the sight of Brodie standing on the chair.

Brodie jumped off the chair and picked up the sword with both hands. It was as long as her leg and weighed a ton but she could lift and thrust it.

"My lady?" the girl quavered again.

"Am I the queen?" Brodie asked sharply. She pointed the tip of the sword at the girl before noticing that the teen's eyes were dark blue. She lowered the sword. "Guinevere?"

"Of course, my lady," the girl answered breathlessly. She darted at the chair, looked at Brodie for approval.

Brodie nodded and the girl put the chair back where it belonged. "Do you need anything, my lady?" the girl asked.

"King Arthur and Lancelot?" Brodie asked. "Where are they?"

"The King has gone to hunt in the New Forest, my lady," the girl said nervously, still eying the sword. "He will return tomorrow. Sir Lancelot is in his chambers."

Brodie absorbed this information without speaking. She was

clearly in the scenario at the end of *The Once and Future King*; Arthur departs to prove to Mordred that Guinevere is faithful, Lancelot goes to the Queen's chambers and their affair is found out, ultimately destroying Camelot.

"All right," Brodie said. "You can go."

The girl disappeared behind the curtain and Brodie stood the sword on its tip, her hands tightly gripping the ornate hilt. The thick blade glinted in the firelight as Brodie anticipated how the dream would play out.

Perhaps Lancelot would have Pedder's white eyes. She hoped the sword would be enough when he tried to kill her for the secret she didn't know.

Pain hit her head like the blow from a wrecking ball.

She let go of the sword to grab her head with both hands before it split open. The sword clanged to the stone floor and the sharp metallic sounds reverberated inside her skull. The pain intensified and crushed Brodie to her knees.

She closed her eyes against the screaming blackness inside her head. The pain was like a crucifying fire.

And then suddenly it was gone.

The smell of dry, dusty urine replaced the stink of mold.

Brodie forced open her eyes to see that she was huddled in a narrow alley surrounded by faded gray cement structures. The walls were pockmarked by age and disrepair. Overhead, the sky was blue and mercilessly bright. The height of the buildings on either side shaded the alley but the heat beat against her like surf. There were no trees, no grass. Everything around her was still and dead except the heat.

Brodie slowly got to her feet, surprised to find that she was dressed like a biblical shepherd in a shapeless beige robe and leather sandals. There was fabric on her head secured by a twist of cording. The fabric trailed over her shoulders, protecting her neck from the sun.

Voices murmured above her, making her start. Seconds later she heard the faint hum of an engine. Brodie looked up to see two swarthy men on the second story roof of a building bordering the alley.

The engine noise grew louder and the men chattered excitedly in a language she didn't understand. Suddenly, Brodie knew whose dream this was and where it had taken her.

Terror surged into the very core of her soul.

She started running down the alley toward the sound of the engines. The air tasted like sand and the heat made it hard to breathe. The long robe got in her way and something dragged against her right side but she ignored it.

The alley emptied into a large dirt area that in better times had probably been a village square. It was bordered on three sides by a motley collection of empty houses and shuttered shops. The fourth side was bordered by a single lane road that stretched into flat nothingness in either direction. On the other side of the road, dun-colored hills hunched against the merciless sun, offering up a few scrubby bushes to whatever gods had forgotten this rocky emptiness.

Brodie could see a convoy of military vehicles approaching the far side of the nearly deserted village. The sound of the engines was like the angry buzzing of bees.

The bloated body of a dead goat was lying on the side of the road near the first village structure. The lead Hummer swerved slightly to avoid it.

As the driver's door drew parallel with the corpse, the goat's body erupted in a ball of fury and fire. The left side of the Hummer lifted and then the entire vehicle rose into the sky, spewing fire and flesh and metal.

The world roared and the concussion wave blew Brodie back into the alley. She fell to the ground like a rag doll, the wind knocked out of her.

Agonizing moments went by as she fought for breath, her

mouth and nose clogged with grit. Her ears rang from the blast. When Brodie was finally able to crawl to the mouth of the alley the scene made her retch with fear.

The road by the far side of the village square was engulfed in flames pumping oily black smoke three stories into the sky. Resting on its side, the Hummer was the center of the inferno. Numerous small fires burned all around the wrecked vehicle. The hard-packed ground was stained with blood and littered with the detritus of war--bits of camouflage fabric, twists of metal, a blood-soaked boot. The heat of the blazing fires, trapped between the cement houses and the hills, cooked the village square with a stink of charred flesh and burning oil. The air was littered with ash.

The roar of the flames competed with the shouts of the Marines and the crack of gunfire. A firefight raged between insurgents on the rooftops and the Marines who'd used their vehicles to create a defensive position.

Brodie could see a small, bloody knot of Marines huddled against a low wall on the far side of the square. They were out of the firefight but perilously close to the burning Hummer.

Joe's helmet was off and his hair was as short as in the picture in Old Forge. His eyes were a wild blue in his smoke-smudged face. The stump of his left leg was a bloody pulp and smoke rose from his body. Blood stained the sand around him. As he shouted the color drained rapidly from his face.

Another Marine bent over Joe and swiftly searched Joe's flak vest pocket for something. This had to be Joe's corporal, Carson.

A third Marine stepped up. Brodie could see the medic's insignia on his bag. Trey Morales.

He's telling me, I've got you, man, I've got you. He's doing two things at once; getting a tourniquet on what's left of my leg and putting out the fire.

As Brodie nearly buckled with relief, the corporal moved aside to let the medic squat down in front of Joe. Carson thrust the package from Joe's vest at Morales.

The medic didn't take it. His movements were unrushed as he took off his helmet, revealing the glossy black hair Brodie remembered from the picture. He rocked slowly on his heels for what seemed like forever, the helmet strap dangling from his fingers, ignoring Carson. Joe and Morales appeared to be talking.

Smoke rose in tendrils from Joe's body.

"Do something," Brodie said, her voice small and lost in the bark of the guns and the snap of the flames.

Carson elbowed Morales aside, sending the medic sprawling, and pressed some sort of cloth over Joe's lap. Joe reacted by turning his head to one side, and Brodie could see how the veins in his neck bulged with pain.

The smoke was smothered but the rusty stain around him continued to grow, the sand absorbing blood like water.

Morales came back at the corporal and flung the younger man away from Joe and toward the burning Hummer. Carson rolled and scrambled back to the protection of the wall as the firefight raged behind them.

Something was very wrong, Brodie knew. She wasn't watching the story unfold the way Joe had told it to her; the way Trey had saved his life. Propelled by a courage she never knew she had, she left the safety of the mouth of the alley and started moving along the inside wall of the square toward the blazing inferno and the three men on the far side.

There was a loud crack. The burning Hummer wobbled and crashed down on its tires. Brodie cringed as the heat wave buffeted her.

Morales squatted by Joe and tipped back his head and laughed.

Brodie saw his eyes and stopped.

Morales's tawny skin threw the diseased white webbing into sharp relief. Pedder's eyes glinted like dirty snow in the handsome medic's face.

Brodie screamed soundlessly, fear squeezing her soul hard.

Morales looked past Joe to Brodie as if he had expected to see her. The white eyes registered amusement and anticipation, as if inspecting a gourmet meal. The medic smiled, ran his tongue over his lips in Pedder's predatory gesture, and laughed again.

Joe's face was gray and bloodless. His eyelids fluttered and his teeth started to chatter. Brodie knew he was going into shock.

"*Joe!*" Brodie started running across the square toward them.

Joe was going to die tonight in a dream in Iraq and at home in Alexandria, too, and Pedder would have his prize.

"You," the corporal yelled. "Stop and drop your weapon."

Still chuckling, Morales felt the pulse in Joe's neck.

"Drop it!"

He's got the long robe on and a turban but he's got a rifle. He's running right at us, through the middle of the firefight.

Brodie realized she was wearing some sort of webbed harness. A rifle dangled from it, bumping against her right hip. Heart pounding with desperation, she grabbed the rifle and tried to detach it from the harness.

"Drop it!"

Her fingers were clumsy with panic and Brodie could not work the catches on the harness. The rifle swung wildly as she struggled. Carson trained his own weapon on Brodie, but his eyes shifted nervously to Joe and Morales.

She could sense the young corporal's panic and fear. As bile scalded the back of her throat, Brodie knew that Pedder would get two souls for the price of one that night.

Another explosion, bigger than the last, erupted out of the Hummer and rocked the air. Brodie reflexively bought up an arm to protect herself against the slap of heat.

Joe's eyes opened and his left hand grasped the front of Morales' flak vest. The medic flinched, clearly surprised.

Something burst inside the burning Hummer, intensifying the fire. Flames spewed high into the sky and sounded like a freight train on the track to hell. Embers showered back to earth, igniting debris close to the medic. Brodie cringed and the rifle swung toward the front. Carson shouted at her, taking her movements for aggression, but his words were swallowed by the violence of the fire.

Joe's right hand brought up his sidearm from the holster on his uninjured hip. He shoved the weapon under the bottom of Morales' bulletproof vest and fired.

The fire billowed closer to the three men by the wall, illuminating the scene with angry licks of red and orange flame.

The medic's body jerked repeatedly, dancing in Joe's grasp. Blood sprayed out of the neck and shoulders as the bullets sliced through the body again and again. Joe fired robotically, until the slide locked back. With what must have been the last of his strength, Joe threw the shredded body towards the fire.

An unearthly scream rent the air as the body sprawled untidily in a pool of blood, the sand too saturated to absorb more. Brodie watched in horror as the unseeing white eyes rolled back into the head. A dirty vapor wafted out of the sockets.

It gathered upon itself, like thickening ashen air. The roiling column seemed alive and Brodie realized it was searching for another host.

"*Joe*," she choked.

The licking flames from the burning Hummer found the medic's body and fed on it as if racing along a line of gasoline. In the blink of an eye the body was fully engulfed.

The ashy vapor boiled above the fire, writhing desperately in the scorching heat, dense and unaccountably alive.

Joe slumped back against the wall, light from the flames flickering across the planes of his face.

The curtain of fire leapt from the charring skeleton to the vapor above it. Vibrant blue tongues of flame licked against the smokiness. Another scream sounded, piercing through the booming thunder of the conflagration and the continuing firefight between the Marines and the insurgents.

The vapor twisted away from the flames starting to devour it and writhed toward Joe. His head lolled and his shoulders sagged as his life drained out into the sand.

"*No!*" Brodie shouted and started running again, the harness pulling the rifle across her body. "*Joe!*"

"Halt or I'll shoot!" Carson yelled.

"*Joe!*"

. . . and this guy is screaming Yaw, Yaw like a banshee.

Suddenly page 362 made sense.

"Yawn!" Brodie screamed. "*Joe! Yawn! Yawn!*"

Joe's eyelids fluttered as the struggle between vapor and flame boiled closer.

"*Yawn!*" Brodie screamed one more time and then she squinted and yawned just as the first of the corporal's bullets smashed into her.

PART 10

It is concluded. Banquo, thy soul's flight,
If it find heaven, must find it out tonight.
(*Macbeth*: 3.1.140-141)

CHAPTER 41

Brodie woke with the nightmare running through her head and Mouse licking her face. Her head throbbed as she pushed the dog aside and sat up.

Books were strewn on the floor around her and sunshine was streaming in through the window. There was blood on the coffee table. Her watch said it was nine o'clock.

"Joe," Brodie croaked. She staggered to her feet and the pain in her head nearly caused her to pass out. Her brain was being crushed in a vise but her fear that Joe's soul was gone and that he was dead was stronger than the pain. Brodie grabbed the edge of the desk and sucked in air to keep herself from throwing up.

She found the phone on the floor and dialed his number.

There was silence on the other end and she imagined her voice echoing around the quiet apartment as Joe lay deaf and blind and dead in the big bed with the Mission headboard.

She redialed the number. A canned recording told her that the service had been cancelled.

Fear twisting in her chest like a knife, Brodie blundered back to the den, found her address book, and called Christine and Marty.

"Hello?"

"Christine," Brodie said, trying to keep her voice even. "Is Joe there?"

"Brodie?"

"Yes," Brodie said urgently. "Joe's not at home. Is he there?"

"Uh, no." Christine sounded uncomfortable. "Look, I don't mean to pry, but is something the matter with you and Joe? Marty said yesterday that--."

"Do you know where he is?" Brodie interrupted.

"Well, I expect he's at the job site with Marty. Did you try his cell?"

"It's not working."

"Do you want me to call Marty and see if Joe's there?"

"Yes, yes," Brodie babbled. "Thank you, Christine." She rattled off her cell phone number and hung up.

For three minutes her life hung in the balance and then the phone rang. It was Marty.

"He hasn't come in to work yet, Brodie." Marty sounded worried. "He's two hours late. What's going on?"

"I'll call you back." She disconnected.

The key to Joe's apartment was on her key ring. In four hours she'd know for sure, know if he was dead, if his soul had been lost in that horrifying dream and he would never wake again.

Mouse followed her to the car.

The adrenaline started to wear off before Brodie even got to Warrenton. She was hungry and dizzy and driving erratically. The Volvo meandered into the oncoming lane and she jerked the wheel to the right moments before hitting a minivan. The driver of the van honked angrily as the two vehicles narrowly passed each other and Brodie knew she had to stop and eat something before she had a head-on collision.

The Volvo turned right, almost of its own volition, went up a gentle rise and into the wide parking lot of a strip mall. A coffee shop, drugstore, and several smaller shops flanked a grocery store. A popular fast food restaurant perched in the middle of the parking lot.

Most of the strip mall shops weren't open yet. The fast food place was open for breakfast, however, with big posters of biscuits and coffee in the windows and a few cars parked close to the entrance. Otherwise, the parking lot was mostly empty. With the last of her strength Brodie steered the car into an open area overlooking the highway and left the Volvo parked across two spaces.

Her legs didn't seem able to support her, but somehow Brodie angled out of the car and stood. She opened the back hatch and Mouse leaped to freedom. The big dog ran to the strip of grass between the parking lot and the sloping verge of the highway and peed thankfully.

Brodie leaned against the side of the car and the summer morning wavered around her, heat and hunger and desolation making the landscape indistinct. People went in and out of the fast food restaurant behind her and she ignored disapproving noises about an unleashed dog.

The loud sound of a big engine revving made her turn around.

Below her on the highway, a big white crew cab truck heading south swerved to cross the oncoming lanes at full speed.

The front tires rammed into the curb of the grassy median. The vehicle went airborne, engine roaring, tires spinning, grass and gravel spitting.

Brodie screamed as the truck slammed back to earth in the middle of the northbound lanes. Traffic spilled away in all directions; the truck seemingly invulnerable.

It came right for her, hurtling up the sloping exit to the strip mall, engine wide open, racing toward her, coming to finish her off. Brodie screamed again in the certain knowledge that she had nothing left to bargain with, no energy left to fight.

Mouse barked madly, prancing around Brodie's legs in excitement.

The truck fishtailed to a stop near the Volvo, squealing and chewing up the tarmac. The driver's door swung open. Brodie saw the right foot touch the ground first, then the left.

"Brodie," he called as he pushed himself out of the driver's seat. "What the hell is going on? What are you doing here?"

He was wearing jeans and a USMC tee shirt and the Oakley wrap-around sunglasses.

She couldn't see his eyes.

It's tricky to go from one to another and only the strongest bodies work, you know. The weak ones just fall apart and there you are, with a mess.

Brodie ran at him, hardly aware of what she was doing. "Show me your eyes," she shouted.

"Sassy, what's going on? Why didn't you answer?"

"*Show me your eyes!*" Brodie reached for the sunglasses but he twisted away.

"What happened to you?" he asked, trying to grab her shoulders. "Who did this?"

"*Show me your eyes!*" Brodie screamed again, dodging his hands. "*Show me!*" She tried to wrench off his sunglasses.

As they wrestled in front of the truck Mouse charged between them, making him stagger.

Brodie managed to snatch off the Oakley sunglasses.

One glance and the ground rushed up at her.

CHAPTER 42

The eyes across from her were clear, honest, mountain lake pure, Oslo blue. Alive with Joe, his essence, his soul.

Yet again, Brodie felt tears slide down her cheeks.

"Hey," Joe said. "Eat your eggs. Then we'll talk."

Brodie nodded, swiped at her eyes, and pronged a forkful of scrambled eggs. She was still an emotional mess, still grappling with the relief of seeing Joe in the parking lot. He'd loaded her and Mouse into the truck, then raced back to Alexandria.

"All right," Joe said when they'd both eaten a few bites. "Tell me why I killed Trey Morales last night."

His meaning hit her broadside.

"You know," Brodie gasped. "You know about the eyes. You saw them last night and you *know*."

"I've had dreams like that before," Joe said grimly. "I know who those eyes belong to."

"Dr. Pedder," Brodie whispered.

"Pedder?"

"He said he was going to kill you, Joe. Take your soul. Unless I told him my father's secret." Brodie choked up, nearly unable to speak. "But until last night . . . in the dream . . . watching you . . . I didn't know what the secret was."

"You told me to yawn and I woke up." Joe's voice was a low rasp. "Was that what your father knew?"

Brodie nodded. "I didn't know if you heard me," she said brokenly. "And it was so awful . . . being there . . . watching you die. Trey didn't save you . . . I thought you were dead."

"You were driving to my place to find out?"

"Yes."

Joe pushed his plate away. "Tell me everything. From the beginning."

Brodie put both hands around her coffee cup, clinging to its lukewarm comfort. The food and coffee had helped, but she felt fragile, as if any moment she might shatter into a thousand pieces of glass.

"I've been having strange dreams," she said awkwardly. "Since my dad died . . . and I thought they were . . ." She trailed off. "But I guess that's not really the beginning."

Joe waited.

Brodie sipped her coffee, trying to collect her thoughts. "My mother's name was Elizabeth Brodie," she started again. "My parents met and married in Edinburgh and had me. My dad taught history and my mother was doing some sort of graduate work in economics, I'm not sure what. When I was just a toddler, she had an affair with a man named Ian something and couldn't decide whether to stay with my dad, who'd been offered a job here in the US, or stay in Scotland with this Ian." She swallowed hard. "Then she died in her sleep. Consensus was brain aneurysm. My dad found her dead in the morning and pretty much never got over it."

"Wait a minute," Joe said. He leaned forward. "Your mother was having an affair when you were little?"

"Yes."

"Is this Ian your father?"

"What?" Brodie looked at Joe, startled. "No. He couldn't be. I mean I don't know anything about him but I look like the Macbeth side of the family. We're all tall, with gray eyes."

"Okay," Joe said slowly.

Brodie took a breath. "Dad and I moved to Charlottesville. He started a diary, writing about how he was still in love with my mother, Elizabeth. He wrote about the dreams he had about Camelot. He always thought he'd see her in the dreams but instead encountered someone with white eyes he called the Keeper."

"Christ," Joe muttered.

"Dad ran into Ian the summer I was 12. Ian apologized for his affair with my mother. That's when Dad realized that everything the Keeper said was true."

"This Keeper had told him that your mother had been unfaithful?" Joe asked.

Brodie nodded. "And that she died because she went looking for answers. That's how he was able to steal her soul."

"He murdered her in a dream so he could take her soul?"

"Yes. Pedder or the Keeper or whatever he is." Brodie started to shake. "God, Joe. I've been talking to the *devil*. I *liked* him. Ellen calls him surfer dude."

"Take a deep breath," Joe said evenly. "So what did your father do about Ian?"

"You would have punched his lights out. Dad just decided that love makes you too vulnerable. Makes you look for answers when it goes sideways." Brodie squeezed her eyes shut against the pain of those words. "To protect me he'd raise me not to love."

"Step one," Joe said softly. "Send her to boarding school."

"Yes." Tears threatened again.

"Your father's suicide is somehow wrapped up in this, isn't it?" Joe asked.

Brodie shook her head. "It wasn't suicide. Pedder killed him in Boston. He admitted it to me Tuesday night."

"Killed him outright?" Joe frowned "Why would Pedder risk being caught for a real murder if he could kill your dad in his dreams? Your dad would have just died in his sleep like your mother, right? No connection to Pedder at all."

"That was the whole point. He couldn't catch Dad." Brodie steadied herself with another sip of coffee. "I kept dreaming about people who asked me how Dad had cheated and I had no idea that each time, in each dream, it was Pedder trying to figure out that Dad knew to yawn and wake up."

"Did your father know that Pedder was this Keeper?" Joe asked.

"He found out about six years ago. At a conference."

"Was it deliberate?" Joe asked. "If Pedder was after what your dad knew, maybe he revealed himself to your dad on purpose."

"He must have. That's when Dad made out his will making me use his license plates." Brodie's mind flashed forward to what must have been a terrible altercation in that Boston hotel room.

Wallace Macbeth had guarded the secret even as he passed it on. *OFK 362.* He must have died wondering if Brodie would ever put all the pieces together.

She told Joe about the license plate's connection to the passage in *The Once and Future King,* the Camelot references in her father's diaries, Pedder's insistence on finding her father's research on King Arthur, the clues in Tuesday night's terrifying conversation with Pedder, and how Lancelot's yawn was what her father had wanted her to understand.

"Pedder offered me a deal." Unconsciously, Brodie began to rock back and forth. "Your soul for my father's secret."

"He never would have honored any agreement." Joe's face showed his own strain of the past few days; fatigue-rimmed eyes, unshaven stubble, worry lines creasing his forehead.

"He said you had a warrior's soul," Brodie said. "Said he wanted to show it off. Like it was a trophy."

"As soon as I saw his eyes I realized it wasn't Trey and that he was going to let me die in that shithole," Joe said. "He said my soul was the price you'd pay for your father's pride."

"You knew who he was," Brodie said, rocking a little faster. It was a statement, not a question.

"I had some nightmares." Joe stood up restlessly and stacked their plates. "After I lost my leg and got the news that Trey had died."

Brodie followed him with her eyes.

"I was in the burn ward," Joe went on. "My parents were there every day. I was pretty doped up, drifting in and out. I'd dream, not knowing if I was hallucinating from the pain or what. Mostly I dreamed about being in ultimate fights. You know, no rules, either knock 'em out or make them tap out. And here I was fighting with one leg. No prosthetic." He paused. "Everyone I fought had those white eyes."

Brodie gave a little gasp.

Joe nodded. "I had four dreams like that. Each fight was tougher than the one before. I kept thinking I'd find Trey, that he'd get me out of there, help me to wake up. I managed to win the first couple of fights but the last one nearly killed me. He tried to break my neck but I got my thumbs into his windpipe. His eyes rolled back and I saw something like smoke."

"His soul," Brodie said. "Just like last night."

Joe nodded. "I was on the edge of passing out. I started to itch all over, as if my skin was coming off, and I knew somehow he was going to take me. I was going to be one of those guys you think are going to make it but two days later you hear from the medics that they didn't and nobody knows why."

"What happened?" Brodie's voice was teary and small. She began rocking in her seat again.

"My mom woke me up." Joe rumpled his hair with a big hand. "She kept doing that, you know. Waking me up every few hours, just to make sure I was still alive. Dad kept telling her to let me sleep but she'd wake me, we'd talk a little, she'd get me to eat something."

"And after awhile, you were able to grieve for Trey and the dreams stopped?"

"That's right," Joe said. "I still have nightmares sometimes, you know, but they're . . . different. Regular."

"Those dreams." Brodie shivered. "It's like being trapped someplace. Someplace real, not just inside my head."

"Limbo is a real place. Where souls go to find answers to their questions."

"And evil stalks them?" Brodie quavered, still rocking in her seat.

"I think so." Joe sat down again, but next to Brodie instead of across the table from her. "Pedder threatened and you told me to stay away from you. Why didn't you just tell me what was going on?"

"How nuts would that have sounded?" Brodie felt herself slipping over the edge, shivering and rocking her way towards the release of hysteria. "I had to protect you. Keep you away. I even offered him my soul for yours but he didn't want it."

"Dammit," Joe swore. "I should have come Wednesday night but I was too busy wallowing in self-pity. Part of me was saying that I'd been right all along. That you'd never stay with me."

"That's not true." Brodie jumped to her feet without even realizing it, hysteria finally gaining the upper hand, feeding on residual fear and emotional exhaustion. "I *hated* saying those things. But it was the only thing I could think of to do. Make you not love me any more. Then maybe Pedder couldn't get to you."

"It doesn't matter what you said," Joe said, looking up at her. "The issue here is that I let you go through this alone."

"You had to. I was trying to protect you the same way my father protected me."

"But it's my fault you ended up in that shithole, too," Joe exclaimed. "With Carson shooting at *you*."

"*You don't understand*," Brodie shouted at him, tears streaming down her face, her emotions in tatters. *"If you'd died the last thing I ever said to you would have been a lie!"*

"Don't, honey," Joe said, startled, but his words were lost as Brodie abruptly started to sob, wracked from the aftermath of the brutal and sharp-edged fear she'd lived with for so many hours.

Joe pulled her to the sofa. Crushed against Joe's chest, Brodie's tears ran down.

Mouse walked around the room agitatedly and resettled by the television.

"That was the bravest thing I've ever seen," Joe said quietly. "You running towards me, telling me what to do. I knew you'd remember about Carson and the old man but you kept on coming."

"You were dying." Brodie's voice was muffled by his shirt. "And then you shot him . . . threw him into the fire."

"It was the only way to get rid of his soul."

"How did you know to do that?"

"I . . . I don't know."

"With all that pain . . . how did you do it?"

Joe rubbed her arms. "If you hadn't been there, I'm not sure I could have done it."

"I love you so much," Brodie said.

Mouse jumped up onto the sofa and for once Brodie let the dog stay. Sandwiched between man and dog, Brodie pulled in a few deep breaths and finally stopped trembling.

Out of all the men in the world, Brodie knew Joe was the only one who could have survived this with her. It would take them a long time to fully understand what had happened, like how she'd been pulled from her father's dream into Joe's, but she knew with certainty that meeting him and loving him was no accident.

When Brodie's cell phone rang, they both tensed. Brodie found it in her purse and looked at the display. It was Sarah Gibbard.

"Hi, Sarah," Brodie said.

"Brodie, can you come into the office?" The history department secretary radiated concern through the connection. "Dean Slocum would like to meet with you right away."

"Sarah, I'm in Alexandria. What's so important?"

"Dr. Pedder's dead," Sarah said with a little hiccup.

"Was it a brain aneurysm?" Brodie asked.

CHAPTER 43

Over the next few weeks everything fell into place with an amazing surety.

Now, sitting at the table in Diana's light-filled kitchen, Brodie was torn between excitement and sadness. She and Joe were moving on, and there was so much to look forward to. But Diana would be 14 hours away.

Brodie twisted the sapphire and hammered gold engagement ring on her finger, loving how it caught the light. The sapphire was as big as an almond and the same color as Trey's stone.

Male voice voices filtered pleasantly from the back yard and Puck barked. Brodie took a deep breath. "I quit my job today," she said.

Diana turned away from the counter holding a big wooden bowl of spinach salad. She blinked rapidly at Brodie. "What?"

"I gave Dean Slocum my letter of resignation."

"It's the start of the semester," Diana said, not moving.

"We're moving to New York," Brodie heard herself blurt happily. "Joe and his brother are going to start building and I'm going to be writer-in-residence at the Museum of the Adirondacks in Blue Mountain Lake. Finish my book about New York and give some seminars."

Diana's mouth formed an O and she dropped the wooden bowl. It clanged onto the tile floor. Spinach sprayed in all directions.

The screen door popped open and Joe stepped into the kitchen, his body tense. *Are you okay?* his expression asked.

I'm fine. Brodie grinned as he took in Diana's stunned expression and the spray of green on the floor.

"You're moving to New York?" Diana sputtered. "You said Warrenton!"

"Joe just told me. Congratulations," Ray said from the

doorway, blocking Puck and Mouse from coming inside. His gaze traveled to the spinach on the floor. "We're not eating that, are we?"

Joe gave Brodie that sideways smile. "I think it's girl talk time, Ray."

The two men went outside again.

"Sweetie, that man loves you like there's no tomorrow," Diana said. She squatted down by the overturned wooden salad bowl. "But he can't just whisk you off to New York. You have *tenure*."

"That's what Dean Slocum said." Brodie plopped down on the floor, too, and picked up a spinach leaf.

The dean had tried to talk her out of resigning, holding out the prospect of her becoming department chair. Brodie had let him talk for ten minutes. Then she'd placed her letter on his desk and told him the university held too many sorrowful associations for her now.

"What about your class?" Diana asked, ignoring the green mess around her. "The semester's already started."

"Ellen Foster is taking it," Brodie said, picking up more spinach. "And get this. Jack Hull is going to be acting chair of the department."

"The walking smokestack?"

"The very same." Brodie grimaced comically. "There goes alumni donations this year."

Diana finally started picking up spinach leaves. "I still can't believe this. All of a sudden you're moving to the kingdom of snow?"

"Where Joe goes, I go." Brodie flipped over the salad bowl and dumped her handful of spinach into it. "Think about it. No more cocktail party fundraisers, no more snarky chats with Jack Hull, no more papers to grade, no more--."

"Pregnant within a year," Diana predicted, grinning broadly.

"Maybe." Brodie laughed and punched Diana lightly on the arm. "We already bought a house."

Diana's jaw dropped. "You what?"

"We went up last weekend and signed the contract." The decisions Brodie and Joe had made hadn't really been decisions at all; they were simply settling into a situation that had been waiting for them.

The surveyors determined the land in Blue Mountain Lake could accommodate double the number of units Brian had planned. Joe and Marty would bring most of the BIRNAM WOOD crew with them to build. Christine found a teaching job, too.

The museum administrators had fallen over themselves when Brodie had called to inquire about a possible position.

And a beautiful house on the shores of Fourth Lake, just north of Hazy Harbor, waited for them.

Brodie felt her grin broaden as she stood up and dusted off the back of her shorts. Buying the big stone lakefront house had made the break with Charlottesville seem real. "It's gorgeous." She opened her tote bag on the kitchen table and hauled out the folder from the realtor. "I've got pictures."

"You got a new job and bought a house in, what, three weeks?" Diana asked incredulously. She stood up and put the bowl of dirty spinach on the counter.

"Dad's house sold yesterday," Brodie said. "Lydia Sue Crosby handled it."

"I can't believe this, sweetie." Diana shook her head but Brodie heard the excitement in her voice.

Brodie took out the pictures as Diana poured glasses of iced tea. The big stone house would be hers and Joe's, where they'd sleep together and raise children and play chess and be warmed by the fire. It had a chimney on either side, a screened side porch with a view of the lake, and a stone terrace. Inside there was a family room with an enormous cobblestone fireplace, a gourmet kitchen, four bedrooms, and four bathrooms. Two of the bathrooms were already outfitted for a person with disabilities. A detached guest house would be the new headquarters of

BIRNAM WOOD.

Diana oohed over a photo of the master suite, with its vaulted ceiling, dark beams, and hardwood floors.

"By the wedding we'll be all settled in," Brodie said.

"Still the last weekend in October?" Diana asked. "You'd better get those invitations out."

"I know." Brodie pulled another folder out of her bag, along with a bridal magazine. "I need to choose invitations. Joe says he doesn't care. And I want you to look at this dress."

They were still studying invitations and wedding dresses when Ray and Joe came in, Puck and Mouse swirling around their legs. Ray had a tray of barbecued ribs and roasted corn. Brodie hurriedly set the table while Diana found rolls and pickles and lamented the loss of the salad.

Joe leaned toward Brodie and brushed the side of her forehead with his lips. Ray said something funny about how they weren't honeymooners yet.

"What do you expect?" Joe asked lightly. "I've found the girl of my dreams."

The move from Virginia to New York was done caravan-style. Inger, Peter, Rosemary, and Caitlin all came down in the Birnam's big SUV, the little girl delighted with the adventure of helping to move Uncle Joe and soon-to-be Aunt Brodie. Peter would drive north in Brodie's Volvo, with Mouse in the back, while Inger, Rosemary, and Caitlin took over the SUV. Joe and Brodie would follow in his truck.

All three vehicles were packed with clothes and books. The contents of Joe's apartment in Alexandria had been sent ahead, to be unloaded at the new house under Brian and Jenna's supervision. The apartment had been rented out.

Brodie took little out of the Granite Castle Road farmhouse for her new life. The tartan curtains and her father's diaries were in Joe's truck. Her father's books, with the exception of *The Once and Future King*, had been donated to the university.

The leather sofa from the den had been thrown away. Odds and ends of furniture were in the big moving truck for Joe and Brodie's house but for the most part, the items that Lydia Sue Crosby had chosen not so many months ago would furnish the first condo built by BIRNAM WOOD as a model for prospective buyers.

The caravan stopped at the Visitor's Center at Arlington National Cemetery. Peter nodded at Joe and Brodie as they got out of the truck. Mouse was sitting in the front seat next to Peter. Inger gave a brief wave from the SUV.

"Thanks for waiting," Joe called.

Joe and Brodie walked through the beautifully manicured cemetery, feeling the majesty and memories of the place. A few headstones displayed small bouquets of flowers or other mementos, but mostly the place was simple and silent, the white headstones undulating over the green grass. Their footfalls signaled that visitors were there to quietly mourn a fallen hero.

Brodie looked at Joe as they walked hand-in-hand without speaking. He had on jeans and a starched white shirt. His sunglasses were hooked into the open collar and the earring glinted. He held a small box in his left hand. His limp was pronounced as they moved over the gravel path winding through the different sections of the cemetery and shaded by the arching trees.

It was a long walk, but they finally found the grave. It was marked by a white rounded headstone, like all the others, with a cross cut the top and the name *Morales* underneath.

Brodie let go of Joe's hand and stepped away to give him some privacy.

Joe stood unmoving in front of the grave for a long time. Then he put his hand to his eyes and Brodie realized that he was crying.

"It wasn't you," Brodie heard him say quietly. "It wasn't

you. I knew it wasn't you."

He bent down and placed the box on the grass in front of the grave. It was his Silver Star.

Brodie felt the tears spill over and run down her cheeks but she didn't move.

Joe stood for a few more minutes as the breeze freshened and shook the stillness out of the air. Then he turned and came over to her.

"Hey." He tipped up her chin and wiped her tears away with his thumb. "It's over."

"I know," Brodie sniffed.

Joe nodded and wrapped his arms around her. Brodie clasped her hands together behind his back and they embraced for a long minute without speaking.

"Have you thought what might have happened if we hadn't been seated together on that flight to London?" Brodie finally asked.

"No." Joe's arms tightened around her. "I was supposed to be sitting there."

"You're the only reason I survived." Brodie's voice was muffled by his shirt. "But there are still things I need to know. How did my father get into the dreams whenever he wanted to? And what happened to my mother's soul?"

"The answers might not be what you want them to be," Joe said.

"I need to know the truth," Brodie said. "As long as you're with me, I can handle it."

"I love you, Sassy." Joe pulled back to stare at her. "With everything I've got. My heart. My soul."

"That's just the way I love you," Brodie said, falling into those blue, blue eyes all over again. "Heart and soul."

They had fought for each other when their own lives were in mortal danger. He had saved her and then she had saved him. Their love would keep them both safe--truly safe, Brodie knew, in a way her father had never understood--for the rest of their lives.

Without speaking, because there was no need, they returned to the path through the rolling landscape of memorials. They walked hand-in-hand as the sun danced on the leaves and warmed the headstones of the warriors who had called their souls their own.

The End

FROM THE AUTHOR

Now that your heart has stopped racing, come join the Mystery Ahead newsletter community.

Every other Sunday you'll get my best book news, special announcements, as well as exclusive excerpts and reviews of mystery must-reads!

In short, not your average email.

Subscribe at carmenamato.net.

P.S. Turn the page for Brodie's Cornish Game Hens recipe.

LEMON-STUFFED CORNISH GAME HENS WITH VEGETABLES

2 Cornish game hens, innards removed
2 lemons
2 tablespoons melted butter
Salt and pepper
Dried parsley
½ cup pinot grigio white wine
2 tablespoons olive oil
½ cup chicken broth
4 large carrots peeled and cut into matchsticks
1 leek, washed and the white section cut into matchsticks
1 small red onion, cut into thin wedges (optional)

Preheat oven to 375

Mix wine, broth, olive oil, and vegetables together in a big bowl, set aside.

Rinse hen cavity with cold water and pat dry with a paper towel. Put in a large rectangular baking dish, leaving at least 2-3 inches between them.

Slice the lemons in quarters lengthwise. Squeeze two quarters over each hen. Stuff hens with remaining two quarters each. Season the cavity with salt and pepper.

Spoon melted butter over each hen. Season the exterior with salt, pepper, and parsley.

Cover hens with foil and roast for 30 minutes. Baste the hens with juices from the pan, then arrange vegetables around the hens. Add wine/broth liquid to thoroughly moisten vegetables . Replace foil. Roast another 30 minutes, remove foil and stir the vegetables. Roast uncovered another 20-30 minutes until the carrots are soft and the hens are crisp.

This is my go-to recipe for special occasions and it is almost foolproof! Enjoy with rice or couscous and a glass of white wine.

ABOUT CARMEN AMATO

A 30-year veteran of the Central Intelligence Agency, Carmen Amato is the 2023 winner of the Silver Falchion Award for Best Historical for *Murder at the Galliano Club*, inspired by her grandfather's experiences as a deputy sheriff during Prohibition. Kirkus Reviews lauded her writing as "Danger and betrayal never more than a few pages away."

Beginning with *Cliff Diver*, her contemporary Detective Emilia Cruz series pits the first female police detective in Acapulco against Mexico's cartels, corruption, and social inequality. Optioned for television, it's a 2-time winner of the Outstanding Series award from CrimeMasters of America and a 4-time finalist for the Silver Falchion award. Her standalone thrillers include *The Hidden Light of Mexico City*, which was longlisted for the 2020 Millennium Book Award.

Carmen is a recipient of both the National Intelligence Award and the Career Intelligence Medal.

Originally from upstate New York, after years of globe-trotting she and her husband enjoy life in Tennessee.

Find out more at carmenamato.net.